'Robertson is a very great [illegible]
Alexander McCall Smith, *Guardian*

'It's like some beautifully ornate kist or jewel box that for most of the encounter you admire for its own sake, only to find a key, near the end, that opens on to even more treasure'
Gavin Francis

'It is another wonderful piece of storytelling from James Robertson, offering a penetrating exploration of the complexities of collective memory and the tenacity of tradition, all played out through a thousand years of life in a single glen. It has all the makings of a timeless classic in its own right'
Professor Gary West

'James Robertson is an extremely fine novelist . . . this is a superb book . . . It is not a book anyone will forget quickly'
Scotsman

'One of Robertson's skills as a novelist is to make both events real and imagined feel equally convincing'
Prospect

'Subtly explores the relationship between place and identity'
Sunday Times

ABOUT THE AUTHOR

James Robertson is the author of *The Fanatic*, *Joseph Knight*, *The Testament of Gideon Mack*, *And the Land Lay Still*, *The Professor of Truth* and *To Be Continued*. *Joseph Knight* won the Saltire Society Scottish Book of the Year and the Scottish Arts Council Book of the Year; *The Testament of Gideon Mack* was longlisted for the 2006 Man Booker Prize; and *And the Land Lay Still* won the Saltire Society Scottish Book of the Year. Robertson is also the author of four short-story collections, most recently *365: Stories*, four poetry collections and numerous children's books written in Scots. He runs an independent publishing house, and is co-founder and contributing editor of Itchy Coo, which produces books in the Scots language for young readers.

By the same author

The Testament of Gideon Mack
And the Land Lay Still
The Professor of Truth
365
To Be Continued

NEWS OF THE DEAD

James Robertson

James Robertson
Cupar 5th September
2022

PENGUIN BOOKS

PENGUIN BOOKS

UK | USA | Canada | Ireland | Australia
India | New Zealand | South Africa

Penguin Books is part of the Penguin Random House group of companies
whose addresses can be found at global.penguinrandomhouse.com.

First published by Hamish Hamilton 2021
Published in Penguin Books 2022
001

Copyright © James Robertson, 2021

The moral right of the author has been asserted

Printed and bound in Great Britain by Clays Ltd, Elcograf S.p.A.

The authorized representative in the EEA is Penguin Random House Ireland,
Morrison Chambers, 32 Nassau Street, Dublin D02 YH68

A CIP catalogue record for this book is available from the British Library

ISBN: 978–0–241–98662–2

www.greenpenguin.co.uk

Penguin Random House is committed to a sustainable future for our business, our readers and our planet. This book is made from Forest Stewardship Council® certified paper.

For Neal Ascherson,
friend, observer, listener,
recorder of stone voices

Readers interested in learning more about some of the Scots words and phrases in this book will find a rich source of information in the online *Dictionaries of the Scots Language* at https://dsl.ac.uk.

Lachie's Ghost

Lachie Darroch came to see me, for the first time in a while. It was autumn, the leaves were turning and falling fast, and most afternoons it was cold enough to light the stove before it got dark. I'd been out in the garden, taking peelings to the compost, and when I came back Lachie was in my house, inspecting the paintings on the walls of the kitchen. No nonsense about knocking at the door and waiting – not from him or anybody in the glen. His schoolbag was on the floor by the kitchen table so I knew he had not yet been home.

'Hello, Lachie. How are you?'

'Fine, thanks. Have you drawn anything new today?'

It would have been an unusual day if I had not. He sat down, and I showed him a sketch I had made of chaffinches at the bird table, and another of Tam, Julia's cat, sitting on the wall between our gardens. Lachie peered intently at each drawing. He stuck out his chin and gave an approving, professorial nod.

'Tea?' I asked.

'Yes, please. Are there any biscuits?'

'Of course. Are there ever not?'

I poured him tea from the pot. According to his mother he never drinks tea at home, but he does when he comes to me. He likes it out of one of my old, thin cups – tea made with real leaves and without milk or sugar. For an eight-year-old he can be very grown up.

'Look, a stranger,' he said, and fished it out with his fingertip. 'What day is it?'

'Wednesday.'

He settled the stranger on one fist and thumped it three times with the other. Whoever it was, they were coming on Friday, apparently.

'I wish I could draw like you, Maja,' he said.

I pushed the biscuit tin towards him. 'You just have to practise.'

'Like with my violin,' he said. 'It's really hard sometimes.'

'But you're getting good. You played well at the summer party.'

'Oh, I'm way better than that now.' He reached out and, without touching the paper, traced a particular line that was Tam the cat's curved back and tail. 'Sometimes when I get a long note right,' he said, 'it's just like that.'

Lachie is a deep, thoughtful boy. I am happy that he feels he can come into my home when he wants. I am happy that he wants to, that there is no sense of obligation about it. I like the fact that he drinks tea here but not in his own home, and that he sometimes has to check what day it is.

He looked at me, then away quickly. 'What's a ghost?' he asked.

'That's an interesting question.'

He pointed at my cat drawing. 'Is it like a dream?'

'I suppose it could be.'

'I don't really mean a dream.' His face scrunched up while he thought about it. 'I mean like something you can't quite remember. A kind of leftover from before.'

'Like an echo?'

'Yes.' He took another biscuit and I put the lid back on the tin.

'I think I saw one when I was having my breakfast, before I went to school.'

This was why he had come. He had this story and he knew he could tell it to me and I would not laugh. Or tell anybody else.

'What did you see?'

'A girl. She had a white dress on. Well, kind of grey. It was quite dirty, I think.'

'What did she look like?'

'Just a girl. She didn't have any shoes on, just bare legs even though it was raining.'

'How old was she? Your age?'

'Not sure.'

'And where was this?'

'In the library. Well, I was in the library but she was outside. I take my cereal there sometimes, to get away from Rosie when she's being annoying. I was at the window and this girl was standing outside on the grass, in the rain.'

'Just standing?'

'She had her arms out like this' – he stretched his own arms wide, the palms of his hands turned upwards, head tilted back – 'and she was getting soaked but she didn't move.'

'Maybe she was enjoying it.'

He nodded. 'Mm.'

'So why do you think she was a ghost?'

'I don't know if she was, but I knocked on the window and she didn't hear me, and I was going to go outside and ask who she was, but then I changed my mind and came back to the window and she'd disappeared. But it was only seconds that I wasn't looking.'

'And you'd never seen her before?'

'No. She was quite strange.'

'Why do you say that?'

He scratched his head. 'Well, she looked older than me. Her face was old but she was wee.' He seemed embarrassed.

'What, Lachie?'

He made circles on the table with the fingers of his left hand. 'I thought it might be you.'

'Me?'

'From a long time ago.'

'But I'm here. I'm not a ghost.'

'Yes, but I didn't know that this morning. And then I had to get on the bus and go to school.'

I tried to remember what it was like, to be eight. I was ten times older than him. Unimaginably old.

'Did you think maybe I had died, and that was me when I was young you were seeing?'

He still couldn't meet my eye.

'Were you worrying about that all day?'

'Sorry,' he said.

I put my ancient, blotchy hand on his, stilling the circles he was making.

'Don't be sorry,' I said. 'I understand. It could have been me, and you were quite right to want to check. That's what I would have done if I were you. I haven't died, though, I'm glad to say.'

'Me too,' he said, and for boyish reasons he took his hand from under mine, and could look at me again. 'So, who was she, then?'

'I don't know,' I said. 'But I like what you said about a ghost being a kind of leftover from before. Maybe that's who she was.'

'You said "echo",' Lachie said. 'I like that better.'

Imagine This

To tell the story of a country or a continent is surely a great and complex undertaking; but the story of a quiet, unnoticed place where there are few people, fewer memories and almost no reliable records – a place such as Glen Conach – may actually be harder to piece together. The further into the past you go, the more you feel you are journeying into a strange, unknowable region. The hazier everything becomes, the more whatever facts there are become entangled with myth and legend. And, when you return to the present, it may seem that fact and fiction were never that discrete from one another after all.

The glens of Angus, famous for their beauty, stretch like fingers from the rich, fertile palm of Strathmore up into the Grampian Mountains. Glen Conach is the least known of them: indeed, there are many people living within an hour's drive who have not heard of it. It is located some thirty kilometres to the north-west of the town of Forfar, and extends approximately twelve kilometres towards the Mounth, a great expanse of moor and mountain where the headwaters of its principal river, the Conach, are found. The glen is supposedly called after a Christian hermit, Conach, but the origin of the name has long been disputed by experts in toponymy. Some say it is related to the *Connachta*, the descendants of the legendary Irish king Conn, and that long ago a branch of that dynasty settled in the glen. The late Professor Donald Collinson of the University of Aberdeen, on the other hand, believed that the name derives from Scottish Gaelic and means either 'glen of dogs' or 'glen of prosperity'; while the late Dr Ken Clavers, researcher in the School of Scottish Studies at the University of Edinburgh, argued vehemently that the name comes from the Scots tongue and means 'glen of waste' or 'ravaged glen'. Popular opinion favours the hermit (sometimes, erroneously, called 'Saint Conach') as its source, and cares little for the claims of these academic disputants.

Today, the main economic activity in Glen Conach is farming: oats, barley and vegetable crops are grown in the lower, more fertile, part of the glen, while cattle and sheep are reared in the upland part. The largest landowner is Glen Conach Estate Ltd, whose assets include farm buildings and agricultural land, shooting and fishing rights, and forestry. Like other rural communities, the glen has suffered population depletion for many years: the census of 1881 recorded some one hundred and sixty people living in Glen Conach, whereas in 2011 the population was less than one quarter of that.

Glen Conach shares a geological history with the neighbouring glens, but has its own particular character. It is made, in its upper reaches at least, of rocks formed more than five hundred million years ago when Scotland was a scattered jigsaw puzzle of four pieces, and the Earth a shifting, cracking, groaning pot of energy subjected to relentless, immensely powerful stresses and strains. It is hard to imagine what was happening on that bygone, unstable planet where nothing was settled, nothing decided, nothing named; where – to adapt the famous words of the 'father of modern geology', James Hutton – if there was any vestige of a beginning, there was surely no prospect of an end. Nevertheless, imagine this –

Enormous expanses of mud, shale and sandstone stretching to every horizon, layer upon layer of this mixture being crushed and folded and heated by the movement of the tectonic plates of the planet's shell, causing these materials to metamorphose into what we now know as greywackes, gneisses and schists, rich in mica, quartz and other minerals. Later, the bits of what will eventually be called Scotland come together – the joins are still visible in its fault lines – and connect also with what will be England and Wales. But this is hundreds of millions of years before these names, or any names, will be spoken – before even a hint of any world we might know. Continents are forming but none that we would recognise. Great passages of time go by so slowly that they are as good as timeless. The continents continue to move, creaking, colliding and re-forming and, as they do, vast quantities of sandstone are pounded into crumbs and borne by tumultuous rivers to lower ground and to the bottoms of huge freshwater lakes. By then the location of this unchristened clump of crust – upon which our glen is as yet neither scar nor scratch – is somewhere near the equator: tropical rainforests grow, coral reefs bloom where land meets sea, and volcanoes spew lava and ash across the southern part of what is not yet remotely recognisable as a country. The clump edges north. The climate changes, becoming drier and hotter; deserts succeed the forests; earthquakes further shake, fold, crease and split the land. And there is life, struggling to survive amid the violence. Unfishlike fish swim; strange reptiles emerge, multiply, perish. The sea rises, flooding the lower land, and dinosaurs make their appearance, exercising their dominion over the fertile boundaries.

The planet is rocked, perhaps, by some juddering collision with another body in space; something happens that brings to an end the age of dinosaurs. The sea flows further, drowns more, until only the highest peaks remain unsubmerged. More tens of millions of years pass. The waters recede; new volcanoes form and erupt, more sediments are carried into an as yet unknown northern sea. Now we draw closer. The planet cools. An age of ice arrives, a mere two and a half million years ago; deep-founded, high-stacked ice, millions of tons of ice upon ice, ice thawing only to be replaced by more ice, grinding, crushing, flattening and scraping the land beneath it. Ten to fifteen thousand years ago – at last, conceivable time! – the lower part of the glen is freed from the ice's grip, the glaciers retreat, the meltwater sculpts and washes loose debris, gravel and soil downhill and eastward. The climate settles into something like a routine.

Winter turns to spring, spring to summer, summer to autumn, autumn to winter. Winter – severe though it can be – is a feeble, faint impression of the long, hard sleep that lay upon the glen for millennia. What is left under the turning seasons? The gouged corries and hard outcrops of metamorphic rock of the upper glen, the widening, sandstone-lined, clay-and-earth-covered strath below, fertile, woody and boggy – and all watered by the constant downflow of the glen's burns and river. Geology has laboured without cease and, for now, appears to be at rest.

Of all this the first people who came to the glen, perhaps ten thousand years ago, knew nothing. They had no sense of the immensity of time and matter and process that had gone into making it. The only way they could read its shape, its rocks, soil and vegetation, was through what was immediate and present to them. They read it by sight and smell, by sound and touch, and gradually they came to understand it, to learn its seasons, its birds, fishes and other creatures, its dangers and gifts, its capabilities and limitations. In order not to lose the learning they acquired, they told stories and sang songs about the glen, and about themselves in the glen, to their children. What they could not explain they considered magical or mysterious, and they either made stories that reflected the mystery or left it untold. They lived and died. No more than this is known about them. From here, they are faceless, nameless and silent. In their wake came others, who perhaps spoke different languages and had different customs, although their primary purpose in life was the same: to survive.

Then, thousands of years later, to the glen came another man, one blessed of God, or so it is said. Although many humans had lived in the glen before he did it is from him, supposedly, that it gets its name. Conach was possibly born in the last two or three decades of the seventh century. He is believed to have been descended from Pictish royalty. He grew up in what is now Moray, became a Christian when a youth, and was educated by monks in the north-east of Scotland, on the island of Iona and in Ireland. After many years both as a missionary and a monk he relocated to Glen Conach, where he became a hermit. He performed miracles and was reputedly much loved by the local people. The precise date of his death is not known but it cannot have been later than about 770.

But there is a problem, because Conach may never have existed, and even if he did his name may not have been Conach. Around the end of the twelfth century a Latin manuscript entitled *Liber Conachi*, the *Book of Conach*, was created which insisted that he did exist and that this was his name – but this document itself no longer exists. An English translation – a *supposed* translation – does survive, full of unlikely claims and assertions, including that Conach performed miracles. The reader may conclude from this that, as proof of anything, the *Book of Conach* is not worth a button. If these stories really are eight hundred years old, they should generate some respect simply for being that age; but, while you may tolerate your ancient neighbour who leans over the wall to tell you how things were when he was a boy, that doesn't necessarily make him any less of a confabulating old windbag. As one historian has put it, 'Since Conach must have lived, *if* he lived, four hundred years or more before the *Book* was compiled, it is as plausible to say that Conach proves the truth of the *Book* as it is to say that the *Book* proves the truth of Conach.'*

Nevertheless, this individual may have existed and his name may have been Conach. Let us give him the benefit of the doubt. Like the other dwellers in the glen he had no knowledge or sense of what had gone into its making but, for him, to live only in the immediate and present was not enough. He needed a story greater than any of theirs, greater than himself, to satisfy his curiosity. *Where am I? Who am I? What am I? Why am I?* These questions were his reason for being, and when he came to the glen he brought with him a story that he believed held the answer to them all. For him, the answer was called God.

* Dr Roland Tanner, 'Myth, Legend and Hagiography: Inventing the Early Celtic Church' in *Studies in Scottish Medieval History*, Volume 32, 2020.

A thousand years passed, and religion no longer sufficed as an explanation for everything. It gave ground slowly, however. James Hutton always carefully qualified his pronouncements about geological time by saying, in effect, *as far as we can tell.* 'With respect to human observation,' he wrote in one of his papers, 'this world has neither a beginning nor an end.' The creationist opinion of the day, which was very powerful, deplored his science since it smashed their timescale to shivereens, but they found it difficult to refute. In fact, Hutton never disavowed the existence of a creator. On the contrary, 'The globe of this earth is evidently made for man,' he wrote in his *Theory of the Earth*. 'He alone, of all the beings which have life upon this body, enjoys the whole and every part; he alone is capable of knowing the nature of this world, which he thus possesses in virtue of his proper right.' And who had given this right to mankind, if not God? Theology and geology *could* coexist, in other words – *as far as we could tell.* Some, who could not reconcile themselves to religious belief, dissented even from this view, but it was politic at that period to keep their dissent to themselves.

In 1809, twelve years after Dr Hutton had confronted the prospect of his own end in his home town of Edinburgh, a young man called Charles Kirkliston Gibb walked into Glen Conach. Whereas Conach had approached from the north, Mr Gibb came from the south, a less challenging yet in his day still arduous route. He came having sought an invitation to visit from Mr Thomas Milne, Baron of Glen Conach. This he had received a fortnight earlier in the following form:

GLEN CONACH, 4TH JUNE 1809

My Dear Mr Gibb

I had your letter on Tuesday last and on the same day coincidentally a letter from Mr Thomas Thomson who says well of you. I hardly know Mr Thomson but he is a gentleman and therefore I do not doubt that you are one too. He says you share his interest in matters antiquarian which I do not doubt either. You ask me to remember you from the occasion when we met at Lord Woodhouselees house in Princes Street when I was obliged to be in Edinburgh last autumn but I regret I have only an indistinct recollection the reason being there was such an immense crowd of people present I lost count of the number who were introduced to me and now after these several months it is quite impossible for me to recall what face I should attach to what name. You do not impose upon me in the least dear Sir or my household by requesting to call on us here in our highland fastness if indeed that description suits as I prefer to think of us as poised at a balance between high and low Scotland in more ways than one as you may find if you make your visit. It is a matter of little consequence to me if you come or you do not and therefore you are welcome if you do and will be no more of an imposition than if you dont. You write that you are anxious to inspect the Book of Conach which is in our possession a very ancient document and you shall be at liberty to spend what time you require with it though you will excuse me from sharing your interest as my Latin is not as good as it should be with my having neglected it since my youth and now I find it tiresome to read and moreover what little I have deciphered in the book does not incline me to try more the script being like something out of Egypt and the characters all crushed together but I trust you will find it less impenetrable than I do. You should come if you are coming as soon as you are able as the glen is at its best just now with the glass settled suggesting a spell of clemency although how long it will last is any mans guess. I know not how you mean to travel or where you may be travelling from but you must reach the town of Forfar and thence continue by horse cart or on foot the journey onward being 20 miles or more and the road quite rough in places so much of a days walking. If you have any baggage disencumber yourself of it at Forfar and we will have it brought on but you will want for nothing as we have spare coats boots linen a good library &c therefore do not fear to bring too little indeed I urge that you do not bring much. You will find us very quiet unlike the bustle and clash of Edinburgh with just myself my wife and our daughter Jessamine here as our son Alexander is encamped with his regiment near Dover having been with us last month after returning from the war in Spain. No other guests are expected so do not think to be much entertained although you may be if only by virtue of our simplicity. Excuse in this letter the absence of any punctuation marks forby stops my spelling is good but my ability to pause in a sentence once I have begun one was never strong and is now entirely dissipated. Although ignorant of what you look like and if your company was agreeable to me when as you say we met at Lord Woodhouselees house I am Sir yours in good faith &c

Glen Conach

P.S. I send this to you as you request care of the household of General Sir Robert Abercromby at Airthrey by Stirling. I do not know Stirling or Sir Robert except of course by reputation but I trust this letter will reach you before you depart his place. Should it not do so I imagine that you will leave instructions for it to be sent in pursuit either to your own residence or whithersoever you may be going next and that the poor thing will catch up with you ere the summer is over but if it does not then I advise against coming here in the winter as you may very well not get out again until spring and we might tire of you and have to eat you.

Journal of Charles Kirkliston Gibb

Sunday, 2nd July 1809

I begin to write – for posterity, I suppose, although God knows I do not expect to have one – in this neat, clean, octavo notebook on the fourth day of my sojourn at Glen Conach House, Forfarshire. The notebook formerly resided at Airthrey Castle, as did I, but since nobody there seemed to have a purpose for it I annexed it, and do not fear that it will be missed. Into it I will now pour my heart, or rather some observations of a witty and amusing nature – amusing to myself, that is, for nobody else presently animate shall ever have sight of it.

I have had until now neither the time nor the energy to record my thoughts about this place and its inhabitants. It will take me some little while to catch up with myself, as there is much to record.

When the family went to church this morning there was no insistence on my going with them, which was an astonishment to me, even though the laird himself told me on Friday that I would not be compelled. It was also a relief, as there has been nothing but a steady downpour all day. In every other part of this self-righteous, God-ridden country one is obliged on the Sabbath not only to attend kirk, whatever the weather, but also to endure additional devotional sessions at home. Here, though, there are no zealous saints to admonish one's backsliding. If laxity is a benefit of remoteness then let me be remote! I stayed in my chamber until noon and have only just now made my way to the library, where there are pens and ink aplenty – I shall take a supply of both back to my room so that I may make entries in this book in either location.

After receiving Mr Thomas Milne's inundation of a letter of 4th June, I immediately prepared to throw myself upon his hospitality. I spoke to him in Edinburgh for only ten minutes last October, but in that time extracted enough information about his place of residence and its antique document to add Glen Conach House to my list of possible future retreats. I am pleased and more than a little surprised that Mr Thomson, the Deputy Clerk Register, wrote on my behalf. Being in charge of the country's public records, he carries some weight when it comes to persuading others of *my* probity. I thought it rather a long shot when I sought his recommendation but evidently my aim was good.

Mr Milne's letter reached me about the middle of last month, at Airthrey, where I strongly sensed that my presence was becoming tiresome to my hosts even though I had arrived scarcely three weeks before and was endeavouring to be as unobtrusive as possible. Having no other offers on hand, and undeterred by Mr Milne's cannibalistic threat, I therefore wrote to him to say that I would soon be on my way. Then, swiftly concluding the 'investigations' into archaeological remains in the vicinity of Airthrey, which were my ostensible reason for being there, and assuring Sir Robert (General Abercromby) that I would compile a detailed account of my findings and send it to him in due course, I took my leave. As the General's eyesight is rapidly deteriorating from a disease he got in India I doubt he will care if the account never arrives, as indeed it never will.

I journeyed on foot through Dunblane to Aberuthven, enjoying the sturdiness and excellent fit of a pair of boots that I had found wastefully unemployed in a press at Airthrey. I then travelled by cart to Perth, on top of a coach to Dundee (at a small cost met by some coins also carelessly neglected by Sir Robert's household), and on foot again from there to Forfar. I was four days and nights on the road. Each night, accomplished as I am in the ancient arts of 'thigging' and 'sorning' (which is to say, *anglicé*, begging and sponging), I found cheap or free food and dry lodging, even if twice I slept in a hayloft and once had to share a bed with a drunken pedlar, than whom the haylofts were far less verminous. In Forfar I secreted myself behind a settle in an inn shortly before it closed, slept badly, and slipped out at dawn ere the landlord awoke. This made a cold and a hungry start to a long day, but ten weary hours later, at half past two last Thursday afternoon, I arrived at my destination.

My second encounter with Mr Thomas Milne, and my first with his wife, Margaret, occurred in what is called the great hall of the house. This is a huge space with a flagged floor from which a staircase of three short flights leads to the upper storeys, while a narrower stair hidden by a door descends to the kitchen and servants' area. The hall is dominated by a fireplace, which, when I arrived, contained an enormous heap of wood – unlit, despite the dampness of the afternoon. Around the fireplace, on a large, faded, red rug that bears many scorch-marks and holes, as an old soldier bears the scars and wounds of battle, are set a number of chairs and a chaise longue. Pictures of earlier Milnes, whose features all but disappear into the oily gloom of their backgrounds, are hung on the wood-panelled walls.

I walked into this scene unannounced, having found the main door of the house open. I was very tired. It was immediately apparent that a matrimonial dispute was in progress concerning the desirability of lighting the fire, she being in favour and he in opposition. It was also clear, when they suspended hostilities to see who had come in, that Mr Milne, or, as I should more properly designate him, the Baron of Glen Conach – or simply Glen Conach – had no notion of who I was. By luck, as it transpired, he had mentioned the possibility of my visit to his lady a few days earlier and, once I had introduced myself, the Baroness seemed perfectly at ease with the fact of my arrival, and if the Baron did not remember me he at least affected to do so – 'Aye, of course, Mr ah, Mr Gibb, good afternoon, Sir.'

'Ye 're gey weet, Mr Gibb, and a wee thing splairged wi glaur,' the lady said, casting a critical eye over me.

Although of course thoroughly familiar with the Scotch tongue, which I myself spoke as a child before my education began, I found her accent quite different from those of the southern part of the country where I was bred, and it took me a moment or two to confirm to myself that these were the words she had actually articulated. She was quite correct: I was dripping from various tips and angles on to the stone floor, and making quite a lochan around my feet.

'I am very wet, yes.'

'In fact, there's glaur a' ower ye.'

'Indeed, I am rather muddy too.'

'That's what I said.'

'He anely speaks English,' the Baron told her. 'I mind noo.'

'Then we will need to do the same,' the Baroness said, changing at once to a confident though still heavily encumbered English, 'otherwise we will be here all night. You really are soaked through, Mr Gibb.'

I nodded my agreement, showering the floor with yet more rainwater. 'The weather is evidently not as settled as it was when your husband sent me his letter,' I said. 'Admittedly that was almost a month ago. It was dry in Forfar when I set out this morning, but it did not last.'

'That's the way of weather,' the Baron said, and made a lurch as if buffeted by a squall. 'It will be different again in the morning.'

I should note here some of the characteristics of this Baron of Glen Conach, the fifth of that title to bear the name Milne. Having observed him at close quarters for three days now, and gathered further information from the household, I may fairly describe him as a shaggy tree of a man who, when upright, always seems on the point of overbalancing and crashing to earth. He apparently spent much of his life wearing a wig, but at the start of the new century abandoned all forms of headdress, in or out of doors, after deciding on no particular evidence that wigs, hats, turbans and nightcaps trap germs and make a man ill. He is about sixty-three or -four, and claims not to have had a single cold since he gave up covering his head. He told me himself that he shaves his face and neck twice a week but, on the

Samsonite principle that it is the source of his strength, does not permit the cutting of his hair, which is sparse, long and unruly, and sticks out in every direction. This makes him appear not only arborescent but also, regardless of the time of day, as if he has only recently risen from sleep. He finds modern life bewildering and ridiculous and tries to avoid it by staying away from overpopulated places such as Edinburgh and Forfar.

'You had better get oot o' thae things and into some dry anes,' Lady Glen Conach said to me, and I realised that it required some effort on her part to make her linguistic adjustments. 'I will have some hot water sent to your room. By the time you come down, this fire' – here she swiftly glanced at her husband – '*will* be lichtit – lit. Where have you left your baggage?'

Of course I had none, but before I could say so she spoke again, to her husband.

'If we had kent, Jock McLeish could have brocht it on his cairt.' Then, to me: 'Jock was here not an hour since with a dozen dining chairs we have been waiting on for weeks.'

'No baggage for me, Madam,' I told her. 'I came on foot.'

'What we need a dozen dining chairs for is beyond me,' the Baron said. 'Four would mair than suffice. We already have chairs. What we want is cheese. Did Jock bring the Dunlop as I asked?'

'The chairs are either rotten or broken, and the breaking was mostly your doing,' his lady replied. 'I have taken the dozen as an insurance against future losses.' (I am writing this down as fully and in as near to the correct order of their statements as I can recall.) 'And aye, Jock did bring a whole cheese. It's as big as a wheel. But Mr Gibb, now that I think on it, he must have passed you. He offered to take you up, surely?'

I knew nothing about any Jock McLeish, but assumed that it was his cart that I had seen departing as I approached the house. That he had not assisted me was not his fault. I explained that I had missed him on account of having taken the wrong road.

'How could you take the wrong road?' the Baron asked or, rather, roared. 'There is only the one.'

I said that I thought I had identified a short cut but it had turned out to be a long cut. And there had been a burn to cross. To be more accurate, although it was probably a burn most days, it was a raging torrent that afternoon.

'Well, you must get dry at once,' the Baroness said. 'Our daughter, Jessamine, will get out some things of Alexander's for you. He is our son, ye ken. He is away with his regiment just now, the Black Watch, waiting to engage the French once more. You look about the same size.'

'Sandy is not so fat in the middle,' the Baron observed, with no thought at all for my feelings. My personal opinion is that I am quite slender, and I once overheard it said that if I were any thinner at the waist I would snap in two. Generally speaking, people regard me as physically feeble, and it is true that although I am quite tall my limbs are not very strong. I had, however, just walked twenty miles and more, in terrible conditions, sustained only by a drink of milk and a bannock, which I had had at the mill where the River Conach joins the Esk. I have since learned that the Baron's erroneous view arose from an unshakeable paternal pride in Alexander, and a belief that no other young man can match the superlativeness of his son's manhood. Therefore, whenever a new specimen of masculinity is put before the Baron, he must find fault with it.

His wife ignored him. 'Did you say you had not brought *anything* with you?' she asked, fixing me with a commanding look (one that I have come to know well in the last few days).

A word about this impressive person, Margaret Milne, or Lady Glen Conach. She is tall and tidy, a garden cane to her husband's unruliness. When she stands at his side they resemble the figure 10. A year or two younger than whatever age he is, she has a long, thin nose above a mouth that seems often about to smile but seldom does, and even then in a restrained manner. On her head she grows a crop of grey curls, which she usually keeps neatly drilled below a lace cap tied under the chin. Her eyes are bright blue and there are little purplish bouquets of burst veins on her cheeks. She is very intelligent and practical, and manages the Baron and the household without fuss and on the principle that nothing will happen unless she organises it. She has a strong desire for order and peace, but whereas in many women this leads to an absence of humour she seems to be constantly amused by life and quite content in herself. Yesterday, for example, I saw her creep up on the Baron with scissors when he was asleep in his chair and snip off the most extreme bits of his foliage, carrying them away without his knowing that he had been pruned. This was obviously both an entertainment and a regular duty to her. The laird must surely wonder that his hair never grows beyond a certain length, but if he suspects his wife of playing Delilah he keeps his suspicions to himself.

As far as I can ascertain, Lady Glen Conach has but two sources of worry. One is the safety of her son, Alexander, lately in Iberia fighting the French and now in Kent awaiting embarkation to some new theatre of war. She understands that the French have conducted themselves abominably for the last twenty years, but she has no personal quarrel with them, thinks that her son is not responsible for their bad behaviour, and objects that his life should be put at risk in order to bring them to their senses. Her other concern is for her daughter, Jessamine, who has reached the ancient age of twenty-four. It is obviously a difficulty, since Miss Milne never gets out of the glen and few eligible men get into it, as to how she is to be wooed, let alone wed. I have felt, these last few days, the mother's assessing eye upon me, but of course being penniless and without pedigree I am completely unsuitable. This is to say nothing of Miss Milne's misfortune in her appearance, of which more anon.

'Only what I carry in my satchel, Madam, which is also somewhat damp,' I said in reply to the Baroness's question. Under her stern gaze I felt obliged to provide further details, and confessed to some linen, hose and a spare shirt, and a book or two, which were, fortunately, wrapped in oilcloth. 'I have brought no more than these,' I said. 'In his letter, the Baron said not to.'

'Not to what?'

'Not to bring anything. He was very definite.'

'Mr Gibb, you will soon learn that one thing my husband is not, is very definite.'

'I told him not to bring books either,' the Baron said. 'We have a whole library of them.'

'That does not stop you adding to it,' the Baroness replied sharply, and a smile nearly broke upon her face. (Again, I have come to know that half-smile well these last few days.) 'Dinna fash, Mr Gibb. We can and will outrig you.'

'I am grateful, Madam.'

The Baron was, I think, beginning to feel superfluous, and intervened as my champion even though ignorant of almost everything about me.

'Mr Gibb is not a man who *fashes* about trivialities such as clothing! He is not a dandy! He is a man of spirit and determination who takes short cuts across hills he kens nothing about. He is – as I seem to recall from our meeting in the capital, Mr Gibb – a man of learning, with a great knowledge of – many things. In short, Mr Gibb is a – is a –'

'What are you, Mr Gibb?' Lady Glen Conach asked, to expedite proceedings.

Having been confronted with this question often in the past, I was able to answer her with great fluency. 'An inquirer into our national relics, Madam. An antiquarian. An interpreter of this country's past.'

'You see?' said the Baron. 'A man of learning, as I said, come to interpret us.'

'You are too far decayed to be interpreted, my dear,' his lady told him. She turned back to me. 'How can you interpret anything about Scotland if you don't speak Scotch?'

Again, I was well prepared. 'I *can* speak it, Madam. I *did* speak it, but I have outgrown the habit. My father was a scholar and was against it, and after he died my mother chastised it out of me in his memory. We also – she and I – were in England for some years, where we got on better by suppressing it. In justice to both my parents, although I comprehend it fully, I do think it a hindrance to progress.'

'That's a fashion, progress,' the Baron said, bristling (though, in truth, he seldom does *not* bristle). 'I am opposed to fashion of every kind, Mr Gibb. I subscribe to a number of different journals purely to inform myself of the latest fashions, so that I can avoid them. As for the noble Scotch tongue, have you not read the work of Mr Burns? If so, you cannot be serious in the opinion you have just expressed.'

'All that can wait, my dear,' the Baroness interposed. 'I gather you have an interest in our *Book*, Mr Gibb?'

Indeed I had. It was what had secured my invitation. 'I do, Madam. I believe the *Book of Conach* to be one of the most important, though neglected, of Scotland's relics.'

'But you have not seen it yet,' the Baron protested.

'No, Sir, but you spoke about it so eloquently when we met in Edinburgh.'

'Did I? I canna mind.'

'You see, Mr Gibb?' the Baroness said. 'Not definite. He contradicts himself at every turn. Well, there will be time enough for the *Book* tomorrow. The first thing is to get you into dry clothes. You are welcome here, but I don't want you dying as soon as you have arrived.'

I had a brief vision of my corpse being bundled in a sack on to the back of Mr McLeish's cart and transported down the sodden track to Forfar, or possibly thrown in a bog. I decided to try a joke on my hostess.

'It would be most impolite of me to put you to that inconvenience, Madam.'

Her lips twitched slightly and I thought I might have scored a point in my favour.

'Therefore,' I continued, 'I would be grateful to borrow a set of your son's clothes and avoid such, ah, impoliteness.'

'Very good.' But she did not smile. 'I will summon Jessamine. You must not think us too intimate, Mr Gibb, but we do not have as many servants as you may be used to in Edinburgh, and that's because we do not need them.'

'Couldna afford them even if we did,' the Baron muttered.

'I am not used to servants at all,' I said. 'Not my own, that is.'

'Then you'll not make yourself a burden on ours,' the Baroness said. 'We are a hardy people, Mr Gibb. We set to with our own hands and get on with things. If we did not' – another swift glance at her husband – 'nothing would ever be done. For example, I am about to arrange our new chairs, while Glen Conach is going to light the fire. We dine in an hour. Excuse me.'

In three steps she was at the foot of the stair. She let out a piercing shriek which I was amazed to hear issuing from such a neat, light-framed woman.

'Jessie! Come doon this meenit! There's a gentleman here wantin your assistance.'

From the floor above, but suspiciously close to the head of the staircase, there came a rustling sound, and then a female voice: 'Did ye call, Mama? A gentleman, did ye say? I am coming doon the noo.'

Nothing happened. I waited expectantly, but no vision appeared. The Baron and his wife glanced at each other. The Baroness said, 'Come along, Jessie. You needna be blate. Mr Gibb will catch his death if ye dinna hurry up.'

'Blate?' the Baron exclaimed. 'She'll be preenin hersel.'

This remark seemed to provoke Miss Milne, who rushed into view, paused on the first landing to say, 'Papa, that is a calumny!' and half glided, half stumbled down the remaining steps in a blue silk dress, a woollen shawl flying at her shoulders. She only brought herself to a halt by putting a hand squarely on my chest. 'You're very kind, Sir,' she said, although I had done nothing but act as a post.

I confess that for a moment I felt less kind than curious, as I found it impossible to avert my eyes from the lower portion of her face. Miss Milne has a prominent birthmark, fully an inch in width and of a fiery red hue, which runs from her left ear across her cheek to her lips and has the unfortunate effect of making her mouth seem stretched and misshapen. I looked away quickly and then, as that seemed ill-mannered, returned my stare to her face and found her staring directly back at me as if pleased to have discovered my embarrassment.

'My daughter, Miss Milne,' the Baron said. 'Jessamine, this is Mr Gibb. I forget his first name.'

'Charles,' the Baroness said. 'You may remove your hand, Jessie. Mr Gibb is an antiquarian.'

'An antiquarian?' Miss Milne's eyes widened and her mouth formed a tiny 'o', reminding me of some kind of bird. She wiped her palm on her dress. 'He's a wee bit damp.'

'He has come to stay with us.'

'What for?'

'To see the *Book*. He has a great interest in it.'

'Oh,' Miss Milne said, 'I hae an interest in it as weel, Mr Gibb, though I confess I hinna read the haill o' it. The glen folk hae a wheen o' tales aboot Conach, or "Saint Conach" as they like to cry him. Perhaps I can tell ye some o' them?'

She tilted her head at me, and gave a brief display of a multitude of teeth before her lips resumed that tight circle. Her ringlets framed her face nicely and I decided that the bird she resembled was a little owl, albeit one with a great scar upon its visage.

'That can all wait, Jessie,' her mother said. 'Mr Gibb does not like to speak Scotch, by the way, so please will you speak English to him as best you can? It will be good practice for you.'

'My English is exemplary, Mama,' the daughter replied.

'There is nothing human that canna be improved,' the Baroness said. 'Away and find Elspeth and tell her to fetch hot water to Mr Gibb. Show Mr Gibb where he is to sleep – the blue room. Then you must select a set of dry clothes for him from Alexander's kist. Linen, breeks, shoes, everything – he's as drookit as a duck.' (She pronounced this, as far as I can represent it, as *djeuk*.) 'A nightshirt forby. Let Elspeth take them to Mr Gibb while you redd yourself up for dinner. Glen Conach, set a lunt to that fire. Mr Gibb, dinner is at four. Go with Jessie. I'm away to make sure that there *is* dinner. Mr Dunning, our minister, will be with us.'

It was evident that when the Baroness gave instructions in this house everybody obeyed. I did not hesitate to obey her myself, but then I have always been quick to learn. It is my intention, if I like the situation, to stay at Glen Conach House as long as I can, perhaps all summer. To winter here, however, does not appeal, even were I not to end up hanging in the larder. I will have to find another nest and fly to it by the close of September at latest.

I followed Miss Milne up the stair, having to catch her at the second turn when she tripped on one end of her shawl. She led me down a passage and dramatically flung open a door. 'Your chamber, Mr Gibb,' she cried, and turned her head in the opposite direction as if the room were a temptation. 'I daurna cross the threshold – imagine! – but Elspeth will see to your needs when she comes.'

I thanked her and attempted to pass her, but she stopped me with an imperious finger that almost took my eye out, and the fiery mark, which for a moment had disappeared from my sight, seemed to leap at me as she spoke. 'A moment, Sir. Let me survey you. Aye, my brother and yourself are not that different in size. How odd, to be choosing garments to clad the person of a perfect stranger! I will send Elspeth directly, and we will meet again in an hour.' And she ran off along the passage.

But my hand aches from having written so much, and I had better at least pretend to be engaged in the purpose for which I have come to Glen Conach, so will pause here.

Monday, 3rd July 1809

The room I entered – *my* room, as I may style it, for as long as I remain here – was sparsely furnished with a bed, a press, a chest of drawers, a chair and a table. On brief inspection it seemed clean enough. The bed was certainly soft enough, the mattress being stuffed with heather rather than straw (as I found on investigating a hole in it, which was perhaps the door of a mouse's nest). I could have lain down and slept at once. The window looked westward towards what I now know to be hills above the trees, but which at the time were obscured by clouds. There was a fireplace, not made up to be lit, and I thought it unlikely, since we were in what passes for summer, that I would be granted that private benefit. (I was right.) The pale blue distemper on the walls did nothing to make the room feel less chilly.

I was untying my boots when the door was knocked and a young woman, barefoot and in a dress that concealed none of her impressive symmetry, came in. She bore a large, steaming pitcher, which she placed beside a wash-bowl on a stand in one corner. I noted also, to my surprise, a commode in this functional quarter of the room. (I scarcely dared hope that I would not have to share the use of this important item with anybody else – but so it has proved.)

'Here's water for ye, Sir,' the maiden said. 'I'll awa for your claes the noo, if ye wid just tak aff whit's on ye.' She left again. I removed the boots but then waited, not wishing to embarrass either of us by being half naked when she returned.

I need not have been anxious on her account. She came back in, this time without a knock, and placed a pile of clothing on the bed. 'Noo,' she said, shaking her head, 'will ye no get oot o' thae things so I can tak them awa to dry them?' Servants in Scottish houses are generally not servile, but this one had an especially forward manner. I loosed my shirt from my breeches and stopped.

ME: 'Are you Elspeth?'
SHE: 'I am.'
ME: 'And you are from the glen? I mean, you were born and bred here?'
SHE: 'Deed aye. Whaur else wid I be frae?'
ME: 'How old are you, Elspeth?'
SHE: 'Nineteen, Sir, but dinna spier me aw thir questions gin it stops ye gettin oot o' thae weet things. Just let them fa on the flair. Here's a towel,' she added, fairly flinging it at me.

She took her stance by the bed, hardly blinking, let alone looking away, and I saw there was nothing for it but to strip off every item and drop them in a sodden heap. She gathered them into her arms while I covered myself with the towel. She was on the point of leaving when she paused.

'Forby, whit's my age to you?'

'Nothing at all,' I said, and she gave a little nod, full or empty of meaning, and went out.

Nothing at all! But my reason for asking was that she made me feel like a small child when I am nine years her senior. She seems to have no fear of me, clothed or naked, and little respect either.

I washed quickly, dried myself off and began to dress in the clothes of the son and heir, Alexander Milne.

Dinner commenced an hour later. When I came down a little early, there was much activity between the dining room, which is really a kind of adjunct to the great hall, and the stair that leads to the kitchen and basement. The Baroness was directing operations: a large, ponderous man who I have since ascertained is the stableman, Davie Nicol, was carrying away old chairs and replacing them with the new ones delivered from Forfar. His wife, Kate, is the cook. I heard Lady Glen Conach tell Kate not to break open the Dunlop that day as the minister, who was to join us at dinner, would go at it in a frenzy and it had to last a month. Elspeth, assisted by a diminutive kitchen maid called Norah, was laying out cutlery and glasses. They also received their instructions: 'Elspeth, that wine is to be poured into a jug, but ca canny wi it'; 'Norah, dinna touch the table linen till ye've washed your hands – they are black wi soot.' I had a notion that Elspeth was clashing the silverware and letting the glasses ring in order to impress her mistress with her industry. I watched for a moment and then passed through the great hall and outer lobby to the door, to admire the vista. There was nothing to admire but mist and rain. Fortunately, dinner was shortly announced.

Our time at table was marked by the hands of a longcase, drumhead clock standing like a sentry in one corner of the dining room, its heavy, disapproving tick contrasting with cheerful hourly chimes. The food, I am pleased to report, was plain but plentiful: first, cock-a-leekie, with a whole bird in the tureen – the Baron masterfully lifted the carcass out with two enormous forks and tore it into chunks, which he then returned to the broth; next, a boiled hare in an onion-rich stock, served with beetroots, kale and potatoes; then, a bread pudding; and all accompanied by a claret that was perfectly drinkable provided one allowed the debris to settle at the bottom of the glass.

GLEN CONACH: 'What do you think of that, Mr Gibb?'

ME: 'Very fine, Sir. There is hardly any French wine drunk in Edinburgh these days.'

GC: 'I ken. One of many reasons for not going there. It's the war, of course. Even my own cellar is much diminished.'

ME: 'And some people think it unpatriotic.'

GC: 'Then they are imbeciles. Is the wine their enemy? It makes a good alliance with the hare, don't you agree?'

I did agree. It was all very acceptable and I can, I am sure, survive on such fare for months without difficulty. Glen Conach eats with enthusiasm, his lady with decorum. Miss Milne has a very efficient way of eating. She fills her fork or spoon to capacity and transfers the load to her mouth while parting her lips so briefly and slightly that it seems impossible that the food will go in without mishap, yet it always does. I had to force myself to stop looking for an accident that never happened. I did find, however, that my fascination with this operation meant that I took less notice of the birthmark.

Mr John Dunning, the minister, did not spare himself at any course of the meal, but attempted to disguise his rate of consumption by frequent dabbings at the mouth with his serviette. He is a fat, dark-haired man with a black beard and a greasy forehead, which he also dabbed and wiped. I estimate him to be somewhat more than fifty years old. He deferred to the Baron throughout dinner and never once disagreed with him, seemed resentful that I had come and even more so when it became clear that I was not soon going away again. Twice I caught him leering at Jessie Milne from behind his serviette. Occasionally he blew his nose into it. By now I was feeling much less dismayed – I will not use a stronger term – by Miss Milne's disfigurement, although it was scarcely possible to pretend that it was anything other than that, but it seemed to me that Mr Dunning's eye lingered upon it almost lasciviously, as if it in some way excited him. I cannot explain this, but record it nonetheless. I record also that I then and there formed a dislike of Mr Dunning which is as yet undiminished: no doubt this is irrational but I cannot deny it. No doubt he has formed an equally irrational dislike of me.

The ladies retired upstairs and, after a short interval involving the circulation of a bottle of whisky, we joined them in a small but comfortable parlour which is the Baroness's day room. Miss Milne played, not well, on a spinet – 'I am aye nervous, Mr Gibb,' she said, 'before strangers.' Dunning said silkily, 'We are not *all* strangers, Miss Jessamine,' and I thought for a moment she was going to be ill. She recovered herself, however, and sang two songs, unaccompanied except for a chord here and there to keep her attached to the melody, and her voice was much better than her playing. The songs were 'The Blackbird' and 'Will He No Come Back Again?' The listeners, myself excluded, were much stirred by these old Jacobite songs, although the romantic effect of the second one was somewhat diminished when the Baron said loudly during the first chorus, 'Guidsakes, lass, he's only just arrived', which made her blush and refuse to look at me for the rest of the performance. When she was done, suggestions were made about some supper, but I pleaded exhaustion and retired to bed.

What shall I say of Jessie Milne? What have I learned of her since that first day? If one could disregard her disfigurement, one might describe her thus: she is tall and straight like her mother, and has a small, heart-shaped face with a dimple in its chin. She has brown ringlets, blue eyes and a rosy complexion from having spent much of her childhood outside in all weathers – and yet the birthmark is not disguised by, but seems almost exaggerated against, this background. In short, it is not *possible* to disregard it: it is there like a creature upon her face that nobody wishes to discuss for fear it will bite or grow even larger.

Like her mother, Miss Milne seems to be amused by her own thoughts much of the time. Following the maternal example, she mainly keeps that small, round mouth pursed, which is as well, for when she does open it the view of her many teeth, rather like a portcullis, is quite terrifying. In other ways she is more like her father, being distracted, untidy and unbalanced. She misses her brother, who it seems was her best friend before he became a soldier. They await word from him, day after day. She would like to sail more in society but would be capsized at once if she did, since all she knows about it is what she reads in the journals and magazines taken by her father. If she is conscious of the effect her mark has upon her appearance she hides it well, yet it must be a perpetual torment to her, for she must believe that her looks are not improved by it. She is as fearful, I think, of being married as she is of not being, and this accounts for her panicking a little in male company, even in mine, and appearing idiotic. But she is not an idiot. I believe, on the contrary, that she is quite cunning.

Maja

I think it is true for most people that the older they get the more disappointing life becomes. The horizon lowers, possibilities diminish, mind and body protest more when made to work, or simply refuse to work at all. This disappointment is, like physical aches and pains, a part of the aging process. I know people much younger than me who feel it, but I don't. I feel lucky.

When I wake in the morning the first thing I do is step outside and breathe in the fresh air. Sometimes it is still dark, sometimes it has already been light for an hour or two. Dark or light, mist or rain, snow, frost or sunshine, it doesn't matter. I open the door and stand there in my dressing gown and breathe. I hear the river thirty yards away. Maybe I hear birdsong, maybe Julia's music is playing next door, maybe an engine is running, or maybe everything is silent. It doesn't matter. It's the breathing that counts. It amazes me to be alive. Still to be alive.

The day that Lachie came to tell me about his ghost started in this way, as every one of my days does. It was raining quite hard, as he said, but then the clouds lifted and my garden seemed to shake itself and dry out a bit. I got dressed, made my breakfast, pottered about at various tasks. I live mainly without noise, which some people find *dis*quieting. Perhaps if they cannot hear noise in the background they think life has ceased all around them. For me, it is the opposite. What sounds there are become louder. I hear my own breath in my nose, the creaks and cracks of my body and of the house, the tick of the cooling kettle, a gust of wind outside, a mouse in the wall. I hear birds all the time. There is nothing more full of life than a bird singing.

Later, I sat in my chair at the window with my sketchbook. I saw three things that morning that moved me. First, I saw a little gang of chaffinches come to the bird table and clean up the breadcrumbs I had spread there ten minutes earlier. I just had time to make some coffee and sit down before they arrived, chattering like bairns let out into the playground at breaktime. Of course, they come because I always put food out. There had been no sign of them in the garden beforehand and yet within those few minutes they all knew the breadcrumbs were there. Word had got around. When they had finished they flew off again, as if they had other important matters to attend to, which they probably had. That was one thing.

Then I saw Julia's cat making his way along the wall that separates our gardens. Tam is a handsome black-and-white beast, sometimes interested in stalking small birds, sometimes not. This morning he seemed simply to be out for a stroll, inspecting his domain – his more than mine or Julia's, since we don't use the top of the wall as a path. I tapped on the glass and he stopped, looked disdainfully over his shoulder in my direction, then carried on at the same casual pace. That was another thing.

I made a few quick drawings of the chaffinches, as I have many times before. Just impressions – they move so fast. And the sketch of the cat on the wall was so vague that he was almost not there, although Lachie seemed to see him well enough when he came in after school.

The third thing was more unusual. I went outside to gather a few leaves, which I wanted to draw in their death shapes, maybe paint them in their beautiful, rich death colours. And also to go to the shed for logs for the stove. The shed was dark and then I opened the door and it wasn't. I put some logs into the sling, a handy item Julia got for me. It makes the logs easier to carry. Just before I closed the shed into darkness again, I saw a stone that shouldn't have been there, lying against the foot of the jamb. I bent to move it. It wasn't a stone. It was a toad. He was very welcome as far as I was concerned but something was not right. I touched him with my finger. He did not move. I lowered the sling of logs and looked more closely. The toad was dead – whole, fresh, but dead. I made sure of this – that he wasn't fast asleep, that this wasn't an ill-chosen spot for hibernation. Then I fetched a trowel and nudged the corpse on to it, and took it outside and buried it in the soft, damp soil.

I did not make a drawing of the toad in death. But I see him, even now. Or her. It could have been a her.

Was the shed the toad's place? Did she know why she had gone there? Was it to hide or to sleep? Did she feel ill? Does a toad know what it is to feel ill? Did she go there to die?

Somebody, I don't remember who, said that humans are the only mortal beings because only we know that death will come to us. Every other creature on this planet – midge, ant, mouse, fish, snake, deer, whale; chaffinch, cat, toad – is blessed with immortality because they do not have that knowledge. They are alive and that is all they know or expect. They do not know that they will die. Or so we, in our arrogance, presume.

If they do not know of death then it follows that they do not know of life either. They are alive but they don't know it. I mean, they don't comprehend it. They don't examine life and worry about death, nor do they worry about life and examine death. Again, this is our presumption – or the presumption of some of us.

But maybe the toad did know. Maybe they all know more than we think. Maybe they know more than we do.

Nevertheless, it is true – whatever we presume – that animals and birds are immortal. We are here, then we are not. The crows, the bees, the mice, they are always here, and they will be when we are gone. We do not know them each, we know them all. It is as *all* that they outlive us.

I didn't mention the toad to Lachie. I thought, with the ghost girl, he had enough on his mind. And maybe I had too little in mine, because I dwelt for quite a while afterwards on what he'd told me. It wasn't that I wondered if he'd really seen her. It was this: if she *was* a ghost, would she know?

I used to go walking in the wood. I don't walk there now. The old, roofless church and its overgrown graveyard is about as far as I venture these days. But whenever I went to the wood, especially in the evening, I would see a deer. Maybe more than one. The wood is their place. Roe deer with their dark coats and white rumps. One would see me and freeze, and I would freeze too. And something would pass across the distance between us. If I stood still she would wait; she became part of the wood. Then quietly, gently, she would move off through the trees. If I began to walk first, she would watch me and sometimes her nerves could not bear it and she would flee. And often she would unfreeze others that I had not known were there. Off they would go. I was no danger to them but they did not know that. They trusted their fear and they were right to trust it.

There is a poem by a poet whose language was Gaelic. It is very beautiful, although painful and sad. I have read the poem and heard a recording of the poet reading it. His name was Sorley MacLean and 'Hallaig' is the name of the poem and of the place it is about. People once lived there, his ancestors, but it was emptied of people, and now its houses are all in ruins. I do not know any Gaelic but even in English it is a beautiful poem. Gaelic has not been spoken in Glen Conach for a long, long time. When I think of the deer in that poem she has stepped out of it and is coming closer and closer to the houses here. A few of these houses are also in ruins. There are gaps where others used to be. The deer sniffs at the grass, at the stones, she skips through the gap in the dyke. I have seen her grazing among the unreadable gravestones where the grass is thick and lush. One day she will come sniffing among the ruins of this house, even those of the Big House.

The deer is Time. That's what the poem says, and it is as true of this glen as it is of Hallaig, which is on an island on the other side of the country. It is too far away for me to go there. Maybe once, if I had kept going westward, but not now. Julia went there. She has a thing about islands: she likes to visit them, ticking them off. It was Julia who showed me the poem and played me the recording of the poet's voice. I felt as if I were hearing something very ancient, from centuries ago. It was a long journey to the island, she said, and even when you got there it was a long walk to the place in the poem. But she went and she came back and she told me about it.

When I used to meet the deer it was like meeting Time. I didn't know that then. I know it now. It was like meeting Time and then Time fled and left me on my own. But Time never goes far. It is in the wood beyond my window, it is in the churchyard beyond my garden wall. If I am very still I can hear a twig cracking under its weight.

What they are trying to do here is change the course of history. For the last two centuries, people have been leaving the glen. Not enough food, too many bairns, no money to pay the rent. In other parts of this country the owners cleared people out and put sheep in instead, or they turned the land into playgrounds for stalking deer, shooting grouse and catching salmon, and only they and their guests were allowed to do these things. Some of this happened here, but it was not so extreme as elsewhere. Still, there were many people living in the glen a hundred years ago, and more if you go back another hundred. Now there are just a handful. Shirley and Peter Darroch, who have the Big House, are not of the glen. Only a very few folk can say that they were born and raised here, and even fewer that their parents or their grandparents were. The Darrochs bought the estate ten years ago, after the financial crash. The people before them, the Duff-Hasties, had had enough. They said it was impossible to make it pay and they were being persecuted by politicians in Edinburgh who knew nothing about the countryside. It may be true that politicians in Edinburgh know nothing about the countryside, or not much, but it was nonsense to talk of persecution unless it was of hares or birds of prey, and that was not being done by the politicians. Most folk in the glen were not sorry when the Duff-Hasties sold up after the crash, the chief regret being the loss of the fun that had been had with their name (they were widely known, among other things, as the Puff Pastries). I cannot say that I had much time for them. Before them were the Grants, who had the estate for a hundred and fifty years. I knew Sir Gregory Grant, who was a good man, and I knew his son, who was not a bad man but who came to a bad end. And before the Grants were the Milnes, whose line died out in 1832.

Peter Darroch is from Perth, Shirley is from Yorkshire. They had enough money to buy the estate but they say they do not own it, they are its custodians. There are some who make faces when they hear this – they say all rich landowners come out with that line – but the Darrochs mean it, and anyway they are not that rich. They have set up a community trust and, in a few years, they say, they will transfer ownership of the estate to the trust. But first they want to make it possible for more people to live here. They are trying to build a more diverse economy – fishing, mountain-biking and holiday lets as well as forestry and farming. They want to do away with shooting grouse and pheasants altogether, but not stalking the red deer up in the hills. They have converted the home farm to be organic. They talk about making things sustainable, about people having two or three different jobs, about the farm shop and café being a hub for locals as well as visitors. To raise funds they made a deal with the energy company to put up six wind turbines. Some people made faces about those too. They said they were ugly and would spoil the views. Now the turbines are here, most hardly notice them. I like them. They are graceful, the way they chop the wind as it turns them, and they bring a lot of money to the glen. The farm shop and café wouldn't have been possible without the turbines; insulating and re-roofing these cottages would not have happened. I moved in with Julia for two weeks last year while mine was done, then she moved in with me and they did hers. When I am no longer around they will be able to rent mine out easily, all through the year. Or they could sell it, but I hope they do not.

Shirley Darroch says her dream is to get people reconnected with the land. She gets quite emotional sometimes, and some laugh at her, but she cannot help it, she feels it deeply. She tries not to be too idealistic. 'Down to earth,' she says, 'that's what I want us to be. Down to earth, literally. But nurturing it, not taking from it and putting nothing back. The earth is thin here, fragile, there is not much of it between us and the rock. You have to be careful.'

Shirley's dream is that the population grows so much that the glen has to have a school again. Lachie and his sister, Rosie, go out of the glen to school and they will be grown up before that change happens, if it ever does. Shirley also wants to turn part of the Big House into a retreat, where people can come to be 'spiritual'. She is not religious, she says, but she likes the tales about 'Saint Conach', who was not a saint at all in the Church's eyes. Shirley thinks his spirit is still floating about. I don't know what makes a person saintly or whether there will ever again be a school in the glen and I don't know about people being spiritual. I do know it will take longer to get a few folk back on the land than it ever took to get their ancestors off it, but Shirley means what she says and so does Peter, so maybe it could all happen, although I will not see it. A dream cannot come true if you do not dream it.

I know something else as well: that the glen can be a place for somebody, if they come here. It can be the place where they hide and sleep, and recover life if they are not ready to die. A place from which they can go back out into the world again, if that's what they choose to do, or stay if they do not.

I know this because of the dumb lass. In these recent days I have been thinking about her more than I have done for a long time. A separate being from me, and yet we are conjoined. I haven't seen her yet, the way Lachie sees his ghost, if it is a ghost. I don't know who it is he sees, but he might be seeing the dumb lass.

That thought makes me wonder if there is a change on the way for me; if I might soon be beyond the animals, treading that line of mortality. I am not afraid. I am curious. But if I have more courage than some it is only because the dumb lass trod that line before me. I took the courage from her, stored it away and then forgot most of how I had come by it.

If a change is coming, it will come in its own time. Meanwhile I will get up every morning and breathe in the fresh air.

Journal of Charles Kirkliston Gibb

Tuesday, 4th July 1809

I slept soundly after my saturation and subsequent dinner, and woke suffering no ill effects from either. My constitution is stronger than others sometimes presume. I rose at six, and found the morning bright and dry. I again put on Alexander Milne's clothes, my own not yet having been returned to me apart from my boots (to which, after the trials I have put them through, I feel nobody else now has a legitimate claim), and made my way downstairs.

The only person in evidence was Elspeth, who was bustling at the fireplace. I should also mention the Baron's two deerhounds, which I forgot to say had lain under the table during dinner, occasionally receiving a bone or other morsel from their master. They were stretched out together and raised their heads and growled at my arrival but did not deign to inspect me more closely.

I am curious as to the position that this young woman Elspeth Carnegie has in the household. She is a servant but does not have a particular role as far as I can determine. There are the cook, the stableman, the kitchen maid and at least one other female servant, a dairywoman and a pair of gardeners, but Elspeth is none of these. She seems to do a little of everything and indeed a *little* is what she does. If she had a title at all I suppose it might be chambermaid, but she would scorn it. Besides, nobody oversees her except the Baroness and even she treats her with some laxity. Elspeth works quite energetically but never for long at any one task, stopping when she feels she has done enough. She has the air of one who believes she should have been born to a higher station. She is the nearest Jessie Milne has to a female friend, but despite being Miss Milne's social inferior and only nineteen she has a greater conceit of herself. She is beauty to Jessie's imperfection. Her hair is thick, black and curly, her eyes dark, her lips red, and she makes no effort to conceal an ample figure and coquettish spirit. Her mother, it seems, died in giving birth to her, and her father has been dead some years also. Perhaps these circumstances explain the favouritism that she is shown. She comes and goes more or less at will between the big house and a cottage half a mile distant, which is occupied by her grandmother, one Alison Carnegie, apparently a frail and very old woman.

But I am getting ahead of myself. Elspeth informed me that the family do not breakfast before half past seven, and further advised that, to be out of her way until then, I should go for a walk with the dogs. She gave their rumps several kicks to encourage them to the door and it would not have surprised me had she treated me in like manner.

'Do they have names?' I inquired.

'Aye,' was all her reply. She lifted a bucket of ash and stepped around me.

'In case I should need to call them?' I prompted.

'Och, they widna pay a stranger like you ony heed. Forby, when it's near breakfast-time they'll ken, and turn back to the hoose directly, ye can be sure. They're that punctual ye'd think they had timepieces in their wames.'

She left me, and I followed the dogs outside, around the house and up the glen. Away they went, bounding and loping through heavy, wet grass and along a stony path beside a burn. This water descends from the western slopes past the house and eventually joins the river, which like so much else hereabouts is named Conach. After a short distance the path left the burn and then ended, and the grass gave way to heather as I climbed. Moorland birds were everywhere, cheeping and trilling, climbing vertically skywards or leading me in little leaping flights away from their nests. The dogs set off a hare and gave chase, but without much enthusiasm and, just as Elspeth had foretold, at a certain point they stopped as if they had heard a clock chime – perhaps they had – and headed briskly back to the house. I returned at a more leisurely pace.

Where I found the path again I paused and took in the view. Looking eastward I noted some black cattle down by the river, a few small enclosures planted out with crops of some kind, and a scattering of turf-roofed cottages half a mile from the stone solidity of the big house; beyond them, two more substantial dwellings and, squatting in a green yard dotted with gravestones, a very small kirk, with a bellcote its only visible outer embellishment. The ground rises quite gently on the far side of the river to rounded, grassy hills. The west side of the glen, which lay behind me, is much steeper. I saw a fine spread of trees below a rugged escarpment, down which poured a cascade which (as I was soon to be told) feeds the burn that passes the house. 'Poised at a balance between high and low Scotland' was the phrase in Glen Conach's letter to me, and from where I stood it seemed an apt description.

A movement above the escarpment attracted my eye: it was a great bird taking off and rapidly gaining height. I have little knowledge of birds and supposed it to be an eagle or similar predator. I searched for a nest or perhaps another bird on the cliff or in the trees below, and spied something that interested me more. The thin white waterfall had over time made a wet black line down the cliff, and close by this I saw what appeared to be a kind of parapet set against or built into the exposed rock. And, close by, there was what I thought might be a stairway up to the top of the cliff. It was hard to discern whether these were natural formations or man-made structures. I determined to ask about them or, if the spot was not inaccessible, to take a walk there to find out for myself.

At the foot of the cliff the water entered a narrow-sided gorge down which it tumbled in a crazed and dangerous fashion, but before it reached the house it outgrew its boisterousness and became almost sedate. I recalled with horror the burn I had waded across the day before, further down the glen. Fatigue must have made me mad to attempt it. There so easily might Charles Kirkliston Gibb have met his end, and none would ever have known what befell him.

The great bird was gliding now, following the course of the burn, passing over the house, and then going above the river. I observed it until it was but a speck against the sky. Then I trudged back to the house. I wiped and scraped my boots at the entrance and entered the dining room, where the family and dogs were already engaged in the business of breakfast.

'Ah, Mr Gibb,' the Baron exclaimed. 'You'll excuse us for starting without you. Elspeth said the dogs had taken you for a walk, but we hadna a notion as to how long you'd be. We thought you might have gone another wrong road.' He laughed in a most uproarious manner until brought up short by one of Lady Glen Conach's looks.

'Sit down, Mr Gibb,' she said. 'There is no ceremony here – you must help yourself or starve. Porridge, eggs, blood pudding, oat-cakes – it is all there on the sideboard. There is coffee in the pot. Jessie, a bowl of coffee for Mr Gibb. Do not feed those dogs any more pudding, Glen Conach, they have had quite enough.'

I thanked her and gave my good-mornings, bowing to the daughter of the house, who rewarded me with a violent display of the portcullis. After I had eaten, Glen Conach invited me to walk round the policies. This did not take long, as the house is not large nor its immediate grounds extensive. I put down here, as nearly as I can remember it but no doubt with more points, commas and dashes than he himself would apply, the extensive commentary with which the Baron illustrated our tour. We began at the main entrance.

'This is the oldest part of the house,' the Baron told me. 'Not the door itself – that is quite new – but the lintel and the hall. My father made many improvements fifty years ago, when I was but a loun. He pulled down almost everything else if it hadna already collapsed of its own accord, but this doorway and the hall would not be shaken, so they survive. The arch above the door is very ancient – from the reign of Robert the Third, I seem to recall. When was that?'

'About the year 1400,' I said.

'Aye, well, they needed stout entries in those days. I mind when I was about six, the whole house was still a kind of fortress, but it was crumbling fast. My father might have let it become a ruin and built a new dwelling somewhere more convenient, but he chose to remain where his ancestors had been for a hundred years.'

'This was not always the property of your family, then?' I asked.

'No, it came into our possession at the time of the Restoration. We – that is to say, my forebears – were loyal to King Charles during the Great Rebellion, and the previous incumbent – a Whig of the most fanatical persuasion – fled the country or died of a surfeit of bile or something, I forget the details. Well, the land was forfeit and my great-great-grandfather, a merchant of Brechin, where we still have kin, decided to become a laird. There have been Milnes in Glen Conach ever since, and unless there is another civil war or the radicals have us levelled I see no reason why we should not be here in perpetuity, if the bloodline does not fail.'

'You mean, through your son?' I ventured.

He seemed to take offence at this, although it was he who had mentioned failure.

'My son? My son is as virile an heir as any man could wish for! He will establish himself when he returns from wrestling with the French, marry and have progeny of his own – and so continues the long march of tradition. Now, to continue ourselves – you threw me off the reel with your question, Sir – we will progress in a clockwise direction.'

As we walked, the Baron explained that his father had extended the house on both sides and 'howked out' the surrounding ground – 'Not personally, Mr Gibb, although he was a strong, muscular man, a Milne trait I am happy to say!' – so that the cellars could have windows put in. This is where the kitchen and other functional quarters – wash house, larder, wine cellar and the like – are now. The old castle had had four storeys to it and a rampart on the roof but was a narrow, dismal pile and the Baron's father, who had in his young days 'battled through some storms' (upon the details of which my guide did not elaborate), had no need to be so defensive, hence the lowering and widening of the edifice.

'And now,' Glen Conach said, 'although we have but two storeys and an attic above ground, the house is airy and bright – its wig has been removed, and it is all the healthier for it. The old folk had fewer chambers than we have. Ours are less capacious but more refined – that window there, Sir, underneath which we are now passing, is the blue room, where you have your quarters. We follow the path along this terrace – mind your footing here, Mr Gibb, the step catches me every time no matter how careful I am. Damn it! You see, I was too much fashed with warning you!'

He recovered his footing and we traversed the terrace to the garden at the rear, where he showed me several beds full of cabbages and other vegetables. I did not recognise them all and asked what they were. The Baron replied that he could not mind all their names but they were too numerous for his household to consume. The glen people got whatever exceeded its needs.

'Nothing is wasted,' he said with some pride. 'My people have their own wee bits of land and grow what they can and keep it for their own use and I encourage that, for if they cannot eat they either die or leave, and neither is a good outcome. Other lairds more ruthless than I doubtless consider me soft but there is cottar blood in us all, Mr Gibb, and without the cottar class there would be no gentry so it behoves us to treat them with kindness and respect.'

Next we passed a pig house, the stables and the dairy. These prompted another lecture: 'We make butter and a fine yowe-cheese, but we are not so good at a hard cheese, hence the Dunlop that Jock brought, which we will sample at dinner today. We pay a price for it, Mr Gibb, but since we no longer have a national parliament a national cheese is not perhaps too much of an indulgence. The burn runs by the garden wall and just there you will see an ingenious dipping place from which we take all the water that the household needs. I say "ingenious" with confidence since I designed it myself. That other wee building is a brewhouse. The water is so pure it makes a very fine ale which our people pay for in kind. You will note the apple trees and plum trees too; some years we don't have enough sun and the fruits do not fully ripen but my lady manages to make excellent pickles from them. Do you see the rose bushes? They are in their third year and are whites and pinks, women are sent delirious by their perfume. They are about to bloom, and when they do I warn you against approaching them if in female company.'

He did not quite wink at me as he said this, but it was a close thing. We had come to the rear of the garden and, going through a narrow wooden *yett* or gate in the wall, we entered a wide, sloping meadow where, accordingly, the Baron's verbosity became still more expansive.

'We call this the high park,' he explained. 'I suppose we call it that because it is higher than the laich parks by the river. There are no beasts here at present but often there are – sheep or kye and sometimes a bull among the kye, but you are safe enough today. I mind when I was a lad the bull who reigned at that time broke down the yett, trampled his way through the garden and made every effort to demolish the walls of the house with his head before he could be brought under control. The poor beast was never quite the same thereafter, I think all those dunches made him doited. Note the stonework in progress along the west and north sides of the park – we are building a dyke that will stand for an eternity, not least because it is taking an eternity to build. That bull – I aye had a sympathy for him, he became very gentle in his senility. Above the high park you will see trees, a few remnants of the wild wood, birch and alder mainly, but most were planted by my father, his father or myself, and then the hills and moorland – you have been up the glen a little way already but perhaps one day we will make a longer expedition to the peaks where my land marches with that of my neighbour, Lord Finbeg. I say "neighbour" but we never see him, there being twelve miles of the roughest country between us. This side of the river there are some steep rocks above the trees, we call these the Scaurs. There is a linn that pours down them, that is where our burn comes from. Turn now, look to the south and you will see the parks by the river. We drained them some years ago and take good crops from them now. They are very neat but I am not used to the look of them yet, we have not enclosed every patch of growing land as farmers have elsewhere. They call it improvement but not everything is improved thereby. The people cling to the old practices and I don't blame them – you can see open land marked out in rigs so that all get a share of the better ground and richer soil, and likewise all join together to help with the ploughing, the hairst, and so forth. We still have oxen for the ploughing and other heavy tasks – they are slow, donnert craturs but very docile, and we could not afford to feed more horses than we have.'

I innocently remarked that I did not know that oxen ate less than horses. He seemed to think I was criticising him and set off again.

'Perhaps you think us backward, Mr Gibb. I am sure I am out of step with the world but the Reformists would reform poor people out of existence altogether. Fortunately, we do well with potatoes and turnips, which sustain ours in hard times. Most of our people stay in that wee group of dwellings, the clachan we call it, though there are some hardy souls further up the glen. There is a forge where they can make and repair tools and shoe the animals when that is needed. Beyond the clachan is the schoolhouse and our kirk. We have Mr Haddow as our dominie, you will meet him this afternoon, he has a great mind but it is as deep as a pool of the river and I am not sure that the bairns catch much out of it. The kirk has a simple kind of charm, we like it even though it requires fortitude and several layers of clothing to sit in it long. It was built in the reign of King James the Sixth after he had gone away to London, so is two centuries old. One day it will fall down but not I hope before I do. It is called Saint Conach's by the glen folk although our famous old resident was never made a saint by the Church of Rome and even if sainthood were allowed by our national Kirk I jalouse he would not have been fanatical enough to qualify since by all accounts he was a peaceable soul. Are you pious, Mr Gibb? I find I cannot tell just by looking at a man. I cannot thole piety, it is just a cap worn to hide cant and I abhor caps of any kind. I myself am not pious, but I go to kirk. My wife and daughter go also, and my son too when he is at home, and I believe they go in all sincerity whereas I go so as not to disappoint my people, who are honest in their beliefs. I do not enforce kirk-going on my guests. Yet I would not like it if religion went out of the glen, it seems to belong here like the trees, so I attend kirk although it sometimes brings me out in a rash. No doubt my reasoning is very confused. Fortunately, our minister, Mr Dunning, whom you met yestreen, is as unmoved by theology as a minister can be and still attend the General Assembly. Not that he has done that more than twice in his time here. I am glad of it, I would not want him bringing resolutions and declarations home and expecting us to adopt them. Once, to our surprise, he brought home a wife. No, no, Mr Dunning keeps clear of religious controversy. Well, he kens how his bread is buttered since I pay his stipend. Mrs Dunning was a poor woman, very frail. She kept to her bed a great deal and finally died in it. The manse is the last building you can see, beyond the kirk, and then you come to the river where there is a ford – that is to say, over the centuries folk have dropped enough muckle stanes in the water so that you can cross more or less dry-shod unless the river is very high. That's where they get the kye across to the hill pastures on the other side. I have considered building a mill on the river but we grow only oats and bere here so it can hardly be justified. There were still querns worked by hand in my boyhood. I used to help the old wives to turn the stones and feed the grain in, but that is all over now, and our grain is milled at the Brig o' Conach, which you passed on your walk yesterday. Here we are in front of the house again and the morning has life in it yet. Would you care to see the library now?'

During this last, constant spate I failed to slip in a single word, despite trying once or twice. It was as useless to interrupt him as it would be to request a bumblebee to stop bumbling, so I held my peace and had an education instead. We entered the dining room, which in the meanwhile had been cleared of the breakfast things, just as the clock was declaring nine. We passed through a second door, which opened into a narrow chamber hung with enough claymores, axes, dirks, targes and guns to equip a small army. 'This is the armoury. Should you wish to assault anybody while you are with us,' Glen Conach said, barely slackening his pace, 'come here to select your weapon. Avoid the muskets and pistols, though. They are either broken or liable to go off in your face. There's a tale behind these armaments I shall tell you another day.' Through another door was the library.

This is a room about thirty feet long by fifteen wide, with a big fireplace – unlaid and unlit – in the east wall, and three long windows looking south. The entire northern wall and the western one, in which the door we entered by is set, are lined from floor to ceiling with bookshelves. There are comfortable chairs near the cold fireplace, a set of steps and a ladder, a writing desk and, in the centre of the room, a leather-topped table big enough to accommodate maps and plans. A heavy-looking wooden casket sits in the middle of this table.

Glen Conach clapped his hands. 'Well, Mr Gibb, is this sufficient for your amusement, or do you need to send for more reading matter from Edinburgh?'

It was now my turn to impersonate a bee, drifting from shelf to shelf, twisting my neck to read the lettering on spines, poking my nose into the occasional volume and emitting short hums which I am not ashamed to record denoted genuine pleasure. There was a very old edition of Holinshed's *Chronicles*, Major's *Historia Britanniae* and many other treasures. At random I picked off a book, blew some dust from it, and read the title: *Ascanius, or the Young Adventurer*. I opened it and saw from the frontispiece who Ascanius was – the young Prince Charles Edward Stewart.

'I have not seen this before,' I remarked. 'Published in 1746 too – very quick off the press.' I tried another, slimmer volume. 'This also is new to me – *Prophetiae Merlini Caledonici*. No author given. I wonder, is it a borrowing from Geoffrey of Monmouth? It was he, as I am sure you know, Sir, who gave us our earliest glimpses of the wizard Merlin of Arthurian legend –'

My host interrupted me. I was, of course, making a deliberate show of my erudition, that being the basis upon which I hoped to secure a long residency in his house, but he seemed irritated more than impressed. He stretched towards me as if bent by a sudden gust and plucked the book from my grasp.

'Let me see that! There is nothing borrowed in this library. Either I paid for it or my father did, or his father. I have never been to Monmouth.'

I hurried to appease him. 'You misunderstand me, Baron. I don't doubt that it is your book. I meant that the anonymous author may have appropriated – forgive me, *adapted*, for his own purposes – the work of the Welsh cleric Geoffrey, or possibly Giraldus Cambrensis, another Welsh scholar, the Archdeacon of Brecon –'

'Why are you deaving me with Welshmen? I know neither of these gentlemen.'

I sought to mollify him with a jest. 'It would be a miracle if you did, Sir. We are speaking of writings from six hundred years ago and more.'

'*You* are speaking of them.' He opened the book, turned a few pages and snapped it shut again. 'All in Latin! That's why I don't recognise it. You threw me off again, Mr Gibb.'

'I apologise. Your library is magnificent. But so much of it must be closed to you if you cannot read Latin.'

'I *can* read it. I choose *not* to. A man of my years has better things to do. There are more than enough volumes not in Latin to engage me, but you are much younger and therefore have more time to waste.'

I said, 'I anticipate happy hours, Baron, but not wasted ones, among your collection.'

He positively growled at this. 'Do not oil me, Sir. I cannot thole being oiled. As for your being happy, you can be as happy as you like here every day of the week, including Sunday, so long as you don't expect me to remain with you. We dine daily at four, though, and we won't wait. And do not address me as "Baron". As an antiquarian you should know better.'

I excused myself on the grounds of being an apprentice when it came to etiquette.

'I don't give a damn about etiquette, it's just not right. Call me "Sir" if you must, but "Glen Conach" is the correct form. Another thing I meant to ask you yesterday – what's the difference between a historian and an antiquarian? *Is* there a difference?'

I was not – am not – entirely sure of this myself, but thought I had better attempt an answer. 'An antiquarian, Sir, is fascinated by objects and relics of the past. He seeks to categorise and describe the remains of former ages. A historian, on the other hand, seeks to *explain* the past. He is interested not so much in objects as in the people who made them or used them, and in what is common in human behaviour to all ages. There is, of course, some shared ground between them.'

'And which are you?'

I said I fancied I was something of both.

'Hmph. That's no use. Perhaps if you are with us for a while you will sort out your fancy *and* come to address me properly. *Are* you to be with us for a while?'

I said I hoped I would not outstay my welcome.

'So do I. My wife and daughter like company better than I do. I don't blame them, I'm not good company myself, and I'm a poor substitute for our son. We all miss him, but my wife misses him like a mother. She will probably want to call you by your first name soon. No doubt that would be frowned on in the withdrawing rooms of Edinburgh – it would offend their *etiquette* – but we're not there so she can do what she pleases. What *is* your first name?'

I reminded him of it.

'It had slipped my mind. Many things do, and I don't miss most of them. My daughter will surely follow her mother's example, if you allow it. *I* don't *dis*allow it. They may as well be friendly to you – I can't be. Are those my son's clothes? They look tight on you. He's a fine young man, Sandy. You missed him when he was home in the spring. He was given leave to recover here after his regiment returned from Corunna. He is in the 1st Battalion, 42nd Foot, along with many other young men from these parts, awaiting the next call of duty.'

The Baron clearly enjoyed talking of his son. I asked what rank he had.

'He is a Captain now. We bought his commission as an Ensign – I make no bones about it, it was what we could afford – but I am proud to say he proceeded by way of Lieutenant to Captain in little time and happily at no additional expense. He was very thin when he reached us – much thinner than you – but we soon had him back to strength. On the march to Corunna all their boots wore out so they were marching on their bare soles, and it was ice and snow. When, finally, they got on board the ships to bring them home, Sandy's boots – what was left of them – were stuck to his feet and he had to bathe them in hot water and peel the leather off, and much of his skin came with it. Aye, but he was marching-fit again by the time he left us. If he were still here he'd call you "Charlie" and have you chase about all over the hills with him. He makes friends with everybody. I daresay he would befriend Bonaparte if he wasn't fighting him. My daughter's name is Jessamine, did I tell you? Jessie for short. You had better continue calling her "Miss Milne" until my wife says otherwise. Speaking of correct forms, if Jessie were my heir she'd be "the Maid of Glen Conach", but she isn't. I mean, she is a maid in the . . . in that sense, you understand, but she is not my heir. Alexander is my heir. He is in camp in Kent, or perhaps somewhere else by now. We have not had a letter for weeks. You've never been a soldier, have you?'

I assured him I was not martially inclined, which is the truth.

'Not keen on a fight, you mean? Or losing your skin when you take your boots off? Well, you're not muscular like Sandy. The army might not take you. You're too bookish. Mind you, they are so short of recruits they'll take almost any man with four limbs and a head. Nothing wrong with books, of course – I've read a fair number in my day, and my father was a great collector, as you can see. But a young man can read too much. How old are you?'

I said I was twenty-eight, which is also true.

'You are ages with Sandy, then. He seems younger than you. He isn't bookish at all. Not a keen reader, nor a keen writer, which is doubtless why we have not had a letter from him. Well, we cannot help what we are. We are all different, but you will make yourself old before your time with too much reading. You'll be wanting to see the Conach book now. It is over here.'

Despite his protestations of unfriendliness he took my arm and led me, in a more or less straight line, to the map table. The Baron released some brass hook-and-eye fastenings on the two long sides of the wooden casket and lifted off the lid, to reveal the *Book of Conach* lying on a faded blue velvet cushion: a small, grubby volume in an untooled, ragged-edged, blotched leather binding, measuring no more than ten inches in height and eight in width.

It was, in honesty, a little disappointing. I assumed from the squeeze of the Baron's clutch that I was expected to be more excited by this than by all the other contents of the library. I therefore swallowed my disappointment and turned it into a wondering gasp.

'Its modesty belies its importance,' I said. 'So unassuming for such a fabled document!'

He seemed to doubt me, as well he might. 'D'ye think so? It's not very bonnie, I always feel.'

I asked if I could inspect it and he assented. I lifted the book and carefully opened it. The folios are of a coarse parchment, probably made from sheep or goatskin.

'It is a great age, of course,' the Baron said, with a hint of apology. 'Remind me, Mr Gibb, what your particular interest is in this book? It is not so *fabled* as all that, surely? Yet when we met you said you were very keen to see it.'

My particular interest is in anything that may win me a few nights' or a few weeks' bed and board. Certain, however, that this was not what he wished to hear, I instead delivered a version of the lines I commonly use in such circumstances.

'You are right, Sir, that the populace at large has never heard of it, but have they heard of the *Book of Deer* or of George Bannatyne's manuscript of our ancient poetry? No – yet these are works which testify that our nation had its own literature, both spiritual and temporal, long before the invention of the printing press. They testify against those who would say we were ever a barbarian race, that it is only in these latter times that we have acquired learning and philosophy, that our past glories are the inventions of charlatans and forgers. And this, the *Book of Conach*, is another witness to those glories.'

'You speak of that rogue Dr Johnson, I think. But how did you, ah, learn of our *Book*?'

This was easy to answer, as it simply entailed the repetition of a number of facts with some decorative embellishments: 'The late Lord Hailes mentions it in a disquisition he wrote on his edition of Bannatyne's collection.' (Fact, although the mention is fleeting.) 'It is referred to several times in the transactions of the Society of Antiquaries.' (Embellished fact – it is referred to only once, and that dismissively.) 'But it was Lord Woodhouselee, in whose house we met, who urged me to write to you.' (Pure embellishment.) 'He showed me' (embellishment) 'some incomplete portions of the work which his father, Mr Tytler, the historian, had transcribed' (fact) 'when he was here some sixty years past as a guest of, it must have been, your grandfather. It was Mr Tytler, I believe, who discovered it.' (Fact.) 'Forgive me, Sir, I am fatiguing you,' I added, for it was a *fact* that the Baron was beginning to sway and his eyelids to flutter.

'Not at all,' he said, shaking himself sharply. 'Mr Tytler, the historian. What about him?'

'He copied out some small parts, but there is not, as yet, a complete transcription. It is my earnest intent to make one, and to provide a translation which I would give into your hands. But it would also be my desire – with your permission, of course – to add explanatory notes and a prefatory essay, and to publish these and the translation through the offices of one of our learned societies. That is my interest, and my purpose in being here.'

This was actually true: the *Book of Conach* has greater possibilities than the ruins lying about General Abercromby's estate. If I can produce such a translation and essay they may open doors for me that lead to years of good living.

However, I had made the Baron anxious. I imagine he saw – as indeed I saw – the roses blooming and fading, the summer turning to autumn, the leaves falling from the trees, and Charles Kirkliston Gibb still installed in the blue room.

'How long do you think that might take you?' he asked.

It is advisable always to be vague when answering such a question at the beginning of a stay. On the one hand, to suggest, when you have hardly got your feet under the table, that you might be *in situ* for weeks, let alone months, is bound to alarm even the most liberal of hosts. On the other hand, it is fatal to specify too early a date of completion, as every hour of every day that you exceed your calculation will be held against you with disapproving looks and sniffs, which is unpleasant for everyone concerned.

'It is not a long document,' I said accordingly. 'Whilst here, however, I must first make an accurate transcription, with accompanying notes, and then a full translation.'

The Baron was quicker off his mark than I anticipated: 'But if you have made the transcription, could you not take it away and do the translating somewhere else?'

'In theory, Sir, yes. In practice, I know from experience that it is always preferable to be able to refer to the original document. Otherwise, it is inevitable that errors creep in which are then reproduced for eternity. Another of my tasks will be to make sketches of any extraneous marks or images on the folios, in order to interpret them if possible. A further difficulty arises where the poor condition of the parchment makes the text difficult to read – on this folio, for example. I will have to be very careful, and record all possible variant readings in such cases.'

I felt that I had very satisfactorily failed to answer my host's original question. Glen Conach screwed his face up and peered closely. 'Only in such cases? The whole thing is so dense and hard to read. I admit it is quite pleasing to the eye, but it looks all alike.' He ran his fingers through his hair, dislodging some leafage that had settled there, which fell on the open book. I blew it away.

'I am used to such script, Sir. I have looked at so many old documents, some in a state far worse than this, that I hardly think about it.'

'If your work were to be published,' he said warily, 'will that not lead to more folk wanting to come and look at this – the original? I have read in my magazines that there are people nowadays who will go on a tour to almost anywhere to gawp at almost anything.'

I assured him that, on the contrary, to be able to read the text in Latin and English would satisfy the curiosity of most scholars, and that his peace would not be disturbed by tourists. Thinking that to touch a little on his pride at this point would be useful to my plans, I asked him if he had any notion of the value of the *Book*. I did not, I explained, mean monetary value, for it was priceless. But was it quite safe here, or might it be better preserved elsewhere?

GC: 'Safe? You mean somebody might steal it?'
ME: 'Or it might be damaged accidentally – by fire, for example, or damp.'
GC: 'It's not damp in here.'
ME (pretending that it was not): 'I meant rather that over time it will inevitably deteriorate. One of the purposes for which the Society of Antiquaries was formed was to establish a secure and permanent repository for just such items as this.'
GC: 'You are not taking it to Edinburgh, if that is what you propose. Much more likely to be stolen or burned there than here. Anyway, this is its home. It must have been in the glen for centuries. How old is it?'
ME: 'Mr Tytler's opinion was that it was compiled no later than the year 1200 – so, some six or seven hundred years old at least.'
GC: 'By whom? Some half-blind old monk, I suppose?'
ME: 'Or a half-blind young one. It was slow and detailed work, certainly.'
GC: 'That word there – is that *sancti*? And the word after it – *magni*?'
ME: 'Quite correct, Sir. Your eye has to become accustomed to the script, and you have assisted it by finding two words together of similar shape and length. *Sancti magni gentis nostrae* is the whole phrase: "the great saints of our people". And here, just below it, is a fine phrase, *umbra oblivionis*.'
GC: 'Something to do with shade, is that not?'
ME: '*Umbra oblivionis eum invasit*: "The shadow of forgetting fell upon him." The compiler, whoever he was, considered himself more than a mere chronicler. Glen Conach,' I added, plucking up the courage to use that form of address for the first time (it felt almost as if I had called him 'Thomas'), 'your *Book* may be humbly clad, but it contains riches. I am eager to begin my labour at once.'

The above exchanges and my final declaration, despite its liberal application of oil, seemed to reconcile him to the notion that I might be settling in for some time.

'Well, then,' he said, 'I will leave you to it. I am going for a walk. Do you honestly consider what you are about to commence to be *labour*? It is my opinion that few men for whom labour is not a necessity like to do much of it. I include myself, by the way. Labour pays very ill and is often injurious to back, limbs and lungs. The only pleasure is when it stops. I distinguish between hard labour, which is always disagreeable, and bodily exertion, which can be pleasurable, especially if one is muscular.'

He looked me up and down as if about to make a fresh, unfavourable comparison of myself with his son.

'Surely,' I said, 'men can labour with their minds as well as with their bodies? Think of the clerk, the clergyman or the schoolmaster.'

'I don't think of them if I can help it,' he said. 'Mr Haddow, our dominie, certainly has a mind and I don't doubt it works in a mechanical kind of way, but I'd hardly call it labour. It is intermittent labour anyway, for he cannot keep the bairns in school when they are needed by their families to work. Mr Haddow is conscientious – he taught my own bairns, to an elementary level – but I think he is not altogether sorry when the schoolroom is empty, as he can then lose himself in books. He is like you, always reading. I let him have what he wants from my shelves, so you may bump into him here from time to time, especially – haha! – if you both have your noses in books. As for ministers, well, ministers more pious than our Mr Dunning din into their flocks the virtues of labour six days a week, but they avoid it themselves like a disease. So do I, and so do most other gentlemen. Not that I do not keep myself occupied – I am never short of things I should be doing or that in my wife's opinion I should already have done. I do not wish to diminish you, Mr Gibb, but what's an antiquarian if not a man filling his idle hours with an amusement?' A sudden horror filled his eyes. 'You're not expecting to be paid, are you?'

'Oh no!' I said, as if the mere mention of money were repugnant to me. His relief was plain. 'And though the work may amuse me,' I went on, 'I too am conscientious. By the end of a day's reading and writing, I know I have laboured.'

'Aye, well,' he replied with a sudden smile upon his face, 'the poor folk here in the glen, or the masons raising all the grand new streets of Edinburgh, might have something to say to you about that. Mind what Robert Burns has ane of his twa dogs say to the other of the toils of men:

'Trowth, Caesar, whiles they're fashed eneugh:
A cottar howkin in a sheugh,
Wi dirty stanes biggin a dyke,
Barin a quarry, an sic like –

'I think I mentioned we are bigging just such a dyke around the high park. Slow work, slow work. I even sometimes heave the stanes about myself and do not deny that there is something heroic about it, but I wouldn't like to have to do it in order to eat. But they were cutting peats on the hill last month, and that is worse, up to your knees in bog and at the mercy of every biting insect while you are about it, so perhaps – och, pay no attention to me, I contradict myself at every turn, as my dear wife told you. Good morning, Mr Gibb. Take care of the precious volume – keep it away from fire and flood. We meet again, if your labours have not worn you out, at four o'clock.'

Wednesday, 5th July 1809

The weather has continued mixed, with bursts of sunshine interspersed with sudden downpours of rain, but the temperature is very mild and the nights so short that it hardly seems worth going to bed. It is now five days since I first opened the *Book of Conach*. I should be at work on it now, but am keen to set down more of these thoughts before I lose them. So much has happened. I am left alone here, so who but myself knows how I occupy my time? Should anybody come in – there is the *Book*, and here am I making notes about it.

After his departure, I considered the character of my host. He is both Mr Thomas Milne and the Baron of Glen Conach, a curious mixture of the astute and the naïve, the simple and the complicated, but made up of what quantities of each it is hard to tell. He makes a pretence of not being bookish yet can summon four apposite lines of Burns without a moment's hesitation. He sympathises with the poor yet does not like the notion of political reform. Is he a Jacobite? When I pulled out the *Ascanius* book and saw Charles Edward Stewart's portrait on its opening page, I tried to gauge his reaction, but without success. He is surely a Tory but even sixty years since that did not oblige a man to be a Jacobite. This part of the country was long inclined to that persuasion, and his daughter sings Jacobite songs, but what do these things signify now? We are on our third King George and the drunkard that the Prince became has been twenty years in his grave. Most Scots are Jacobites to some degree, whether they own it or not. Perhaps even I harbour such sentiments. Lamenting 'what might have been' eases the guilt of having thrown in our lot with the English. It is a part of our character, I think, to love a lost cause.

As for myself, I have but one cause – not yet lost, though I am always on my guard against the possibility – and that is Charles Kirkliston Gibb. From the age of ten my life has been an unbroken campaign of not being found out. The death, when I was six, of my father – a schoolmaster, or *dominie* in the Scotch tongue – turned the life of my mother and myself from thriftful but relative stability into near destitution. We removed to Carlisle for a year or two, where we lodged with a cousin and my mother found work as a seamstress, but she became unwell, the cousin could not keep us on charity and we returned to Linlithgowshire to throw ourselves on the mercy of my uncle, the elder brother of my father, a cloth merchant, with whom my mother was not on good terms. God knows what would have been my fate had I not shown signs of scholarship. My uncle was friendly with a minister who, having tested me pretty thoroughly, recommended me for a bursary available only to the sons of deceased dominies. This enabled me, aged ten, to attend the High School of Edinburgh. I then, at fifteen, received another bursary, or *mortification*, which bought me a place at the same town's college. For two years I studied Latin, rhetoric, law and philosophy. I did not leave that institution with a degree, but I tucked away much learning in my time there.

Every day until I was twenty was a day of hunger – of both the mind and the body. I understood that only by assuaging the first might I form a plan for ending the second. At the college I hid from my fellow students the true extent of my poverty but I could not hide my lack of connections in society. Again, I determined that the only way to rise from the former was to cultivate the latter. At every opportunity I ingratiated myself – I do not shrink from the phrase – with whomsoever might, wittingly or not, provide me with a handhold or foothold on the precipitous cliff of advancement. And Edinburgh about ten years ago was full of opportunities.

I learned that if one gentleman believed me to be the friend of another gentleman and vice versa, then both of their doors would open. I requested letters of introduction whenever I could, and hoarded them like gold coins, to be spent one at a time. The great and growing interest in antiquities, genealogy, artefacts, historical remnants and the like – the interest, that is, in the ancient fabric of this country – has been to me what mariners call a lifeline. It became my business to know, or seem to know, as much about all of these things as I could. This has been what I style my invisible calling card, my way into symposia, lectures and meetings of learned societies from which, had I been only what I was – a poor boy from Torphichen – I would have been excluded. (I also left real calling cards wherever I could, especially in the grander houses of the Southside and in Charlotte Square, Queen Street and Heriot Row, which was then beginning to be built. The custom that only your name should appear on your card saved me much embarrassment, since where I then resided – the meanest of lodgings in a dingy quarter of the Canongate – was not disclosed.) Men became used to seeing me at these social gatherings. Some even began to notice if I was absent. No gentleman felt threatened by me. Women found me inoffensive. When an obscure historical fact was disputed or a name forgotten, the cry went up, 'Ask Gibb! Where's Gibb?' And I was always ready to supply an answer, often the correct one.

I suppose I could have despised this ignoble mode of living and gone a different road. I could have become a Reformist or even a Revolutionist. The trouble for any man who decides to take up such an occupation is that success inevitably brings him to the notice of authority, which then sets out to catch him and hang him, or send him to the colonies; and even where a Revolutionist is so successful as actually to usurp authority, as happened in France, he soon discovers that other Revolutionists think him either too extreme or not extreme enough, and they chop off his head. I had enough brains to see that I could achieve more in the political field by being a parasite rather than a Jacobin.

When I was twenty, I received an invitation to attend a soirée in Buccleuch Place at the town house of Sir John Dalrymple, fourth Baronet of Cousland. To this day I do not know through what connection this came about. Sir John had been a judge and was a founder of the Royal Society of Edinburgh and author of an *Essay Towards a General History of Feudal Society in Great Britain*. The *Essay* was then forty years old and had been a turgid read even when first published, but its author was immensely rich through inheritance, and had influence in proportion to his riches. I went, of course, and was introduced to the Baronet, who was in his seventies and universally considered a pompous bore. But pompous, rich, influential bores are bubbling fountains to me, the more so if they have written history books which I have read and about which I can say flattering things. Sir John talked at me for half an hour, then passed me round the room like a trophy, and when I left at the end of the evening I was handsomely endowed with invitations to stay at houses all over Scotland whose owners desired me to inspect, study, transcribe or catalogue any number of mouse-nibbled documents they had in their possession, or to write a dissertation on this or that rickle of stones that had lain since time immemorial on their land. A new occupation thus presented itself, for which I shall ever be grateful to the offices of that dreadful bore Sir John Dalrymple.

I called on my mother, whom I had not visited for some time, and told her that I was going on a long journey to seek my fortune and that she might not see me again for years, but I would endeavour to write to her on my travels. I am afraid that I have not kept that promise well – indeed, not at all. Returning to Edinburgh I quit my lodgings, packed a very small bag, deposited a few books and one or two other possessions with an advocate acquaintance, Mr Douglas Bartholomew, who also undertook to forward letters to any address I notified him I was at – and became a peripatetic antiquarian. And, somewhat to my surprise, I have prospered, at least as well as a kind of intellectual vagabond can be said to prosper. I have survived, anyway. For eight years I have seldom had a night without a bed or a day without a meal and a glass of something, and these are the fruits of my learned profession.

Money, on the other hand, is much harder to come by – and a man, however fixed in his purpose, can only endure so much fruit. The people who patronise me are generally so wealthy that it never occurs to them to hand me any money. After all, I am not doing a job, I am pursuing an interest, am I not? *They* are not paid for their interests, so why should I be? Hence the way my fingers instinctively scrape a few coins into my pocket if nobody is looking. Hence too the acquisition of items of clothing that nobody else seems to want. I have praised my excellent boots, but not the fine breeches I wore on my long walk from Forfar, now dry, clean and returned to me, which once belonged to another guest at Airthrey. I feel no guilt about these appropriations. The former owners have not raised the hue and cry upon missing their possessions – because they have *not* missed them. Life is too short to worry about such matters. I have greater concerns. My pleasant but precarious existence continues, the cause not only of self-congratulation but also of constant expectation that one day I will be unmasked or dislodged and plummet to the bottom of that cliff upon which it is my fate to scramble.

It was the tension between these two feelings, I realise, that spurred me to commence these scribblings. I have a dread of mortality: however short or unedifying my existence, I cannot bear the notion of all I have seen and done being consigned to utter darkness as soon as I draw my last breath. What if I left no evidence, not just of my wit and wiliness, but of my having been here at all? This record of my adventures gives me some assurance that I am actually alive. Strange to write down such a thought. Even if this journal be preserved only to serve as a warning to others, in some future time, to lead a better, more improving, less selfish kind of life, I should greatly prefer that to oblivion. Hence my striving to be honest even when writing of my own dishonesty. The future may make of me what it will, but at least (if this volume survives) it may make *something* of me.

But enough of the history of me, and back to the history of Glen Conach. I approached the great table, where the *Book of Conach* lay on its cushion like a dirty, half-asleep eaglet waiting for its parent to bring it meat. I decided to carry it to the desk and begin my work there. The opening phrase, inscribed by that long-vanished monk with the rheumy eyes, rose before me, as if in anticipation. *De beato Conacho ego scribam in his paginis . . .*

Book of Conach

Chapter 1

Of the lineage and childhood of Conach

Of the blessed Conach I shall write in these pages, telling of his character and lineage and how he came to dedicate himself to God; of his years of ministry among the Picts; of his retiral to the upland place that is named after him; of his wisdom, miracles and prophecies; of his humanity; of his temptation by the Devil; and of his last days and the manner of his death.

Although not renowned as are the great saints of this land such as Kentigern, Fillan and Blane, and Columba the greatest of all, yet Conach was a man of beautiful holiness and righteousness, who carried the Gospel to those of the Pictish people who had not received it from Columba, Drostan, Machar, Walloch and others who lived before his time. For in those days the people were scattered unevenly across the land, and there remained many who did not know Christ. Conach wrought miracles and made prophecies as did his predecessors, and those that lived near him loved and honoured him. But he made his own path and would not conform to the rule of others, and because he dwelt in obscurity in his latter days and turned his face from the world, the world knew him not, and the shadow of forgetting fell upon him. And because, above all else, he stumbled, and in stumbling revealed his sinfulness, his name was expunged from the memory of the Church, which loveth not the good man as it loveth the perfect man, though no such man hath there been nor ever shall be. For every man, whether or not he walk in the light of Christ, is cursed by the sin of Adam, and every woman is the daughter of Eve, and the fruit of knowledge is in her womb.

What of the lineage and blood of Conach can I tell? Some say that he came from Ireland to Iona with Columba but this I deem to be nothing but a fable, for he was still living a hundred and fifty years after Columba's soul departed this world. Nor was he an Irish man at all, but was of the Pictish race, and most probably descended from the house of Bruide, that king whom Columba visited in the north country. This I understand to be true because once, in the kingdom of Fortriu, where he lived as a monk for some years, Conach fetched a pure white stone from a river and, having blessed it, used its touch to cure an old woman of her crooked and stiffened joints. Then he returned the stone to the water where it did not sink but bobbed like an apple, and floated away downstream. 'Yonder goes the white stone that the Dove of our church blessed,' he said, 'in the days of my forebear Bruide, who saw the power of healing that was thus given unto it.' 'Brother, how do you know it is the same stone?' they asked of him. 'Because it hath upon it the mark of Columba's hand,' he said, 'and now of mine, and I send it on its journey to the next generations.'

Again, another time, he was lying in great sickness in the hut where he dwelt in the glen of his name, and his servant said unto him, 'Master, the women of this place hath still their heathen knowledge of herbal concoctions and cures. Let me go and bring the cleverest of them to you, even though she be not a true Christian, that she may visit her knowledge upon you and make you well.' But Conach forbade him, saying, 'Think not that I deride the women, for they are wise and gentle in their ministrations, and their knowledge cometh from God though they know it not. But fetch none hither, for the blood of mine own heathen ancestors is in me, the blood of Bruide and Melcho and Kinet, and it is strong, and it will chase out the sickness in three days' time.' And his servant obeyed him, and Conach sweated like a river for two days and on the third day he arose and was well, and went up into the mountain to pray.

Thus it is shown through his own words, not once but twice, that he was of a noble line. Because of this, from an early age he was expected to become a great warrior or counsellor, or a leader of some other kind. But while he was yet a child God called upon him to be his servant, and he forsook all violence and all disputation on temporal matters. This happened at a time when the pagans, though many were still to be converted, had let the monks settle among them. One day he was with other boys, shooting at targets with bows and arrows. A hare appeared in the meadow not far distant. The boys, on seeing it, all turned their aim and loosed their arrows at the poor creature and by chance, as it seemed, one arrow struck it and wounded it sorely. Then the boys fell into argument as to whose arrow had hit the mark. While they brawled and even came to blows, Conach walked calmly among them and lifted the hare. 'See, the arrow bears my feathers,' he said. 'It was I who did this cruel deed, but from this moment forward I shall not use a weapon against another, neither man nor beast.' He carefully removed the shaft of the arrow from the hare's body, and placed his hand upon the wound, and it was healed, and he let the hare go.

The others ran home to tell their families of this miraculous event, but Conach did not go with them. When he returned some time later they asked him where he had been. 'I have been talking with a stranger,' he said, 'and he has told me to go to the monks and give myself into their care and instruction, and become a servant of Christ.' 'Who is this stranger, and where is he now?' they asked. 'I know not,' Conach said. 'He was beside me and when I looked again he was gone.'

Chapter 2

Of his education, and his adoption of the precepts of Columba

It was through his quiet example as much as by his preaching that Conach impressed upon the Pictish people the virtues of the Christian faith and the salvation promised to all men through the sacrifice of our Lord Jesus. Once, when he was sharing a simple meal with a large company, a nobleman noticed that while everybody else was eating and talking, the wisest man among them spoke not a word and that he ate only a small portion compared with what was consumed by others. After the meal, the nobleman asked Conach why he had not joined in the conversation. 'I heard much of what was said,' Conach answered, 'but I made no reply because I found my soup of more interest.'

On another occasion, he said to a monk who was overfond of idle chatter, 'Weigh up your words against silence, Brother, and you will find that the more words you add to the scales, the heavier silence becomes.'

After the boy Conach had declared his commitment to God he was taken in by a monastery which then existed in Moray under the protection of the king of the Picts. The monks taught him to read and write and were astounded by his intelligence and by the diligence with which he applied himself to acquiring these skills. When he was not yet twelve he was sent to Iona for further instruction. Thence he travelled onward to Ireland before returning, still a youth, to his own country.

It is said that he knew Saint Nathalan, he who gave up his land and wealth and became a labourer in the fields, growing vegetables to feed the poor and the weak. Nathalan lived a humble life, dwelling in a cave in utter poverty, and it would appear that Conach inherited his own dedication to the ascetic life from this great saint. It was through the example of such as Nathalan that he adopted the precepts of Columba and practised the following, adapting and sharpening the saint's rule for his purpose, which was to glorify God through his own abasement:

Be alone in a separate place, and let your shelter be a fast and narrow enclosure.

Whatever you possess of clothing, food or drink, give nine tenths away. Supply only your real and smallest needs from what remains, and give the rest of that away also.

Waste not time with idle talkers who murmur at what they can neither remedy nor prevent; hear them but once and turn from them, and admit them not another time.

Let your servant attend you only for the purity of your days and nights, not for your comfort; and let him be a true, discreet man, whose tongue is free from tattle.

Be always ready for red martyrdom; that is, violent death in the service of faith.

Be always fortified for white martyrdom, the life of self-denial, which is itself not a violent but a slow death.

Pray for those who trouble you, and for the dead as for the living.

Eat not until you are hungry.

Drink not until you thirst.

Sleep not until your body has no power to resist sleep.

Let your labours be prayer, preaching and contemplation.

Resist the Evil One, and be not deceived by his salutations of friendliness and flattery.

Love God with all your heart and all your strength.

Chapter 3

Of his ministry among the Picts; his encounter with a squirrel

The blessed and venerable Conach lived in the north country for some twenty years, sometimes in the kingdom ruled by Drest on this side of the great firth of Moray, sometimes in the distant land of Ross. He made many journeys alone into unheard-of places, taking with him only his psalter, a crucifix, and oil for the rite of baptism. The psalter he himself had made from calfskin, and had illuminated with ornate lettering and with pictures of boars, eagles, fishes, wolves and other beasts. This book contained, as well as some of the Psalms, short passages from the Gospels from which he could elaborate and tell the whole of the life of Christ, His teachings, sufferings, death and resurrection. Conach's psalter was a thing of such beauty that when he invited people to look at its pictures, and slowly turned the pages for them, they were moved to tears by what they saw, though they could not read the words. Then they would beg him to read to them, and would listen to his words both spoken and sung. Thus he carried the message of salvation to people who were yet living in darkness, and brought many into the light. What became of the psalter is a wondrous miracle of which I shall tell in due course.

In those times any person travelling the country alone faced many dangers, from wild animals, fierce weather, murderous brigands or men who would enslave those they captured, but it was customary among the Pictish tribes to allow poets, chroniclers, magicians, physicians and holy men free passage. So Conach wandered, barefoot, clad in but one robe, the cross about his neck, and on his shoulder a sack containing the flask of baptismal oil and the precious book, which were far better wrapped against the weather than he was himself. If he carried food it was a gift from others, and when he had consumed it he ate no more until he received the charity of his next hosts.

Once, it is told, when Conach found himself far from human habitation and very hungry, he noticed a squirrel gathering nuts from the ground beneath a hazel tree. Conach was loath to deprive it of its store for the winter, and so sat down to wait until the squirrel had acquired enough nuts. But the animal did not cease but went on collecting, carrying nuts up into the tree, then returning for more. While he waited, Conach talked to the squirrel, remarking on its beauty and its wisdom in making ready for the harsh season ahead. The squirrel showed no fear of the gentle watcher, stopping and turning its head towards him whenever he spoke. And in a while Conach noticed that for every nut that the squirrel took away to its nest, it left one on the ground, a few feet from where he was sitting. Soon, a little pile of nuts had accumulated. Then the squirrel itself sat and seemed to wait for Conach to eat. Conach chose two stones, a flat one and a round one, and placing the flat one on the ground used the other to break open the shells on it. The squirrel neither flinched nor fled, but patiently watched as Conach opened and consumed every nut that it had set apart for him. Then at last it ran up into the tree and he saw it no more, and Conach, his hunger somewhat relieved, went on his way.

Maja

The stranger Lachie fetched out of his teacup arrived on the Friday, just as Lachie's three thumps had predicted. To be fair, he was expected, as he had already made an appointment with Shirley and Peter, but Lachie didn't know that. His name was Dr Matthew Tybault, from Edinburgh University. He came to discuss our old hermit. He was doing some research which had brought him to Conach.

Dr Tybault was not the first of his kind to visit the glen. He was a cultural anthropologist. The earlier ones were called folklorists or collectors, but enough years had gone by for those designations to have become old-fashioned. Shirley and Peter thought that they would learn more from a cultural anthropologist than he could possibly learn from them, and perhaps he thought so too, but Dr Tybault came anyway because he had not been to the glen or the Big House before.

Something happened, however, between the making of the appointment and his arrival which shifted the balance of power a little. Shirley and Peter are turning the old stables behind the house into holiday accommodation. They had been emptying a lumber room there, clearing out rusty tools, boxes of bric-a-brac, broken furniture and other junk, and burning what could be burned. One of the things they found was an old commode, all bashed about and full of worm, not good for anything. So it was destined for the bonfire, but it more or less disintegrated when they threw it on, and something fell out of it. Peter reached in and got hold of it before the fire did. It was an old leather-bound book. When they opened it the first thing they found was a letter sent from the glen, dated 1809. The book was a journal somebody had kept all those years ago. Although the ink had faded the writing was still quite legible, and they could see the name 'Conach' on several pages. They thought it would interest Dr Tybault. When he came, they showed it to him.

Dr Tybault grew quite excited and wanted to take it away so that he could study it in detail. The Darrochs were not sure about this. What if it were damaged or lost? What if – they did not voice these particular questions – he refused to give it back, or sold it? In the end they were persuaded that Dr Tybault was an honourable man whose sole interest in the journal was its connection with his research into Conach. He promised to look after it, and to return it within a fortnight, and he wrote out a receipt on headed paper and gave this to them. Then he drove away with it, and they wondered if they had done the right thing.

But he was true to his word. Two weeks later he came back with the journal. He wanted to know what were they going to do with it. They said they thought it belonged in the glen, and specifically in the library of the Big House. Dr Tybault nodded his head gently – to show, Shirley told me, that he disagreed with them. He thought it should be somewhere else. It was a great survivor, but only by chance and through the quick actions of Peter. If they agreed, Dr Tybault could arrange for it to go to a place of safety, perhaps the National Library in Edinburgh, where there were already other items by the same man who had written the journal. The Darrochs said they would consider this, and meanwhile they would keep it and treat it carefully. Dr Tybault said he had taken the precaution of typing up the whole thing on his computer and had printed out some copies. He had brought one of these with him, which he gave to the Darrochs. It would be a shame, he said, if anything should happen to the journal itself, given what had happened to the *Book of Conach*.

He was referring to the great fire of 1832. This is something everybody in the glen has heard of even if they know nothing more about it. You don't have to be an architect to see that one part of the Big House looks very different from the rest of it. The fire destroyed the library and the rooms above it, and all of the library's contents, including the old manuscript.

He asked them what they knew about the 1832 fire, and of the history of Conach, and if they had ever heard of Charles Gibb, the man who had kept the journal. With each question the balance of power shifted back towards Dr Tybault, since the Darrochs did not know much about any of these things. 'Peter was getting edgy and I felt a bit stupid,' Shirley said, 'so we took him for a walk up the glen and showed him some of the work we're doing. He said he'd come back again once he'd done a bit more research, and then he drove off.'

When Shirley dropped in to tell me all this, a few days later, she had the typed-up copy of the journal with her. 'You have a look at it,' she said, 'and tell me what you think.'

'Why me?'

'You're a better reader than I am. I can't sit still. You have more patience.'

She was right on all counts. I have read an awful lot of books over the years, and I'm still not done with reading. Frank, who drives the mobile library, calls me his best customer, and then corrects himself – 'I shouldn't call you a customer. It's a service. You're my best reader.' The library van has been coming to the glen every week for as long as I can remember. Before Frank it was driven by a woman called Jill, and before her there were others whose names escape me now. I used to give them lists of books and they would bring as many of them as they could, and if they didn't have them in stock in Forfar they would often manage to get them from somewhere else. Julia next door is another good reader, but she admits she hasn't read anything like the number of books I have. 'Well,' I tell her, 'you are half my age. Just you wait.'

When I open a book, even though it is just black print on white pages, to me it is like opening an album of pictures. I don't know how that happens. Perhaps it is because I don't have a television or a computer and I never went to the cinema. Perhaps my brain still works in some old way that is dying out; is still able to make its own pictures. When I used to go for a walk in the woods it was like reading a book, and when I read a book it is like seeing everything for real, things I have never seen in places I have never been. Reading is the way I have gone out of the glen. I have hardly ever gone out of it any other way.

Julia once asked me to join her on one of her island trips. All I had to do was get in the car and off we would go. She said, 'We could go to Islay or Jura or anywhere. Or Orkney, I've never been there.' I said no. 'Don't you want to see some more of this country?' she said. 'It's so beautiful.' I said, 'I am sure you are right, but I have no need. Everything I need is here.' I did not say that the idea of going frightened me, that I was afraid in case I could not get back.

I felt something else too. I felt it then and I feel it now – about myself and how I fit in the world. It is the feeling I sometimes have that I am not here at all. Not just in my mind, but even physically. If someone – Lachie, say – were to come into the cottage when I am 'away', I really would be away. I don't know where it is I go or if I leave a trace, an echo, behind. My life is full of absence. I am sure any doctor or scientist, anybody rational, would tell me I am wrong, that I don't go anywhere, and I would not argue with him (it would most likely be a man). But this is not a matter of right and wrong, it is a matter of feeling. It is strange and yet I am so used to it that it hardly bothers me. I am much less afraid of it than I was at the thought of physically going out of the glen with Julia and not being able to find my way back. I think this is also why, so long as I am here, I am not afraid to die.

I am wandering. I asked Shirley how Peter was. Fine, apparently. And Rosie? Rosie was great, just overflowing with life. And what about Lachie? She stopped to think about that.

'Lachie's Lachie,' she said. 'He's my little boy, but sometimes I think he's about ten years older than me. He can be so serious.'

'Yes,' I said. 'He'll be fine too. He came in to see me a few days ago, after school. Did he tell you?'

'No. But, then, he doesn't tell me anything unless he wants to. What did he want?'

'A cup of tea and a biscuit,' I said.

She made a face, then put a smile on it. We've discussed Lachie's tea habit when he's with me. I think it makes her jealous.

'Was he all right?'

'Yes. I showed him my latest artistic efforts, and he told me about practising his fiddle. He just wanted a chat. You don't mind him coming here, do you?'

'Of course not.' And she did mean it, I know. But I said nothing about Lachie's ghost. That was between him and me.

I spent most of the next day reading Charles Gibb's journal. I was not much taken with Mr Gibb. He seemed mean-spirited, and conceited, and not nearly as clever as he thought he was. But, then, if I hadn't read it I would not have met all the other people who were here in the glen at the same time as he was. I would not have known about Elspeth Carnegie. I wish he had written more about her. I took to her at once. I took to wee Mary, the minister's housekeeper, too. Such irrepressible young women, in spite of their lowly positions. So I should give Mr Gibb credit for that. And when I think about what he wrote, and when he wrote it, he was not all bad himself. There were two of him on those pages, squabbling, one trying to be better than he was, trying to distance himself from his other self, the other not letting him get away. Charles Gibb was no different from any of us, I suppose. And I am grateful to him for showing me Elspeth, especially.

I gave the journal back to Shirley and I told her what I thought of Mr Gibb. She laughed. 'You see?' she said. 'You have more tolerance than me. I'd have thrown it against the wall.' I realised I had given her an excuse not to read it at all.

It would be wrong to say that I forgot about it after this. Elspeth and Mary and Jessamine and the others came around me from time to time. Once, I almost went to the Big House to borrow Mr Gibb's journal again, but I didn't go. If I had, Shirley might have remembered that I had read it once already and, when Dr Tybault came a third time to the glen, just before Christmas, she might have told him so, before she sent him to me.

Journal of Charles Kirkliston Gibb

Thursday, 6th July 1809

I received a visit later that day (which was last Friday – I arrived here one week ago) from Miss Jessamine Milne. Time had stilled and I had entered the world of the medieval Latin I was reading, when a movement caught my eye and brought me back into the present. Miss Milne was standing to my left – not quite at my side, but close enough to make me start. I had not heard the library door open. I had the impression that she had been watching me for some time.

'I beg your pardon, Mr Gibb, if I flegged you,' she said. 'You have been here alone some hours, and I thought you would be in need of sustenance.' She spoke quickly and quietly, yet her lips hardly moved, and the mark on her face seemed asleep. The strong accent was still there, but the words were cool and practised and, for the most part, English. She indicated a wooden tray which she had laid down on the large table. 'I have brought you tea, which I hope you will take, and a scone and jam forby.'

I noted not only the teapot, the jugs of hot water and milk, the sugar, and the dish of jam, but also that there were two teacups and not one scone but four.

I rose from behind the desk and said that she should not have gone to such trouble. She said it was no trouble and that, as she had made the scones, she had brought the tray herself in case they were not to my liking and I blamed Kate Nicol for them. She apologised for interrupting me.

I said that she had not, but of course she had. The monks and warrior kings of yore fled before the teapot and sugar bowl. I fetched two chairs, set them at the side of the map table and asked her to join me, which she did willingly.

Jessie (as I think of her, although I have not yet addressed her thus) poured the tea. The scones were still warm. I had a strong urge to lift one and inhale its smell. I broke it in half. 'I will not insult this one with jam,' I said.

Her teeth flashed at me. 'As you wish. We are not formal here.'

I ate, and she watched me with a most disconcerting, somewhat dreamy, gaze.

ME: 'Please, will you not help me? I cannot eat all four.'

JESSIE: 'I am not hungry. They are for you.'

ME: 'They are very fine. Will they keep?'

J: 'They will, but they are better eaten fresh and warm.'

She said this without at all diminishing her gaze. Being not quite sure that she was really speaking of scones, I changed the subject.

ME: 'Miss Milne, you mentioned yesterday that you have not read much of the *Book of Conach*, but you have heard stories about Conach from the people here. What do you know of his history?'

J: 'No more than what I have read and what I have heard, Sir. However, I did not say that I had not read *much* of the *Book*. I said that I hadna read *all* of it. I find the Latin trying.'

ME: 'Who taught you Latin, Miss Milne? Your father said you were educated here in the glen.'

J: 'Educated? There's a word! What need has a young woman in my circumstances to be educated? But you are right, I had my letters and numbers from the dominie, Mr Haddow, as my brother, Sandy, did, when we were young. Sometimes we went to the schoolhouse and sat with the other bairns, and sometimes Mr Haddow came here. He taught us in this very room. Then Sandy went away to the Grammar School in Dundee and Mr Haddow taught me on my own, and he taught me Latin. You have not yet seen Mr Haddow?'

ME: 'Not yet.'

J: 'You will meet him later. He is invited to dinner.'

ME: 'Mr Dunning one day, Mr Haddow the next. It is almost a salon. Should I like one more than the other?'

J: 'We all like everybody as well as we can, Mr Gibb. There are not enough of us that we can afford to dislike anybody for long.'

ME: 'I hope I may like Mr Haddow, then. From your father I understand that there was once a Mrs Dunning?'

J: 'There was. She was a poor, sick creature. I liked her as well as I could. She was here six years altogether, and spent half of them wasting away and coughing. I cannot think of her without hearing her terrible dry crochle. I used to sit with her and read to her, but my mother put a stop to that for fear of infection. It was very sad that she died but I cannot say that I miss her or that anybody much notices she is not here. It was a heavy burden for Mr Dunning, naturally.'

ME (remembering how little I liked the minister): 'A heavier one for his wife. They had no children?'

J: 'Oh, no, she didna hae the strength. A bairn would have carried her off even sooner. The gentlefolk of the glen are not very productive when it comes to bairns. The glen folk seem to magic them out of nowhere, but we have none. Though, of course –' (She fell silent.)

ME: 'Miss Milne?'

J: 'I was only thinking of Liza Dunning. If she had had a child it might have made her happier, but it was not to be. I am not sure that Mr Dunning would have been happier. He is not fond of bairns. He was in the glen some years alone, like Mr Haddow, and nobody thought he would be married, and then one summer he went away for a week and came back with Liza. That was ten years ago and he has been a widower for four, which I think he likes better.'

I turned the conversation slightly. 'Mr Haddow is not married?'

'No, indeed,' she answered. 'Mr Haddow is too timid to wed. If *he* went out of the glen he would never come back with a wife – but I doubt he will ever leave. Consequently, he will never marry, for there is no woman suitable *in* the glen. He is younger than Mr Dunning – somewhat younger – but has been here longer. Mr Dunning, of course, came after old Mr Gillespie died – I hardly remember Mr Gillespie – but Mr Haddow was here before then. He taught me as well as he could – very well – including Latin, as I said, and a little French, but at last he said he could do no more for me. I supposed that was because of my sex, but he said no, it was because my mind was fully capable of finding out what it wished without his assistance. I did not believe that could be true, but it was generous of him to say so. I do have the advantage over him of this place' – indicating the library – 'although my father allows him to borrow what he wishes. He borrows prodigiously, unlike Mr Dunning, who I don't think has read a book for years apart from the Bible, and that only because he has to. Forgive me, Sir, I tend to speak overmuch when there is a visitor. We have so few.'

I could not speak at all, as my mouth was full of a second scone and raspberry jam. I gesticulated an apology and swallowed some tea. She was, I thought, when in full flow, much like her father.

'My father –' I began, and stopped myself. I normally avoid all mention of my parents when sojourning in great houses. I was very surprised to have begun the sentence at all; when I do it usually ends '– died when I was a child'. It is my way of forestalling inquisitions. On occasion I have even uttered the lie 'My mother is no more' to the same purpose. But at that moment Glen Conach House seemed far removed from any society that would judge me for my humble origins, which I suppose is why the words slipped out.

J: 'Mr Gibb?'

ME: 'My father was a dominie. He was not so timid as your Mr Haddow, from what I remember of him. He died before I was of an age to sit under him in a classroom.'

J: 'Then you learned your Latin from somebody else?'

ME: 'Yes, a Mr Philip. He was not a timid man either. In fact, he was a harsh teacher.'

J: 'And do you also find the Latin of the *Book* trying?'
ME: 'I don't find it very difficult.'
J: 'Then either Mr Haddow was too gentle, or I must be a dullard.'
ME: 'But, Miss Milne, I have only just begun to read it. I may find it trying later.'
J: 'Perhaps it is not so much the Latin as the story. The stories the old people tell of Conach are more – engaging. But you are concerned with history, not idle tales that must become more absurd and impossible with every generation that tells them. Do you think history must always be duller than fiction?'
ME: 'I could not say. I do not read many works of fiction.'
J: 'Nor do I, if by that you mean novelles. There are very few of those on these shelves. I meant, rather, legends and romances. Your task must be to eliminate everything that cannot be proven to be true. My task is to imagine whatever men such as you eliminate.'

I thought this a striking remark, although I did not quite understand it. Was Miss Milne wise or innocent? She certainly seemed – seems – capable of disguise. She went on to talk about her brother, of whom she is evidently very fond. He had had, she said, a wild and romantic imagination when he was a boy, and shared his adventures with her. The glen was their playground. They never cared about the weather and escaped the house whenever they could. They had no fear of Mr Haddow, for it was not in his nature to discipline them. But as they grew up they had to learn to be serious, especially Sandy when he went to the Grammar School.

'I wish he were here all the time,' she said, 'but as long as the war lasts he will come home only rarely. And then when he does settle he will have to find a wife. I hope, whoever she may be, that she will be my friend.'

She fell into a silence and three wrinkles appeared on her brow.

'My brother was much changed, Mr Gibb, when he was with us last month,' she said. 'Whatever my father may tell you, Sandy was not well. He told me he had seen terrible deeds in Spain. The retreat to Corunna was heroic, no doubt, but the winter was very severe and the British troops did not always behave as they should have to the Spanish people. Forgive me, I did not mean to say such things. I *should* not be saying them – not to anybody, and least of all to a guest of ours.'

ME: 'Perhaps there is no one else to whom you can say them.'
J: 'I know I could not breathe a word of this to my father.'
ME: 'Your mother?'
J: 'But she would tell Papa – she is very loyal to him. Sandy felt that *he* was being *dis*loyal to his fellow officers yet he had to speak. I do not think I am breaking a confidence but he would be angry if he knew.'
ME: 'It is between us alone, Miss Milne. I will say nothing.'
J: 'He told me that he would still be an Ensign if there had not been so many casualties in the ranks above him. I said he surely would not have been promoted if he did not merit it. He said that merit means very little in the army. Some of those same officers look down on him because while they paid for their promotion he had to work for his.'
ME: 'Then it is very good of him to be so loyal to them.'

At once she brightened. The wrinkles vanished. 'Thank you,' she said. 'With Sandy away, it is pleasant to have somebody new to talk to, even though you are only here because of the *Book*. I hope we may have more conversations about that – if not about these other matters.'

I confess that a little wave of sympathy broke upon my breast at this moment. It appeared that her life was very solitary.

'Miss Milne,' I said, 'you are right. My interest is in the *Book*, but not to the exclusion of all else. It is, however venerable and fascinating, only a book.'

'That seems almost sacrilegious from one who styles himself an antiquarian,' she said.

'Not at all. As an antiquarian, I cannot blindly accept the authority of its text. I accept the *fact* of the *Book* but not necessarily the *facts* of what it says. After all, I do not even know who wrote it. Does that make sense to you?'

'*You* sound very sensible, Mr Gibb,' she said, not answering my question. 'Mind, though, that you came here only yesterday. What is clear to you today may be veiled in the mist of time if you remain with us long.'

I said that that sounded something like a siren's call, and she said that perhaps it was. I suppose I had been playing a game with her. Suddenly I saw that she might be playing a game with me.

'We will see,' I said, probably rather too coolly. 'My task is to produce as faithful an English translation as I can of the *Book*. It will be for others to decide what credibility it has. Miss Milne, I thank you for your kindness in providing these refreshments and restoring me to this world, but I must travel back a thousand years and work another hour before dinner.'

'Forgive me, then, for delaying your journey, Sir,' she answered, with equal coolness. She rose and gathered everything on to the tray. 'I will see you at the dinner table. Whenever you wish to be diverted from your studies by foolish tales, or should you require a guide to point out some of the places in the glen where Conach is said to have done this or that, I will be at your service.'

I rose too, bowing. Jessie moved proudly off, accompanied by the gentle rattle of porcelain. At the door she struggled momentarily with the handle, and the rattle increased as if presaging disaster. Too late I moved to assist her, but she got through unaided. 'Do not trouble yourself, Sir,' she called triumphantly, and slammed the door hard behind her.

Dinner that afternoon was barley broth followed by roast mutton with leeks, kale and potatoes; rice, instead of bread-and-butter, pudding; and Mr Haddow instead of Mr Dunning. *After* the pudding there were oatcakes and cheese – the Baron had wanted to save the precious Dunlop until last.

By my calculation, Mr Haddow, to have schooled Alexander Milne as a child, cannot be less than forty-five and is perhaps fifty or more, but you would never guess it to look at him. He has the soft, hairless face of a boy, and his red hair and plentiful freckles only add to his boyishness. During the meal he sat upright in a clean but faded white stock and a black suit shiny with use, speaking seldom and very quietly when he did. He put his food away, though, and seemed grateful for the opportunity to do so. If, on lifting his eyes from his plate he happened to exchange glances with Miss Milne, he looked away quickly and then checked to see if her mother had noticed. I doubt that the Baroness cares whether he looks at Jessie or not, or *how* he looks at her. She cannot consider him a serious proposition and neither, I suspect, does Jessie. In support of these conclusions, I also caught Mr Haddow looking in a similar way at me, so I think he is simply afflicted with an acute shyness.

Miss Milne ate with the same efficiency as on the previous day but said almost nothing. She hardly glanced at Mr Haddow, nor was I favoured by her attention. She may have thought we had quarrelled earlier, although in my opinion we merely sparred. The Baron, who even when seated tends to blow about in an autumnal way, kept the *Scots Magazine* to his left side and the *London Miscellany of Knowledge and Pleasure* to his right and between courses read out, from each, passages illustrative of his belief that the world had taken leave of its senses. When he came upon anything he considered to be mere stuffing he excised it and replaced it with grunts, groans and the expedient expression 'blah blah'. It was not until the cheese was brought in by Elspeth Carnegie – who was so undaunted by social niceties that she sometimes waited to hear what the Baron read, and even offered a comment before being shooed out by her mistress – that the Baroness managed to get ahead of him.

LADY GLEN CONACH: 'Have you made progress with the *Book*, Mr Gibb?'

ME: 'I have, Madam. Today, I translated the first folio.'

GLEN CONACH (cutting himself a wedge of cheese): 'Only the one?'

ME: 'I must be thorough, Sir. I have made the transcription of the second folio, and taken some notes. I am also sketching a copy of each folio, so that I have an accurate representation of each, with all its marks, stains, tears, marginalia, and so forth.'

GC: 'Well, Mr Haddow, what do you think? You would be long at your desk if you had to make a copy of all the marks and stains of your pupils, eh?'

HADDOW: 'I would, Glen Conach. I keep the bairns on slates until they can form their letters, but ink is a challenge to some of them. I can only admire Mr Gibb's attention to detail. Meticulous, I am sure.'

Mr Haddow gave me a smile that seemed halfway between sorrow and hope. I could not make him out but, liking him so much more even on a slight acquaintance than the minister, I smiled back, which lightened his expression considerably.

'It is slow labour, Mr Haddow,' I said, 'especially at this early stage. The more I labour, the quicker I will become.'

Glen Conach growled a little on hearing the word 'labour' employed so freely by me, but forbore to say anything.

'And how many folios are there?' Lady Glen Conach asked.

I said I thought about one hundred and fifty.

'One hundred and sixty-four,' Jessie said, and seemed to surprise herself as much as she did the rest of us.

'I didna ken you were so familiar with it,' her mother said.

'I mind counting them a long time ago,' Jessie replied. 'I don't know why the number stays in my head.'

'So many?' the Baron said, almost to himself, and probably computing how long I might be on the premises. I decided to change the subject.

'When I was out walking before breakfast,' I said, 'I spied what looked like a parapet or rampart. I was too far away to see it clearly. I wondered what was its history – whether it was ancient or modern.'

'Rampart?' the Baron said, feigning, I thought, a kind of ignorance.

'And a kind of stairway too. Below the cliffs and beside the waterfall you showed me on our walk later in the morning,' I explained.

'Cliffs?'

'He means the Scaurs,' Elspeth volunteered as she lifted some dishes.

'And Conach's Linn, and the hermitage,' Jessie said.

'Your father's folly,' Lady Glen Conach said, addressing the Baron.

'Ah, that,' Glen Conach said in a dismissive tone. 'Hardly a rampart, Mr Gibb. More a length of stone ledging along a path, and not much of it left in place. There is a cave, which of course *is* ancient, but as for any stairway or rampart – no, no, not old at all. As my wife has intimated, that work is from my father's time. He was persuaded, against his better judgement I should say, to let the thing – what Jessie calls the hermitage – be built. There was a fashion then for such dwellings.' (Here began what I see in retrospect was an attempted diversion from the subject.) 'I don't care for fashion. It is a tincture concocted by mountebanks and fed to innocent folk until they are obliged to like it at great cost and by the time they do the mountebanks have developed a new flavour that makes the old one bitter. London,' he said, getting quite blustery and thumping the *London Miscellany* with his fist, 'is awash with fashion, according to this journal. I don't know, not having been there. But Edinburgh, as you yourself can attest, Mr Gibb, is not immune. I keep my wife and daughter away from Edinburgh – to save them from temptation.'

'To save yourself a few pennies,' the Baroness remarked. 'You may go now, Elspeth.'

'You say pennies, my dear, but I say pounds. Women are wilful, Mr Gibb.' Elspeth, from behind her master's chair, quite brazenly pulled a face. 'They must have everything they see, so the less they see the better. These dining chairs, for example. The old chairs, I admit, were past their best –'

'They were past repair,' the Baroness said. 'Elspeth!' she hissed, and that young woman made her departure with a toss of her head.

'– but my wife,' the Baron continued, 'could not order three or four or six to replace them. No, there are a dozen so she must have a dozen. And so it would be in Edinburgh. I keep out of it for the most part – it was a legal matter that obliged me to go last year but I got away again as soon as I could. If the women went their heads would be quite turned and then they would turn my head and insist on having fashion all through this house and its policies and in no time we would be ruined.'

'A *little* fashion would surely not be ruinous,' Miss Milne said quietly.

'Ye ken na what ye speak aboot,' her father said with a sudden vehemence.

'I ken that I am never in Edinburgh.'

'Nonsense! You were there some years ago. It has not changed at all, forby that it grows ever more crowded.'

Jessie fixed her eyes upon me, realising that I could be of use to her after all. 'Mr Gibb,' she said, 'has Edinburgh not changed greatly? Are there not more shops than ever before? And are the streets of the New Town not clean and wide and the houses beautiful to see? And are there not dances and card-playing parties and piping contests and musical recitals three or four times weekly at the Assembly Rooms?'

'You are well informed, Miss Milne,' I answered. 'I cannot deny that all the things you mention –'

'She reads this,' the Baron interrupted, loudly suppressing the *Scots Magazine* with the flat of his hand, 'so she kens all she needs to ken about Edinburgh. As for the new streets being clean and wide, well, some of them are wider than they were, but that merely allows more filth to accumulate.'

'That problem,' I suggested to him, 'is better than it was not so long ago, even in the old closes and wynds.'

'Aye, but foul enough, especially in summer. Don't encourage her,

Mr Gibb. Her head is half turned already, just from reading. This yearning for new things, it's a form of madness. Don't you agree, Mr Haddow?'

Mr Haddow blushed red above his off-white stock and threadbare suit. The Baroness came to his rescue.

LADY GC: 'You have too little faith in us, my dear. I am sure we would remain perfectly sane if you took us to Edinburgh.'

GC: 'Ye widna like it if I did. *You* dinna like to leave hame ony mair than I do.'

LADY GC: 'That is true, but it does no harm to have experience of other places and people.'

GC: 'Well, Mr Gibb is with us so we do ourselves no harm and without having to go away. And we have had other visitors and no doubt still more will come, and thus fashion finds its way here in spite of my best efforts to keep it out. Not that you seem very fashionable, Sir. I mean that as a compliment and hope you take it as such. You are like our dominie here, an excellent example of immunity to the disease of fashion. Mr Haddow and I are as one on this matter, eh?' (Mr Haddow mumbled some kind of agreement.) 'Na, na, we do not fall for such nonsense here.'

LADY GC: 'Your father did.'

GC: 'Well, he tripped upon his own feet, but he regained his balance, as you might say. And the hermitage, as Jessie designates it, is the memorial to his temporary loss of equilibrium. What do you say, Mr Haddow?'

HADDOW: 'It was your father who gave me my position. It is not for me to judge.'

GC: 'To judge what? Our family history? But you've heard it all before.'

H: 'I hear much from our people, some of it true, no doubt. But they are of the glen.'

LADY GC: 'And Mr Gibb is not, is what Mr Haddow means. Am I right?'

H: 'Quite right, Madam. I mean no offence to Mr Gibb.'

I began to notice something in Mr Haddow's voice and demeanour that I had not suspected until then – a hesitancy, yes, but a strength, a principle, behind it. I favoured him with another smile, to demonstrate my complete equanimity.

'Mr Gibb will think we have dark secrets,' the Baroness said. 'We might tell him *something* of how the hermitage came to be.'

'Aye, or we might no,' the Baron answered.

At this moment Jessie put her serviette to her mouth and said, 'Mama, Papa, Mr Gibb, Mr Haddow – will you excuse me? I have a sore head. I think I will retire early.'

Neither parent seemed unduly concerned by this announcement. The Baron, running a hand through his hair, said, 'It *is* gey early, lass, but as ye wish,' and waved the same hand in dismissal.

The Baroness eyed her daughter in a quizzical manner. 'Will I send Elspeth to you?'

'No, Mama, it is nothing. I am just tired.'

'Very well, my dear.'

Jessie rose from the table. Mr Haddow and I rose also. The Baron pulled himself up in his chair by an inch.

When the door had closed behind her, I addressed the Baroness. 'I am sorry that your daughter is unwell,' I said (although I did not think that she was).

'She does tire,' the Baroness replied.

'Och, she is fine,' Glen Conach said. 'I doubt she is out of sorts because I said she canna go to Edinburgh. She'll be away to write in her journal. She keeps one, Mr Gibb. What she finds to write in it, I have no idea. The days are all the same here. I'm not complaining! I like the sameness! But for Jessie –'

'These last two days have not been *quite* the same,' the Baroness said, nodding meaningfully in my direction.

The Baron was not in the least abashed. 'Oh aye, *you'll* be in it, Sir!' he cried. '*And* Mr Haddow came to dinner. But I merely speculate, for I really do have no idea – she keeps it very private, and that's her ain concern. Sometimes my daughter wishes for no other companion than that book, as you have just witnessed, Mr Gibb.'

I made a mental note to hunt down Jessie's journal at the earliest opportunity. The Baron reached for the *London Miscellany* again, and started to leaf through the pages.

'Where were we?' he murmured.

'The rampart,' I said quickly.

The Baron seemed – or chose – not to hear. 'A shopkeeper in Bristol,' he said, 'has trained a monkey to sort buttons by colour. Mr Blank says – that Blank is a line, by the way, why do they omit his name?'

'Because the story is very likely an invention,' the Baroness said. 'Three quarters of what is written in that magazine is untrue, I am sure.'

'But if a quarter is true, it proves that the world's gane gyte. This Mr Blank says that if he had ten monkeys trained to different tasks he could dispense with his other workers and the monkeys would toil for nothing but food, and the novelty of being served by them would bring him customers by the thousand. What d'ye think of that, Mr Haddow? Could you teach monkeys to read and write?'

Mr Haddow coughed which – again, in retrospect – was equivalent to a puff of wind filling his canvas before he set sail.

'I daresay, Glen Conach,' he began, 'they could be taught to form the shapes of letters and even of whole words and sentences, if subjected to very long hours of practice and with sufficient inducements or punishments. But even if it could be done it would be an untidy business, and the poor creatures would have not the slightest notion of the meaning of what they had written, or I should say *drawn*, any more than the parrot knows the meaning of what it has been taught to repeat. The reason of animals, even of those that most closely resemble us, such as monkeys, or of those that *live* closest to us, such as dogs, is derived purely from experience, and can never pass beyond it. We may marvel at a creature's agility, its dexterity, its instinctive knowledge, its intelligence even, but we cannot admire its wisdom or its power of logic, for in truth it has none. Thus, though a monkey might hold a pen and even scrawl characters of a sort on a page, it is impossible to conceive of a monkey that could read, that is to say, actually decipher those same characters and understand the import of what they represented. Mankind alone, as far as we can tell, possesses that faculty.'

I record the above speech as accurately as I can remember it. The Baron's question had been facetious; the dominie's response was far from that, and delivered with the calm assurance of one who has pondered his subject deeply. I stared but could get no sense of the brain that lay behind that boyish, ferny-tickled face. He caught my eye and this time I thought I detected a glimmer of fun in the glance. Lady Glen Conach's eyes were sparkling, from which I deduced that though she might not consider Mr Haddow good enough for her daughter, she was proud to have him at her table, the glen's ingenious schoolmaster.

'Mr Haddow is quite a philosopher,' the Baron said. 'He has read Locke, Hume, Smith – any others, Mr Haddow?'

HADDOW: 'Some, Glen Conach.'

GC: 'Och, but which ones? Impress Mr Gibb, I implore you.'

H (somewhat embarrassed): 'Rousseau, Voltaire, Diderot, Ferguson, Reid. To say nothing of the ancients.'

GC: 'And all of them in my library?'

H: 'Aye, Sir.'

GC: 'Even Voltaire? I had no notion. Was he not a terrible rogue?'

H: 'Your father was sympathetic to the French. For myself, I read these men as much to argue as to agree with them.'

GC: 'They are all inside Mr Haddow's head, Mr Gibb, quarrelling and insulting each other. I could not thole it. Where were we?'

ME: 'The rampart.'

GC: 'What?'

ME: 'The hermitage, as Miss Milne called it. May I ask how it came to be built?'

GC: 'I am weary of the subject.'

Now Lady Glen Conach interposed on my behalf. 'But Mr Gibb is not,' she said. '*I* will tell you, Mr Gibb.'

The faint smile played on her lips, and the Baron gave way before it. He lowered the magazine, reached for his glass and sank down, his neck retreating into his shoulders as if he anticipated, and not for the first time, a long siege.

Mr Haddow receded also, though somehow without moving.

'There was a man from Manchester,' Lady Glen Conach began, 'who had a reputation as one who designed and built hermitages. There was, as Glen Conach mentioned, a craze for them at the time, more than forty years ago. It began in England but spread northwards and even across the Irish Sea, I am told. They came in all sizes and forms – pavilions, cells, towers, grottos. There were even, I understand, small houses made of tree roots under which the resident hermits were supposed to creep. Not that these habitations were all occupied – most, I think, were meant merely to please the eye. Well, now, this Mr Riddell came recommended, and Glen Conach – I speak now not of my husband, but of his father – took the recommendation.'

'*I* would not have,' the Baron interjected.

LADY GC: 'I am not so sure of that.'

GC: 'I was a loun – fifteen or sixteen or thereabouts, and I was away a great deal at that time, staying with my cousins at Brechin. If I had been here I would have resisted. But the decision was not mine in any event, it was my father's. I could not overrule my own father. Could I, Mr Gibb? Could you overrule your own father?'

ME: 'I was only six when he died, Sir, but no, I could not.'

GC (trumpeting at his wife): 'You see? And another thing. Mr Gibb here – *he* came recommended. Does that mean I am blind to his faults? I am not. Perhaps he has none. Perhaps he is all virtue. Perhaps he is wicked through and through. I don't rely on a recommendation. I make my own assessment on the evidence before my eyes.' (I nodded slightly, in case this were a compliment.) 'You are welcome, Sir.' (Apparently it was.)

LADY GC: 'Be quiet for ten minutes, my dear, so that I may tell our guest the tale of John Riddell. My husband's father, Mr Gibb, was a kindly and sentimental man. I knew him in the last years of his life. He was much affected by poetry, and especially by the poems of Ossian, as presented by Mr James Macpherson. As a man of letters yourself you will know how many people were affected by Mr Macpherson's *Fragments*.'

ME: 'And are to this day. Even Bonaparte, I am told, has a taste for Ossian, and carries the poems with him on his campaigns.'

GC: 'That's something in his favour at least. There is nothing wrong with liking poetry.'

LADY GC: 'Indeed not, if it does not become a ruling passion. Sixty years since, Mr Gibb, there were still speakers of the Erse tongue in the glen. They are all gone now. Glen Conach's notion was that he would build a shrine to that ancient language and to the people he remembered speaking it in his own childhood, but that it would be in the modern taste.'

GC: ' "Taste" is but another word for fashion. As for the modern taste –'

LADY GC: 'You will not put me off, however much you try.'

I do not think however that her husband *was* trying to put her off. He seemed at once to wish to prevent *my* hearing the story and yet to derive some curious, disgruntled pleasure from hearing it *himself*. In the end, I heard it in fits and starts from *both* of them. But, my fingers no longer having the strength to hold the pen, I will stop here, and return to the fray tomorrow.

Book of Conach

Chapter 4

Of his disputes with the abbot and his decision to become a hermit; of his servant Talorg

This was the manner of Conach's departure from the land of Drest.

Faithful though he was to the Church, he was yet more faithful to the teachings of Christ and sometimes he disputed with the abbot of the house on matters of theology, or on the proper duties of men of their calling. The abbot desired him to be silent and to content himself with the gentle life of the monastery.

Then Conach said to him, 'Father, are we put upon the earth to lie on it and not to till it? Are we put among the poor and the hungry to be comfortable and fat? Are we to shelter in safety when so many are in danger?'

The abbot, who was a man of great girth, chastised Conach and said to him, 'Do we not labour? Do we not tend the sick? Do we not take in and feed the stranger? Is it the vanity of your blood that makes you quarrel, or do you claim to know God's will better than I do?'

Conach said, 'It is not vanity but humility that makes me as I am. For Christ said that the first shall be last, and the last shall be first, and that a rich man shall hardly enter into the kingdom of heaven.'

The abbot said, 'Brother, we are not rich.'

Conach said, 'The poorest, most abased man is closer to heaven than we are.'

Then the abbot was angry and turned away from him. From this moment Conach determined to betake himself to the eremitical life, to become a despiser of the world, a voice crying in the wilderness, and by harsh martyrdom and pain in mind and body to repel the temptations of the Devil and bring himself closer to God. For he took literally the word of Christ, who said that everyone who did forsake houses or brethren or father or mother or lands for His sake would inherit an hundredfold and have everlasting life.

Not long after this, Conach asked a young man called Talorg, a servant to the brothers who was much loved by Conach, to go with him to the river to fetch water. So they carried pails to the river and filled them, and there they spoke of the coming spring.

'It is a good season to make a journey,' Conach said. He told Talorg that he felt not only spring but old age approaching and that he needed to change his ways before he died.

Talorg said, 'Master, you are healthier and stronger than men half your age.'

'That means nothing,' Conach said. 'A man can die at any moment, however old he is and however strong. You yourself are half my age, Talorg. Do not pretend that I am healthier and stronger than you. See how my skin is rippled like the sand on a beach when the tide goes out. See how my fingers are knotted like old wood. When you came among us ten years ago you were a hand's length shorter than me. Now you are a hand's length taller. Look at my feet, how the toes are crushed and bent, and the flesh hard and veined as marble. Who knows how much longer they will support me?'

Now Talorg had often looked at Conach's feet, and thought them so ugly that they should rightly belong to some creature that was not human. But he had said nothing, being ashamed of his thoughts.

Conach told Talorg that ten years was a long time to a youth, but little more than a short sleep to an older man, and less than the blink of an eye to God. He said that he had looked into a dark, still pool of the river recently, and had been surprised to see an old man staring at him whom he did not recognise. He told Talorg that his work in that place was done and he was going away, and that the abbot would not be sorry when he went. And he offered Talorg a choice: either to stay in the monastery, or perhaps find himself a woman to be his wife, and have children and live a life that was blessed by God though it were outside the Church; or to go with Conach as his servant. But if he chose the latter, Conach could offer him nothing but hunger, cold and discomfort, and beyond these things only the certainty of death through white martyrdom or, if they fell among enemies, the possibility of red martyrdom.

And Talorg said that he would go with him. 'I fear nothing if I am with you, Master,' he said. 'You have taught me that this life is short and death but a moment, and that after these comes eternal life.'

'You are a brave young man,' Conach answered, 'and I will be glad to have you beside me when my strength and courage fail.'

When Talorg remonstrated against these words, Conach stopped him. 'Such a time will come to pass. We are weak because we are human. I will know fear, and so will you. Fear is the greatest weapon of the Devil. But trust in God and even though you stumble, even though you quake to your heels and to the emptying of your bowels, He will not let you fall.'

At that part of the river there was a bank of pebbles, and the water as it ran over them made a constant sound as of laughter. Conach said to Talorg, 'Hear how the river mocks the cares of mankind. Yet one day this land will be a dry, dead desert, and the river will not laugh then.'

'When are we to leave, Master?' Talorg asked. 'And where are we to go?'

Conach said that they would journey south, to the other side of the great mountains, where the ruler was Oengus, or Unust, as was his name of old, a cousin of Drest. Conach was acquainted with Oengus and had stayed among his people on some of his earlier travels. He intended to ask Oengus to give him a lonely place where he could devote the rest of his days to the contemplation of God. Long had he taken the Word to people across the land but he would do so no more; yet if they came seeking him in that remote place he would not turn them away.

'See on that bank of stones,' Conach said, 'a heron stands, patient and unmoving. I have a premonition about that bird. She has been waiting, but she will wait no longer.'

Even as he spoke, the heron flapped its wings and rose from the stones in an arc of gleaming spray. She flew over their heads, in a southerly direction.

'There is no sustenance for her here,' Conach said, 'so it is her time to leave. Take up the pails, Talorg, and we will return to the monastery, but only for a little while. It is our time to leave too.'

Chapter 5

How Conach and Talorg came into the land of Oengus

When Conach came into the land ruled by Oengus, cousin of Drest, he was guided by the hand of God over the mountains into the glen that to this day bears his name. He, with his servant Talorg, left the north country in the late spring, when the weather was bright and mild. They walked hour after hour together, singing psalms, and were not afraid of the high hills, still with snow on their peaks, that rose before them. As I have said already, Conach wore only the one robe that he possessed, and no shoes upon his feet, and he supported himself with a stout staff of hawthorn. Talorg had sandals made of deer hide, and bore a sack of tools, food and other necessities upon his back. Each day Talorg gathered a bundle of wood as they walked, so that wherever they rested at night they could build a fire. Water was always close at hand, and Talorg mixed water with oatmeal and made porridge in the little iron pot he carried. Also, they ate dried pig meat, which Talorg kept in another, smaller, bag. They chewed pieces of this meat until their jaws ached. Afterwards they lay curled round the fire like dogs, and before going to sleep they lay together to keep warm. Talorg shielded his master's back from the cold and damp, and Conach told him stories about Columba and other saints and heroes. And the voice of his master rolled like a river against the bank of Talorg's chest until he fell asleep.

I have learned that one story which Talorg never tired of hearing was that of Columba and the heron. One day on Iona, Columba told one of the monks that on the third morning thereafter, at the ninth hour, he must wait on the western shore of the island for a heron, a stranger blown from Ireland by strong winds. It would be hungry and weak, and would lie down on the beach in front of the monk.

'Take the bird to a house nearby,' Columba said, 'and there let it be nursed and fed for three days and three nights. After this time the pilgrim bird will not wish to bide with us but, restored to strength, will fly back to its home in Ireland. Treat the heron kindly because that is our own native place too.'

So the brother did as he was instructed, and on the third morning, at the ninth hour, the bird arrived on the beach just as Columba had said it would. The monk took it up in his arms and carried it to a house nearby. He fed it and left it in the care of those who dwelt there. When he returned to the monastery, Columba, without asking anything about what had happened, blessed the monk for his kindness. And after three days and three nights, the bird, restored to strength, took flight and set its course for home.

At daybreak, Conach offered prayers to God, thanking Him for sparing them during the night. During this time, as I have been told, the mind of Talorg was filled with questions. As the shape of the land began to reveal itself in the growing light, Talorg remembered the stars and the stories of the night, and he thought of strangers also looking out on the world, in places of which he knew nothing. Who were those people, and what were those places? And how was it that he was where he was, and not somewhere else? But Talorg held these questions in his mouth because he feared to interrupt his master's prayers.

Then they continued on their way without having anything to eat, for it was too cold to linger. And although they were master and servant they laughed with one another, making comments about the condition of their feet, and each seeking to outdo the other in absurdity since they were both in pain from the arduousness of their journey.

'Your feet, Talorg,' Conach said, 'are like two deer running across the hills, barely touching the ground. Mine are like an old man and his wife who have nothing left to say to each other but cannot be separated.'

They rested, and bathed their feet in the icy water of a burn. 'My feet, Master, are salmon swimming upriver in search of their birthplace. Yours are two rocks over which they have to leap. How can a holy man like you have such feet?'

'How can a fool like you serve a saint like me?' Conach replied. And Talorg was ashamed, until his master laughed, and said that he considered neither Talorg a fool nor himself a saint.

Sometimes on this long journey there was a path, but more often there was none. Sometimes Conach led the way and sometimes Talorg did. Sometimes rain or snow fell. For two days and more they saw no other person. 'Only a saint and a fool would be up here at this season,' Conach said. 'Who else would believe that God would keep them safe?'

Chapter 6

Of a pair of sandals and Conach's lie

One morning, when Talorg was some distance in front of his master and approaching a narrow passage in the rocks through which they must go, he heard men's voices coming towards him, and the sound of iron and leather. He turned and ran back, signalling to Conach that they should hide. Conach acknowledged the warning, and

Talorg hid behind a boulder, but his master kept on walking. Six men with two horses came through the passage. The men had swords and axes, and Talorg, not knowing who or what they were, was afraid of them. He remained hidden while his master walked towards the men. On Conach's shoulder was the bag containing all his worldly possessions, a book and a flask of oil; around his neck, on a leather thong, was a bronze cross; in his right hand was his hawthorn staff.

When Conach was but a few paces from the men, he laid his staff and bag on the ground and made the sign of the cross. Then he opened his arms, extending them towards the earth, and turned his face to the sky. Thus he made himself defenceless. The leader of the band opened Conach's bag and took from it the book and the flask. He unwrapped and inspected them, showed them to his companions and then carefully returned them to the bag.

Talorg watched as Conach and the men began to talk, even to laugh, and he was jealous. He saw the leader fetch something from one of the horses and give it to Conach. Conach blessed the man, touching his brow with his fingers. Likewise, he blessed all the others. Then the men journeyed on to the north, and Conach watched them go.

Talorg emerged and ran to his master, prostrating himself on the ground and kissing his feet.

'What are you doing?' Conach said.

'Forgive me, Master. I failed you,' Talorg wept. 'I deserted you as you have told me Peter deserted Christ in the garden.'

'No, Talorg,' Conach replied, 'you did not desert me. Get up at once. You warned me, and I chose not to hide. I was worthless to those men but they might have enslaved a strong young man like you, or even killed you. But they did not search for you because they thought you were only a child of six years.'

Talorg arose, saying that he did not understand.

'They asked me if I was alone,' Conach said, 'and I said that my grandson had run away at sight of them, and was probably halfway down the mountain wetting his legs. They thought it a great jest. They are Picts like us, traders from the coast, so despite our different accents we understood one another. They gave me a gift, which I pass on to you.'

He handed Talorg a pair of new sandals, better than any he had ever worn. The leader of the band had looked at Conach's feet and decided he needed them. Conach's gift in return was the blessing of Christ. This, Conach told his servant, was a good exchange, for although the men were pagans, God smiled upon them, and in time they would be brought into the light.

Talorg was ashamed, both because he had run away and because his master had pretended he was a little boy.

'I understand that you told them what you did to save me from danger,' he said. 'But was that not a lie, Master? And have you not always said it is a sin to lie?'

'Sometimes there is good in a lie,' Conach replied, 'although usually there is not. God knows the difference. It is not for us to judge the judgement of God.'

And Talorg gathered this into his heart and pondered upon it, and trusted his master's words. For he could do nought else.

Chapter 7

Of a storm and Talorg's lie

A great storm arose while they were on this journey, even as they descended from the mountains. Thunderbolts shook the hills, a mighty wind brought destruction to the forests, and beasts and trees alike were swept away by sudden floods. Night fell, and it was so dark that they could not see their hands in front of their faces. Talorg was frightened, and said that they should have remained high in the hills where the ground was firm; for the lower they came, the more they floundered in bog and the more they were obstructed by fallen trees and rushing streams. But Conach was resolute. 'We cannot go back,' he said, 'and we cannot stop here to rest, so we must go onward.'

Soon after this, they came upon a large flat rock like a raft in the sea of mud around it. They climbed up and lay on it while the rain fell heavily upon them.

'God is watching over us,' Conach said, 'and has guided us to this rock.'

Then Talorg said, 'If He has found somewhere better to shelter from the rain, I wish He would tell us so we could join Him.'

At this, his master fetched him a mighty blow to the head, that left one ear ringing like a bell.

'Do not blaspheme,' Conach said.

'It was but a joke,' Talorg replied, nursing his ear.

Then Conach struck him on the other side of his head, saying, 'That is a lie, for you know better than to defend blasphemy.'

Talorg, with his ears ringing, was left to ponder the nature of a lie, and fell asleep with the rain falling on his eyelids.

Maja

Lachie came to tell me he had seen the girl again. It was a Saturday afternoon in late November, a few days after his mother had called in. He had been in the woods before his breakfast when he saw the girl. This time she was in the high park.

'What were you doing up there so early?' I asked. We were sitting across the table from each other, the teapot and the biscuit tin between us. Outside the light was beginning to go.

'Just playing,' he said, which was his polite, eight-year-old way of telling me to mind my own business. They are free-range children, Lachie and his sister. I approve of that.

'And what happened?'

'I was climbing over the dyke and she was there.'

'What was she doing?'

'Just standing still again but not looking up at the sky. Just standing still.'

'Same dirty old dress?'

'Yes.'

'No shoes?'

'I couldn't see. She was quite far away and the grass is long. I think she was looking at something.'

'What?'

He shook his head, impatient with me. '*I* don't know. I couldn't see anything.'

'Were you frightened?'

'Not this time.' Which was an admission of a kind.

'Good,' I said. 'It's quite a while since you came and told me about her before. Have you seen her in between times?'

'Not really,' he said.

'What do you mean?'

'Well, sometimes I think I'm going to see her but then she isn't there. Which is annoying because I'd like to talk to her.'

'Okay. So did you talk to her this time?'

'No. I walked towards her, to see how close I could get before she disappeared again.'

'Oh, you thought she would?'

'Well, if she's a ghost. It's what happened before.'

'And did she?'

He nodded. 'She turned round and kind of started waving at me and then stopped. And then she wasn't there. When she waved it was like she knew who I was, but how could she?'

'Maybe she mistook you for somebody she did know?'

'Maybe.' He hesitated, but only for a second. 'I thought she could be you again. Then she would know me.'

'But when I was young, I didn't know you.'

'Yes, but maybe there's some way she might if she was you, because you know me now. I don't think ghosts care about time and stuff.'

'Well,' I said, 'why don't we see if she looks anything like what I looked like when I was a girl?'

I switched on a couple of lamps and the gloom retreated. I went over to the chest where I put things I am not ready to throw away, and took out the cardboard box in which I keep some postcards, letters and photographs. Something has to be quite special to go in this box.

I picked out three photographs and spread them on the table in front of Lachie.

'These are of me when I was about ten,' I said. 'So, a bit older than you but not much. They're only black and white but they're quite clear. That's me on top of one of the horses we had before tractors. They were called heavy horses. That one was so big they had to put a ladder against him for me to climb up, but he didn't seem to mind. And in this one I'm sitting on one of the first tractors in the glen. I think it was the same year, or maybe the one after.'

'The tractor looks smaller than the horse,' Lachie said. He helped himself to a second biscuit.

'Tractors didn't have cabs in those days,' I said. 'They just had wee metal seats and your bum got sore very fast so you'd fold up a sack and sit on that. It didn't make a lot of difference, to be honest. Your bum still got sore and usually cold too.'

'Is that why you're not smiling?'

'I'm not smiling on the horse either. I didn't smile much then.'

I thought he would ask why not, but he didn't. He said, 'How old did you say you were?'

'Ten or thereabouts.'

'You were wee, weren't you?'

'I've always been wee, Lachie, but I was tough. I wasn't that strong but I didn't give up easily.'

'Is that what you did when you left the school? Drove a tractor?'

'Not just that. I did all kinds of things. Farm work. I helped at the lambing and at harvest time, and I lifted tatties and neeps and all of that. Just any job that needed to be done, I would have a try at it. Anyway, do I look like the girl you saw?'

'A bit. She doesn't smile either.' He spent some time looking at the photographs, looking at me. 'Aren't there any in colour?' he asked.

'No,' I said. 'Why?'

'You've got browner skin than that.' He kept looking. Eventually, he said, 'I don't think she's you.' Then he pointed at the third picture. 'Who's that?'

'That's a man called Geordie Kemp. He's just a young man there.'

Geordie and me standing in front of the post office when Mrs Pirnie was the postmistress. When the glen still had a post office.

We're squinting into the sun and Geordie has said something funny and is looking at me, testing my self-control. I remember that but not what he said.

'Who is he?'

'Was, Lachie. He died when you were about three, so you won't remember him. He was a good friend to me back when this photograph was taken. He did all sorts of jobs on the estate, even more than me. He gave me a lot of tips but he kept a few to himself so he was always better at things than anybody else. He could do almost anything, and if he couldn't he'd learn. You know that dyke you were climbing over? He built that. Well, he *re*built it because a lot of it had fallen down. You'd have liked Geordie. He told good jokes.'

'You look like you're about to cry in that one,' Lachie said.

'I was trying not to laugh,' I said, 'and he was trying to make me. Well, what about this ghost? You're not frightened of her. Do you think she's frightened of you?'

'I don't know if she even knows I'm there. I mean, I *thought* she was waving at me, but maybe she wasn't.' He hurried on. 'I've not told anybody else about her, only you.'

'That's all right. I won't say a word. It's just between us.'

'My dad would just laugh. My mum would get worried and think I was ill or something.'

'What about Rosie? What would she think?'

His look said he expected better of me than that.

'She wouldn't think anything. She's only six. And she's so stupid.'

'Don't say that. That's not a good thing to say about your sister.'

'Well, she is.' I raised an eyebrow at him. He made a concession: 'Sometimes.'

'Some people are stupid,' I said, 'but most aren't. If you think they are, it's because they're seeing the world differently from you.'

'But that can still be stupid.'

'You've told me about the girl who might be a ghost and I don't think you're stupid but some people would call you that. Wouldn't they?'

He nodded. I knew he would take that away and weigh it up. For now, he voiced the thing that was bothering him at that moment.

'Why do people have to die? Like your friend Geordie, and the girl. She must be dead if she's a ghost, mustn't she? I mean, I know about biology and stuff, but what's the point if we all die anyway?'

'If somebody had the answer to that, you wouldn't even have to ask the question.'

He scowled at me, not very threateningly, as if he thought I might be playing tricks on him. Then he said, 'Okay,' and got up to go. 'Thanks for the tea and biscuits.'

'You're welcome. You're always welcome here, Lachie. Any time.'

'Okay. Thanks.'

'You can let yourself out. Mind how you go. Do you want a torch?'

'I've got one,' he said, and took from his pocket a little flat disc which, when he pressed its side, shot a thin but powerful white beam into a shadowy corner of the room. I raised a thumb to show that I was impressed.

'Take care of Rosie, Lachie,' I said, 'even if she gets on your nerves sometimes. She's your wee sister and she's the only one you've got.'

'I know *that*,' he said, and we both laughed, which was a good way for the visit to end.

Afterwards I thought about his mother worrying about him, and I worried if *he* would worry about our conversation. Maybe I should have been less mysterious. The thing is, though, it *is* all a mystery, and each of us has to discover that in our own way. It's no good an adult telling a bairn they know something if they don't.

We are all still bairns, whatever age we reach. Even the bravest of us don't like the dark, but sooner or later we will have to walk out into it, torch or no torch.

Journal of Charles Kirkliston Gibb

Friday, 7th July 1809

This is the curious tale, as well as I can record it, told to me by the Baroness, with occasional interventions from Glen Conach.

LADY GC: 'It seems that, to begin with, Glen Conach's father wanted only a small monument, a statue perhaps, to honour the old people of the glen and their language. But his wife, the late Lady Glen Conach – whom I never knew – had been on a tour of England, and this had given her other ideas. She had been encouraged to develop these ideas by a certain Acquaintance, who came to the glen at her invitation. I do not know much more about this gentleman than that she had met him on her southern tour –'

GC: 'I know that he was English and didna deserve the title of "gentleman". I have no objection to the English, on the whole, but I dinna like a rogue who pretends to be a gentleman.'

LADY GC: 'Well, it was he, anyway, who proposed to Glen Conach that what he wanted, whether he knew it or not, was a retreat in the wilderness, the kind of bower where an ancient bard – not Ossian, but one such as Ossian – might have composed his works. It should not, however, be so deep in the wilderness that it could not easily be reached and admired by those who wished to admire it. More than an hour's walk from this house would be too far, less than a half-hour's walk not far enough. So said the Acquaintance, and Lady Glen Conach concurred.'

GC (intoning): ''Tis distance lends enchantment to the view, And robes the mountain in its azure hue.'

LADY GC: 'Charming, my dear, but not relevant. My husband's father, Mr Gibb, who *was* a gentleman in every sense, did not always respect his wife's opinions but wanted, if possible, to gratify them. Several inspections of secluded spots in the glen were made by the Acquaintance and Lady Glen Conach, who undertook these surveys by themselves and were sometimes away for hours at a time. At length the Acquaintance suggested to his host that the Scaurs would be a highly suitable situation for the retreat, especially since a cave already existed there. This was a great relief to Glen Conach, who had spent more than he had meant to on the house. "Then there is no more to be done," he said. "That cave has sheltered a man or two in its time, and needs no alteration." Oh, but there was much to be done, according to the Acquaintance. The cave was too low and narrow and must be enlarged. The access to it must be improved, the view from it was imperfect, and there were probably other faults that only an architect would be able to discern and correct. Glen Conach said that he had an architect, the one who had planned and executed the changes to the house, but evidently he was the wrong kind of architect, as the skills needed for making a retreat for a bard were of a different order to those needed for making a house for ordinary folk. "Ah," Glen Conach said, "then we are sunk, and the cave must remain as it has been since the days of our first ancestors. And I am not sorry for it."'

GC: 'My wife, Mr Gibb, although having the appearance of a woman of sense and order, has a wayward and fanciful mind. She puts words in my father's mouth and everybody else's as if they were characters in a play – even though she was an ignorant wee lassie in Montrose at the time of which she speaks.'

LADY GC: 'I have never been ignorant, and I put no words in your father's mouth. I had them directly from him when he was lying sick in his bed and I sat with him and we passed the hours in gossip. I have the tale by heart. He liked to tell it against himself, both his lady and the Acquaintance being dead by then. Dinna fash, Mr Gibb, Glen Conach and I will not come to blows. See how placid Mr Haddow is – he kens us well.' (Mr Haddow was so still that I suspected him of having entered a trance.)

'Then ensued a mighty debate. Glen Conach had a fondness, almost a passion, for the cave, and wished to leave it as it was. But his lady was equally passionate for changing it, and furthermore she reminded him of his own desire to memorialise the old people he had known, their language and customs, and how could this be done if nothing were altered? The Acquaintance took the side first of one and then of the other. Glen Conach, honest man that he was, did not detect that this was a subtle play by a man he suspected but could not prove to be his enemy, and so he was worn down until he said at last, "Very well, but if we are to proceed how are we to know what this retreat should look like? And who is to build it?"

'The Acquaintance said that happily he knew of the very person to answer both these questions. His name was John Riddell, than whom no finer creator of these little dwellings existed. He had in the last year designed a poet's house for Lord Camborough, a hermit's house for Sir Richard Duroc and a three-roomed grotto for Lady Tamworth. Lady Glen Conach added her endorsement of Mr Riddell, whom she had met when in England. The Acquaintance offered to write to Mr Riddell on behalf of Glen Conach, and Glen Conach with an uneasy heart said that he would be obliged if he did.

'The Acquaintance warned that Mr Riddell's reputation was such that he was greatly in demand the length and breadth of Great Britain, and that therefore he might not be able to attend to Glen Conach's anxious desire for months. "I shall write to him nevertheless, in case he is able to find a space for you in his calendar." And Glen Conach said, "Aye, write to him," and because he had said "Aye" began to think that it truly was his anxious desire to have a home for a bard or hermit, even though he had never before dreamt of it. And in half the time it took in those days to come here from Edinburgh, John Riddell arrived from Manchester, a miraculous journey which cast some doubt as to whether he had been quite so distant or in such demand as had been averred.

'Undoubtedly, though, Mr Riddell was a busy man. He busied himself producing the references and testimonials of satisfied clients; he busied himself admiring the grandeur of the glen; he busied himself at sketches, elevations and diagrams; and he busied himself about the wine and the whisky and anything else consumable that came within his reach. He and the Acquaintance carried out more inspections of the Scaurs, and Mr Riddell declared that it was a fine site, wanting only a few adjustments to make it ideal. Chief among these was to alter the approach. It was very difficult, in fact it was dangerous, to scramble *up* to the cave, and so he proposed building a stair *down* from the top of the Scaurs, and a walkway along to the cave, and a frontage to the cave so that it was less exposed. Glen Conach said that as a loun he had scrambled up to the cave himself without much trouble, but he supposed that would not suit the ladies. Mr Riddell said it would not, and furthermore the alteration would save visitors from being drenched by the waterfall as they would not have to climb up beside it. It would also be a more picturesque and romantic route: the steps cut into the cliff would make a steep but secure descent to a narrow path, happily already in part provided by nature, which would lead to the cave. Thus visitors would not come upon their destination until the last possible moment, which would produce in them the greatest effect of surprise and delight. The cave itself needed some refinements, such as raising the height of the roof and carving some alcoves and seating from the rock, and making a window in the frontage through which a spectator would be able to enjoy the cascade of water without being made wet by it. And, finally, there should be a fireplace complete with a chimney to take away the smoke.

'Glen Conach, seeing the cost mount with every sentence uttered, questioned the need for a fireplace.

'"Oh, there must be a fireplace," said Mr Riddell, and the Acquaintance, in an excruciating imitation of a Scotch accent, said, "A wee bit hawth wee an ingle aglow in it."

'"Indeed," Mr Riddell said. "The hermit must be able to sit at his ingle-cheek while he muses or composes, inspired by the patterns of the flames. By day he must cogitate, and by night he must rest."

'Glen Conach protested that there had never been a fire in the cave in all the years he had known it. "Surely," he said, "you do not intend that anybody should actually *bide* there?"

'"My dear Sir," said Mr Riddell, "whether a hermit *bides* there or not, the impression made on your visitors must be that one does. For what purpose would you build a hermitage, if it were not to house a hermit? Therefore, when your guests descend the stair to the cave, there must be all the signs of occupation – the ingle aglow, a candle in an alcove, a bench with simple bedding on it, a half-eaten meal, a half-written poem even. It must be, if there is no hermit to greet them, as if he had just stepped out a few minutes before – shy of company perhaps, and keen to retain his privacy and solitude."'

GC: 'Ah, Mr Gibb, would Shakespeare not envy my wife's powers of invention?'

LADY GC (ignoring him): 'After further bombardments, Lady Glen Conach, Mr Riddell and the Acquaintance combined in a cavalry charge to overwhelm Glen Conach and put all his objections to flight. The plan was agreed and a price estimated. It was early summer, and the work was to commence as soon as possible. Mr Riddell had to return to England to complete another commission, and departed with one half of his fee, which he had most reluctantly requested, having had some unhappy experiences with gentlemen whose honour he had no wish to impugn by naming them. He left the Acquaintance in charge of procuring three masons and their apprentices, who set up a camp at the foot of the Scaurs. This, too, required an advance of money in addition to what Mr Riddell had already had. Mr Riddell, the Acquaintance and Lady Glen Conach were all satisfied with these arrangements. Glen Conach alone was unhappy. But he was a proud man, and he tholed the Acquaintance's presence and his too-familiar attachment to the lady, and he bore the costs, which before long far exceeded the estimate. First the masons found the rock too hard, and it took longer than expected to cut the steps into it. Then the path to the cave was too soft, and crumbled under the masons' feet, and a fresh path had to be cut, and a ledging built along it to prevent anybody from falling. The carving of the cave's furnishings, such as the benches, and the construction of the frontage with its window, were more problematical than expected, and the creation of the chimney to draw away the smoke from the fire was a feat of engineering such as had never been undertaken in the history of mankind. Mr Riddell returned from time to time, and ate and drank his fill, and advised this or that addition to the original plan, and if Glen Conach protested it was soon made clear that not to proceed with the addition would be tantamount to not having begun the work at all, and Lady Glen Conach's hopes and happiness would be confounded and Glen Conach's money spent in vain.'

At this point the Baroness broke off from her narrative and fixed me with a steady eye. 'You may imagine the position he found himself in, Mr Gibb,' she said. 'I am sure there are schemes afoot in Edinburgh all the time in which knaves are deemed great artists and honest men are played for fools.'

'I have not been in Edinburgh of late, Madam,' I replied, 'but I do not doubt it.'

The room was warm, yet I felt a chill at my back. The Baroness's ghostly smile still hovered upon her lips. Was her comment a kind of warning to me? My own fear of being found out preyed upon me. Again I turned to Mr Haddow for a helpful sign but he was staring at the clock as if it were a gorgon and had petrified him. The Baron was so quiet that I thought he might have dozed off, but when I looked more closely I saw his eyes glowering under the thatch of his brows.

LADY GC: 'But at last the works were concluded. It was the middle of September, and the weather fine, when Glen Conach and his lady walked from here to the top of the Scaurs. Mr Riddell led the way – he would not have missed the occasion for the world, he said, and had even postponed an appointment with the Earl of Sandwich in order to be present, and by the by he hoped it would be convenient to Glen Conach to settle the account before he left for that purpose the next day. The Acquaintance awaited them at the top of the stone steps. The masons and their lads, being neither beautiful nor sublime, had been banished from the scene. Down the steps the party went, slowly and in single file, the Acquaintance reaching Lady Conach a hand whenever her shoe rested on an uneven step, of which there were a surprising number. They went along the path, made exceedingly narrow because of the ledging, and arrived at the cavern. All within was as had been promised – more or less. The water fell past the window and only a modest portion of it splashed in when it hit the projecting sill. Glen Conach could stand erect in the middle of the cave although he dunched his head elsewhere. The seats carved from the rock were charming to look at but the stone was cold and he thought it rash to sit on it long. There was a quantity of rubble in one corner which he thought should have been removed. The Acquaintance had already been at work with his tinderbox and had lit candles in two or three alcoves but they burned feebly in the close, damp air. In the very small hearth the makings of a fire were laid. Glen Conach asked why the fire was not lit.

'"Well, it is a warm day, and we thought it would discomfort you," Mr Riddell said.

'"But I must see it working," said Glen Conach. "It is the thing I most wish to see."

'"I fear we will be somewhat hot if it is lit," Mr Riddell said.

'There was a rumble, as of thunder, from Glen Conach. "You will be somewhat hotter if it isna," he said.

'Here the Acquaintance interposed himself. "The fact is," he said, "we are still not quite satisfied with it, are we, Mr Riddell?"

'"The fact is, we are not," Mr Riddell answered, and began to discourse at length about the height and angle of the chimney, the distance from the hearth to the outlet, the draw being best when the wind was in the west whereas today it was hardly blowing at all, and so forth. And Glen Conach listened for a few clauses and then he listened no more. "Mr Riddell, if you please! I wish to see it lit. I have paid a small fortune to see it lit."

'"Very well, if you insist," Mr Riddell said, as if whatever transpired would be Glen Conach's fault. So the Acquaintance took one of the candles and touched it to the kindling in the hearth, and soon it was ablaze. And soon after that the whole party had to evacuate the cave as it filled with reek which seemed determined to go everywhere but up the lum. And as there was not enough space for them all to stand on the path until the fire was out, they made their way back up the steps and into the fresh air atop the Scaurs and there, between coughs, Mr Riddell, having first reminded Glen Conach that he had warned him against lighting the fire, entered into a further explanation about the chimney not being warm enough, and that once it was the fire would draw much better and indeed was probably doing so as he spoke.

'"Do you think so?" Glen Conach asked, also between coughs. "I do," said Mr Riddell. "And what do *you* think?" Glen Conach asked the Acquaintance, and the Acquaintance said he thought what Mr Riddell thought, and added that it had been unwise of Glen Conach to go against Mr Riddell's advice.

'Then a change came over Glen Conach, a transformation into some other kind of being. He stopped coughing and seemed to expand to an enormous size and he eyed the Acquaintance dangerously. "Unwise, was I? Aye, indeed I was – very unwise!" And with a roar like that of a rutting stag he rushed upon the Acquaintance and struck him so hard on the side of the head that he fell senseless to the ground. Lady Glen Conach gave a shriek and her husband turned on her and commanded her to hold her tongue – which, to be just, she did very well for the next few minutes. Then Glen Conach seized Mr Riddell by an arm and the collar of his coat and led him to where the chimney emerged from the rock and asked him to judge if the reek was yet issuing from it, as he himself could not see so much as a wisp. Nor at first could Mr Riddell, but on closer inspection – Glen Conach twisting his collar and arm so that his neck and head were mechanically inclined towards the ground – it seemed that thin lines of smoke were making egress through certain fissures in the rock and rising among the whins, but these fissures were nowhere near the actual, supposed lum head, which was capped by a clay pig like those normally seen on roofs. Then Glen Conach, still gripping Mr Riddell's coat, obliged him to sit on the pig and asked if he found it at all warm, to which Mr Riddell replied in the negative. Glen Conach wondered if Mr Riddell could estimate how long he would have to sit there before he did feel it warm, and Mr Riddell said that that estimation was beyond him. Then Glen Conach asked Mr Riddell if he could fly, to which Mr Riddell said he had not that capacity either. Glen Conach said that this was excellent news as he had a mind to pitch him over the precipice to see where he landed. And, keeping a tight hold on him, he marched him to the edge and asked him if the account was all settled, to which Mr Riddell said that there was not a penny left to pay. Glen Conach said that this too was welcome news and gave Mr Riddell a push in the lower back and Mr Riddell gave a terrible scream as he thought himself about to be pitched, but Glen Conach kept a hold of his collar and pulled him in and kicked him hard on the *dowp* (so the Baroness designated this part of the man's anatomy) and at last let him go. Then he advanced on the Acquaintance, who was just rising from his stupor, and kindly assisted him to his feet and, having remarked that *his* account was all settled too, carried out a similar administration and released him so that he danced dizzily away like a man on hot coals, squawking and moaning. Mr Riddell and the Acquaintance staggered a few paces together, stopped to see if Glen Conach was still dangerous and, deciding that he was, took off back down the ridge of the Scaurs, Glen Conach following after them like a hound snapping and barking at their heels, and when they came to the house he allowed them fifteen minutes to gather their gear and be on the road to Forfar, and they were on it in ten. And Lady Glen Conach was abandoned and had to find her own way home, which of course she knew very well from her frequent and lengthy perambulations in the company of the Acquaintance, and she managed that fine but there was no polite conversation between herself and Glen Conach the rest of that day and for days after it, for in truth they had nothing polite left to say to one another.'

Saturday, 8th July 1809

I was hard put to it, when the Baroness concluded, not to bring my palms together and clap, for it was truly a performance. I felt however that she was not a woman to welcome applause. Instead I raised my glass to her without a word, and she gave me back her half-smile. This almost melted me, and I resolved that, though I might not be as good as I should be, I would try my best *not* to be a Mr Riddell to these people. I do not, however, understand why the Baroness chose to relate the tale to me, a stranger, on the second day of my visit, nor why her husband should have permitted it, even slyly encouraged her, when what she said reflects so poorly on the wisdom of his father and casts a worse light on the behaviour of his mother.

The Baron wriggled his way northward, and astonished me by laughing through his nose as he too raised his glass.

'My wife, Sir – my wife, my dear Gibb – spins a good length of yarn. She omitted to say, however, that my father, from that day forth, had a renewed sympathy for the cave. I think he was sorry that he had let it be knocked about when he had liked it perfectly well in its natural state. He went himself with a big shovel and cast the rubble out and over the cliff but there was not much he could do about the other alterations. After that he didna go back at all, at least not that I ever kent. He didna prevent me from going there when I returned from Brechin, but he never discussed what had happened. It was not until some years later that he would speak about it, and when he did it was not to me but to Peggy – to my wife, I mean, as she had by then become. Did he ever speak about it to you, Mr Haddow?'

The dominie somehow shrugged off the gorgon's spell, and looked younger than ever.

'No, Glen Conach. I came here – when, now? – in the year 1784. I was but twenty or thereabouts. Your father was very kind to me – he took me on the strength of a recommendation, and I believe he never had reason to be displeased with my work – but of course he did not confide in me on any such matter.'

The Baron laughed again. 'Recommendations, eh, Gibb? Dangerous things. I expect somebody recommended to the Trojans that they take that horse in. One thing I mind my father did say to me not long after the events just described, when he kent I had been exploring up there, was that he would be grateful if I would take some big stones and block up the lum. The cave had been perfectly dry before, but that lum was a funnel for all the moisture from on high to enter the place and make it uninhabitable. And with the aid of one of the lads from the clachan I did that, we fitted some stones in at both top and bottom and fixed them with mortar, and the lum has never been used since. It's some years since I was last there. Mr Haddow, have you been there of late?'

H: 'I whiles take a walk along the Scaurs, Glen Conach, but to the cave itself, no, not for some time. Mr Dunning, I think, finds some solace there or at the linn.'

GC: 'Does he? I didna ken that. Solace, eh? Well, Mr Gibb, one day soon, perhaps, when you have worked at a folio or two more – I must not keep you from your *labour* – we will take a dander up there and see what we can see. But that is quite enough of these affairs for one night.'

H: 'Indeed, I must go home. I have some reading to do.'

GC: 'Mair philosophy? Are you wanting to borrow another book?'

H (pushing back his chair): 'Thank you, but no. I have some to return to you. Lady Glen Conach, I thank you for your hospitable table. Mr Gibb, I am honoured. Glen Conach, as ever I am your servant.'

He waited not a moment longer but slipped from the room. As the door closed, the drumhead clock struck seven. The Baroness rose, and I did as well.

'I will call Elspeth to clear away the things,' she said. 'Then I am going up the stair. You will have to do without me or my daughter to amuse you tonight, Mr Gibb. I hope you will excuse us.' And she too made her way out.

'If you wish to drink whisky we will need to go elsewhere,' the Baron said. 'Do you wish to drink whisky?' I saw his eye was upon the *London Miscellany* as if he would rather lose himself in its lies and exaggerations than converse any more.

'I have drunk very well, thank you,' I said. 'I was thinking I might return to the library. The light will be good for another hour or two.'

GC: 'I'll not stop you, then. Some nights we have supper, sometimes we dinna. Tonight, we dinna. Will you be hungry?'

ME: 'No, Sir.'

GC: 'Mr Haddow is an interesting young man. Not young at all. He reminds me of that clock with his round, gash face and dark attire. A very deep man. He should be a professor of something and let everything that's in his head skail out of it to the benefit of others, but he canna. And it might not *be* to their benefit. I'm not sure that it's to his. It must be a sair thing, to have a mind like that and only doited bairns to show it to. I think that without the library to ease his brain he would go quite mad, but perhaps it only inflames it. He has been here twenty-five years. I can hardly believe it. My son, Alexander, was an infant when he came. Mr Haddow schooled him from when he was five and schooled him well, but Sandy was not keen on books. He did not enjoy the Grammar School at all. He is a man of action not words, Sandy. He has not written to us since he went away. How old are you, Mr Gibb?'

ME: 'Twenty-eight, Glen Conach. The same age as your son.'

GC: 'Aye, I mind that now. You look older than him, and Mr Haddow looks younger than either of you. He has hardly aged at all since he came here. I expect him to turn back into a bairn one day. Perhaps it's being with the bairns that keeps him bairnlike. What a strange, heeliegoleerie world we bide in. D'ye ken what that means, *heeliegoleerie*?'

ME: 'I think so.'

GC: 'I used to think so too. Here is Norah. Is Elspeth no wi ye, lass?'

NORAH: 'Na, she's awa to her granny's. I'm no sure if she'll be back. I doot she'll bide the nicht there. She whiles does.'

GC: 'I ken, lass, I ken. And she's left ye to redd up? Shame on her. Is Kate aye in the kitchen?'

N: 'Aye, but she's thrang. I'll hae to tak a'thing doon by mysel.'

GC: 'Well, Norah, ca canny and dinna tell your mistress. She disna trust ye no to drap things.'

N: 'I dinna trust mysel. I'll just dae what I can.'

GC (excavating himself from his chair): 'Guid lass. We'll get oot o' your road, and I'll gie Elspeth a tellin for desertin ye. Mr Gibb, I will not keep you from your labour either. I think I'll take a walk round the policies with the dogs. Good evening to you.'

He left the room, and Norah went off in charge of a precarious pile of plates. There was a dribble of claret left in the jug. I helped myself to it, keeping back the gravel, and drained my glass. Then – acting on the sound principle that one never knows when one will next be hungry – I cut a wedge of the Dunlop, wrapped it in a serviette, and made my way through the armoury to the library.

The house felt heavy around me, and yet I was curiously excited.

As I write this, that feeling has scarcely subsided though a week and more has passed since my arrival. I cannot easily explain it. These few folk hidden away, far from the salons of Edinburgh – as far from London as the moon – are interesting to me. Even the lubricious Mr Dunning, who for some reason seeks solace by a waterfall, is of interest. They have their own expectations and inquiries, they read, they form their opinions of life, they imagine the things they cannot experience – and they are full of stories and half-kept secrets. They are at one and the same time very like people I have encountered elsewhere – including those who think themselves much above the common herd – and very different from them. What do they have that is lacking in the froth of Edinburgh and London? I think it is time: time immeasurable, stretching the length of the glen.

'The days are all the same here,' Glen Conach said. I begin to know what he means. Once, at Dysart in Fife, I was taken out in a fishing boat. Not being able to swim, I was afraid, but the wind dropped and the water flattened. Though this pleased me, the fishermen (who could not swim either) complained at the dead sail, and at last had to row us back in. For me, being out on the sea in that stillness – so still that we did not even drift – brought an *inner* calm. And I think that is what I feel now, thirty miles from the nearest coast: becalmed.

That evening, while I pondered such things, the Baron passed in front of the library windows, his wild hair made beautifully golden by the last of the sun. He reached a gate in the east wall of the garden and let himself and his dogs through it. That way, as I now know well, leads to the clachan. It is the route Haddow took home, and Elspeth too, on her way to her grandmother's. Half a mile away, there lies another world again.

I was not aware of my host having returned when, an hour and a half later, replete with the extra portion of cheese, I decided I had had enough of the *Book of Conach* and went to my bed. My last thoughts before sleep were of walking on the Scaurs, and descending the stone steps to the never-inhabited hermitage.

Book of Conach

Chapter 8

Of Conach's first coming to the glen, and of his meeting with Oengus

When Conach came into the glen, the people who dwelt there gave him food and shelter, and were astonished that he had survived the storm, alone but for his servant and unprotected as they had been from the fearsome elements. But he told them that their deliverance lay in the hands of God, and that if the people opened their hearts to Christ Jesus they too would be saved, not during a passing storm but for all eternity, through the blood He had shed for all mankind.

Then Conach said to Talorg, 'Remain here and rest with these people, while I travel on to visit their king, Oengus, and seek his permission to stay in his domain. Restore your strength, for you will need it to build a cabin for me and a cabin for you when I return.'

Talorg said, 'Should I not come with you, in case that king does not let you settle, and we have to go elsewhere?'

Conach said, 'Oengus will not deny my request.'

And so the holy man journeyed on alone to the court of Oengus, bringing messages of goodwill to him from his cousin Drest. And he asked Oengus for a place where he could lead a quiet and separate life, worshipping God without fear of persecution.

Now Oengus neither forbade nor encouraged his people to accept the Christian faith. He was not a Christian, nor did he ever become one, but he respected the missionaries who visited his people, and Conach among them. He asked if Conach had somewhere in mind.

Conach said, 'Where I came down from the mountains into this country, I found a place that is both close to God and far from the bustle of the world. It is there that I would spend what years are left to me.'

Oengus conferred with his counsellors and said that this was a good choice, and he would grant Conach his wish. 'But,' said he, 'that place is far away from here, and although it lies within the bounds of my realm I cannot assure you of protection from any uncivilised person who might disturb your solitude.'

Conach said that he sought no such assurance since God would protect him until He was ready to receive him into His arms. The venerable monk and the pagan king then parted on the most cordial terms, never again to meet in this life nor indeed in the next, because Oengus saw not the light when it shone upon him.

Chapter 9

Of Conach's return to the glen

When Conach returned to the glen, he found Talorg much rested. Great was his servant's joy on seeing him, and happy too were the people. He told them that their king, Oengus, wished that he and his servant be allowed to live without harm in that location. The people of the glen said to him, 'Though we have heard of this king, we have never seen him. But we have seen you and that your God shields you wherever you go, so we are content for you to stay.' And they offered to build a dwelling for him near to their own houses. But Conach said it was his desire to remove himself as far as possible from the world, to be a hermit in some more remote part of the glen.

'My servant will be a messenger between you and me,' he said, 'and we will meet from time to time, but were I to live always among you the pillow of your hospitality would be a barrier between me and God.'

Then they said to him, 'But there is already one who dwells alone among the trees and high rocks, and he is a true hermit, being without even a servant.' And they said that this man communed only with the wild beasts and the moon, that nobody could remember how he came to be there or for how long, that they thought him insane and that he would resent Conach's coming. Conach said, 'We will go and make ourselves a place in which to dwell. Should we meet with this man we will treat him with respect. He need not resent us if he treats us likewise.' And forthwith he and Talorg set off into the wilderness, although not before the people had given them food to carry with them, and promised to help in the building of their cabins.

Chapter 10

A song made by Conach after he came to the glen

The founds of my house are unhewn stone
Gathered from where they lay in the wild:
A layer of stones and on it a second layer.

Rough are the roofbeams of my house,
Fallen branches from the forest
Cut and bent crudely into shape.

The walls and roof of my house are of turf
Laid on the stones and across the beams,
Sealed and patched with heather and clay.

The floor of my house is but the cleared ground.
I have no window, chimney or hearth,
And I cannot pass through my door without stooping.

When the wind blows my little house rocks.
When the rain falls my little house weeps.
When the sun shines my little house sweats.

And I am not worthy of these guests
Sent by God to me, a sinner,
Nor worthy of the grace of Christ His Son,

Who was sacrificed to save me and all who believe,
That these slight trials shall come to an end,
And we shall dwell in comfort and glory for ever.

Maja

All the stories about Conach were Geordie Kemp's. He had a wife, Betty, but she died years ago, long before he did. She and Geordie shared the Conach stories between them, and after Betty went Geordie had to keep them all in his head, because he was the only one left that had them. It was Geordie that those earlier folklorists – Dr Tybault's predecessors – had come to see. They were mostly young men with beards and dark-framed glasses and they came with heavy reel-to-reel tape recorders, and later with smaller cassette machines, and they recorded him telling stories until he ran out, and then they would ask for more. He didn't like to disappoint them, so he would say he was tired and would have to have a think and they were to come back in a month and be sure to bring another bottle of that fine whisky when they did. And by the time they returned he would have another batch of stories for them. He was a rogue, Geordie. He would order books of folktales from the library van and read up on the kind of things the students liked, and change the names or add a new twist to a story that came from somewhere else, and they loved it. I remember he told me once, 'That's them awa wi a Norwegian tale and a Russian ane, and they'll never ken the difference.' They couldn't get enough of him but he was canny, he knew what would make a good story and what would make a bad one. A good story, he said, had to have some element of truth in it, even if he had made it up or stolen it. If it did not have that truth, even if it was the best tale of them all, it would fail. But, anyway, some of his stories *were* very old and as good as anything else the academics had in their collections, and Geordie swore he'd had these ones, from folk who were now dead, long before anybody from the universities was interested.

Another thing about Geordie was that he was of the glen and it was deep in him. If you wanted to know some fact about the glen and its history you went to Geordie Kemp and you might get what you asked for but you would get a few stories too, and you could check the fact later but not the stories. You just had to take them as they were, for *what* they were. I don't think he would ever have told you something that showed the glen in a bad light. That would have been insulting to himself.

Geordie was a labourer all his days, an outdoors man, he worked with sheep and cattle but, as I told Lachie, at many other jobs too. He was just the kind of person the Darrochs could do with now. The thing he did best was building walls. He was a drystane dyker and he was famous for it. His hands were like big claws and he could use them like the bucket on a digger to move stones but he could use them like a musician or a potter too, you could see his mind shaping the dyke as he worked, the thoughts went down his arms and into his fingers and he shifted and shoved and slotted stones into place like a conjurer. 'It's jist fillin in spaces,' he said, but it was much more than that. It was Geordie who repaired all the dykes around the estate. The last job he did was the big dyke in the high park. He was eighty-five when he started that, it took him two summers, a day here and a day there, but one day he finished it. That afternoon he went home with a sore back and looking forward to a dram. 'That's the last bloody stane I'm pittin on tap o' anither stane,' he said to Peter Darroch, who met him on his way home. Peter went on up to see the finished dyke. 'I'll come in later and settle up with you,' Peter said, but death got there first.

That was five years ago. Apart from when he was away in the army at the end of the war, Geordie was in the glen all his life, and nobody could remember it without him. It was as if he had been here for ever, like the birds and the other creatures. And that's something else about him – he was as close to being an animal as any human could be. There was a roughness and a heat about him, sometimes his eyes flashed at you and you thought there was a dog or a fox or even some beast long gone from the glen hidden away in the depths of him, a wolf or a bear.

But none of that made any difference at the end. One day he was building a dyke and the next he was gone. Death came for him and I think he knew it was coming. He felt a change, maybe the way I'm feeling it now. I think when he said that about the last stone he wasn't just complaining about his back, he was saying that that was him, done. Peter went in to pay him what he was still owed and found him in his armchair with his boots off and his slippers on, and his bunnet still on his head, and an empty glass on the table beside him. And that was Geordie Kemp's place, he was in it when death came calling, and he didn't even have to get up to open the door.

Geordie's cottage – I still think of it as his, even though my neighbours Kristina and Sean have been there for the last three years – is not that far from mine, at the other end of the clachan. I often went to see him in the evenings and we always had plenty to laugh and talk about, but I hadn't been for a week or so because he was feeling tired after those days working on the dyke; he said he wouldn't be good company. So I left him alone. It was a great shock when Peter came to my door to tell me what had happened. We went back together, and then Peter went home to tell Shirley and phone for the doctor while I waited with Geordie. He seemed quite at peace. I tried to be cheery even while I was wiping my eyes. 'Och, Geordie, Geordie, could you not have poured a dram for me too?' I poured myself one anyway, and raised it to him. He could have been sleeping. I checked a couple of times to make sure that he wasn't, but the coldness of his cheek told me he was away. I felt the world settling around me: I was sad, but it began to be all right that he had gone. We are all going, we just don't know when it will be our turn.

I am getting distracted again – by my own meanderings, I suppose. If it was stones you wanted to know about, or if it was local history, or if you were after a Conach story or any other kind of story, Geordie was your man. If he'd still been alive when Dr Tybault came, Shirley would have sent him to Geordie. 'You have to speak to Geordie Kemp about this,' she'd have said. But it was too late, so she gave me the typescript of Charles Gibb's journal to read and sent Dr Tybault to me instead. I couldn't help him much. What was in that journal was all new to me. It would probably have been mostly new to Geordie too but, then again, you could never tell what he had stored away under that bunnet of his; he might have been able to fill in a few spaces to help Dr Tybault out.

The one story you wouldn't get from Geordie was the one about the dumb lass. You would not get it from him because he didn't know it.

That's not quite right. He did know it, or some of it. He was *in* it, near the end. He never told it, though, because it wasn't his to tell. Och, that's not right either. We would talk about it, but that was just between him and me. But it didn't *belong* to him. The Conach stories were his and Betty's, but the dumb lass's story wasn't, and he knew that and he respected it. Betty too, she understood. There were certain things, certain ways of behaving. That's the kind of people they were.

Journal of Charles Kirkliston Gibb

Saturday, 15th July 1809

It is now more than a fortnight since I came to the glen, and a week since I last wrote here. The weather turned to heavy rain again, that first weekend of my sojourn. As I have already written, I stayed away from church on the Sunday and was not condemned for it. The Baron, his wife and daughter and the rest of the household went, and came back very bedraggled about midday. The weather being as it was, there was no possibility of a visit to the cave.

On the following few days I sat undisturbed in the library from after breakfast until late in the afternoon, drawing imitations of the folios, transcribing the Latin and, on separate sheets, making a rough translation. My progress was rapid – too rapid if I were to remain here all summer – and in order to slow down I regularly left the desk in order to find something on the shelves to distract me from my task. Indeed this has been both ploy and principle during the whole of the fortnight – to find diversions in the library and elsewhere.

On one occasion, the Baron himself colluded in my time-wasting – unwittingly, I assume, although it is not always easy to determine if conscious purpose lies behind his actions. A parcel of new books arrived from Edinburgh and he brought them to me with something like humility, as if I were the keeper of the library and he my assistant. Three items were enclosed: a long poem by Thomas Campbell called *Gertrude of Wyoming*; the first number of a new periodical, the *Quarterly Review* (which I heard some time ago was to be established in

London to counter the Reformist influence of the *Edinburgh Review*); and *Bibliomania, or Book-Madness, a Biographical Romance* by one Thomas Frognall Dibdin, a Doctor of Divinity. Glen Conach was at a loss to explain why he had ordered this selection and thought that the bookseller had made a mistake. I suggested that the books might have been sent on approval and could be returned if not desired.

'That is possible, Mr Gibb,' he replied. 'Certainly it is possible as far as this new journal is concerned. Or I may have subscribed for all of them by accident, thinking I was subscribing for something else – it would not be the first time. Or Mr Haddow may have mentioned them to me, I really cannot say. I have asked my wife to explain it and she said she could not as she does not know what goes on in my head, which is true, she does not, any more than I know what goes on in Mr Haddow's. I must break the subscribing habit – it is very costly. Well, well, for now I will take this *Gertrude* away. I know some of Mr Campbell's work – *The Pleasures of Hope* is a fine poem. I leave you the *Review* and this other slim volume, which may be a joke of some kind, if this is representative: "In laying before the public blah blah an account of a disease which blah blah has entirely escaped the sagacity of all physicians . . ." You decide, Mr Gibb, you are the scholar among us. Or hand it to Mr Haddow – it will kill or cure him. How are your labours?'

But he swept out again without waiting for a reply, and I spent the rest of that day reading the *Quarterly Review*, which was good despite its being very Tory. My host should find it to his liking. I skimmed over Dr Dibdin's treatise, which is satirical after a fashion, but tedious even though short.

To become more familiar with the house and its grounds has been my other business, and this I have accomplished to the extent that I feel as much at home here as I have anywhere in the last few years. Being long practised in the skill of not drawing attention to myself, I have moved quietly and watched carefully, trying this door and that passageway until I know where everybody sleeps, sits, works, prepares food or consumes it; who is likely to be where at different times of day; who speaks much, and who is mostly silent; which rooms are warmer, which draughtier, and so on. I have observed how the Baron goes out bareheaded in sunshine, rain or wind, sometimes with his dogs, sometimes without, and hardly seems to notice, let alone care, what the weather is doing. He walks over to the clachan at least once a day, but for what reason he is so regularly drawn there I have yet to discover. Elspeth Carnegie too goes back and forth along the same route on her visits to her grandmother. Perhaps there is something secret between the laird and his handmaiden, but I think not: it would be impossible to conceal for long, and I cannot think that Lady Glen Conach would tolerate it. Elspeth continues to act with an impunity that none of the other servants enjoys. I have noticed how she wears shoes in the house but casts them off when she steps outside, as if she wants to rise above her station but cannot endure any consequent discomfort for long. Norah the kitchen maid, by contrast, never wears shoes indoors or out, and quite possibly does not have any.

What else have I learned? That Elspeth and Norah share a room and a bed under the baulks (I slipped up the narrow attic stair in order to establish this). That Kate Nicol sleeps over the stable with her man, Davie. That one of Davie's daily chores is to go through the house emptying the chamber pots and adding the contents to a midden, which consists also of horse dung, situated at a good distance from the house. That two men come in most days from the clachan to work among the vegetable and flower beds, and one of their tasks is to dig this waste into the garden soil. That there are three horses kept in a paddock behind the stables, sturdy white garrons with thick necks and broad rumps. My horse knowledge is small and they look to me like rough, bad-tempered creatures, and whether they can be either ridden or persuaded to pull the two-wheeled cart in the stable, or are good only for hauling timber and bringing game off the hill, I have no idea. (Mr Dunning has an old nag, but that appears to be the sum total of horse ownership in the glen.)

Then there are the habits and habitat of the Milne family. To ascertain what these are, I have discreetly entered and inspected each of their chambers at a time not inconvenient to the occupant – that is, when he or she was out. I am especially keen to see what Jessie has written about me in her journal but on two separate visits I have been unable to locate that volume among the clothing, bits of needlework, books, papers and other items scattered about her bedroom. I have put my head round the Baron's door and found his room as windswept as the Baron himself, partly because a stick has been used to wedge the window open, thus ensuring a permanent blast of fresh air. He and his wife keep separate bedrooms, an unusual arrangement in most houses with which I am acquainted, and which I think must be due, in part, to the incompatibility of their habits of tidiness. The Baroness's room, next door to his, is neat and ordered, a reflection of *her* character. I am not so far aware of any night-time trade between the two. Next door again is Alexander's room, very sparse and soldierly, though perhaps his mother is responsible for keeping it that way. The one thing common to all these rooms, ignoring the chaotic condition of the Baron's and Jessie's, is what little they contain: a bed, a chest or two, a press, a mirror, a pitcher, a basin, chamber pots (the ladies, like me, have commodes, a luxury I assume the Baron disdains), some grooming items, a few pictures and tapestries on the walls, some rugs over the rough floorboards; nowhere an abundance of clothes, and those they possess all old and well used. Mr Milne, I conclude, may be a baron but he is not a wealthy one, and I do not wonder that he is reluctant to expose his family to the outrageous extravagances of Edinburgh.

One bright afternoon this week – I think it was Wednesday, but the days merge one into another so it may have been Thursday – I took advantage of the sunshine and strolled over to the clachan. It consists of two dozen cottages spilled across the low land near the river; their walls are built of random stone, and peat smoke issues from open holes in their turf roofs. At a slight distance from this metropolis stand the schoolhouse, the kirk and the manse. Children of various sizes, dirt-clad from tousled head to naked foot, came at me from every direction, clamouring in a dialect which I struggled to interpret. I could not decide whether they were expressing curiosity, hostility or a mixture of both. Some of these infants were barely able to walk by themselves, others were carried inexpertly by their slightly larger siblings. Hens and geese wandered freely; I saw two very scarred and mangy cats, the one disputing the right of the other to cross its domain; further off I could see boys herding dark, hairy cattle up to the higher ground, away from the crops in the enclosed parks. On the distant slopes were numerous greyish dabs which I at first mistook for stones but which were, in fact, sheep.

At the door of one of the cottages an old man sat on a stool; at another, three women of indeterminate age stood watching me. I nodded at them as I passed, but they made no acknowledgement in reply until my heel slipped on some sharn and I was nearly pitched on my back. This entertained them greatly, as if the disadvantage of wearing boots were proved beyond a doubt. The children, who also found my narrow escape amusing, followed a few yards behind me until I had got beyond the last cottage and was making towards the schoolhouse, kirk and manse, when they fell away, as if they had done their duty in seeing me out of their jurisdiction, and returned to their playing and shouting.

From afar, the clachan might be a setting for *The Gentle Shepherd*; an Arcadian idyll, in other words. Close to, it looks rather as if one failed harvest could topple it into destitution. I do not see how the glen can sustain its present population. There are few young men here. The Baron spoke to me of men going off to join the army, but how much of a soldier's pay finds its way home? What if more men stayed in the glen? Would there be work for them, or would they simply have to go somewhere else and find a new way to live, perchance to live better? And where would they go? To the towns, to the seaports, to the manufactories springing up everywhere, to the Americas? And when they do return, whole or maimed, what then for these soldiers? And if they never return? Who will then care for the children and the old people? The women of the clachan appear hardened against life but also bowed down by it. What is it, to be alive in this place? Is it only to be not yet dead?

Tuesday, 18th July 1809

Having written the above, I almost scratched it out, but have left it. It was my old fear of being found out, rising again. I too have learned the game of survival, though the rules are different for me. It is a game at which we all play, some more knowingly than others, but play it we must. The winners are those who cheat poverty, pain and death the longest.

I paused outside the schoolhouse. This is not a grand edifice. It is all on a level. There is a long room at one end with two shuttered windows, not in very good condition: this is the schoolroom. Adjoined to it is a much smaller, more humble part, which is the quarters of the dominie. The roof is of thatch and a stone chimney rises in the middle, serving two fireplaces, one in the schoolroom and one in Mr Haddow's accommodation.

I peered in through a window of the schoolroom. There was Mr Haddow, with half a dozen older children in a row in front of him. I could not hear what Haddow was saying, but his pupils were all upright and apparently attentive. No doubt had I chosen to enter he would have welcomed me and had his monkeys perform their tricks for me. But what can he say to them that will change their lives one bit? If he tells them to think for themselves, will they not become dissatisfied with their lot and leave the glen as soon as they can? If he tells them to be docile and obedient, what is the point of teaching them at all? If he teaches them numbers and words and puts ideas in their heads, does he make the world seem a better place or only awaken them to the poverty of their existence? These gloomy thoughts make me think of my father. What did *he* intend for the children in his care? I doubt even my mother would be able to tell me.

Mr Haddow talked on. I did not enter the schoolroom, but quietly investigated his accommodation instead. This appears to consist of two halves, a snug area by the fireplace separated from his sleeping chamber by a thin partition. Both are clean and well ordered. I know not if any woman from the clachan assists him in keeping house, but there is little to suggest that he leads anything but a quiet, rigorous and solitary life. Likewise I am not sure how he subsists when he is not dining at the big house, except that it must be sparingly.

I gave thanks that I was not condemned to such an existence, and that I had made it a law to myself that I never would be, and continued my walk.

The kirk is a low, narrow thing, like some ancient creature crouched in sleep. It is two hundred years old, according to the Baron. The stone tiles of the roof ripple below the twisted spine, as if their weight is almost too much for it to bear. The bellcote resembles a horn and the arched door a closed mouth. In each side wall there are five very small, very grimy windows, which must allow only a dim light into the interior on winter days. The lack of furnishings inside is remarkable. Near the front are three short pews on either side of a narrow aisle, but the rest of the space is open: most of the congregation must either stand for the duration of a service or bring their own seats. Beyond the pews the floor is flagged, but behind them it is of earth. There is a stone font, a low table, a lectern on which rests a large Bible, and a dark, wooden pulpit like a tiny pavilion or summerhouse, with a flat roof and a short spiral staircase leading up to it. It looks hardly big enough to contain Mr Dunning, certainly not if he gesticulates much when preaching. I don't imagine that he is the gesticulating sort.

The kirk is the simplest I think I have ever been in, in a land renowned for the austerity of its temples. Even on such a warm day, it was cold enough to make me shiver. Nevertheless, I did not dislike being there. Alone in its silent gloom, I felt quite cut off from the outside world. I waited a minute, breathing so shallowly that I could not even hear evidence of my own vitality. Then I stepped back into the afternoon.

The mossy, uneven graveyard is enclosed by a low stone wall that cannot be much of an impediment to grazing animals. Most of the marker stones are uninscribed or their legends unreadable, and so weathered that they resemble humped, headless bodies buried upright in the turf. I deciphered a few dates, the oldest I could find being 1690. One of the most recent stones, modest in size and inconspicuously placed (I came upon it by chance), bears the name 'Eliza Anne Dunning' and the brief information that she was born in 1776, was the cherished wife of John Dunning, minister of this parish, and was taken into God's everlasting care on 15th April 1805.

There is an area, separated from the rest by a rail, where I discerned, from the names and dates carved on a slab of red sandstone adjacent to it, that several Milnes are interred. I picked out the Baron's grandfather Alexander and *his* father, Francis, and their spouses, and their children (most of whom did not survive infancy). The Baron's father, also Alexander – he who finally turned against the Acquaintance and Mr Riddell – lies there too. No wife shares *his* pre-resurrection sleep; in fact, the stone bears no mention of her, or indeed of their son. This seems very curious. I believe I am missing some obvious explanation.

Not far away I found the lair of 'old Mr Gillespie', Mr Dunning's predecessor. The flat stone under which he lies is one of very few that are clearly legible. I memorised the inscription and reproduce it here:

SACRED TO THE MEMORY OF
DAVID GILLESPIE
BELOVED OF THE PEOPLE
OF GLEN CONACH
WHO DEPARTED THIS LIFE 20TH JULY 1790
IN THE 75TH YR OF HIS AGE AND THE 47TH YR
OF HIS MINISTRY IN THIS PARISH

By my calculation, Gillespie was minister when the present Baron's grandfather was alive, and during the Rising of '45. He must have baptised the Baron, buried his grandfather and father, and baptised Sandy and Jessie too. He died the year after Glen Conach inherited from his father. Mr Haddow will have known him.

I moved on again. There was only one building left – the manse – before I must either return the way I had come or find another route back to the big house.

Yet 'manse' is too grand a word. Some manses I have seen – and some I have stayed in – are three times its size and ten times better appointed. I daresay this is a reflection on the impecuniousness of the patron, or in fact of his father, for the manse was (I have learned) erected some forty years ago when Mr Gillespie was the minister. It is stone-built, with a slated roof, and has two storeys, but much more than that cannot be said in its favour. It has no grace nor does it look settled in the landscape but rather as if it has been dropped accidentally by somebody who meant to put it somewhere else. It is a narrow, shallow, squat, mean house. Its architecture is very simple, and easily discerned: there are two rooms upstairs, crammed under the eaves, and two downstairs, with a scullery stuck on at the rear.

A bony old horse was tearing feebly at the tough grass nearby, giving no impression of either pleasure or purpose as it ate. This beast presumably transports Dunning to some of the more remote members of his congregation should he ever deign to visit them, but I think it might be quicker, safer and more comfortable to walk.

The sashes of all four windows were open, but the front door was shut. I was about to pass on when I heard a dull yet vigorous and repeated thudding sound close at hand. It seemed to come from within the house, and to my ears had something of a violent tone, as if a beating were being administered. It is one thing to stop one's ears and pass by on the other side of a crowded Edinburgh street; quite another to ignore such a noise in a quiet spot such as Glen Conach. I walked up the path and knocked loudly.

Nothing happened. I knocked again and called out to ask if all was well. The thudding sound ceased, so I knew that I was noticed, but again nobody came to the door. 'Are you there?' I shouted – a ludicrous inquiry, but I fancied I heard whispering and scurrying noises. Another minute passed. Scarcely satisfied, but at least hopeful that a murder was not being committed (although it was possible that one just had been), I turned to walk on. As I did so a skinny, flushed, bare-armed lass with her hair tied back in a cloth, and in possession of a mighty clothes-beetle, poked her head round the end of the house.

'Was that you chappin?' she asked breathlessly.

I looked about me, as if to check whether it could have been anybody else, then admitted my guilt. The damsel, whose dress was somewhat at odds with decorum, was not impressed by my attempt at levity. The following exchange occurred.

'Weel, whit for were ye makkin sic a din?'

'Because you did not come to the door.'

'Whit for wid I come to the door? I was thrang wi the washin oot the back.'

'I knocked to attract somebody's attention.'

'Attention? Wha was to tak tent o ye?'

'Well, you, as it happens.'

'But I was oot the back. I didna hear ye.'

'That is my point.'

'Eh?'

'I knocked twice because nobody came.'

'Naebody *came*?' she screeched, evidently astonished. 'Weel, whit for did ye keep chappin?'

'That is the normal procedure. One knocks at a door, and in due course somebody comes to open it.'

'That isna normal. Ye jist walk in or ye gang awa. But ye're here noo. Whit is it ye're wantin?'

'I have come to pay my respects.'

'Is somebody deid?'

'I mean, to Mr Dunning.'

'Is he expectin ye?'

'No, but as I was passing by I thought to call on him.'

'But ye said he's no expectin ye.'

'He can hardly *expect* visitors here, surely? Should I have left my card beforehand?'

'Eh?'

'Is he at home?'

A wily look came upon her countenance.

'He micht be.'

I tried again.

'Perhaps you could tell him I am here.'

'Whit for?'

We were not making progress. I tried another tack. 'What is your name?'

'Whit for d'ye want to ken my name?'

'I thought that if I addressed you by it I might melt your heart.' She returned me a look from which it was plain to see that such gentle sarcasm was wasted on her. 'Mine is Charles Gibb. Please tell your master I am here. I am staying at the big house.'

'Weel, a'body kens *that*,' she said, rolling her eyes heavenward. Seeking to assure her of my good intentions I took a step towards her, but she seemed to interpret this as preparation for invasion and raised the beetle like a battleaxe. I could not but admire her determination to block me even with physical force. This proved unnecessary, however, as another figure appeared around the house-end, in an open, loose shirt with the sleeves rolled above his elbows. His brow and ample beard were wet with either sweat or water, and his chest was black with hair. This was Mr John Dunning, the minister. He was not in a good temper.

'What keeps you, Mary?' he said. 'You have not yet hung out all the sheets.' Then, laying eyes on me, he added with exaggerated surprise: 'Why, Mr Gibb! What brings you here, Sir?'

'He's come to visit ye,' Mary said helpfully. 'But I widna let him by in case ye werna in.'

'Away you go, lass. Quickly now. I will attend to the gentleman. You find me ill-prepared, Mr Gibb. My housekeeper and I are engaged in a washing of all the bedlinen.'

As she went past her master, I had a sudden, unannounced vision of them as a couple – coupling, in fact – the flabby cleric and bony Mary. I wondered how I could have been such a fool in my persistence, for it seemed obvious to me now that I had interrupted something other than a washing. There was a predatory look about Dunning, the same goatish leer he had let slide over Jessie Milne at dinner, that was most disturbing. This was the main reason, apart from a complete lack of faith, why I had not been to church on my first Sunday, nor intended to go at all if I could avoid it: I could not bear the prospect of being preached at by such a man.

Mr Dunning was quick to make a thrust at me for non-attendance.

'I am surprised that *you* wish to see *me*, even on a weekday,' he said. 'Do you come on a matter of conscience, or something less weighty?'

'I happened to be out for a walk,' I replied. 'I did not mean to intrude, but I heard a noise and that was why I knocked.'

As soon as I said this I remembered the thumping sound, and now it seemed more like a headboard in repeated contact with a wall than anything else. Mr Dunning sensed my discomfiture and pounced upon it.

'I thought,' he said, 'you did not mean to intrude.'

'I was concerned,' I answered, 'that somebody might need assistance.'

'I assure you, nobody did.' He made what seemed a supreme effort to be gracious. 'I thank you for your concern. This great washing is an annual task, in which I always involve myself. I have done so for years, since before –' He broke off, then added, 'It would be heavy work for Mary alone.'

'I would suppose there are plenty of women in the clachan willing to help her.'

The graciousness, such as it was, vanished again.

'Oh, you are familiar with the local populace?'

'You know that I am not.'

'Then what you would suppose is of no import.'

I ignored this insult. 'You may surely call on them to assist you from time to time?' I said. 'They are your parishioners after all.'

Dunning said, a little menacingly, 'Aye, they are. I know them body and soul, out and in, as only their minister can.'

We faced each other for what seemed an age but was no more than a few seconds. In his open shirt, with his head lowered and eyes staring from under that darkening brow, he looked more like a prizefighter than a pastor. Then he turned and retraced his steps to the back of the manse, calling on Mary. I hurried away, ashamed. I was especially ashamed of the image I could not shake from my head, of slippery Dunning groping and thrusting at his sinewy housekeeper.

Tuesday, 25th July 1809

Another week has passed. I have had to count out the days to verify this to myself, so completely am I losing sense of time. My task goes on at its irregular pace. Food and wine are daily placed before me. I sleep in comfort every night. Surely this is a blessed dispensation, yet I am discontented. The weather continues changeable, but nothing else changes! Everybody goes about their affairs quite independently of everybody else. We meet at mealtimes, eat, talk and disperse again. I feel I have become a kind of distant cousin who arrived so long ago that the family has quite forgotten a time when I did not draw up my chair at the breakfast table; but, should I one day not appear, would they not immediately forget that I was ever there? I have the library to myself for hours at a time, and cannot settle. There lies the *Book*, disturbing my conscience, and I shy away from it. I am reading my way through everything else, but sometimes I must escape altogether and so I set forth on a reconnaissance. I still have not found Jessie Milne's journal despite being systematic in my searches. There are few places left in her room where it *can* be.

She, having been somewhat cold, is again quite friendly to me, and occasionally 'visits' me at my labours and questions me as to how far I have got with them. She knows more about the *Book* than I appreciated, and has told me one or two charming tales about 'Saint Conach' which she learned as a child from some of her father's people but which as far as I can see do not appear in any form in the manuscript. She gives a strong impression that she wishes they did, or even that they *should*.

The Baroness, a most accomplished conductor of daily and seasonal routines, is always busy at something. She is not at all averse to working like a servant in the kitchen or the dairy – almost as if she has only so much patience to expend on Norah or Elspeth and once it is used up must do the things herself that they have failed to do. Fashionable society would greatly disapprove of her and not hesitate to let it be known.

The Baron, on a contrary principle, adores her but does his best not to show it. He has not his wife's attention to detail but he too has routines of a sort. I have several times seen him, when he sets off on one of his excursions, carrying a gun, by means of which he brings home occasional small game, such as hares and rabbits, which are plentiful. He also shoots foxes, although not of course for eating. When the sky is threatening rain, he substitutes a fishing rod for his gun. There are many fishes in the river, especially brown trout and salmon. I feel we have had rather too much salmon at table of late, but I cannot complain aloud. Last week he returned with an eel, fully a yard in length. Kate Nicol cooked it and presented it in slices but I liked it even less than the salmon and rather hope he does not catch another. On days when he is not at his sport, he 'oversees' the two or three men building the new wall round the high park, and sometimes (as he intimated to me) sets to the work himself as a kind of entertainment. He reads his magazines, continues – in spite of his resolution not to – to order new books, and writes letters. And he visits the clachan. I have ascertained that he has a great affection for Elspeth's granny and goes to see her often. He also likes to exchange news and opinions with the clachan's male worthies. From these exchanges come further plans of work, such as making drainage ditches, planting trees &c, which never seem to begin or, if begun, never seem to finish.

I have long made it a rule not to take up the burden of other people's cares, but when amusement is as hard to come by as it is in Glen Conach I am forced to disobey my own statute. My curiosity about Mr Dunning – who inspires revulsion and fascination in me in equal measure – stayed with me. Not wishing to give the Baron, his wife or daughter the impression that I am a meddler, I did not press them for more information about the minister. Instead, I took another walk to the clachan last Saturday afternoon, intending to seek out the dominie. A certain understanding already existed between Mr Haddow and myself, I felt: we had not disliked each other when we first met at dinner, and he had called at the house several times since, usually to return and borrow books from the library, and on these occasions our meetings had been cordial. He, surely, would have something to impart concerning his clerical neighbour.

The day was dry but dull. Eyes were once again upon me as I passed through the clachan, but I felt they were more friendly than on the previous occasion. Indeed, a man I had not seen before waved and gave me a cheerful greeting. Not so many children were about, but those that were also seemed to regard me as an old acquaintance. It seemed that this change had come about, without any effort or intent on my part to win favour, or on theirs to grant it, through the simple fact of my having been resident at the big house for more than a fortnight.

I thought it unlikely that I would find Mr Haddow washing sheets in his shirt-sleeves. Indeed I did not. Through the window of his snug I saw him seated on a chair by the unlit fire, in his old black clothes and white stock, yet still unconsciously boyish, bent over a writing slope on which were a number of sheets covered in a close hand. So absorbed was he that it took two taps on the glass to win his attention. He looked up, startled, then hurried to the door and ushered me in with flustered animation. 'Mr Gibb, what a pleasure, come in, please sit here, forgive me, I don't know that I can offer you anything to eat' etc. – a stream of apologetic friendliness which I cut off by saying that I required nothing but had simply come to pass some time with him if that was not an imposition. 'Imposition? My dear Sir, you cannot imagine, you are very welcome' etc. He laid aside the writing slope, seated me on the best, in fact the only, chair (the one he had vacated), brought a cutty-stool from his bedchamber and perched upon it and, then, having apparently used up in five minutes all the words he would usually spread over an hour, lapsed into silence.

The writing slope looked primitive but effective, I observed. Mr Haddow bashfully admitted that he had made it himself. It comprised a smoothed and polished square of wood mounted on a frame made of rougher pieces and, nailed to the underside of these, a cloth stuffed with some soft matter so that the whole could rest comfortably upon the thighs. I indicated the handwritten sheets and said I was sorry to have interrupted him.

'I was only at my usual dabbling, Mr Gibb. I am – I aspire to be – a man of letters. Now that the term is ended – just a week ago – and the bairns are away to the shielings – a location they much prefer to the schoolroom – I can indulge my aspiration. I would be like yourself, one who lives by his writing, but you are far ahead of me in progress – and alas I am far ahead of you in years.' He said this with a shy look that only made him look younger than ever.

'I have published very little,' I said (and spoke the truth if 'very little' and 'almost nothing' are the same, which they are). 'What is your subject?'

Haddow glanced at me as if I had unknowingly touched on something intimate.

'My subject, Mr Gibb –' he said, and abruptly halted. 'Must I always call you "Mr Gibb"? My name is Daniel. Would you care to address me by that name?'

I saw no reason why not. I invited him to call me Charles, and we shook hands on it.

'My subject, Charles,' he resumed, 'is not easy to describe. I have been in the glen for so long – have been thinking for so long – that I sometimes wonder if my subject has not gone away in exasperation and left me to chase my own tail. And yet, were I not here in this wild yet settled place, with all the time to contemplate and with that whole library to read, I doubt it would concern me at all. Forgive me, I am so very pleased to see you here. I do not explain myself well.'

'Not at all,' I said, meaning to put him at ease, but he thought I was agreeing with his self-deprecation and leapt to his feet.

'I *can* offer you something which may help to clarify matters,' he said.

He slipped behind the screen again, and returned bearing two thick little glasses and a *pig*, or earthenware jar, which he set down on the floor.

HE: 'Do you drink whisky, Charles?'

ME: 'Very seldom. I find it dangerous to the brain.'

HE: 'Some whisky is. This, however, contains *good* whisky. It is made by men who know what they are about. *Yet it does not exist*. Do you understand me?'

ME: 'I *think* I do.'

HE: 'You would scarcely believe how much whisky is made secretly in the hills hereabouts, Charles. It is an ancient craft, and has been for generations. In the past the people made it in small quantities chiefly for their own consumption. But in the last few decades a great demand has grown for it in the towns. Whenever a market for any commodity appears some men will set out to control and dominate it, and the government too will seek both to regulate it and to benefit from it through taxation. This is what has happened here. Almost as soon as it became possible for the people of these glens to produce a surfeit of whisky and sell it to their advantage, other men sought to capture that advantage from them, and the government made efforts to restrict its production to those same men, who are skilled at commerce and can afford to pay the tax on it and still make a profitable return. And so one of the few products of these parts that can be exchanged for money becomes worthless to the local people unless they sell it illegally. Thus, as I said, it exists but it does not. If the gaugers come looking for it, they find nothing. It trickles away invisibly, and the people receive a trickle of coin in return, poor recompense for breaking the law.'

As on that previous occasion at dinner, it was evident to me that the dominie, whose natural disposition when not teaching children was to favour silence, constructed careful paragraphs in his head which he could at an appropriate moment deliver as if he were reading from a book. I looked again at the sheets of handwriting and wondered if the little treatise on the illicit whisky trade I had just heard had been not long written down. Meanwhile, he took the cork from the pig and filled the glasses. Handing one of them to me, he lifted his own, wished me good health and tossed off most of the contents. I returned the compliment, sipping cautiously. The whisky was fierce and caught at my throat, which came close to rejecting it, but the liquid had a delicious flavour and once it had descended further it caused a hot and most exhilarating sensation to spread, as it seemed, through my entire frame.

ME (coughing slightly): 'That is certainly superior to some of what I have tasted that purports to be whisky.'

HE: 'It is a perfect illustration – Charles – of how, as a nation becomes ever more regulated by the rules of commerce and property – by the division of labour and the laws of a settled, ordered society – the quality of virtue declines. *That* is my subject, and what I wrestle with continually in my head and on paper.'

ME: 'Do you equate whisky with virtue?'

HE: 'No, it is only a symbol. Whisky as good as this stands for something old and pure and vigorous and – may I say? – heroic. That is something I never can be. No, no, Charles, hear me out. I am neither pure nor heroic. I wish it were otherwise, but I am a man built upon books. I have read everything in Glen Conach's library at least once, and what I have not read in its entirety I have acquainted myself with enough to know that I have no wish or need to read it further. I have been transfixed, seduced, by this parade of words. I have watched it go by me for a quarter of a century, and yet when I reach out – there is nothing there. There is no implement with sharp blade and well-shaped handle. There is no musket, shield or axe. There is not seed to sow, nor stone to place, nor animal to slaughter. All the words dissolve and I think that I have wasted every minute I have spent trying to make sense of them.'

Despite the import of *his* words, Daniel, far from being woeful and despondent, spoke with great animation. It was as if the single gulp he had taken were not of whisky but of an elixir of life. I myself took another sip, larger than my first, and he hurried to refill our glasses.

D: 'Nearly all of our great writers make a distinction between the savage and the civilised. Some find nobility in the former, but most prefer the safe, regulated life of streets and farms to the dangers and surprises of the forest. We avoid confrontation and strife, and if we must have them then we raise armies and send them to fight one another on our behalf. We think this a superior way of living to that of the savage who contends with nature and with other savages. And perhaps it is, but there is no heroism in it, there is no courage.'

ME: 'What would you have, then, Daniel? Would you wish us back to whatever miserable lives people lived a thousand years ago?'

D: 'Miserable to you and me, Charles, from our present view. But our view is no less obscure than theirs. Was Conach, with whom you are presently engaged and who lived in the era to which you refer, less noble or civilised than us?'

ME: 'You have read the *Book*?'

D: 'I already said, I have read everything in that library yonder. I don't believe Conach was more or less saintly, noble or cultivated than you, me or Jean-Jacques Rousseau. The truth is, no single rule can measure the advantages or defects of different ages. *I* do not wish to live a thousand years ago, but if I had done I would not have spent my time resenting that I was not born a thousand years later.'

ME: 'You mean, there has been no progress? Things are not better now than they were then?'

D: 'Things are *changed*. I cannot say if they are better. I wrestle with words and their meaning, but what is that effort to the struggle of men against the elements, or against other men? A wise man once wrote that he who has never struggled with his fellow creatures is a stranger to half the sentiments of mankind.'

I do not know to what sage he referred. I wished to oppose his argument, which seemed so dispiriting, but he was now as lively as I had ever seen him and, pausing only to fill our glasses again, he rushed on with great vehemence.

D: 'And when I spoke a minute ago of civilisation and savages, I meant to say that the philosophers, on whichever side of that argument they stand, are wrong. It is a false antithesis. When man is a savage, he is yet a social animal. He does not live alone in the wilderness like a tiger. But when he is in Edinburgh or London or Paris, has he left all his savagery behind him? No, he has not. Humans are the same in whatever condition they are found, though when men from different societies are by chance thrown together they may perceive themselves to be so unalike that one takes flight, while another worships, a third enslaves and a fourth murders his fellow creature. This is tragedy, my dear Charles, but is it not true? When Cain slew Abel he slew himself also. Does not the slave-driver draw his own blood when he lashes his slave?'

ME (hesitantly): 'But if we do not improve – if society does not improve, and we with it – then what hope is there? Do we simply shrug and put all our faith in the deity?'

D (eagerly): 'From the framing of your question – from that phrase you use, "the deity" – may I assume that you do not, or cannot, have such faith?'

ME (cautiously): 'I did not say that I thought faith futile.'

D: 'And nor do I, Charles. Indeed, I must on occasion say the opposite to the bairns I teach. But I try to exclude the deity from the schoolroom. Mr Dunning comes in from time to time and tests their knowledge of the Bible, but that is different. And forby, Mr Dunning cares little enough about it.'

ME: 'I was going to ask you about Mr Dunning.'

D: 'Later, Charles, later. Don't make me lose the thread of what I wanted to tell you. I will be frank – I *can* be frank here, far from the hot cauldrons of opinion. I feel I can be frank with *you* anyway. I do not know of a deity. I do not have proof of one and I deny that anybody can give me such proof. It goes against all rational thought. There! I have said it.'

ME: 'But a believer does not need proof. The believer is no rationalist. Proof is an obstruction to him. He needs faith, not proof.'

D: 'You are correct. And what gives him his faith? If God has not miraculously appeared before him – and let us be honest, even among the most fervent believers there are few who claim that this has happened to them – his faith must rest on something else. Some powerful inner feeling, perhaps, which cannot be denied. But not only have I not seen God, I lack such a feeling too. No matter how hard I may wish it, I cannot persuade myself of God. And yet – and this is important, Charles – that is not to say that he may not be watching over me, his ignorant creation. If I displease him I cannot help it, for if he made me at all then he made me as I am. And there is another thing.

Try as I may – stretch the sinews of my rationality as I may – I cannot close my eyes and think of myself *not here*. I cannot *un*imagine myself. And so I tread a path somewhere between faith and atheism, and commit to neither.'

He tried again to fill my glass, but I put my hand across it. 'You are quite right,' he said, and put the pig down, but I noticed a minute later he took another dram to himself.

'Now,' he continued, 'I come to another matter, which you touched on just now – misery. Or rather, I wish to speak of its opposite, which is happiness. Christianity teaches that all the wealth in the world will not buy us a place in paradise, and also that it cannot buy us happiness. But it also teaches that we should thole misery in this life because we will have happiness in the hereafter. Again, there is no security that we will be happy in that future state because there is no *proof* of that future state, let alone of how we will feel if we attain it. And the crueller kind of religion that exists in this country – and elsewhere, of course – says that if we are happy without God in this life it is very likely he will make us miserable *for ever* in the next. More than miserable – he will cause us to suffer torture and pain unending for the crime of having being naturally happy. That is – I am sorry if this offends you – that is a monstrous imposition on a mere human creature.'

I assured him that I was not offended. I was more concerned, as the whisky worked upon me, with following his argument than with taking issue with any part of it. He went on:

'Yet despite what Christ taught, good Christian people acquire riches and possessions, they eat and drink to excess, they play at games, they enjoy music, and so on. These things may make some of them happier but less righteous, but there is no assurance of that either. Are the inhabitants of America or Africa – the "savages" as we are wont to call them – are they less happy though they have so few possessions? You will find, among the poor, men and women without a penny to their name who are happier than a duke or a duchess, though assuredly you will also find many who are miserable.

Happiness is not determined by position or wealth, nor by age or the continent in which one lives. And although a man may say, if asked, that he is happiest when he is at leisure, it is seldom true. He merely thinks, when he labours or exerts himself in some other way, that he will be happier when he stops. But it is his labour and his exertion that make him a man, and when he stops he is at a loss what to do.'

ME: 'And do you apply this theory to women also?'

D: 'Certainly, although I cannot pretend to know them so well. Women are always occupied with something, and complain less than men who are not half so busy.'

ME: 'That they do not complain does not mean that they are happy.'

D: 'True, but their busyness may be a shield against melancholy. I have read of one woman who thought that men should learn to knit and sew, as this would prevent them, when time weighed upon them, from being a burden to themselves and to others. And another woman agreed, saying that she dreaded bad weather when men could not get out of doors, as then they did not know what to do with themselves and became irritable – and irritating! But again you are leading me astray. I spoke about treading a path between faith and atheism: in the same way, I believe that between savagery and civilisation lies another condition, in which mankind is neither overmastered by nature nor has quit his place in it. And that is perhaps the happiest state, the happiest *place*, in which he can dwell.'

ME: 'And where may we find this Garden of Eden?'

D: 'Why, it is here, Charles! Glen Conach!'

He said this with a shout and a laugh, and I joined in the latter, for the elixir had by now quite affected me and I felt as if I were floating above my chair. But at once he brought us back to earth, though still he was as excited as a puppy. 'Yet it is a dying garden,' he said, 'and here am I in it, a schoolmaster. There is no heroism in schoolmastering. My work is to make my charges unfit for the life into which they were born, and scarce able to flourish should they go elsewhere. And in either case, I make them less happy than they might have been.'

I said, 'I cannot pretend that the same thoughts did not occur to me a week ago, when I peered through a window and saw you teaching the children. And though they seemed attentive they were, in fact, as you have told me, eager to be away to the shielings. But you are not responsible for their fates, let alone their happiness. And I must ask you this: would you and I rather we had been kept in ignorance than be the men we are?'

He looked at me. 'Ah, Charles, the men we are. You do understand me,' he said. 'Or do you?'

His entire frame was shaking, I did not know with what emotion. He lifted the pig and indicated to me to present my glass, which he filled again. As he did so he steadied himself upon me with his free hand, and then he squeezed my shoulder in a manner that I could not mistake.

I have been misinterpreted in this way before. I neither welcome nor resent it. It is almost flattering. Other men, if they think of it at all, are frightened by what they conceive to be a bestial perversion. That is because they are frightened of themselves. Once, I confess, some years since, I allowed things to progress a little further than I liked in order to get a lodging on a winter's night. On that occasion I was somewhat surprised at myself, but I was not frightened.

'I think, Daniel,' I said, remaining quite calm, 'that *you* have misunderstood *me*. If I have in any way led you to suppose . . .'

He at once retired to his stool and to his own glass. 'Ah, an error of judgement, a philosophical error. Dear Sir, another offence.' I told him again that I was not offended, and begged him not to think of it any more.

'I will not, I do not.' I thought he might start to weep. Poor fellow, I suppose he has meagre fare here and must take what he can, but I won't encourage him. I decided to take no more of either his whisky or his philosophy. 'Tell me about Dunning,' I said.

(But here I must desist as my fingers are numb and I have yet to apply myself to Conach today, and had better do so.)

Wednesday, 26th July 1809

Mr Haddow was greatly relieved to be able to change the subject. In ten minutes I had the whole history of the minister. Dunning is the only man in the glen, other than the Baron, with whom Daniel may have a sophisticated conversation, but they are not friends. This is not surprising to me. If Daniel has difficulty believing in a deity he must find it almost impossible to believe in Mr Dunning.

As I had already learned from Miss Milne, Mr Dunning came to the glen after the death of Mr Gillespie, some nineteen years ago. It was not a charge, from its isolation and poverty, likely to attract the most ambitious or capable of men. Daniel, who had been here several years by then, soon found that in place of the old minister – a kindly man, he said, yet one fervent and firm in his faith – had come one whose faith and kindness were alike equivocal. Mr Dunning's moods changed as often and as quickly as the weather. He could be tolerably polite and forthcoming at noon, and by two o'clock short-tempered and withdrawn. He would deliver a sermon extolling the virtues of charity and forgiveness on Sunday but on Monday reduce a child to tears over some petty misdemeanour. He liked to sit down to dinner at Glen Conach's table but not to bow his head and enter the cottages of his nearer parishioners. And it soon appeared that he had a habit of absconding altogether from his duties. Sometimes he was not seen for days at a time, either because he was locked away in the manse or, it was said, because he had taken himself off into the hills.

I asked if this latter were true and if so what reason might lie behind such absences. Daniel said it was quite true, for on one occasion, to pacify a girl who was then acting as housemaid to Dunning and had got it into her head that her master must be lying dead in his chamber, he had entered the manse and searched for him in vain. The old nag, which was then a young nag, was grazing in its customary pasture, so the minister had evidently not gone to call on a distant parishioner. The next day, however, Daniel had met him walking home, very bedraggled and muddy as if he had been out all night. He had refused to give any explanation of where he had been. The men of the glen did not like it any more than the housemaid, who was resolute that she would not go back to the manse. But what had he been about, out there in the wilds? That was what folk wondered. In the same way that some fishermen (such as those I knew at Dysart) have their superstitions, and will not put out to sea if they encounter a minister on the way to their boats, the Glen Conach people were not keen on a minister loose in the hills, and thought he would bring mischief upon them.

This, I said, was simply explained. It surely related to the illicit stills, and the worry that he might betray them to the gaugers.

'Aye,' Daniel said, 'but that would be too easy for these people. They prefer tales of mysterious meetings with the Devil or some lesser species of bogle, of hearing screams and shouts in the night, to an admission of anything so mundane as that.'

'Surely,' I said, 'they don't believe that nonsense?'

'But it is wonderful nonsense in which to believe,' Daniel replied, 'and to tell such stories between songs is a pleasing way to spend a long winter's evening. And you must remember that the minister came among them, literally, as an intruder, for he was the nominee of the laird, not the choice of the congregation. That is, he came among them whether they wanted him or not. It has always been that way in Glen Conach – this is no hotbed of democracy – but it means that the people do not see Mr Dunning as *their* minister, but as the laird's minister. It is true that Mr Gillespie was also intruded, but he was here so long that he came to be theirs.'

'But they have not taken to Mr Dunning?'

'Not in nineteen years, and I doubt not even in ninety.'

'Then why does Glen Conach not get rid of him and bring in somebody else? Does he not care that his people do not love their pastor?'

He looked at me with as straight an eye as he could manage, given the combination of what he had imbibed and his recent embarrassment. 'You must understand, Glen Conach is not a religious man. He is not an irreligious man either, as I am. What matters to him is that life should continue here much as it has done for centuries. He does not want to put out a minister that he himself put in. And then, what if he put in another whom the people liked even less? He hates the thought of any such fuss. Do not mistake me, Charles – I greatly respect Glen Conach. I am indebted to him for my living but, that aside, he is a good man, a good master to his people. He wishes to keep things as they are. And I, like an actor playing Third Attendant in *King Lear*, have my part in that – I attend church every Sunday although I believe not a word that issues from Mr Dunning's lips. I attend because it is expected of me. What have I been saying to you all afternoon? This is an Eden. Why would a man like Glen Conach not wish to preserve it, and why would a man like myself not dissemble a little to assist him?' After a moment he added, 'Yet it cannot be preserved. It is dying.'

'Do you think Mr Dunning believes much of what issues from his lips?' I asked.

'In all honesty, I do not know,' he replied.

'Whether he does or does not,' I said, 'and whether he consorts with bogles or not, he does not strike me as a contented native of Eden.'

'And there, Charles,' he said, 'you are quite right. He is a most unhappy man.'

I pressed him to tell me about the late Mrs Dunning. How had he acquired her? Had *she* made him happy?

According to the dominie, Liza Dunning was supposedly a native of Dundee. It seems that Dunning and she knew each other as children, and that ten years ago, on one of those rare occasions when he was a commissioner to the General Assembly, they met again when he was on his way to Edinburgh and were married on his way back. This seemed to me an improbable tale. I said as much to Daniel, who was at first cautious in his reply, saying that, improbable or not, folk accepted it; but then acknowledged that he agreed with me. It was the case, however, that the minister's overnight absences ceased when Mrs Dunning came to the glen. Daniel was not convinced that Mrs Dunning really was from Dundee, or that it was there that they had met. He thought that she and her husband might have become acquainted elsewhere. He had heard it said that not all commissioners to the General Assembly spent *all* their time debating Kirk law, but some expended *some* of their energies in other ways under *other* roofs whilst in Edinburgh. Was that true? he asked me.

I said that it was not *improbable*, and asked in return if he was insinuating that Mr Dunning had found the future Mrs Dunning in a house of ill repute and removed her from it. Daniel made an exaggerated shrugging gesture but said nothing. I said that I did not condemn a woman or a man for where they came from or what they might once have been or what they were. We let that lie between us.

I asked what kind of character Liza Dunning had had. Daniel said she had been pleasant enough but would say hardly a word even if you were to speak directly to her, and when in the presence of her husband had always with a glance sought his permission before she would venture an opinion. More than anything her character had been marked by illness. She was sickly when she arrived and was never fully well in all her six years in the glen.

ME: 'What was wrong with her?'

D (shrugging): 'She wasted away. She was consumptive.'

ME: 'Was a physician ever brought to her?'

D (shaking his head): 'No. Dunning used to say that Christ was her physician, and she needed no other.'

ME: 'But she did.'

D: 'We are back where we were, Charles – faith and misery. I believe he loved her, but her illness wore him down, and in the end he neglected her. He was not alone. We who should have befriended her were not friends enough. We share his guilt. I am sorry for it now.'

ME: 'Her headstone says she was his cherished wife.'
D: 'He chose the words. I do not judge his love or lack of it. He was an unhappy man then, as he is now. A tormented man.'

Shortly afterwards I left Haddow. He began to make apologies again, and said he hoped I would say nothing of what he called his 'secret' to Glen Conach, since he was no danger to the bairns in his charge. I refused his apologies. I said that I had not the least concern that he was a danger to anyone, and I urged *him* not to torment himself, since no possible benefit could come of it. He thanked me, said that I was a good man and he did not deserve me for a friend. I said that he did not know me, that I was no better than he was. All human creatures, I said, carried their own private burdens, and I preferred to think of these not as secrets but as stories of which others were ignorant. We shook hands. I felt the whisky in my head as I swayed out of his house into the afternoon light. 'Goodbye,' he called. I turned and waved farewell. For the first time since I came here, I thought he looked older than his years; older than myself, which he is by twenty years or more.

Thursday, 27th July 1809

It was remarkable that, despite what I had consumed, I seemed to see the world with the utmost clarity and even now, days later, can recall with no great difficulty the details of my movements and of the conversations I had. I use the plural form for I did not converse only with Mr Haddow that afternoon. I was passing through the clachan when I met Elspeth Carnegie coming gaily in the opposite direction, and we fell into discourse. Unquestionably she is a very bonnie creature. She was friendly to me and seemed not at all disturbed if she detected, as surely she must have, my state of inebriation.

I asked her if this was a holiday for her, and she laughed. 'Ye should ken better,' she said, 'than to think ony day but the Sabbath is a holiday for the likes o' me. There's aye trauchles and toil for us, even on the Sabbath, while gentles tak their ease seven days in the week.' There was a martyred tone in her voice, and yet she spoke and smiled so cheerily that I replied, 'Then, Elspeth, you must be one of the gentles yourself, for you are often at your ease and never seem bowed down with care.' 'Weel,' she answered, 'they dae say blood will oot,' and laughed again.

She asked me where I had been and when I told her she said that she liked Mr Haddow and always had. He had taught her as he had most of the bairns of the clachan, but she had not had the patience to sit still in the schoolroom and had got out of it as soon as she could. She would rather be in the fresh air, she said, or in the company of her grandmother, to whom she was just then going. 'Ye had better come wi me and let her see ye,' she said, 'for the laird has tellt her a' aboot ye, and she aye likes to pit a face to a name.'

The cottage to which she led me was, looked at externally, no more or less palatial than any of the others, but on entering I was glad to find it neat and dry, with the earthen floor swept clean and a good number of wooden furnishings placed around the walls, including chairs, a spinning wheel, a table and a kind of primitive dresser – which goes by the name of a *haik* – full of cooking pots, plates, jugs, a bannock spade, and the like. This was the human end of the house, there being a lower part, separated by a wooden rail, for beasts, but that was empty and swept clean too (the beasts, presumably, being in the high pastures). The stonework of the walls appeared in good condition and so too was the wooden frame supporting the turf roof. A box-bed made up the sleeping arrangements. A curtain, which for modesty's sake could be extended to create two separate quarters, was tied back to a hook in an upright beam, but the cottage was so murky even in the afternoon that I could hardly think it necessary. In the centre was the fireplace, built around with blackened stones, and over it was a kind of canopy made of wood and skins to direct the smoke through the roof.

There was also the usual crane-like apparatus, called a *crook*, for the swinging of pots. The peats were glowing, causing a light drift of smoke, but owing to the canopy the air was not as thick as is sometimes the case in these houses, when the motes float before you like so many gnats and your eyes are perpetually weeping. Various items of food – a cheese, some sinister smoked fishes and hunks of what looked like salted mutton – were suspended from the roof.

Elspeth did not hesitate to introduce me, at a considerable volume, to her ancestor, a person I understand to be more than eighty years of age. 'Eh, Granny Ally, here's a young callant to see ye, Maister Gibb, that's bidin at the big hoose eenoo. D'ye mind Glen Conach was speakin aboot him to ye?'

Her grandmother was yellow as old parchment and her skin as brittle to the touch when she reached out a hand to me. I took it and bestowed a kiss upon it, much to her amusement. She was of a different structure to Elspeth, thinner and more angular, and yet in her prominent cheekbones and dark, lively eyes I could see a resemblance, and clearly there was a strong mutual affection, evinced in the warm embrace they gave one another.

'Aye, I mind fine, Elspet,' she said. 'Sit ye doon, Sir, and let's hae a keek at ye. A young callant, ye said? He's no that young. I hear ye're a scholar come to look at thon auld book up at the hoose. Ach weel, I could tell ye a wheen o' tales aboot Saint Conach, and mine are a' true.'

I asked her what made her think the tales in the *Book* were not true, and she said, '*Because* they're in a book, ye gomeril!' and I saw that I was diminished in her estimation. I could not draw out of her any of the stories she claimed to have, and when I said that if she would not tell them to me I would have to rely on Miss Milne's versions she snorted derisively. 'As muckle use as a book! But dae ye no hae ony ither purpose in mind?' she went on. 'There's lassies in the glen just desperate to be wad gin there were suitors to wad them. But a' the braw laddies are awa for sodgers, sae if ye're quick ye micht tak your choice, eh no, Elspet?'

The crone directed winks of a most deplorable sort at both of us, which I chose to ignore. Elspeth simply laughed and said, 'Och no, Granny, I'll wait on a sodger comin hame or else I'll gang awa and find ane for mysel. But dinna fash,' she added, observing a look of what was probably exaggerated anxiety in her relative's face, 'ye'll no be left alane. Ye'll aye hae Glen Conach to mak sure ye're lookit efter.'

'Glen Conach takes good care of his people, then?' I inquired.

'There's mony a laird that's waur,' the old woman said. 'Some hauds their folk in penury and some wants to clear them oot a'thegither, but Glen Conach is nane o' that breed. He has a saft hert, though it's no aye to his advantage.'

It was hardly ringing praise. Elspeth, I thought from her expression, was still less admiring of the laird's beneficence, but she held her tongue. I asked her grandmother if she lived alone in the cottage, to which she replied that she did, although Elspeth came back and forth and often stayed the night, which she found a comfort in the winter – 'But in the summer I'll no hae her in the bed for she gies aff sic a heat as wad melt me intae seerup.' And there was sometimes a neighbour's daughter that helped her about the place, for she was not as able as she once was. And Glen Conach stopped in to see her almost every day, whether or not he had much to say. She wanted for nothing but her husband, her two daughters and Elspeth's father, all of whom were long dead and, she said, there was no profit in wanting them back for they would not come, and Elspeth was a fair compensation when she felt their loss.

I took my leave soon after this, puzzled both by what I had learned that day and what I had not learned. There were things about the glen that were confusing and obscure to me, and I felt this was not due only to the power of Mr Haddow's 'good' whisky. I made my way back to my room in the big house, where I thought I would stretch myself out for a few minutes' contemplation before dinner. Unfortunately I fell into a deep sleep, and nobody either summoned me or kept me back a morsel for when I awoke, which was at about nine in the evening. Glen Conach might look after his people but his house guests must look to themselves, it seems. He warned me of this when I first arrived, of course.

Book of Conach

Chapter 11

Of the questions of his servant Talorg

Conach loved his servant Talorg, who was ever loyal to him and stayed with him over many harsh seasons even until his death. And though Conach was often apart from the world, and for days together did not see Talorg, let alone speak to him, at other times they shared a meal and sat together in conversation. On these occasions Talorg was eager to partake of his master's wisdom, and if Conach's mood was benign he would teach him.

'Master, how do we know?' Talorg asked one evening.

'How do we know what?' Conach replied.

Then questions burst from Talorg like the sudden melting of a frozen waterfall.

'How do we know anything? That the world is as it is? That there is water? That there are trees? That a deer is a deer and a fish a fish? That there is cold and dry and sharp and rough and light and dark? That the stars are the stars and the moon is the moon? That I am me and you are you? How do we know all this?'

Conach touched Talorg's face. 'What do you know of this?' he asked.

Talorg said, 'I know you have touched me.'

'How do you know it?'

'Because it is your hand. I see it, and I feel the heat and touch of your flesh.'

Then Conach pointed to the moon. 'And what do you know of that?'

'That is the moon,' Talorg said. 'I can see it. It is bright.'

'But you cannot feel it. Sometimes it is there, sometimes not. It changes shape each night. What do you truly know of the moon?'

'Even though it goes away, it always returns,' Talorg said.

'That is all you need to know,' Conach said. 'The world is the world, the moon is the moon, you are Talorg. Do not concern yourself with how you know these things. Know only that you do.'

Talorg said, 'Master, how, then, do we know things that we can neither touch nor see?'

'What things?' Conach replied.

Talorg said, 'Master, do not be angry with me, but I am troubled. How do we know that God is God? That there is no other god? That our faith is the true faith? That there is a heaven? That we will live after death?'

Conach said, 'I am not angry. He who does not seek will not find. But you are seeking in the wrong place. You are like a bird searching for food on the ground who does not see the stalking cat. To live, that bird must fly. You are seeking in your own mind, and the answer does not lie there. The answer lies in faith.'

'But what is faith?' Talorg asked.

'Faith is knowledge that is revealed, not learned. It is given, not found,' Conach said. 'We know because we know. The truth of our faith has been revealed through miracles. I did not see the miracle of Christ risen from the dead but I have been told by others who knew others who knew the ones who saw Him. And Christ's teachings and His deeds have come to us through the words of these men, written down in the Bible. That book contains the truth as a bowl contains food. The bowl is placed before the hungry man; he eats. But even if I had not read or heard of these things, I would still have faith, for we have miracles in our own times. All these things tell us that our path is the right path, and that it leads to the resurrection and to life ever after.'

So they would talk on a good day. But there were other days when Conach's mood was dark like a storm upon the mountain. Then Talorg knew not to pester his master even though his curiosity was not satisfied. For in those times Conach descended into himself, and would neither sing nor speak. And whether he went out among the trees and upon the hills, or whether he sat like a stone within his cabin, he was a man of sorrow, and the Devil was at his elbow.

Chapter 12

Of the wild man of the glen

It was true what the people had said, that a wild man lived high up in the glen. They were afraid of him. He was a mighty man, fleet and agile in his nakedness. He could climb the tallest tree in the time it took an ordinary man to walk the same distance on a flat piece of ground. He could creep up on a hare and catch it before it could run the length of its shadow. He lived on berries and nuts and the raw flesh of fish and other creatures. Yet he was wretched as an ape, and cut and bruised himself upon the rocks and howled so piteously at night that even the wolves were silenced when they heard him.

One day not long after Conach's arrival, while Talorg and some others were building him his dwelling, the holy man was led by the Spirit into the wastes to pray. As he was praying aloud the wild man came upon him, beseeching him to desist and to leave that place. Conach conversed with the man, who said that he too had once been a faithful servant of God but had fallen into sin, and must suffer on earth until the day he was taken up into the arms of Christ. Conach asked him his name but the man said he had none. Conach asked what was the nature of his transgression and the man wept but would not say, begging only to be left alone. But Conach refused to go. Then the man seized the psalter that Conach had made and that he kept always with him, and ran away with it into the forest. And he cast it into the river and the river carried it away and it was lost. And fierce was Conach's rage against the wild man.

But the next day, as I have been told, it happened that an otter hunting for fish far downstream found the psalter and took it in its teeth and brought it to the holy man and laid it at his feet. And the book was not marked by the teeth of the otter, nor was the writing in it spoilt by the water.

When the wild man appeared again Conach showed him the psalter, saying, 'See how your wickedness is repaid. For evil is powerless against the Word and cannot defeat it. Even a creature that lives below the bank of the river knows this, yet you know it not.'

Then the wild man gnashed his teeth and cried out against Conach, 'The Devil shall tempt you as he tempted me, and you shall do penance even as I have done.' And he fled again into the forest.

And Conach gave thanks to God for the salvation of the book, and prayed for the salvation of the demented man.

Conach and the Wolf

(School of Scottish Studies Sound Archive: Geordie Kemp, Glen Conach, Angus, recorded by Dr Ken Clavers, 1985; transcribed by Dr Matthew Tybault, 2020)

Weel, ye're spierin whit stories there are aboot Saint Conach, miracles an siclike. The thing is, naebody kens the half o whit's true an whit's made up aboot him. Naebody really kens if he was even a saint or even if he wis ever alive, it wis aa that lang syne. But there's ae story that if ye were born an brocht up here ye wid ken it, an that ane's aboot whit happened when he met wi the wolf.

Ae day, Conach wis awa up the glen whaur he liked tae go tae meditate as they ca it, a bit prayin tae God an thinkin intae himsel, an there he wis up there an a wolf comes by an they fell intae a dispute. Noo there's nae wolfs in Scotland nooadays as ye ken but in thae days there wis an awfie amount o them an it wisna a wise thing tae argue wi a wolf because if it wis feelin crabbit it could summon the lave o the pack tae come an tear ye intae bits just the richt size for eatin on the spot, or mibbe for cairryin awa tae their dens for a wee bit supper. Weel but Conach wisna feart, ye see, because he wis a holy man an God wis on his side, even if Conach couldna aye see him he kent he wis there or there aboot. But in fact Conach wisna just no feart, he wis ragin mad because the wolf hed twa wee lambs in its teeth, jist hingin there like cloots, an Conach kent that thae lambs belanged his freens that kept sheep doon at the fit o the glen. There wis nae ither place they could hae come fae. So he says tae the wolf, 'Oh aye,' he says, 'an whaur dae ye think ye're aff tae?'

'I'm gaun hame,' says the wolf. It wisna easy for her tae speak because she hed these lambs in her jaas. 'Whit's it tae dae wi you?'

'Weel, they're no your lambs,' says Conach. 'Ye shouldna hae hurtit them an ye shouldna hae stolen them.'

'But I'm a wolf,' says the wolf. 'That's jist whit I dae.'

'Weel, the folk ye've taen them fae will go hungry because o you,' says Conach.

'Na, they'll no,' says the wolf. 'There's plenty mair lambs whaur these cam fae. And onywey,' she says, 'I've three bairns masel, three cubs tae feed.'

So Conach says, 'I order you,' he says, 'I order you tae let the lambs go, so they can live an hae their freedom again like they did afore ye took them.'

The wolf must hae thocht he'd gane gyte. 'But they're deid,' she says. 'I killt them awready.'

'You jist pit them doon,' says Conach. 'You jist drap them fae yir jaas an ye'll see.'

Sae the wolf thocht he wis haiverin ye ken, speakin nonsense, an she wis sure that the lambs were deid, sae she drappit them fae her jaas on the gress. An as soon as this was done, did the lambs no spring up an loup awa? They were oot o her reach in a second, ane's awa tae the left an the tither's awa tae the richt. Sae she couldna catch them baith, ye see, she couldna catch either o them, an they ran awa doon the glen back tae their mithers.

'That's aa very fine,' says the wolf, 'but noo ma bairnies'll sterve an you'll hae the wyte o it.'

'Aye, weel,' says Conach, 'you gang awa tae yir den the noo, an see whit ye find. An if ye like it, come back an tell me.'

Sae the wolf gaes awa hame, an when she gets hame her cubs are feastin awa on aa this fine fare. There's a brace o grouse an a hare an the fawn o a roe deer, in fact there's food eneuch there for the wolf tae eat her fill an aa. Back she gaes tae Saint Conach an she says, 'I never brocht them aa that grouse an hares an that.' 'Aye,' Conach says, 'is that richt? Weel, somebody's been daein yir job for ye. Noo, if ye swear never tae tak anither lamb or sheep while ye bide in this glen, then I swear tae you that there'll aye be plenty o wild beasts for ye tae hunt for you an yir bairns.'

Weel, the wolf swore it, an fae that day on the shepherds never hed ony trouble wi wolfs in Glen Conach, an that wis the wey o it for centuries tae the last wolf wis killt in Scotland by a man cried MacQueen, but that wis hyne awa up in Moray. Sae that wis three miracles that Saint Conach performed. He brocht the deid lambs back tae life, and he filled the wolf's den wi food, and he made the wolf promise no tae steal.

Journal of Charles Kirkliston Gibb

Friday, 28th July 1809

After having written here as much as I had yesterday, I was about to set myself to the tedium of transcribing a new folio of the *Book* when the house was turned upside down by the arrival of letters from Captain Milne. These have been looked for every day since before my arrival, and at midday at last they came – one for his parents and, enclosed with it, one for his sister. A man brought them all the way from Forfar with a fresh Dunlop cheese. The Baron, having broken the outer seal on the letters, marched from room to room waving them above his head with one hand and clutching the cheese against his chest with the other, shouting for his wife and daughter to gather in the great hall at once. He burst into the library and demanded my attendance also – 'News frae Sandy!' he shouted. 'Abandon your labours!' – and burst back out again.

We assembled, the Baron, his family and myself. I think he would have gathered the servants, minister, dominie and all the folk from the clachan had the Baroness not restrained him. She did summon Kate Nicol from the kitchen, wrested the cheese from Glen Conach and handed it to Kate, telling her to take the messenger to the kitchen and feed him preparatory to him making his return journey. The Baron passed his daughter her letter and unfolded the other. In their mutual excitement they clean forgot that I was there, despite the Baron having summoned me himself.

'Noo, Jessie, will you gang first or will I?'

'You, Papa, but ye'll hae to read it a' and no pit in ony blah blahs.'

'I'll read ilka word oor Sandy has written.'

'Aye, but ye're likely to read just a hantle o' them aloud and the lave into yirsel, and syne we'll miss some vital pairt o' whit he has to tell us.'

'Haivers!'

'*I* shall read it,' Lady Glen Conach said, reaching for the letter in her husband's hand.

There was a brief skirmish between them, from which the Baroness emerged triumphant. While this was going on I saw Jessie quickly turning over the sheets of her own letter and slipping one of them into the sleeve of her dress. She glanced about guiltily, to see if she was observed, and when our eyes met I made sure that she knew she was. Then, thinking to make myself less obtrusive, I retreated a little. This movement recalled my presence to Glen Conach, who demanded to know where I was off to.

'The library,' I said, although I had no intention of leaving. 'This is surely an occasion for the family alone.'

'Stay, stay! We dinna mind ye. If you don't hear Sandy's news from him now you will hear it from us at dinner time.'

So we all sat down – except the Baron, who went back and forth across the hall like a newspaper blown by the wind – while Lady Glen Conach read the letter.

It was quite a long letter, but not an interesting one. More interest, I felt certain, lay in the sheet secreted by Jessamine, which I made up my mind to see before the day was out. Captain Milne is no great stylist, and makes military affairs seem extraordinarily dull. That may be because they are. He wrote from encampment near Deal in the county of Kent, and apologised for not having written sooner (his letter was dated 13th July), but he had had much to do. It seems that His Majesty's Ministers of State have instructed the Earl of Chatham, who commands the army being amassed in those parts, of which the 42nd Foot is only a small fraction, and Sir Richard Strachan, who commands the Royal Navy in the North Sea, to prepare for an immense operation against the French, who command large portions of the Low Countries and need to be persuaded to go somewhere else. The responsibility for making sure that everything happens according to plan in the forthcoming campaign, if I understand Captain Milne correctly, has descended in rapid stages from the Prime Minister, via the aforesaid Earl of Chatham and Sir Richard and numerous elderly generals, colonels and commodores, to land on the heads of lesser commissioned ranks such as masters, midshipmen and military captains, and in particular on the head of Captain Milne himself, who somewhat resents the way his duties encroach upon his leisure. 'Had I known what delays would occur here I would have stayed longer at home,' the scion of the glen complains. Nonetheless, he will overcome all obstacles placed in his way by quartermasters and suchlike. He has great faith in the rough honesty of the men, not just the Scots but the Welsh, Irish and various shades of Englishmen, all of whom scrape along together well enough unless they are idle and drink is taken, when hostilities commonly break out. He finds some of their accents difficult to penetrate. He expects embarkation to begin at any moment and is proud to be a member of one of the greatest expeditionary forces ever assembled, with a destination which is widely talked about but which he must not write down even in this letter in case of spies, as the French are cunning rascals etc. Captain Milne concluded with love dispatched to them all, a plea to be remembered to all the good folk, not forgetting Elspeth (I detected a slight tremor in his mother's voice when she read this out), and kind regards to Mr Haddow and Mr Dunning.

No sooner had Lady Glen Conach finished than her husband snatched the letter from her and read it to us again at twice the pace, ignoring what few commas and stops Sandy may have inserted. And then we had to have Jessie read her brother's letter to her, which – in its excised form at least – was identical to what we had just heard except in a different order, as if Sandy believed that by moving his paragraphs around he would delude his family into thinking he had written them two letters instead of one. I knew that he *had* written two letters, and was as eager as Jessie evidently was ('I am quite overcome, Mama. I shall go and lie down for an hour') to find out what the other one contained.

I too excused myself, hurried to the library, where I paused only to collect Dibdin's *Bibliomania*, then darted up the back stair and along the passage to Jessie's room. Risking the instant termination of my residency, I entered without knocking. I wanted to catch her by surprise with the letter in her hand, and fortunately this was how I found her and not in some other state of unpreparedness. She gasped once when I said, loudly, 'Miss Milne, here is Dr Dibdin's book, which you were so eager to look at,' and then again when I closed the door behind me and said, 'Now, be good enough to share with me the contents of your brother's private missive and nobody else will know of it.' It was wicked of me, but I did not think she would be able to refuse.

'What possible business is it of yours what my brother writes to me?' she said, putting the letter behind her back and blushing so hotly that her birthmark glowed and twitched.

'Now, Miss Milne,' I said, 'when we had our first tête-à-tête – you brought me delicious scones, if you recall – you were forthright about your brother's experiences in Spain, and about his ill health when he returned. You were not able to relate what he told you, or your worries about him, to your parents, so you took me into your confidence. Have I breached that confidence?'

'On that occasion, Mr Gibb, I *chose* to speak to you. You have no right to breenge in here and make demands of me. Your manners are detestable.'

'I cannot believe, however,' I answered, 'that you will not wish to share whatever Sandy has written with *somebody*, since you could not read it out downstairs. If not with me, then with whom? Elspeth?'

It was a lucky hit – though not altogether lucky. 'I'd not let *her* see it,' Jessie said. 'She is fond enough of Sandy already, without getting his kisses from afar.'

'Well,' I said, 'you have revealed so much now that you may as well let me see the rest. Or read it to me, if you prefer.'

She simmered a while longer, then sat herself down (I still stood with my back to the door) and said, lightly touching her disfigurement, 'You must think me a very easy conquest, Mr Gibb, but I must tell you, I will not be bullied.'

'Jessie,' I said (taking another risk), 'let us be friends. You are far beyond my reach if I had any thought of conquest, and as for bullying, well, I am not coarse enough for that.'

'Nor, I hope, so stupid,' she said, and held out the letter.

Sunday, 30th July 1809

I had written so much of Friday's entry when my journalising was again curtailed by interruptions, chiefly brought about by a requirement to practise manoeuvres (I have adopted military parlance, thanks to Captain Milne) around the manuscript. I spent hours of that day pretending to make progress in my study and transcription of it, and perhaps one complete hour actually doing so. All my supposed concentration on this task was caused by Lady Glen Conach, who kept appearing on some pretext or other, asking me deep questions about the *Book* and desiring to see examples of what I had so far achieved. Her visits were so frequent and yet so irregular that I felt I could not leave the library for fear of being discovered, as it were, absent from my post. I suspect her of espionage; I am sure she feels I should be marching more rapidly than I am; and she has also, as I shall relate, apprehended too great a cordiality between her daughter and me which she seems determined not to let grow into a full-blown alliance. At any event, these last two days I have been confined to barracks – that is, the library – but, this being the Sabbath morning,

I am at present in my room. All the family went to kirk, and I in their absence carried out another search of Jessie's chamber and at last located *her* journal. It was beneath her mattress, where I certainly looked before. Such an obvious priest's hole! I either gave her too much credit for ingenuity or perhaps not enough, since she may have prolonged my hunt by moving the 'priest' around. The extra sheet from Sandy's letter was pressed within the book, and I hastily copy it here. It is marked at the top, in capital letters, KEEP FROM PRYING EYES, and runs as follows:

Dearest Sister,

I trust to our father's sense of propriety that you will receive your letter unopened, & to your cleverness – you were always cleverer than me – that you will not let him or Mama see this portion of it. It would dismay them to read what I will now write. They are so proud of he who was Ensign & is now Captain Milne but they might think me traitor to King & Country if they suspected my inner thoughts. Our commander is nicknamed 'the late Lord Chatham' on account of his slowness in determining on any course of action, & Sir Richard Strachan of the Navy is called 'Mad Dick' for his impetuosity. This is a bad combination as between these two extremes many things are begun but left unfinished while many others are not done at all. At lower levels of rank the soldiers and sailors have a mutual sympathy with one another, but the truth is this army & not just this army but the entirety of His Majesty's forces are poorly led & the men are not well looked after & resent their neglect at the hands of their officers. I do what I can for my Company but they are inured to bad food, bad treatment, bad quarters, harsh punishment for small misdemeanours & they themselves, even braw country lads, soon turn to brutes if they were not already so when they listed. Their only pleasure is tobacco & beer, rum or other liquor, whatever they can get, usually of the worst kind, & the same when it comes to female company. Yet in Spain I saw the roughest of men be the gentlest nurses to wounded comrades, & the cruellest weep for their mothers when in their cups. Yet too some forgot their own mothers when they mistreated folk as poor as themselves, as I told you before, depriving starving women & bairns of food, stealing & looting, sometimes I am sorry to say encouraged by the examples of their officers. But now we enter a new campaign. We are bound for Zeeland any day, the greatest army ever to leave British shores. You would not believe the extent of this camp & others nearby, they contain 40 thousand troops, enough you would think to send the French scuttling for home but I greatly fear, dear Jess, our numbers may be a burden not a boon to the expedition & to our chances of success. I dare not speak to my superiors on these matters, they are deaf to the notion that anything they devise could be improved upon. Nor would I scatter seeds of discontent among the men – greater than what already exists – for that would amount to an incitement to mutiny. So I am caught between the twain. Well, I am a loyal officer to the King & will serve him to the best of my ability or die in the attempt. Do not fret for me, Jess, I was made for this life despite its harshness & if the worst should happen I will take a sword thrust or a musket ball happily in my Country's service, it is the best way a man of spirit & vigour can die. But O I do miss the craggy hills & soft rains of home. It is so damnably flat here, & hot too. I write these things only to you because as you know I love you dearly & with God's grace I will be with you again soon. Kiss Elspeth for me & tell her to be good & save her daffing ways until I am back in the glen. She is your friend as well as mine, & something more forby, let us never forget.

Your loving brother, Sandy.

I must not jump ahead of the chronology by putting down at this point what Jessie has written of me. So, having carefully reinserted Sandy's page in the journal, and then having replaced the journal in the exact position from which I removed it, I have just now returned physically from Jessie's room – only to return to it in my mind in order to describe what next occurred between us there on Friday.

When I had finished perusing Captain Milne's words, I looked up and was surprised to see Jessie's head bowed and tears running down her cheeks. I was at once stung with remorse for having silently mocked (as I have recorded) Sandy's epistolary style. It was evident from what I had just read that he was not just a fond brother but a passionate man obliged to suppress his feelings and opinions in the situation in which he found himself; evident too that Jessie was much moved by his sharing his troubles with her and having faith in her discretion. He would be touched by her tears, I thought; but unhappy that the 'prying eyes' of a complete stranger had also seen what he wrote.

'Please try not to distress yourself, Miss Milne,' I said. 'Your brother shows himself to be a conscientious and good officer who will not rashly endanger either himself or his men.'

'I hope you are right,' she said. 'There is no end to the war, though, and remember what I told you, that he was only made a captain because all the other captains were maimed or killed. I dread that before long some other young man will be promoted because my brother has fallen. And he was so unwell, in mind as well as body, when he was home. He may be the most conscientious officer in the regiment, but that will not keep him alive. And then –'

She broke off to wipe her eyes and blow her nose, and looked at me most mournfully. I felt another internal sting, which I took as a warning to be on my guard.

'And then?' I said.

'And then he and Elspeth have always played with each other's affections, although it can come to nothing. I fear that as well – and that it will end in tears. He plays too soft and she too strong. Do you know the words of Mrs Elliot's lament? "Nae daffin, nae gabbin, but sighin and sabbin"?'

I indicated that I did. 'You think he will break her heart?'

'No. I think, if he comes home, he will be greatly changed. The broken heart will be his.'

'I am not in a position to dispute what you say, Miss Milne.'

She gave me another mournful look. 'I liked it better when you called me Jessie,' she replied. ' "Let us be friends," you said.'

It was a delicate situation, calling for the utmost restraint on my part. In five minutes she had gone from detesting me to – something else. I said, 'If your parents do not object, it would please me very much for us to address each other by our Christian names.'

'Papa will hardly notice. Mama will notice, but how can she object? You are our guest – Charles.'

She stood up and moved towards me, and as she did so I fancied I saw the dental portcullis beginning to open. My instinct for self-preservation was suddenly transformed into a terrible bout of cowardice. Whether I was repelled by the combined effect of her unfortunate birthmark and flashing teeth, whether I did not trust myself to treat her kindly because I was unsure if I pitied her or was attracted to her, or whether I saw myself ejected from Glen Conach House without having arranged my next safe haven – whatever my true motive, I understood that it was time to leave.

'Jessie,' I said, 'I have compromised you enough simply by being here. We should continue our conversation another time. Meanwhile' – putting my finger to my lips – 'let us not breathe a word of it to another soul.' Thinking by thus making us conspirators to forestall any loud protestation, I found the door handle behind me, turned it and rapidly departed. It was unfortunate that Lady Glen Conach appeared at the head of the main staircase as I was about to make my way to the back stair.

'Mr Gibb!'

'Lady Glen Conach?' I answered, as though not in the least surprised.

'You were in my daughter's chamber.'

I swung upon my heel and approached her, thankful that I had taken precautions before invading Jessie's privacy. 'I was, Madam. Miss Milne had requested me to look out a recently arrived book, one that your husband had recommended to me and I to her. I have just brought it to her.'

'What book?'

'*Bibliomania* by Dr Thomas Dibdin. A kind of satire on over-affection for books.'

'My daughter is surely capable of fetching any book she wants for herself?'

'Of course. But, as she said she was tired, I took the liberty of taking it to her.'

I have previously noted that my hostess's mouth seems always to be on the brink of smiling. It looked now as if smiles had been abolished altogether, at least while I was in view – and yet, in the bright blue eyes was still some glimmer of mirth. I think she was daring me to elaborate on the liberty to which I had just referred. I chose not to but, pleading that I needed to get back to the old hermit, I excused myself. Before I descended the stair I glanced back and saw Lady Glen Conach knocking on Jessie's door and entering. My honour, like Captain Milne's, depended at that moment on the discretion of his sister.

Here I am, then, up to date with my own adventures, and I may now jot down a summary of Miss Jessamine Milne's impressions of Charles Kirkliston Gibb. My vanity is hardly flattered by either their extent or content. As Glen Conach advised I would be during my second dinner here, I *am* in her journal. I only wish she might have written more, and with more enthusiasm, each point she makes in my favour being cancelled by one less positive. I did not have time to copy her words verbatim, but recollect the following: 'Mr Gibb, an antiquarian, arrived. I have not heard of him.' 'He is to make a copy of our Book and translate it. Well, he may try!' 'I selected some clothes of Sandy's that I thought would suit him, since he has none of his own. He must be very poor.' 'I took him tea in the library and we talked on various matters. He has *some* learning.' There was this too: 'Elspeth says he is very white and not as manly or as well made as Sandy, and that she saw his pintle and it resembled a newborn rat in a nest. I told her to keep her sauce to herself.'

Lastly, this – as well as I can remember it – which is more revealing: 'I asked Papa how long Mr Gibb would be here. He said, as long as he needed to be, to complete his task. I said that he seemed in no great hurry, and did Papa not think he was being too generous a host? Papa said he didn't care about that, what was one extra mouth, and it was pleasant to have a young man about the place with Sandy away. I said I would rather have Sandy. Papa agreed, but said that since we cannot, Mr Gibb was not bad company, spoke back when spoken to etc., so I must make do and mend. Mama keeps her own counsel, as ever. Everything would go to ruin without her.'

I begin to comprehend the politics of this place.

Sunday, 6th August 1809

A week has passed, and I have little to report. There has been no further communication from Captain Milne. The Baroness continues to watch me and I am left in no doubt that, while always polite and even friendly, she wishes to prevent any intimacy between Jessie and myself. I am not sorry about this, but the mother's assiduous attention has had two unfortunate effects. One, it has encouraged the daughter to think that she must be in love with me, and I with her, and therefore every mealtime and any other occasion spent in each other's presence is full of sighs, lowered glances and, if she can arrange it, touches of hands and arms. Two, it means I have had to spend hours every day in the library with the holy hermit and his servant and, to be frank, I am growing weary of them. I have read through to the end of the manuscript, so the 'particulars of the denouement', as Mr Smollett expressed it in *Humphry Clinker*, are known to me, which makes the effort of transcribing and translating what precedes it mere drudgery. Still, I keep plodding, and I keep not being barred from the dinner table, and the weather has been bright and dry, so matters might be worse.

Last night it was made pretty plain to me by the Baroness that for once I should be expected to go with the family to church. This I took as a sign of her determination to know where I am at all times. We all went – Glen Conach and his lady, Miss Milne and myself – with Elspeth, Norah, and Kate and Davie Nicol a few steps behind us. A crowd of glen folk was waiting outside the lowly little kirk, some carrying stools and even chairs. It is the custom for the laird and his party to enter first and everybody else to crush in behind them. Daniel Haddow, in his usual sombre attire, was among the assembly, somewhat diffident in his role of hypocrite-at-large. I saw other familiar faces – men and women from the clachan, Elspeth's grandmother, the dirty children with the dirt wiped from their faces at least, and Mary, 'the Maid of the Manse' as she might be styled, also quite scrubbed and decently covered up. We entered. I sat at the end of the laird's pew, and was glad to be separated from Jessie by her parents, the Baron rustling and creaking next to me and quite obscuring mother and daughter from my view. Daniel sat directly across the aisle, and gave me a smile and a nod to which I responded in like kind. A moment later, the standing folk parted, and Mr Dunning came through them like a prophet of olden times and ascended the pulpit stair. Once he had squeezed himself in, the service began.

The usual dreary process of worship followed. When I have been in England I have, though my soul was unmoved, envied that country its cathedrals with their choirs, organs and sung liturgy, if for no other reason than that these help to make the time pass more quickly and pleasurably. Mr Dunning is not enough of a devotee of suffering to stretch a service of an hour and a half to one of three hours, but still it was a grinding affair. The psalms were led by a precentor who kept wandering off his line like a lost sheep and had to be called back by the rest of the flock. Dunning read from the scriptures and offered some convoluted extempore prayers including the usual pledge of loyalty to the King. Like the precentor he lost his way during the prayers, once coming to a complete halt in mid-sentence. When I looked up, his face was stricken as if in horror at something he could see in the beams of the roof, and he had to shake himself in order to continue. But I was pleased to see he did not indulge in the common practice of summoning miserable sinners and castigating them before the rest of the congregation. I also sensed – and occasionally, by twisting my neck, saw – that the people were attentive and sincere in their worship; more so than their dominie and their laird, in my estimation.

The minister gave a sermon on that verse from the first Book of Samuel in which David says that the Lord that delivered him out of the paw of the lion, and out of the paw of the bear, will deliver him out of the hand of the Philistine, and Saul replies, 'Go, and the Lord be with thee.' David was all the men gone from the glen to be soldiers, Alexander Milne among them (he alone was identified by name), and I took Goliath to represent Bonaparte and Saul to be King George or at least the Prime Minister. It was all very clumsily expressed and not very apposite since the expedition about to be launched is equipped with considerably more than five smooth stones and a sling, but I declined to raise an objection. To my left, the Baron slumbered but at least did not snore. Beyond him, the Baroness was upright, and to my right, across the aisle, Daniel Haddow adopted the trance-like state I had seen him in before, which was very politic of him. All in all, the whole ninety minutes was a reminder of why I avoid attending kirk if I can and also suggested to me why the venerable Conach left the monastery all those centuries ago. The common folk of Scotland yield to none in their religiosity but I do wonder sometimes how deep it runs, and if one day they might suddenly discard it as the Baron flung away his head coverings.

If Mr Dunning improved his popularity with the people during the service they did not show it afterwards as he stood outside the kirk. He nodded his head and shook hands with the men but they did not linger. It is as if they consider him a foreigner who does not speak their language, as indeed he does not. Consequently they must regard him as a barrier rather than a conduit between them and their God. He exchanged a few words with our party. When it was my turn he stared at me with something close to that ghastly expression he had in the pulpit, before recovering and saying my name very coldly. Daniel Haddow called him tormented – a fitting description. I felt almost sorry for him.

Daniel drew me aside as we were dispersing and asked how I had enjoyed the service. 'Not much,' I said, 'but I think the people could have taken more of it, and spicier.' 'Oh, you are right,' he replied, 'it is their weekly theatre. The pity is that the company consists of but one poor actor. They used to sit happily through hours of fire and damnation from Mr Gillespie. He was a gentle body when out of the pulpit, but a veritable rioter when in it. Oh, they sorely miss a player of Mr Gillespie's quality.'

Monday, 14th August 1809

I have not neglected my journal. I have simply had nothing of interest to write about. For more than a week I have been left completely alone and uninterrupted in the library. This has been partly through the strategy of the Baroness, and partly that the time of year has brought extra duties upon herself, Jessie, Elspeth and the other womenfolk. The sheep have all had their coats cut and the fleeces have been steeped and washed and carded ready for spinning. Fruit both wild and garden-grown is ready to be picked, herbs likewise to be cut and dried, and many other tasks arise in preparation for the time of harvest. There have been days when I have been quite alone for hours. The house is abandoned to mice, me and Kate Nicol, whose clatterings sometimes float from the kitchen up the stair or through an open window.

The Baron, partly I think to occupy his body since he cannot long stop his mind from worrying about how his son is faring, has had a burst of enthusiasm for completing his stone dyke – that is to say, he complains that it will never be done if he does not set to it himself – and, the weather having been fresh but dry, he has been a builder most days. No other men being available, he dragooned me into assisting him last week, declaring that even if I did not enjoy the physical work it would do me good. He was so insistent that I felt I could not refuse without incurring his severe displeasure.

One day of dyke-building was enough for Charles Kirkliston Gibb. By the end of it I had the bent back of an ancient crone, legs and arms so stiff I could scarcely get into my bed, bruises, cuts, blistered fingers and broken nails, and a determination never to have to toil like that for my bread if I could possibly avoid it. My discomfort was not diminished by Glen Conach's frequent references to Captain Milne's strength in lifting the stones and his ingenuity in placing them. One would think, to listen to the father, that the son could finish the entire work in an afternoon simply by throwing boulders into the correct positions. I think all my efforts extended the dyke's length by about a yard. 'You are no faster at this than at the Latin,' the Baron said jocularly – or so I believe he meant it, but I was by that time in too foul a mood to be amused.

I never saw a laird and his household so unlairdly. They come home in the afternoon brown and dirty and tired, and caring not at all what they look like, and Glen Conach, if he happens to pass through the library, starts at me as if I am that half-forgotten sojourning cousin. Yet at dinner his wife and daughter have restored themselves to order and even he has wiped himself down and put on a clean shirt. Of them all, only Elspeth Carnegie seems to resent her toil, and huffs and puffs well above her station, but her mistress takes no notice of her, not even when she neglects her evening duties and takes herself off to her grandmother's.

Excepting that one day when I was pressed into service by Glen

Conach, I have spent the time in quietude and boredom. I dabble in the *Book*, read my way through another – I picked up *Gertrude of Wyoming* and was pleased to find it far better than I expected – go to my room and stretch myself out for an hour, stare from the library window for two, and so make the days pass. Jessie is kept so busy that she has not written in her journal either, so no pleasure is to be had there. In short, I am on the point of expiring from ennui and only the absence of anywhere else to go keeps me here. Mr Bartholomew has forwarded no letters to me – probably he fears I may not repay him his expenses, although I have promised to do so whenever I am in Edinburgh (if I can amass any money, that is) – and I am doubtful as to whose hospitality I can next call on, so for now I am stuck. I do have a mind, however, to seek lodging at Oxenfoord Castle, the country residence of my early patron Sir John Dalrymple. I believe I can persuade him to receive me and feel I could endure a week or two there not least because it is but a few miles south of Edinburgh and would therefore be a convenient place from which to renew other connections. As he is very ancient I should not delay. Accordingly, I have written to him, begging to be permitted to pay a visit in order to benefit from his wisdom and expert knowledge regarding certain points of feudal law, etc. The composition of this fawning letter (which may not set off on its journey from here for a day or two) took the better part of an hour, after which I once again dozed away the afternoon.

Friday, 18th August 1809

Fortunately for the exercising of my brain, on Tuesday Glen Conach received a fat package of newspapers from his bookseller – numerous copies of *The Times*, *Caledonian Mercury*, *Morning Post* and others of the last several weeks, which he pores over in the evenings and allows us to look at when he has finished with them. We have thus learned more about the expedition in which Captain Milne and his regiment are engaged. The latest issue of the *London Miscellany of Knowledge and Pleasure* also contains a piece, laden with phrases such as 'it is supposed that' and 'as we are given to understand', in which the chief aims of the campaign are laid out, how accurately it is impossible to determine. Taken as a whole, however, the news is, I suppose – speaking as one not martially inclined – mainly encouraging.

From the *London Miscellany* I have gathered the following. The objective, long fixed in the minds of the Government, has been to keep Napoleon from using Antwerp as a base from which to launch an invasion of Great Britain. Antwerp is a large port, heavily defended, far up the Scheldt estuary. At the mouth of this river lies Flushing, another well-fortified town with a deep anchorage, on a low, flat island called Walcheren. If this island and another called South Beveland were captured and the river blockaded the French fleet would be prevented from reaching the sea. The British army and navy could then between them advance on Antwerp and destroy both Bonaparte's ships and his arsenals, thus ending his invasion plans. The anonymous author is 'given to understand' that Walcheren is under-garrisoned, mainly by former convicts and deserters put there because they cannot escape. He also states that it is a low-lying, unhealthy place in summer, but as the intention is to remain there only as long as necessary to carry out the attack on Antwerp, and then to withdraw, he considers this of no great importance. 'It is supposed' that the French have no means to reinforce their positions as so many of their armies are engaged in Spain and in Germany, where our Austrian allies keep them at bay.

It is a disappointment, therefore, to read in the more recent newspapers that even before the expedition sailed, which it did on 28th July, word arrived of a great victory for Napoleon over the Austrians at somewhere called Wagram. This battle seems to have taken place even before Sandy wrote his letters. Austria has since sued for peace and Bonaparte has, no doubt, hastened to march his troops to Antwerp. I am no soldier, but if I were he that is what I would do.

However, in *The Times* and others we learn that the island of Walcheren has been occupied with great ease and few casualties, most of its towns have been captured and the port of Flushing is surrounded and under siege. So, although there are no letters from or news of Captain Milne, we must assume that the campaign has begun well and that soon Antwerp too will be invested.

Monday, 21st August 1809

I caught Elspeth alone this morning. I was going from my chamber down the back stair to the library and met her coming up.

'Not at your work with the others today, Elspeth?' I asked. If I startled her she did not show it but fired back at once.

'You're not at yours,' she said.

'Oh, but I am going to mine,' I said. 'Where are you going?'

'I'm awa for a message that's nane o' your affair or ony man's,' she said, 'and syne I'll be back oot. And at least when I'm at *my* work, I work.'

'You don't think I do?'

'Ye widna ken work if it was a dog and bit ye,' she said poetically, trying to go past me.

I stepped in front of her and said, 'Why don't you come to the library and I'll show you what I work at?'

'I ken whit ye dae,' she said. 'Ye just gove at the books a' day.'

'Have you never looked at them yourself, Elspeth?' I asked. 'Did Mr Haddow not teach you to read a little?'

'A little?' she cried. 'I'm as guid a reader as you or onybody.' But she asserted this without conviction, as though she would struggle if put to the test.

'Show me,' I said, but she thought I meant to play a trick on her, or make her look foolish, or even try to kiss her, and would not come with me. She slipped by me and went up two steps but once in that advantageous position stood a while longer, and we spoke some truths between us. I asked her for her honest opinion of me, and she said if it was her opinion of my honesty I wanted that was easily given, for she thought I had none. I asked for what reason she cast such a slur upon my character, and she said for no reason, only an instinct. I said that I thought I did very well if her perception was that I had only one fault, to which she answered that she could readily add another based upon what she *perceived* of me, which was that I was very idle. I said, if that were true, did that not make us like two peas in a pod, for I had *perceived* that she did not like to work. She said she could work as hard as any person but did not always choose to. I had no notion, she said, of the endless *darg* of women, to say nothing of many other tribulations with which her sex was encumbered. It was all very well for a man to sit at a table all day, pulling this volume or that from the shelves as it pleased him, but let a woman try it for ten minutes and she would be called a bluestocking or have her conceits mocked or beaten out of her, according to her station.

I was impressed that she was acquainted with a word such as 'bluestocking' and knew how to use it, and told her so. She told me she was *acquent* with a great deal more ('a hantle mair' was her actual phrase) that I might not guess at. Such as what? I asked. She shook her curls at me and laughed. I should say that this conversation was conducted in a good spirit, not an unfriendly one, and that even when she was bellicose she could hardly help being coquettish. I suddenly felt a great urge to clasp her and kiss her, which she clearly and at once *perceived* for she danced up another stair or two to keep a distance between us. I asked again why she thought me dishonest.

'It's the way ye aye keek aboot yirsel,' she said. 'Whit are ye here in the glen for a' this time? Ye cam wi naethin' but I doot ye'll no gang awa wi naethin'. There's something no richt aboot ye, that's a' I can say.'

Again, she spoke without malice, as far as I could determine. I could not fault her as a judge of character, although really there is little in Glen Conach to make away with. I felt warm towards her. There we were, together on that back stair and nobody else in the house, and something was passing between us and I believed we both recognised it. Perhaps that was what it was – a recognition. But when I stepped towards her again, and even put a hand on her arm, she chided me.

'Na, na, Mr Gibb, dinna mak sic a fool o' yirsel. Ye're like maist men, that try their luck as soon as they find their courage for fear they'll lose it again. Ye may dae whit ye will wi some ither lassie, but ye'll get nae cuttins frae me.'

I did not press the matter, for I saw that she was not to be persuaded, but only asked if she were saving herself for someone.

'Save mysel?' she answered. 'That's nane o' your affair either, but d'ye think that's a' lassies can dae, save theirsels? I could hae whitever man in the glen I wanted, gin I wanted ane. I'll say this, I widna save my breath for a dissembler, or a man that comes here wi nocht. And I dinna want a man that spends ower muckle time amang books. Books are fu' o' fykes and fykerie. I'll just bide till the army comes hame to get whit's mine. A strang and simple sodger will dae for me.'

I knew very well what soldier she must have in mind, and admired her ambition, for surely the Baron, let alone his lady, would never allow the match. After these last remarks of hers she hurried away, and I went on to the library, and I have not seen her again the rest of this day.

Saturday, 26th August 1809

Another week has passed. I had lost all interest in making these entries but the last two days have restored it. The weather turned exceptionally warm last Monday and it seems that sultry air does not agree with the redoubtable Baroness. She is mistress of all things but close heat, which caused her to retreat to her chamber with a bad head. For three days at dinner we were just three. The Baron was quite morose without her. Jessie on the other hand was lively, keen to cheer her father and to please me. She had a glass of wine more than she might have in front of her mother and was more relaxed and personable than at any time since I came here. She also once or twice slyly addressed me as 'Charles' on Monday, and again on Tuesday, and by Wednesday Glen Conach had unconsciously caught the habit from her. I felt it would be churlish not to respond in like manner (to Jessie, not to her father!) and by Thursday when there was a thunderstorm and the Baroness re-emerged, much restored, we were all a happy family. She perceived it at once and saw that it could not be reversed without warfare, so let it be, and in fact it has made us all more easy with one another and perhaps herself less fearful that I will seduce her daughter, which I have no intention of doing.

Jessie did leave off her other tasks and come much more about me during these days. She told me another Conach tale that she said she had got from Elspeth's granny. She made me show her some of my translation, and when I asked her if she had read right to the end of the *Book* she said she had.

'Did you ever hear from Elspeth's granny about what Conach did to himself?' I asked.

'I did,' she said. 'That's a tale many ken but few like to tell. Granny Ally whispered it to me once as if it was a secret.'

'But you knew of it before you read the *Book*?'

'Aye, but not in all its horrible detail. Please dinna speak about it again, Charles, it makes me feel faint just to think on it.'

So I left that alone, but she is better acquainted with the Latin than she let on at first. I wrote earlier in these pages that she was cunning and she is. She has stopped being in love with me and treats me now like a kind of brother. This is a relief and indeed I grow to like her much more. On Thursday evening she sang several songs very well and her playing of the spinet was much better. The songs were again mainly Jacobite ones.

I don't know if these songs set off something in her father's head but at breakfast yesterday, which dawned fresh and clear after the rain, he waited until we were alone and said to me, 'Charles, leave your studies for a day, and let us take a jaunt together. I feel a need to stretch my legs and get up a height. I know you are not as robust a young man as you should be, but I would be grateful if you would join me.'

I at once agreed, and half an hour later we were on our way. To my surprise, Glen Conach took neither his dogs nor his gun. Kate Nicol appointed me porter and presented me with a canvas bag containing cheese, oatcakes and portions of a mutton pie. We went up across the high park, pausing so that the Baron could remark on the progress of his accursed dyke. Its intended purpose, he told me, is for keeping the cattle and other beasts in at certain times of year, so that they do not get among the rigs and trample and eat the corn, as they are wont to do when the louns who are supposed to herd them are distracted by games or fall asleep. Glen Conach (I mean the glen but it is true also of the man) seems to be twenty years behind other parts of the country when it comes to agricultural improvements. I mind the enclosure of open pasture to make planted parks happening all over Linlithgowshire when I was a boy. In some places, even as the cottars and their families were being evicted, the very stones of their cottages were being taken to build the farmers' new dykes, a haste which seemed unnecessarily cruel. Perhaps I harbour an antipathy to Glen Conach's dyke for this reason, although I hope I am not that sentimental.

We continued out on to the moor in a steep climb that prohibited much conversation between us. For such a large, ungainly man he is powerfully agile and I had to work hard to keep pace with him. We stopped every ten minutes or so, when he would expatiate on the view while I caught my breath. He referred several times to Lord

Finbeg, the neighbouring landowner, and at first I feared, remembering the 'twelve miles of the roughest country' he once mentioned, that he might decide to take me to be introduced to him. However, it seems that he does not much like this Lord Finbeg, who has turned some people off his land and leased it to sheep farmers, and so my fear was allayed. We continued our vigorous walk, dropping down an incline, crossing a burn and ascending another slope until I had lost all sense of direction, when suddenly we emerged as high as we could be on the west side of the glen, with magnificent vistas in all directions.

'D'ye see where we are?' the Baron asked me. 'We have come as it were by the back stair – a route with which my wife tells me you are not unfamiliar – to what we call the rig of the glen, and we shall now proceed down from it until we reach the top of the Scaurs, which I have pointed out to you before. The ground is boggy in places and hard in others, and will be slippery after the storm, so take care as we approach the edge for it is a long drop if you should accidentally go over it.'

I said I hoped I would not go over it any other way, and he laughed and said, 'D'ye mind how my father threatened to put that Riddell chiel over it? For all you ken, my dear Gibb, that is how we dispose of unwanted guests here. Och, dinna look like that! You are perfectly safe! You are not unwanted and, what's more, you have the mutton pie.'

We proceeded, and after a few more minutes arrived at the head of the stone stair of the Baroness's tale. Glen Conach kicked about among the undergrowth for a few minutes, attempting to locate where the flue had emerged which he had covered over, but he could not find it. Some fifty yards to our right the ground became very wet, and my companion pointed out a dark, deep pool into which the ground's moisture drained. This was the source of Conach's Linn which, he said, could not be seen from above without great risk of a slip. We then descended the steps and made our way along the path, which was strewn with fallen debris, until we came to the cave.

It was very much as the Baroness had described it, with its stone seats and window and dampness. Glen Conach stamped about in it, apparently dissatisfied, and then declared that we would sit on the ground at the cave mouth, where the air was fresher, and eat our victuals. I did not altogether like this idea, as the ledging that according to the tale had been built to make the place safe had mostly fallen away, so that when we sat down our feet dangled over the edge of the cliff. This did not appear to perturb the Baron, so I pretended that I was not perturbed either. In the canvas bag were two pewter cups. By going to the cave's 'window' and stretching his hand through it he was able to fill these from the waterfall, so we were well provided.

Between mouthfuls he was again lyrical about the panorama before us. Impressive though it was, I could not look too long without it inducing a nausea at odds with the mutton pie.

'You're like my dogs,' Glen Conach said. 'I brought them here when they were young but they didna like it, and made a terrible fuss about getting up and down the steps. But does it remind you of anything, Charles?' He rolled about on his rump a little more than I could have wished given his proximity to me and my proximity to the drop. 'Have you heard stories of the Highland chiefs who were out with the Chevalier, whose people protected them when the soldiers were hunting them down? For example, there was Ewen MacPherson of Cluny. He lived in a cave or a cage, or a combination of the two, high up on Ben Alder, so I am told. I have never been to Ben Alder. Have you?'

I said that I had not, and that I understood it was very remote.

'A great deal more than a half-hour's stroll from Cluny's castle. If you were needing a place to hide in at short notice, a cave like this would be more convenient, would you not agree? Not for MacPherson, of course, but if your home were here, in Glen Conach.'

I agreed with a nod.

'This part of Angus supplied a great number of soldiers in the Rising of '45. There was not a company raised in this glen – my grandfather who was the laird then forbade it. He believed the cause was doomed to fail and wanted as little to do with it as possible. He was a cold-hearted, hard-headed man, so my father always said. I knew him a little when I was a bairn but he did not care for me much, and I did not care for him. Well, during those troubled times he kept his hard head as low as he could and tried to dampen the excitement of the glen folk, but many of them were enthusiasts for the old cause and the men went over the hills and joined Lord Ogilvy's regiment, and were in the Prince's army all the way from Edinburgh to Derby and back, and then north to Culloden. Many young men, aye, Sir. It must have been a stirring time to be young. It *was* a stirring time. Would you have been stirred, do you think?'

I said that I was prejudiced in favour of a settled government, and that I would have done my best not to be stirred. He would have none of this.

'But your prejudices *now* – when the country has been shaken by radicals and threatened by French invasion – are not what your prejudices might have been *then*. We are of our own time. We cannot be sure how we would have behaved in an earlier time.'

'I am sure,' I said, sounding more priggish than I meant to, 'that I would have objected to French invasion then too, Sir. It was, I think, threatened.'

'The threat came to nothing, however. France never sent the men or the money that had been promised. But let that be – I am speaking of what inflames the heart, not calculations of self-interest. Does a man join or oppose a just cause for the sake of some shillings or even some sovereigns?'

'It is clear that men often do exactly that,' I said. 'But such men do not consider the justice of the cause. They think only of what they will gain from it.'

'I despise them,' he said. 'But sometimes a man feels bound to act on his passions because not to do so would be, however rational, a kind of betrayal of himself. I speak hypothetically, my dear Gibb. I have a liking for hypothetical questions. How would a man act if his passion overcame his reason?'

I said that that was a simple question, not simply answered. He took a mouthful of pie, chewed on it for a minute, then spoke again.

'The clarity in the air today, since the rain, is excellent. If you lean out a little you can see the distant outlines of the great hills to the north, the Cairngorms. I do not know their individual names. Ben Alder is not in that direction, it lies behind us. My father, now, *he* was a passionate man, a romantic man, as Peggy – as Lady Glen Conach – may have said when she spoke of him.'

I leaned out and then quickly back again. After that I sat as still as I could, which made the view below us, of the green glen stretching north and south with the river a silvery-black snake winding along it, at least bearable. It occurred to me that we were engaged in the sort of companionable, filial outing that I had never shared with my own father. Of course, my father was dead and Glen Conach's son was at the war, and the laird was speaking of *his* father. And all at once I saw that this was the reason why he had brought me to the cave. He wanted, perhaps he *needed*, to tell me about his father.

'You may have thought, my dear Charles,' he said, 'that my wife and I were sparring that night, when she told you about my father and this place. So we were, but we like to spar. It keeps us lively. There is no man so fortunate as he who can argue with his wife at the dinner table and be friends with her before bedtime.'

'I did not think you argued,' I said. 'You seemed, as I recall, to enjoy the story she related. Perhaps not at first, but as it progressed.'

'She tells it well,' he said, 'but she did not tell it all. Look – directly in front of us, beyond the river! Do you see it?'

He indicated a great bird flying on a level with us. I said, 'I believe I saw it my first morning here. It has the same size and the same motion. Is it an eagle?'

'It is a kind of eagle – what the folk here call a fishing eagle. Mr Gilbert White of Selborne names it an osprey. That bird and his wife have a nest in a tree on the far side of the glen, and one will guard the nest while the other goes fishing. If they were both always on the nest they would doubtless spar but they take turn about with their duties and are very faithful to each other. Every spring they return, and always to the same nest. Where they go in the winter is a mystery. Some gentlemen like to shoot these birds because they steal their fish but I prefer to see them fly. And forby, I think it more correct to say that we steal their fish than that they steal ours. Now, you have distracted me. What was I saying?'

'That Lady Glen Conach did not tell all the story.'

'Aye, aye. Well, I always feel uneasy when she begins it, especially in the house and if our young people are present, but then Jessie excused herself and went to her chamber. Not that we have kept her ignorant of it, but it does not confer much honour on the family history. She is less fashed with matters of honour than her brother, though. If Sandy were here – I mean *here*, in this nook with us – I would not tell it. He would think that by doing so in presence of a stranger I was demeaning my own father and myself – demeaning the name of Milne. But he is not here. He is away besieging that Dutch town, Flushing, or perhaps marching on Antwerp. I hope we will hear from him again soon, but if he is fighting he will not have time to write, and even if he had what possibility is there of a letter reaching us from across the sea?' He produced a large red handkerchief and mopped his eyes with it, and then his forehead. 'Forgive me, Charles, I have something of my father's passion. Sandy was not so well when he came home. He was, thankfully, much better when he left again. When I think of him in uniform, leading his brave lads, I am very proud to have such a son.'

I held my peace and followed the flight of the osprey while the Baron composed himself.

'When the Prince made his landfall in the West, my father was twenty,' he said after a while. 'He cared very much for the common people – felt easier in their company than he did in the big house under the rule of my grandfather, who, as I said, had little interest in anything but work and money. And reputation – that was also very important to that dour old man. When word came flying through the country about the coming of the Prince, all my father could think of was joining the cause. He knew that it would be forbidden, but his prejudices were all on that side, and so he was determined to go.'

'But why?' I asked. 'Your ancestor, as you have told me, was loyal to the Stewart dynasty at the time of the Restoration, but were there Milnes out with Claverhouse at Killiecrankie, or in the 1715 Rising?'

'No, no,' he said, smiling. 'Those generations were sensible that what they had gained from the political mistakes of others could be lost at a stroke if they were not canny. My grandfather was aye canny. Like yourself, Charles, he did not favour disturbing the status quo.'

'But your father did. He was not a Jacobite by faith or tradition or what was in the family interest, and yet you say his prejudices –'

He interrupted me: '– were all for that young adventurer. Faith? No, that had nothing to do with it. We Milnes must have been Episcopalians once, I suppose, but after bishops were finally ousted from the Kirk my forebears seem not to have missed them, and we became good Presbyterians. We turned a blind eye to those folk in these parts who adhered to that form of religion, for if they held services behind closed doors, what harm was it to us? We had a kirk and a minister and that was enough. No, my father was not inspired by faith. Do you ken what I think it was? The Jacobite cause was a way for him to rebel against *his* father. They really did not much like each other. And there was another reason. He loved a woman, Charles, a young lass of the glen called Alison Murray, and *she* was all for the Prince. And so, defying his own father, my father slipped away out of the glen, and the lass went with him, and they joined the Jacobite army at Perth.

'Well, they went to Edinburgh and my father was, shall we say, present at Prestonpans. I will not say he *fought* there because he never let on to me that he did – it was advisable not to make too much of these matters during his lifetime. Then he marched into England, and the lass by his side, and then they came back again. But she by now was with child and my father found a safe place for her near Perth where she would be cared for. He stayed there with her for two days and promised to return for her whatever the fate of the army. Then he set off northward to rejoin the Prince, but somebody who kent him had sent word of his whereabouts to his father, who came after him with a party of men and detained him at Blair Atholl. My grandfather's sole intention was to bring him home and if possible erase all proof that he had been out, for he could see, if my father couldna, the way the thing was going to end. Well, they argued and even came to blows, and the other men had to restrain them, until at last my father said that he would obey and come home, but only if they brought his sweetheart too and she was treated as well as the mother of his child should be. And my grandfather, being a practical man, agreed, for it would not have been the first time a laird's son had bairned a cottar's daughter. But he made my father promise that no mention of his adventure must ever be made, for my grandfather saw not only a price on his son's head or a rope about his neck but also a gathering of ravens to see if they couldna get a morsel of the estate should it be forfeit. And so the bargain was made and they brought the lass home to her father's cottage and she gave birth to a laddie, and as you're nae daft laddie yourself, my dear Gibb, you will ken who that bairnie was.'

I was two steps ahead of him. This, then, explained the sparseness of the lettering on his father's gravestone. I said nothing, but simply nodded and kept my eye on the distant river. I had lost sight of the osprey or fishing eagle. Glen Conach continued to relate the tale he must have told himself many times.

'After Culloden, the precariousness of my father's situation was greatly increased. It needed only one person to name him and he would be hunted down and God knows his fate thereafter. There were redcoats making sweeps through all the glens in search of rebels in hiding. They had lists of names, from the humblest to the highest, of those who had been out and were said to be lurking in or near their homes. That was the term they used, "lurking". My grandfather knew that some of the young men had slipped back again, hoping that with the passage of time they would not be arrested. It would do *him* no good if they were convicted of treason. So he discreetly let it be known that if there were arms hidden in the peat stacks or in the roofs of cottages they should be brought to the big house for safe-keeping and not a word more would be said about them. And in the course of a few days a heap of blades and guns was gathered in, and my grandfather put them away in the eaves of the house, and it is those weapons that now adorn the walls of the armoury.

'My father for the most part remained in the house, as if he had never left it, but sometimes word reached the glen that soldiers were on their way and there was always that anxiety that somebody had spoken a quiet word in somebody else's lug, and so my father would come here and wait out his time until the danger was past. And all the while his son was growing in a cottage in the clachan. My grandfather, to his credit, kept his word and made sure that mother and bairn were well looked after. So you can see why, Charles, when all that trouble had blown over, my father maintained a great affection for this cave.'

'But of course,' I ventured, 'the bargain he had struck with your grandfather would not extend to his being allowed to marry the mother of his son.'

'*My* mother, Charles – let us not be blate. If you look in the kirk register you will see me there, baptised as her natural son. Mr Gillespie, the minister, knew that he was not to put in the father's name, even though he kent it – it is written there now, in case of any dispute at law, but that did not happen until years later. Aye, but you are right, my grandfather was set on increasing his standing in the world and vowed to disinherit my father if he did not marry on a wife of at least equal standing. As for me, well, there were bastards aplenty in this world and my grandfather did not see, when I had reached a certain age, that I should merit any special attention. So, when I was nine, I was sent from the glen to my cousins in Brechin while my father was married on a woman whom my grandfather deemed suitable. It was an alliance of convenience but it produced no convenience, no happiness and – much to my grandfather's dissatisfaction – no children either. My father tried to please my stepmother, even to allowing this place of sanctuary to be desecrated, but his heart wasna in it. She did not like the glen and stayed away whenever she could, and made . . . friends, elsewhere.

'She was not told this story – all that she knew was that I was her husband's bastard. She did not like me if I came home, and I did not like her, so when she was here I went back to Brechin until she left again. I last saw her a year before the events Peggy described to you. By that time my grandfather had been dead three years and more. My father was emerging from his shadow but that took a while and he tripped over himself in the process, as you have heard. When finally he regained his footing and ejected the Acquaintance, my stepmother did not tarry long but removed herself to London. She led a dissolute life there and died of it a dozen years later. I do not bear grudges if I can help it, Charles, but that woman was a blight upon us, and I did not shed a tear when I heard of her end. Yet, when I think on it, she too was a pawn in my grandfather's game, so I should be more merciful towards her memory.'

He fell silent. It was tempting to fill that silence, but I restrained my tongue. I felt that all the questions forming in me would be answered – if only he continued to speak. We had both drunk our water and so, sliding back from the precipice upon the seat of my breeches, I got to my feet and refilled our cups by the same method he had used, holding them through the glassless window. The Baron took some sips and, when I had settled myself again, recommenced.

'Naturally my father could not remarry while my stepmother was alive. There was but one woman he might have married, and that was Alison Murray, but she was not free. She had remained in the glen and married a cottar and they had two daughters – my half-sisters – and of these one survived to womanhood. As a child I used to play with her and the other bairns of the clachan, and I would often see my mother but we were not intimate. I have no recollection of when I was told she was my mother, but I certainly knew that she was from an early age. Her husband was not cold or unkind to me, but he perceived that if he favoured me overmuch difficulties might arise between himself and the laird, my grandfather. I mind when I was about eight he took me aside and said I would be better staying away from the clachan, and not long after that my grandfather sent me to Brechin, so they were of the same mind although for different reasons. I did not care, Charles. I was a solitary but spirited bairn, and I would be deceiving you if I said I suffered for want of my mother's affection or anybody else's. And indeed, as I later discovered, she did not lack affection for me, but she kept it to herself for my sake.

'Well, I came home again, and for ten years nobody stayed in this house but my father and myself and the servants. Those were the years when he completed the work on the house and its policies, and encouraged me to take an interest in tree-planting and suchlike. I did not then have the general antipathy to physical toil that affects me now. My father and I were mechanics and seedsmen, and the books that came into the library then were manuals of husbandry, drainage and livestock. There was little female influence upon either of us.

'It was about the time of the American War that both my stepmother and my mother's husband died. Perhaps, you think, my father and my mother might then have been reunited? It is true he began to make visits to her cottage, and to ensure that she had whatever comforts she required, which were few indeed, but long years had passed since their adventure with the Prince and in truth they were very different people. I went to her myself, but quite separately. He and I never spoke about these visits. It was less that we had secrets than that we had nothing we wished to share. And Alison, my mother, was proud, and loyal to her husband's memory. Her daughter, Ellen, then in her teens, lived with her and they were as content to live without men as we were to live without women.

'One day, however, I woke up and found that I was somewhat past thirty and had a great desire to have a wife and bairns. I cannot tell you how this change came about, but once upon me the mood could not be dispelled. You are not married, Charles. Have you no wish to be?'

'No, Sir,' I said, emphatically.

'How old are you?' (I have lost count of the times he has asked me this.)

'Twenty-eight,' I said. 'The same age as your son.'

'Ah, that explains it. Sandy thinks he does not wish to marry, but both you and he will soon think differently. Well, the urge was upon me. I saw that I would wait a long time before a wife came to me here, therefore I began to roam the country in search of one. I started at Brechin and ranged through all my cousins and their friends but I wanted none of them. I went to Dundee and Arbroath and had no more success in either place. At last I found Peggy in Montrose, where her father was a lawyer. We were soon fond of each other, and neither parent made an objection, so we were married. My father was not very precise about my origins, and her father, as I thought, was too polite to question them. It was only after we were united that Peggy told me that certain rumours had reached her father's ears, but he had steadfastly ignored them, having, in a professional capacity, met with too many bairns born out of wedlock to be alarmed by one more. She too had heard some of these rumours, and her father had advised her that, while she was at perfect liberty to accept or reject my suit, she should take no account of them in making her decision.

She herself was more amused than shocked when she learned – from me – the circumstances of my birth. It was only then that my father got Mr Gillespie to add his name to the notice of my birth in the kirk register.

'I liked Peggy's father. He was a very easy man for a lawyer. And Peggy was fond of *my* father and was good to him in his declining years, and he loved her for that – and for giving him two grandchildren. And that is how you find us today, with those children grown and our people reduced but around us still.'

'And,' I said, 'your mother nearby and in good health. But her daughter, Ellen, what happened to her?'

Glen Conach sighed. 'She died. Her history was what her mother's might have been. She was enamoured of a soldier, and went away with him, and he deserted her. So she came back to her mother's and gave birth to a child, but she didna long survive the ordeal. The bairn did, of course, and was cared for by its grandmother.'

'Of course,' I said, recalling Elspeth's remark that blood will *oot* – and her more recent assertion to me, on the back stair, that she intended to get what was hers by marrying a soldier. But I thought that it was not for me to mention that.

We sat in silence for a while. At last I said, 'Forgive me, Sir, but you have made me, a stranger although your guest, party to your family's most private affairs. Why have you told me all this?'

'Why would I not?' he said. 'You have been with us long enough, and these are not great secrets. Half the glen knows them, half does not, and neither half cares. You are not a fool and had probably guessed some of it yourself. And then –' He broke off and fell again into silence. 'And then,' he resumed, 'Sandy is not here.'

Before I could reply, he set off on another track.

'What's a wee thing like a bairn to fash about? We are a small, unremarked place, Charles, yet some of us have seen remarkable things. There were old men in the clachan who once were away on the far side of oceans. One was a soldier in the French and Indian wars half a century since. He is dead now, but he told me great tales. He said he never knew heroes like the Iroquois warriors he fought beside. After the war he left the army and worked in the distant wastes of Canada for the Hudson's Bay Company. The coldest winter here, he said, is as nothing to winter there. Snow to the depth of three men, and rivers that are frozen solid for months. There is another man, living yet, away up the glen, who set off for Edinburgh and went on to London and then to Paris and Rome, and even to the island of Sardinia where he narrowly escaped being taken into slavery by pirates from Tunis. He came home again because he found the sun too hot, and chose to bide on his own where he would never again be in danger of captivity. And these are the ones who returned. Others – men and women and their children – have left, and what became of them I do not know. Perhaps they are hungry and sorrowful and wish they had remained. Perhaps they are farmers in Pennsylvania or foresters in Ohio. Perhaps they are dead. What marvels could they tell us if they were here? Who cares about a bairn's legitimacy when he has all that to wonder at?'

This was the end of his musings. I have recorded all of the above as accurately as I can remember it. The Baron spoke at times with such emotion that I seem to hear his words even now. In writing them down, it is as if he were here in the library and I simply acting as his amanuensis.

We gathered ourselves together and made our way back to the foot of the stone stair. Here, he suggested that instead of mounting them we take another way home, along an old, overgrown path which he had frequented as a boy and had a yearning to retrace. It ran below the cave and would lead us by the foot of Conach's Linn, he said, which would be a fine sight after the thunderstorm. What occurred there, I will write down next. However, my fingers will no longer grip the pen and I must put this notebook aside and turn again to Conach and what Elspeth might call his *trauchles*. I will complete this tonight or tomorrow.

Sunday, 27th August 1809

(No kirk for me today. I keep to my room until noon, and so I resume.)

The Baron led the way down a sometimes precipitous, thoroughly muddy track, his bulk dislodging stones at every step. I say 'step' but we slipped as often as we placed our feet securely, and I had to clutch at clumps of grass and the low branches of trees in order to keep myself upright. The undergrowth was so thick that the light of the afternoon was all but blocked out, and I began to be angry at my host for taking me on such a hazardous route. After twenty minutes or so, the ground levelled and the going became slightly easier. I was uncomfortably hot, and resentful that I had been bitten, pricked and stung by every insect, thorn and nettle in the glen. I felt dizzy and weak-limbed, and fancied that some whining creature had lodged itself in my ear and was maddening me with its song. Glen Conach's broad back was my only view. All at once and without warning he halted, and I crashed into him. He turned round and signalled to me to be quiet. Miraculously the whining ceased, and then recommenced, and I realised that it came not from within my ear but from some source a little distance ahead of us. Glen Conach advanced more slowly, and as quietly as he was able. I followed. In another minute we emerged into a kind of glade: there, twenty yards away, was the cascade of gleaming water, clear against the black rock that was its passage to the burn below. A man was visible, standing up to his knees in a pool at the foot of the waterfall, and it was from him that the 'song' emanated – a kind of skirl above the water's thunderous bass. My vision became clearer, and I saw that the person thus revealed was the Reverend John Dunning, and that he was entirely naked.

The Baron and I stood side by side for about a minute. I think we were both a little awestruck by what we could see and hear. Unclothed, the minister was no prettier than when suited. He was as hairy as an ape, and as pale-skinned beneath the black hair, and his belly was pendulous and very great. He took another pace or two until the torrent struck him full upon the chest, the temperature and the force of it together causing him to gasp and bellow. He dipped his head into the water and nearly lost his footing, then returned to the former position and resumed his singing, which was more like the sound of a cow needing to be milked, or of a dog in pain, than of a man. I tried to discern a tune and words, sacred or otherwise, but could not. And I realised suddenly that this was because he was not singing, but howling. He was truly in anguish.

It was Glen Conach who broke the spell, if spell was what held us. Dishevelled and bedecked with bits of leaf and twig, he made a stumbling rush towards the minister. 'Mr Dunning! Mr Dunning! What the devil are you at? Wait, Sir! Do not go! I demand that you wait!' For at the first indication that he was discovered, Dunning had bolted from the pool with unexpected agility, scooped up his clothing from a rock and scampered away at great speed, like the grotesque prodigy of a hare mated with a toad.

We stood beside the rock where the minister's clothes had been and stared at each other. It was almost as if we had seen an apparition, but we knew we had not.

'Extraordinary!' the Baron said. 'I didna mean to fleg him, but I did. Do you think he is not well?'

'I thought that weeks ago,' I said. Then I added, 'But when we are alone, or think that we are, perhaps we all behave strangely.'

'*I* don't,' Glen Conach answered. 'I behave the same whether alone or not. He will have to stop somewhere and dress himself. If anybody else sees him – well, how will they sit under him again in kirk without laughing? How will *I*?'

'He was only washing himself,' I said. I do not know why I sought to defend a man I did not like.

'But what a noise he was making!' the Baron said. 'We might almost have heard him from the cave. Washing himself? Is that what he was doing? Perhaps we should do the same. Do *you* want to wash, Charles?'

The thought of the Baron and myself stripping our clothes off together was abhorrent to me. 'I think I will wait,' I said.

'I think I will too,' he replied. 'By, but he was unco-looking! I would not want to look like that and be seen. I do not mean his body – but I don't know what I do mean. And I must sit under him on Sunday! Say nothing of this to my wife and daughter. It must be a secret between us. Say nothing to anyone.'

I assured him I would not, and we continued on our way. The water flowed from the pool in a series of smaller cascades towards the glen floor, and the path went down beside it. We saw no more of Mr Dunning, nor did we speak again until we reached the house. The Baron said, almost as if to himself, 'I will speak to him. Aye, I must speak to him.' Then he called for water to both our rooms, and we parted until dinner.

Sunday 27th August 1809 (continued)

The next day (Saturday) being fine again, I worked away in the library until noon, then escaped from the house by myself for several hours, walking down the glen on the road to Forfar. It occurred to me that I could keep on going and not return, for I had left very few possessions behind me. But where would be the profit in that? I was somewhat afraid of Jessie, yet somewhat fond of her; fond of her father too, and even of her austere mother. I was surprised at both the strength and confusion of my own feelings. More cynically, I reckoned there was surely a month of provender left for me at Glen Conach House. So I stretched my legs, admired the countryside, felt all the better for it, and walked back again. The heat lay on the land like a blanket. I encountered not a soul the whole afternoon until, a mile or two short of the house, I spied the Baron sitting on a stone, mopping his head with his red handkerchief.

'I have been waiting for you,' he said as I came up. 'They told me you had gone this way. I wished to tell you that I have spoken with Mr Dunning. I went to the manse two hours ago. D'ye ken what he did?'

Obviously, I did not.

'He *apologised* – for having surprised us! I said I thought we had surprised him! He told me that he went to the linn when he was feeling *especially* dejected. He says the force of the water and its coldness have a restorative effect. I asked him what he meant by "especially". Did he *commonly* feel dejected? He said he did, on account of his wife being dead. "Mr Dunning," I said, "she has been dead four years." "I cannot help it," he replied. "She was very dear to me. Nothing compensates for her loss." "Not even the certainty of being reunited with her when –?" I began, but he interrupted me as if he could not bear to think of heaven: "Not even that." It is odd, because I have sometimes thought that there *was* compensation. In the manse, if ye ken what I mean.'

I said I did, thinking of Mary, the Maid thereof.

'But whether there is or there isna – weel, it does him nae good. He says he is overwhelmed with sadness almost daily. I never thought him capable of such feeling. I almost wept in front of him, Charles. It makes me think better of him, and I will listen to his sermon more closely tomorrow. He was sorry for the shock he gave us but I told him to think no more about it, and that you and I were sworn to secrecy, for which he was grateful. I think he thought I had come to expel him, but how could I? What a terrible, private thing to have witnessed! And where else would he go? I invited him to come to dinner instead, on any day next week, but he declined. He said he would be poor company and would be better to be on his own for a while. How little we ken the folk we live beside. We must be tolerant, my dear Gibb, we must be kind. Dear God, I cannot imagine such grief.'

Together we walked slowly to the house. Glen Conach had again come out without his dogs, but they came looking for him and accompanied us for the last mile. They are quite used to me now, and pay me little heed. They love only one man, and that is their master.

The Baron informed me quietly this evening that Mr Dunning's text today was Isaiah 53:3 and that he preached the best he had ever heard him. I had to look that verse up: 'He is despised and rejected of men; a man of sorrows, and acquainted with grief: and we hid as it were our faces from him; he was despised, and we esteemed him not.' Mr Dunning said in his sermon that whatever we choose to see or not see in others does not alter them one iota; nor if we shun those whose grief spoils our own happiness will we be truly happy; for of one thing we can be certain, that sorrow will come upon us all in time. Glen Conach said he found it very moving, and even when he had a sudden vision of Mr Dunning naked he did not laugh at all, but almost wept again.

Book of Conach

Chapter 13

Of a man struck by a stone thrown by Conach

The people of the glen knew that Conach desired above all things to be alone. For the most part they respected his wishes and did not disturb him in his forest abode. They communicated with him only through his servant, who went between that place and their village. But on one occasion some of the men, curious to see how he lived, came to enjoy his wisdom and, as they hoped, to receive his blessing. They even, without permission, entered into his cabin, where he was at prayer. Astonished at their audacity, Conach flew into a great rage and cast them forth, and would not bless them. For, he said, they came not in humility but as gapers and thieves, to steal his tranquillity and carry stories back to their families. And he pursued them from his cabin and threw stones at them as they ran away.

Now it happened that one of the stones struck a man on the head, and he fell to the ground. His companions, seeing that he lay motionless, returned and sought to rouse him, and when he could not be roused they lifted him to carry him away. They said to Conach, 'See what you have done.' And Conach stood before them and cried out, 'Now you have caused me to break my vow never to use a weapon against another living creature. Lay down your friend and let me tend him, as once before I tended a wounded hare.' But they said, 'He is not wounded. He is dead.'

Conach wept. Then, putting his anguish aside, he laid his hand upon the wound that the stone had made, and said, 'Lord Jesus Christ, forgive Thy servant who in his righteous fury hath done this wicked thing. Let him abase himself and be punished as Thou seest fit, but spare the life of this man.'

Then before their eyes the man who was dead began to groan, and sat up and rubbed his head. And when he saw the blood on his hand he said unto Conach, 'Father, do not be angry with me. We should not have come.'

And Conach said, 'My anger is all spent.' And forthwith his friends carried the man home, and Conach departed into a field of nettles, grasping them in great handfuls until his hands were so swollen that he could not close them. Then he took off his robe and lay among the nettles, first on his back and then on his belly, and made long prayers to God in gratitude for saving the man he had struck with the stone.

When Talorg his servant found him later, he hardly knew him, so swollen and empurpled was he by the stings of the nettles. And Talorg wished to bathe his body and cool the heat of the stings, but Conach forbade him. 'Then,' Talorg said, 'surely you have punished yourself more even than God would wish, for did you not repent of your anger?' But Conach said, 'My punishment is not one hundredth of what I deserve for my sins.'

Chapter 14

Of a conversation between Conach and a wolf

It is said that one of the blessed hermit's great gifts was an ability to communicate with animals. I know not how this was accomplished, whether by speech or some other means, but he would sometimes be found standing or sitting close to a deer, a bird or some other wild beast, which was not at all afraid of him. These creatures would even take food from his hand or allow themselves to be stroked by him, but would flee as soon as another human approached.

Once, so I have heard, Conach was alone upon the mountain when he met a wolf carrying two dead lambs in her mouth. Conach rebuked the creature for stealing from his friends, the people of the glen, but the wolf spoke back, asking how else she should feed her cubs. Conach said that the earth was home to all kinds of animals, each species with its own station in the order of life, and that she should eat only the wild beasts that were her natural prey. 'It is natural to eat what is most easily taken,' the wolf said. 'But this sets you and your kind against man,' Conach replied, 'and a day will come, if you do not change your ways, when men will kill all your children's children and not one of them shall be left alive.' 'This they will try to do whether I change or not,' said the wolf, 'for men are more cruel than we are, and their hatred for us is without limit.' 'I do not hate you,' Conach said. 'Yet I say to you, if you resist temptation and steal no more, and stay away from human habitation, your children and their children will be in less danger.' 'You speak of temptation,' the wolf replied, 'but a wolf is not tempted. My sole intent is to defeat my enemy, hunger, and to feed my children. Who visits temptation upon me?'

Then Conach said, 'You are both more and less wise than I am, because you know nothing of good and evil. My God is your God, for He made you, but you do not know Him. Now I ask God to intercede between you and my friends who hate you. I tell you this, if you let go the lambs you hold in your mouth and promise to steal no more of them, your den will be filled with food for you and your cubs.' The wolf said, 'You are wiser than I am, Conach, and because you do not hate me I will do as you ask. But you are also more foolish, because these lambs are dead.' No sooner did she lay them on the ground, however, than they sprang to life and ran away down the mountain. Then the wolf complained to Conach that her cubs would starve, but he told her to go home and see if they were hungry. So she went, and found all manner of food in the den, and her cubs fat, full and contented. And it is said that ever since that time no sheep or lamb has been taken by a wolf in the glen.

Maja

I don't know what Shirley had said to Dr Tybault about me. He was, at first, quite tentative, almost apologetic. He hoped I would not mind the intrusion. He did not want to tire me, and would not take up too much of my time, but he was keen to talk to me about Conach. I already knew this, because Shirley had told me that much. I made a pot of tea. While the kettle boiled he hovered uneasily, looking at my pictures. He didn't make any comments about them, not then.

When we sat down he slid a mobile phone out of a pocket on to the table. He explained that he would like to record our conversation. Would that be all right? I said I would rather he didn't. I didn't know what he was going to ask or what I was going to say and so I would not be comfortable. He looked disappointed, but put the phone away. Then he brought out a notebook and said that instead he would make a few notes as we talked. As a matter of fact he made hardly any. He did not ask many questions and he seemed not to need long answers from me. Mostly, he talked and I listened, nodding or shaking my head at appropriate moments in case he thought I had fallen asleep. He chatted on, at times almost as if to himself. Maybe he is like that when he is teaching students. It was a cold but bright day, and it was not unpleasant to sit in the afternoon sunshine that filled the room. I gave him more tea. Occasionally I offered an opinion, and he nodded in his turn and – once or twice – jotted something down.

'We have two documents to consider,' Dr Tybault began. He had a clear, precise way of speaking. I realised I was to receive a lecture.

'The first of these is a translation of the *Book of Conach*. What do you know about the *Book of Conach*?' I felt as if I had neglected to do some set reading.

'Nothing,' I said, 'except that it used to be kept at the Big House long ago. I know some of the legends about Conach, but –'

He put up his hand. 'Please don't tell me about those yet,' he said. And he gave me the story of the *Book of Conach*.

'It was a manuscript written in Latin, *Liber Conachi*,' he said, 'compiled, probably by a monk, about eight hundred years ago. It is not known how it came to be in the library of Glen Conach House or where it might have been before that. In 1809, a man called Charles Gibb came to the glen to make a transcription and also an English translation of it. Years later, in 1832, a fire broke out in the east wing of the house, and most of the library and its books, including the ancient manuscript, were lost.'

'Yes,' I said, 'everybody here knows about the fire.'

Dr Tybault looked slightly annoyed. 'What they won't know,' he said, 'is that after that event Charles Gibb tried several times, without success, to publish the work he had done on the *Book*. On one of these occasions his Latin transcription suffered the same fate as that of the original manuscript – it was destroyed by fire. After his death, Gibb's papers were deposited in the Faculty of Advocates' Library in Edinburgh, and are now in the National Library. These papers include his English translation of the *Book of Conach*, but as neither the original nor his transcription survive it is impossible to know how accurate a translation it is.

'I came across it quite by chance. I was searching for references to lesser-known Celtic saints and I saw Conach's name mentioned in an entry in the online catalogue, and it led me to Charles Gibb's papers. His translation of the *Book* is an interesting read, but it also has some unusual characteristics. Its tone is suspect, if you understand my meaning.'

I said I did not understand his meaning.

'Similar works of that vintage,' he explained, 'I mean of the Middle Ages, tend to be very reverential, not just towards the holy person being written about but also to the Christian Church. The *Book of Conach*, or at least the only version of it that we have, Gibb's translation, is not only critical of the Church, it also portrays, in some detail, Conach's weaknesses and failings. It feels quite modern or, at least, not quite medieval. There is something not right about it. Until now, however, we have had no way of verifying the accuracy of the translation.

'Now we come to the second document. We have a journal written by Charles Gibb when he was here in Glen Conach in 1809. I think you probably know that this was rescued from a bonfire by Mr and Mrs Darroch?' I nodded, and was about to say that I had read it but he did not pause. 'This changes everything. It is full of interesting information about the glen, and about the Milne family who lived in Glen Conach House – Thomas Milne, his wife, Margaret, and their daughter, Jessamine. After my first visit to Glen Conach House I took the journal away and examined it closely. Among other things I was looking for references to the *Book of Conach*, especially to any specific passages from the original. There are a few, including some phrases in Latin. I then went back to the National Library to compare these with Gibb's English translation. For the most part, the references fit, although some do not. But something else was bothering me, something I was only able to confirm when I looked at the translation document, and it was this: the handwriting of the translation is not always Gibb's handwriting. There are small additions and amendments, crossings-out and suchlike, which have been written by somebody else. The bulk of the text is definitely in Gibb's handwriting, so it is not as if he was dictating, but sometimes – it is hard to explain this without showing you examples – it looks as though somebody may have been dictating *to him*. When I came back here to return the journal to Mrs Darroch, she was good enough to look out some estate documents dating from that period, in fact from a little later, and a comparison of the handwriting leaves no doubt as to who wrote those additions.'

He paused, presumably for effect. I, for effect, raised my eyebrows.

'It is perfectly clear,' he said, 'that the translation was a collaborative effort between Charles Gibb and Jessamine Milne.'

'Does that matter?' I asked.

Dr Tybault looked rather shocked when I said that. I had thought he would be, which was partly why I said it, to see if I was right. But I also asked the question sincerely. After all this time, *did* it matter?

To him, it mattered greatly. He reminded me that because of the accidents which had destroyed the original manuscript and Charles Gibb's transcription of it, the *Book of Conach* now existed only in the form of Gibb's translation. With the discovery of the journal and following Dr Tybault's own detective work, it seemed that what was held by the National Library was an adulterated and therefore entirely unreliable document. This was deeply frustrating, but it could not be helped.

'Why is it unreliable, just because Jessie Milne had a hand in it?' I asked.

'Well,' he said, 'there are things in Gibb's diary that cast some doubt on her, well, her motivation and objectivity.'

'Oh,' I said. 'And was Mr Gibb beyond reproach? I mean, when it comes to being reliable?'

Dr Tybault looked annoyed again. 'Not entirely,' he said.

I said, 'At least you will be able to write an interesting paper about it. But it doesn't change anything, does it? It was all so long ago.'

Now that his lecture was over, he became the slightly awkward, shy man he had been when he first came in. He said, 'I suppose on one level you are right. But this is what I wanted to ask you about. Mrs Darroch says you've lived here nearly all your life. You are one of the oldest inhabitants in the glen. So it may be possible for me to do some, well, what we call data triangulation. What I would like to know is, what stories about Conach did you hear when you were younger? I'm interested in comparing them with the stories in the translation and also, now that we have it, with those that are mentioned in Gibb's journal. Gibb reports Jessamine Milne as saying that the glen people have a whole store of Conach tales, and later he writes that she told him one or two of these, which he describes as "charming". I would love to know if any of these were still current within living memory.'

He seemed to veer between being an ordinary man and an academic. The academic was back. No doubt he had thought carefully about how to say what he had just said, but I thought it quite careless. It seemed to me that he was only interested in me for what I could give him. I did not expect him to want to be my friend, but still, he spoke as if 'living memory' were shortly to be extinguished, which was a little hard to hear even though it was true. I began to feel impatient. There were moments when he was talking, as the sunlight passed across certain objects, when I just wanted to draw or paint. I told myself there would be other days for that, and hoped I was right.

'You should have come before,' I said, 'when Geordie was still alive. He would have told you all those stories. But you don't need me to tell you that. You can listen to them all in Edinburgh anyway.'

He did not know who or what I was talking about. I told him about the bearded and bespectacled ones who came in the 1980s to record Geordie Kemp, and he became very animated and made some notes and said that this information alone made his journey worthwhile.

'I see,' he said. 'It is just as well I came to interview you. It never ceases to amaze me,' he continued, chuckling in a serious kind of way, 'how often academics working in the same city, in the same institution, perhaps even in the same building, have no idea that their researches are connected. Now, about the stories you heard about Conach when you were younger?'

I said that the only ones I could recall had been told to me either by Geordie or by his wife, Betty. One was about Conach meeting a wolf, another was about his psalm-book being rescued from the river by an otter, and another was about a madman who died three deaths. He put up his hand again, like a policeman.

'That story is highly suspect,' he said. 'It bears a strong resemblance to the legend of Saint Kentigern and his encounter with a wild prophet called Lailoken. Do you know of it?' I shook my head, and asked for the second name again, and he even spelled it out for me. 'Well, I won't go into the details now, but the Kentigern story appears to have been appropriated and inserted wholesale into the life of Conach, probably by the original chronicler, although now we shall never know. The story of the otter, on the other hand, is one of the passages in the manuscript where there are marginal notes in Jessamine Milne's hand and then what looks like an additional paragraph inserted in Charles Gibb's hand. I wonder if you can tell me that story now.'

I said that there was no point in me telling him that one or the others, since they would all be on the tapes in Edinburgh, told properly by Geordie. So I was not much use to him, especially as I couldn't remember much more of them than were in Mr Gibb's journal.

His face fell when I said that. 'You have seen the journal?'

I said that Shirley had left the typescript with me and I had read the whole thing, from start to finish.

'Ah,' he said, 'I didn't know this. Mrs Darroch didn't tell me. That's disappointing. I was hoping, you see, that you would tell me only what you remembered, whereas it transpires that you have seen what Gibb wrote down.'

'Is that a problem?'

'It's a little like a witness giving evidence in a court case after having heard another witness giving evidence about the same events,' he said.

'Do you think I would make things up?' I asked.

'No, no,' he said. 'I don't mean that. It's just that it would have been better, in terms of corroboration – of data triangulation – if I'd spoken to you *before* you had read Gibb's journal. It's about authenticity. I am not questioning your memory, but your memory might have been coloured by what you read.'

This I did understand. I said that memory was coloured by many things and circumstances. Sometimes it was not coloured but erased. But perhaps none of this mattered anyway, because from what he had told me the authenticity of the 'translation' of the *Book of Conach* could be neither proved nor disproved.

'I suppose you are right,' he said, and chuckled again, more sad than serious this time. 'When I am back in Edinburgh I will go and find those recordings of Geordie Kemp and listen to them. From the 1980s, you say? At least we know that *they're* authentic.'

I thought it would really upset him if I said that the recordings might be authentic but some of Geordie's stories weren't, so I didn't. Perhaps it was wrong of me but I was beginning to tire.

He wondered if the glen children today would know any of the old legends. I said I didn't think so. He asked me if I had children or grandchildren. I told him no, that had not been my destiny. That word, 'destiny', seemed to make him uneasy. I do not know if Shirley had said anything more about me, but he did not ask about my life in the glen. So I turned the question back to him, and he told me about his own children, a boy and a girl. He seemed quite relieved not to have to ask me more questions. Well, I could give him nothing more about Conach: he had a better source to go to now.

His boy was still at school, his girl had just begun university. She was studying law. I asked if that was what she wanted to be, a lawyer?

'Yes,' he said, 'she is interested in human rights. The world makes her angry, all the hatred and persecution that's in it. People who are on the move because where they are is too dangerous or there are no jobs or not enough to eat. People who drown looking for a better life. She has a very strong sense of right and wrong. I try to tell her that not everything is clear-cut, but she says some things are. She wants to make a difference.'

'That's a good ambition to have,' I said.

'It is, but I'm not sure how much difference any one person can make.'

'What about your son? Does he know what he wants to be?'

'He is not academic at all,' he said, 'but he is musical – plays guitar and piano – and he's good with his hands. He makes things out of wood, beautiful things, little boxes and caskets. I am not sure what he'll end up doing. My wife worries about them both, she doesn't want them to be disappointed. I don't think there's much point in worrying.'

I offered him more tea. 'No, I must go,' he said. 'It's a long drive.'

I took the cups to the sink and he gathered his belongings. Before he left he had another look round the walls. He spent some time peering at my flower paintings. 'There are so many,' he said. 'Do you exhibit? Do you sell them?'

'I used to,' I said. 'If there is one you like, you can have it.'

He was embarrassed. I was not sure how much he liked them so I did not repeat my offer, and he did not choose one. Maybe he will take one if he returns, but why would he return? There is nothing for him here.

The light had gone by the time he left. It was too late to do any work. I went to bed early and lay in the dark, thinking about Geordie and Betty and all those other folk who used to be here. And I thought of Lachie's ghost girl and if she might be the echo of any of them.

Journal of Charles Kirkliston Gibb

Friday, 1st September 1809

My relations with the Baron have certainly benefited from our recent excursion. He treats me now half like a son, half like a close friend. We share a secret about the minister, of course, but I think he was also impressed by my walking and climbing prowess, as he has not disparaged my vigour or my physical shape all week. Indeed, I do feel healthier and stronger than I can ever recall. Daniel Haddow was at dinner on Tuesday and complimented me on my appearance. The fresh air and braes of Glen Conach were agreeable to me, he opined. I said they were and hoped that I was agreeable to Glen Conach. The Baron, who had not been listening properly, at once agreed that I was agreeable to him. Miss Milne stared at her plate, her mother at the ceiling – both, I think, conscious that so long as I remain in the laird's favour I will not be served notice to leave, even if it were discovered that I had translated the *Book* not only into English but also into French, German and – for mere amusement – Arabic. I have been here nine weeks, one of the longest encampments I have ever made. However, already Daniel's Eden begins to pale, and soon it will turn to brown. I am ever mindful of the Baron's own warnings about the winter, but have heard nothing back from Sir John Dalrymple.

Daniel's compliment was, I am sure, sincerely meant, and came with no suggestive intent. I fear no further attempt from that quarter. He is almost *too* shy, but how else can he be? Were he to make one ill-calculated approach to the wrong man, he would be utterly ruined. I was on the point of writing that I cannot imagine what it is to live like that, but I can. I live like it myself, though my dangers are of a lesser magnitude.

Still no word from Captain Milne, but the latest newspapers carry reports of the surrender of Flushing. This has apparently been accomplished with few losses to the British forces, but the bombardment of the town has left scarcely a house unmarked and many buildings lying in ruins, and the inhabitants are left in a very sorry condition and ill-disposed to the liberators who have destroyed their homes. Many French troops have been captured, which must always be a great inconvenience to a victorious army, as they must then guard, feed, and attend to the wounds of the men they were intent on killing the day before. It must be tempting in such circumstances either to disarm them and let them go, or starve or shoot them, which of course would not be gentlemanly and also, once word got out about it, would lead to reciprocal behaviour on the part of the enemy. But as the two sides were only trying to achieve the same result previously, though by different methods, the moral outrage rings somewhat hollow. I will, thank God, never make a soldier.

Saturday, 2nd September 1809

I have not long woken from a most vivid and detailed dream which has disturbed me greatly. I woke while it was still dark and found myself in a sweat and very confused as to where I was and what was dream and what real. It is lighter now and I am less confused, so I will write down everything exactly as I yet see and hear it.

Jessie came to me in the library. She seemed listless, almost mechanical, and had neither a smile nor a frown upon her face. She held a plate before her but it was empty. One moment she was at the door, the next she was putting the plate down on the great table and standing directly opposite me, very dull-eyed. The *Book* was resting on its cushion, open somewhere about the middle.

She said, 'You are surely nearly finished with that by now, Mr Gibb. You have been here nearly three months.'

'Not quite so long as that, Miss Milne,' I replied.

'Oh, are my calculations wrong? More than sixty days, then. If you have managed two or three folios a day, which would not be very burdensome, then your work must be all but complete.'

'Some parts of the text are more difficult than others,' I said.

'I did not find them so,' she answered in the same flat tone.

I said, 'I thought – that is, I remember *you* saying – that you found the Latin trying.'

'Yes, but did I not correct myself and say that it was the story that tried me? I suppose it is easily checked.'

Then she turned and seemed to glide, very swiftly but as stiff as an automaton, to the nearest shelves, and ran her finger along the spines of the books, as if searching for one that would corroborate her memory. Her finger came to rest on a large volume, and she stood very still.

'But in truth,' I heard her say, 'I am not surprised at the slow progress you have been making, when so much of your time is taken up with writing about *us*.'

'Miss Milne,' I said, 'whatever do you mean?' But it was as if somebody else spoke and I only mouthed the words.

'Oh, please, Mr Gibb,' she returned sharply. 'Do not pretend you have not been keeping a record of our faults and failings.'

'Miss Milne,' I said, 'have you been spying on me?'

She continued to face the shelves. 'Have *you* not been spying on *me*?' she said. 'One person's private journal is as interesting to read as another's, I suppose – although you need not think yours so fascinating that I have read every word of it. I have read enough, however. You must think me very naïve, or perhaps just idiotic – what with the ugly mark that you say perpetually torments me, my too many teeth and my too low estimation of your wealth and genius. Yet you also have the arrogance to believe that I have fallen in love with you.' Suddenly, as if mounted on a revolving disc, she spun round to look at me, and now her voice grew loud and shook with emotion. 'Oh, but you also think me cunning! Is it cunning of me to appear idiotic? Or does my idiocy destroy my cunning? Is it cunning that causes me to sigh when you come near me, or can I not help it? And then there are your opinions of my brother whom you have not even met, and of my mother and father, into whose house you have slid like a snake. Impostor! Abuser of my father's kindness and hospitality! Thief! Do you deny what you have admitted in writing, that you stole money and chattels from some of the very people who have given you food and shelter? I wonder what you intend to steal from us before you depart.'

I stood up and found that I was no longer by the desk but at the windows that look down the glen – among the dream's curiosities were these unnatural sudden movements. 'Miss Milne,' I said, 'I am caught in a snare set by myself. You have every right and reason to despise me, not only because of what you have read but also because I was so arrogant as to think you would not find me out. I beg you to believe that I never thought you an idiot. I never thought any part of your appearance ugly. I only admire and respect you. I admire and respect your parents too, though I am as wholly undeserving of their generosity as I am of yours. I cannot expect you to welcome the esteem of a dishonourable wretch, but I would plead that if you had not seen the things I wrote down in private you might at least not dislike me. You are right to call me a thief. If you wish me to go now to your father, to beg his forgiveness or be delivered by him to the nearest custodians of justice, I will do so. If, however, you simply wish never to see or hear of me again, only say the word – or do not even speak, but make a sign of assent – and in five minutes I will be gone from here for ever.'

I remember thinking – that is, in the dream I thought – that this was a rather fine speech, and that I hoped Jessie would agree. But her stern expression told that she was not impressed. 'I will settle this,' she said. 'That damned old charlatan is the cause of it.' She sprang without any effort on to the table and, lifting her skirts a little, began a regular march, stamping each shoe in turn upon the *Book of Conach*, which was rapidly demolished amid a cloud of feathers as the blue cushion also disintegrated. (Is it not wonderful how, when we dream, such behaviour does not strike us as at all singular? If Mr Dunning had appeared naked under a cascade issuing from the library cornice I daresay I would not have been surprised.) Jessie's disfigurement, which I realise now had not been visible until that moment, was at once larger than ever, and throbbed in time with her marching. When she spoke she sounded just like her mother. 'You may prefer to slip away, Mr Gibb, but I will not permit it,' she said. 'You may attempt to disguise your offer of flight as a service to me, but I am not beguiled. You have a task to complete, and I demand that it be completed, even if it takes you until your last breath to do it!'

This was the moment when I awoke, perspiring freely and in great terror. I may even have cried out. My first thought was that it would be impossible to fulfil Jessie's order since she had destroyed the *Book*, and this filled me with a profound despair. It was only when I reviewed the sequence of events that I understood that the whole thing had been a dream.

It nevertheless contains a very clear warning to me, which I have taken to heart. I *was* arrogant not to consider that Jessie – or somebody else – might find and read this journal, as I found and read hers. The consequences of that are so awful to dwell upon that I have been dwelling upon them with a morbid pleasure for the last half-hour. What would happen to me, were my words to be read by another? What would happen to Mr Haddow, or Mr Dunning? One of us would be hanged, another loaded on to a boat to Botany Bay, and the third put in a hospital for the insane; but I am not sure how the allocation would fall, nor which would be the worst fate. I therefore determined to secrete this book, when it is not in my immediate possession, in a place where it will never be discovered. For some minutes I hunted in my chamber for such a spot, testing floorboards, looking under the bed and in the press, but without satisfaction. At last I came upon the very location. In the commode, behind and below where the chanty is stored, is a space just wide enough to accommodate the journal. Conveniently there is a loose piece of wood which, when fixed in position, entirely hides the fact that the space exists at all. It is as secure a retreat as I can hope for, and better than many that in the past kept safe Catholic priest, rebel Covenanter or fugitive Jacobite.

Wednesday, 6th September 1809

The oats have ripened early because of the good weather. Glen Conach tells me that in some years they cannot fell the oats until late October, and even this year the bere must wait several more weeks. There are also some clover meadows that were cut earlier and can now be cut again – this is good fodder to get the beasts through the first part of winter, so the Baron says. There will be potatoes to lift next month too. So, all are employed in some manner, although I am relieved to find that the family do not stoop quite so low as to wield sickles and gather stooks themselves. I might otherwise have been recruited to join them. Instead, the women help Kate Nicol prepare and carry food and ale to the harvesters at intervals during the day, and Glen Conach loiters near the rigs with his gun, and takes shots at rabbits and other creatures as they break cover and flee from the reapers' blades.

I walked out with him yesterday when they were in one of the parks by the river, and saw a more efficient though also more barbarous way of collecting game. Some boys stretched a net between the riverbank and a tree, and as the last of the crop was felled others drove a dozen displaced rabbits and a hare towards the water. When the creatures turned in their panic to escape drowning they were caught in the net, whereupon they were set upon with clubs and sticks which occasioned a terrible squealing and crying, mercifully soon over. The boys offered the laird the choice of their catch and he took two rabbits but left the rest to be divided among the inhabitants of the clachan.

'My people are at their happiest when life is like this,' he said to me at breakfast this morning. 'When they are happy, I am happy. With a good hairst comes the promise of better times to come. When the last sheaf is cut – what we call the clyack sheaf – it is dressed in ribbons and the youngest lassie brings it hame to us here, and we have a feast and a dance. We will have dancing when all has been ingathered, will we not, my dear?' (This addressed to the Baroness.)

'There is plenty to be done before there is any dancing,' she replied, but I could see that his excited mind was racing ahead of all practicalities.

'Two or three times in the year, Charles,' he said, 'such as now, or at Hogmanay, we clear the hall, put chairs and the pews from the kirk round the walls, and the people come and eat with us and then dance through all the evening. Strathspeys, Scotch reels and jigs – we do them all. It is a great occasion, the clyack feast, is it not, Jessie?'

'It is, Papa,' she replied.

'It sometimes becomes very high-spirited, Charles,' her father went on. 'I will not say that there are not visits to the whisky bothies beforehand. And we take a few of the old swords down from the armoury walls and the best dancers show off their skills at skipping over them. Oh, it is a great occasion. It is like a dramatisation of "The Piper o' Dundee".'

'It's a shame, though, that we do not have a piper,' the Baroness interjected. 'The last piper in the glen went to the army and has not come back, Mr Gibb.'

This remark cast a sudden gloom across the table, which I

attempted to disperse by inquiring, since I could not imagine Mr Haddow dancing or teaching the children to do so, if a dancing master came to the glen. Glen Conach almost choked at the notion.

'We have no need of dancing masters here, my dear Gibb. The bairns start to dance as soon as they can stand. There are fiddles aplenty hanging in the houses, and men that ken how to play them. They play not for payment but as a pastime when their work is done. It is true they are mostly old men, but one or two of the young lads show some talent. As for the bagpipe, I have no great love of it and do not mourn its absence from us. The fiddle is the true Scotch instrument.'

I said that if I were still here I would look forward to the dance, which was an untruth, and the Baroness pierced me with a stare and said, with equal sharpness, 'I think you will be away before then, Mr Gibb.' Then she rose from the table and left the room, but not before giving an imperious nod to the Baron, which, quite accurately, he interpreted as an instruction to follow, and which he did not disobey.

After they had gone, Jessie said, 'You *are* surely nearly finished with the *Book* by now, Charles?' and I experienced a moment's confusion, wondering if I were asleep or awake, since her question was so similar to the one her likeness had asked in my dream.

'I am still labouring, Jessie,' I said.

'Well, I would like to see what is needed to make your labours complete,' she said. Again, I was struck by this echo of my dream, and half expected her to say something about my last breath. What she in fact said was, 'Let us reconvene in the library in half an hour, when we can make a plan of attack.' And she too rose and departed.

Her use of the plural pronoun disturbed me. I did not know what she meant by it but I sensed that the time for taking my leave of Glen Conach House was approaching faster than I had anticipated. I have looked daily for a letter from Sir John, as eagerly as the Baron looks for one from his son, but we both remain disappointed. God forbid that I am obliged to go back to my mother.

I had left my transcription of the Latin and my English translation in a drawer of the desk in the library and, after a hurried retreat to my room to ease a certain queasiness of the bowels, I went there at once, intending to remove a good number of the sheets and put them out of sight, so that Jessie would not discover that both transcription and translation were finished. Alas, when I entered the library I found that she had been too quick for me, and was already seated at the desk with all my sheets, covered densely in my handwriting, spread out before her. She gathered them and took them to the great table, where she sat down again and asked me to place the *Book of Conach* in front of her too. She then began to read, turning my sheets and the folios of the *Book* – as if she were comparing the transcription with the original and making a judgement of the quality of my translation against both. I tolerated this for a few minutes and then begged her to ask me any questions she might have about my work. She looked at me as if I were an impudent boy and she my governess.

'Please, Charles, let me read in peace. Amuse yourself among the other books for a little while. Then we will talk.'

I saw that she was deadly serious, and also that there was no pretence at all in the manner of her reading: she *was* judging my work! This was a more formidable Jessie than I had ever thought to encounter. Somewhat piqued, I roamed the shelves in search of something I had not yet read, but I could not settle. It was not long, however, before she summoned me to sit with her.

'Oh, Charles,' she said, in a chiding though not too severe tone. 'What would Papa think of you if he knew of your deceit? What if I were to tell him that you are *not* still labouring, but lazing at his expense? Well, he might not be surprised or even much care. Mama, I am sure, would care very much if I told *her*. But what fashes me more is what I said to you weeks ago – the story of Conach is not very engaging. Your translation is accurate enough, but do you not find him the dullest of heroes? He is so priggish and superior I want to slap him, and his extreme forms of penitence are revolting. He is a rank hypocrite too – I don't believe he was any holier than the abbot he so despised. As for his wandering about clad only in a sack all the time, it is quite ridiculous – he would have died of cold his first winter here. Well, we must work with the clay we have, but we cannot let *our* hermit go out into the world half finished. We must add the other stories about him – the ones I have told you – and one or two more.'

ME: 'There are more?'

JESSIE: 'I am sure there must be. The more miracles he performs, the better.'

ME (attempting to reassert my authority): 'Jessie, this is a document of antiquity. I am not writing a romance.'

J: 'Oh, but whoever composed it was doing just that. You surely don't believe any of it is true?'

ME: 'I believe it is *genuine*, which is not the same. I cannot invent things and add them simply to make it more interesting.'

J: 'But writers of romance do that all the time.'

ME: 'I am a historian, Jessie.'

J: 'And historians do too, I am sure. They want their heroes to look as heroic as possible. Besides, I thought you were an antiquarian. Have I shocked you, Charles? Surely no more than you have shocked me. And *surely* it is not unreasonable to include, in a book about Conach, *all* the stories that exist concerning him?'

ME: 'It might be acceptable to mention them in an introduction or an appendix, but not as if they were part of the original document.'

J: 'I am glad you concur that they should be included. Very well. Let us proceed with that as our plan for the time being. We can make a decision on how to arrange these items later.'

I could not let this pass, and asked her if she meant to be involved in the work which hitherto had been mine alone. She said she had decided that this would be both amusing and instructive to us both, and had already added a few notes in the margins, to which she hoped I had no objection. I said that I had very strong objections, and observed that it was strange that her father had invited me to undertake the translation when there was an erudite scholar already under his roof. She answered very firmly that she understood I had invited myself, that she was her father's daughter so it was not in the least strange that she resided here, and that, given my past behaviour towards her and what she knew of my character I was in no position to refuse to agree.

Had we been playing a game of draughts that would have been a king of hers capturing three of my men in one move, I think. I recalled my dream and felt a little more unwell, for when she mentioned my character it occurred to me that she might have found and read *my* journal before I hid it, and yet be too cunning to tell me. I determined that, for now, I should acquiesce to her proposal, and said so.

'Then I am happy again, Charles!' she said, clapping her hands and transforming herself instantly into the Jessie over whom I once thought I had some mastery. Her face was bright with pleasure – I was both repelled by and attracted to her. Mr Gibb, I said to myself, you are swimming in deep waters now.

She announced that we should do no more manuscript work for the rest of the morning, but celebrate our new alliance with a walk up the glen. I had been to the so-called hermitage, she said (this part of my adventure with her father being no secret), but she herself was doubtful that the cave had ever been the home of the venerable hermit. She wished now to show me two other places that had long been associated with 'Saint Conach' in the minds of the local people. The day was fine and if we left quickly and discreetly then nobody – by which she surely meant her mother – would miss her. 'Certainly nobody will miss *you*,' she added.

So it was that ten minutes later we had slipped away and were walking up the glen, the Scaurs on our left and the river and the harvest work some distance to our right. We crossed the burn that flows from Conach's Linn, and far above us I could see where the cave must be, but this was not our destination. I thought I was in good marching trim but Jessie is sturdier and swifter than I am ever likely to be. After going half a mile or so further, the way began to narrow, and drew us towards the river, where the hardy alder and birch trees grow quite thickly. But as we approached the water the path suddenly turned away again and we climbed a short, stony incline on to a mossy sward, about fifty yards in length and half as wide, sheltered on three sides by rocks and pine trees. The damp green carpet was dotted here and there with clumps of bog-cotton and a few boulders, but was otherwise unremarkable. It was here that Jessie stopped, and spoke.

'Elspeth's grandmother – Granny Ally, as we call her – has a story about this place. She and others older than her say that this is where Saint Conach had his cabin.'

'Why do they call him a saint?' I asked. 'He was never canonised by any church.'

'Is that what causes saintliness?' she answered swiftly. 'Perhaps it is enough that the common people thought him a good man.'

'But you have read the *Book*,' I said. 'You know he was no saint. Not an hour since, you called him a prig.'

'That is how I read his character as it is in the *Book*. But the *Book* tells also of the sacrifice he made of himself,' she said. 'I told you before, *that* story is known to the people too, although they seldom speak of it. He refused to betray those he was protecting. Our people would judge that a saintly act, a heroic act.'

'Ah, now you are confusing saints and heroes,' I said. Her reasoning was quite unreasonable. 'But did you not describe Conach as the dullest of heroes?'

'I am not confusing anything,' she replied. 'What the *Book* says and what the old folk think are different. And, whatever he was, they also say that this is where he had his abode.'

'On what evidence?' I asked.

'The word of their ancestors,' she said. 'It is what they were told by their grannies, and their grannies by theirs, and so on all the way back to when Conach lived.'

'The tales of old wives!' I said.

'See how the bog-cotton has been left unpicked?' she answered. 'Everywhere else the women pick it in June, when it is new. They use it to make candle wicks, and great quantities of it go to stuff cushions. It is also used to staunch intimate blood. But here they leave it, because this is Conach's place.'

'But why, on that account, would they leave it?' I asked.

'Because it is like him. When the seeds first turn to cotton, it is pure and white. But as the summer passes bits are blown away and only the scraps of an old man's beard are left – as they are now.'

I could not stop myself from laughing. If that was evidence, I said, then I had better take lessons in antiquarianism from the old wives.

'Perhaps you should,' she said. 'Old wives' tales they may be, but they are still told. What would you put in their stead? You may search all you like but nothing remains of Conach's cabin. The *Book* mentions a stone carved with a cross, under which Conach's bones should lie. There is no such stone here. Only the stories remain.'

'But to pretend that this is where he lived, because bog-cotton grows here and is like his beard, is ridiculous. Even if there were traces of a dwelling or a grave, it would still be nonsense.'

'I pretend nothing. And that is not what I said. They believe he lived here because they were told so, not because of the superstition about the bog-cotton. It is plain that the superstition must have grown upon the story that was handed down, not the other way round. Whether the story is true or not is another matter.'

'If they are right,' I said, 'which I do not concede for an instant, then this must also be where Conach wielded the knife with such terrible effect.'

But she either did not or chose not to hear me. Already she was marching onward. 'Come with me, Charles,' she called, 'and I will show you something else.'

We returned to the path by the river, and proceeded still further up the glen. The way grew very steep and rugged and the river narrowed, but it was not tumultuous because, apart from the thunderstorm, there has been so little rain of late. Jessie sprang on ahead and I clambered behind, until she brought me to a spot by a pool, made shady by the overhanging branches of birches covered in moss.

'You will recall the passage in the *Book*, Charles,' she said, as I regained my breath, 'in which Conach goes away to pray, and meets the madman.'

'And they argue, and the madman steals his psalter,' I replied. 'Yes, I recall it. Are you about to tell me that this was the scene of the wicked act?'

'So our old people maintain.'

'And what is the evidence this time?'

'None of the kind you seek,' Jessie said. 'The only evidence is in the stories and the situation itself. Is this not a very wild and romantic spot? Can you not imagine the scene? Can you not hear the argument between the two hermits, the one saintly and the other insane?'

'I can,' I said, 'but anybody can imagine such a scene. It does not make it fact.'

'Oh, I detest facts!' she cried. 'If we had only facts, we would not have the part the otter plays when it rescues the psalter from the river – such a bonnie detail!'

'But that,' I said, 'is nothing more than a fairy tale, even supposing the first part of the story to have some basis in reality. And, if I may remind you, the otter is *your* detail.'

'Is it?' she said. 'I can hardly remember. What does that matter anyway? I could also show you where Conach spoke with the wolf, or where he threw himself in the bed of nettles, but I have no evidence to persuade you of the truth of those locations either. Charles, do you not see that it is quite impossible to *prove* anything about Conach or any of what that dirty old manuscript says about him? It is all lost in the mist of time. Do you not mind that I warned you of that mist on your second day here?'

'And do you not mind, Jessie,' I said, 'that I told you I accepted the fact of the *Book* but not that what it contained were facts? I am not interested in fairy tales and the prattling of old women. I am interested that the *Book* exists, that it *is* a dirty old manuscript. It is *not* lost in the mist of time. It has survived. That is why it matters.'

'It matters to you,' she said, 'only as a means to an end, which is to be provided with food and shelter at my father's expense. That is your sole reason for being here. You do not care about the *Book* at all.'

'Then we are the same,' I said.

'No,' she said, 'we are different. I am like the old women you disparage. If I grow old I will tell the same stories that they do, because the stories belong here. Do you not see how completely apart we are from the world? You have come and you will go, and other men too, but we women – we cannot leave. We care about this glen. If the stories die then so does a part of the glen. But you, Charles, when you grow old what will you care about? I fear you may not even care about yourself.'

'You misread me, Jessie,' I said, knowing that she did not.

'No,' she said. 'I read you very well. My flaw is visible to all. Yours is hidden, but it is there just the same.'

She had come very close to me. We stood with only two feet between us and yet, in that wild and romantic spot, as she had designated it, I felt that we were as far apart in our thinking as two stars, which seem so near to one another when seen from our own planet but which are in fact separated by a greater distance than any of which we can conceive.

More immediately, I found that her face, flushed with emotion, the ringlets that framed it and were damp from physical exertion as was her brow, her tall, ungainly figure which yet was shown to its best effect in the simple dress she wore, her eager blue eyes, the little red 'o' of her mouth, even the birthmark which seemed not ill-formed but to be a part of her natural being – in short, I found everything about her enticing and endearing, while everything within me fought against that discovery and wished to flee from her and from it and from the place to which she had brought me. But I did not flee. We were such strange companions, neither liking nor disliking one another, and unmatched in our social positions, and yet there was a mutual understanding of what was to take place. I put my hands upon her hips, and she put hers upon my shoulders, and I did not draw her into me any more than she voluntarily came to me, and our lips met. And then very quickly our hands strayed elsewhere, and things became undone, and in reply to an urgent inquiry which I made she whispered in my ear that *lassies ken mair than just auld wives' tales*, and what I will next inscribe here, in order to draw a veil over the occasion since even to think on it now, several hours later, both excites and appals me, is a device used (so I believe) by authors of a certain class of novel to represent the closing of the bedchamber door, viz:

*****

Friday, 15th September 1809

I have been too busy this last week to write anything in this journal. The harvest is in full progress, and every able body from the clachan is out from dawn until dusk assisting with it. Jessie and I have had some further, somewhat rushed, lessons in what M. Voltaire calls natural philosophy, but we have neither of us been able to avoid being recruited for other duties – in her case, by her mother, in mine by her father. All the other men being occupied with the harvest, the Baron insisted on my returning to the occupation of dyke-builder on three separate days. I thought I would be killed by this, but to my surprise found my blood invigorated and my limbs given new power and skill, perhaps as a consequence of my educational endeavours with Jessie. Mr Dunning does not toil in the parks, but Daniel Haddow does. He is as brown as a nut and has had all his youthfulness restored to him.

For a week I have not even entered the library, let alone looked at the *Book* or my translation, and indeed even to think about them nauseates me. It is a peculiar thing that, despite our new intimacy, I see no prospect of Jessie and I resolving our differences about what a new presentation of Conach's life should or should not include. I suppose it does not much matter, as I will take both transcription and translation with me when I depart this place, which will be soon enough whether I have somewhere to go to or not. I only hope that I leave no trace of myself behind. She assures me that all is safe in that regard but I do not altogether trust her.

The Baron, when he is not anxious for news of his son or building the dyke, now has his head full of the coming festivities to mark the hairst. He has set a date for the dance, the last day of this month, which falls on a Saturday. Thus there will be a pagan thanksgiving one evening, and a Christian one the next morning under Mr Dunning. But I shall be away before these things happen.

I should say that Dunning has been civil to me since the Baron and I saw him naked under Conach's downpour, and seems quite calm. On Monday morning we exchanged greetings as he rode by us in the high park on his old nag. He said he was going far up the glen to see an old man who lived alone and had been reported by a shepherd's lad to be very ill. Glen Conach said that this was the man he had told me of, who was once nearly made a slave by pirates. On Wednesday I learned from the Baron that the minister, on arriving at the remote habitation, had found his parishioner dead, and had had to ride back again and call on Davie Nicol to go with him next day to help dig a grave, for it was too rough and too far to carry a coffin all the way to the kirkyard. After they had interred the body and Mr Dunning had said prayers over it, they came home, and he entered the death in the register. The Baron says that with that old fellow's decease there is no person now living more than four miles beyond the clachan this side of the mountains. He sees this as a mark of decline.

We had word yesterday from Jock McLeish, the carter, that the army in the Low Countries has abandoned any attempt to capture Antwerp. As this was the whole purpose of the expedition, it seems an extraordinary turn of events. McLeish was adamant, however, that the people of Forfar, who are as keen for news of their sons as Glen Conach is for news of his, believe that a large part of the army is being withdrawn across the sea, and that many of the troops are sick with a fever. The carter brought with him some newspapers from August which contain none of this, and we must await a further batch before we may learn the truth.

Wednesday, 20th September 1809

In one more week the present work in the fields will be complete, although other crops will be taken in during October – potatoes, neeps, bere, etc. – and the garden vegetables such as cabbages and kale will be cut as long as frost does not kill them. I am no expert when it comes to inspecting the quality of grain but the quantity amassed is impressive, and everybody seems pleased. Very soon, some of the men and boys will choose the cattle they intend to sell and drive them a hundred miles to join the throng at the Falkirk Tryst, and that will be the end of the season's work.

I have received no letter from Oxenfoord. I must be away from here before the month is out, and it is therefore too late to write anywhere else to beg a temporary haven. On the subject of havens, the one where I have been mooring often this last fortnight has been declared out of bounds owing to the risk of taking on unwanted cargo. I miss our lessons but the truth is, it is too deep a harbour for me. When we are not philosophising I have little to say to Jessie that does not lead us into dispute. I see her mother in her more and more and this is disquieting now that I have been where I have been.

I always did intend to leave before summer's end. I have resided here nearly three months, my work on the *Book of Conach* is done, and it remains for me only to make my excuses to my host and take to the road.

Still, I will be sorry to say goodbye to these people, and will not soon forget them. My fondness for them is however not greater than my desire to be in or near Edinburgh – that is, to be in a place somewhat more touched by civilisation than Glen Conach ever can be, and having more to amuse a man of my intellect than this house, despite its library, ever can possess. I am, moreover, highly uncertain how much longer my present relations with Jessie can be sustained without leading to one of several falls, all unfortunate: either she falls in love with me again and I am obliged to be cruel to her; or I fall so out of favour with her that she denounces me for the villain I am; or she falls victim to a common female indisposition and I am obliged to marry her; or we are discovered hypothesising and I am felled, beaten, murdered or eaten – or some combination of these – on the orders of her father. Any of these eventualities would be undesirable. On the other hand, if I go within the next week, the least damage will be done to me, to Jessie and to her honour. It is plain to me that, as things stand between us, I will not break her heart, since I am clearly not the first to have toyed with her affections or engaged her in scientific investigations. She will be very angry at first, especially as I will have to leave without saying farewell, but I do not think she will regret my going, indeed may even be glad of it. I will not be here, of course, to see if I am right.

Saturday, 23rd September 1809

Another carrier was here from Forfar with, among other things, some copies of newspapers from the past fortnight. The reports are thin, yet seem to confirm that there has been a general retreat from the Dutch islands and that the bulk of the great force assembled has been brought back to England. We do not know whether the 42nd was involved in the siege of Flushing or in some other part of the campaign, and therefore have no indication of what dangers Captain Milne faced or what heroics he may have performed, and this ignorance causes the Baron much frustration. When the Baroness tells him that he must calm himself he becomes more impassioned still and has to go to the high park and work it out of himself with a yard or two of dyke. I must say, for a gentleman who claims to disdain that kind of labour he has a remarkable capacity for it.

Thursday, 28th September 1809

Jessie in a private moment this morning asked me if I was avoiding her by chance or design, and did I not wish to resume our acquaintance, as she would be able to receive me in another day or two? I made some exculpatory mumbles by which even I was not persuaded, and knew – know – that I must leave at once, for if I take her up again I dread what might be the outcome. I then told a downright lie, which was one concocted and intended for the Baron but which I suddenly thought could serve as well with his daughter.

'Jessie,' I said, 'I beg your forgiveness if I am out of sorts. These last three nights I have been disturbed by a most unpleasant dream. My old mother, who ever since my father's death has been an example to me of fortitude in the face of adversity, came to me in my sleep, pale and weeping, and when I asked her what was wrong she said that she was terrified that I would not be at her bedside in her last illness, nor bear her coffin to the grave. I remonstrated with her but she faded before my eyes.'

I said that I thought my sleeping mind must have been influenced by the story of the man who died alone far up the glen but, the dream having recurred on two successive nights, I was left with a great fear for the health of my mother, and this was what was preoccupying me. The fear was so strong that I felt I might have to go to her.

Jessie gave a kind of snort and said that in all the weeks I had been at the house I had not once mentioned my mother or her fortitude, and that she did not believe I put any more store in dreams than I did in old wives' tales. Furthermore, I had been 'out of sorts' for a week. In short, she scoffed at the notion that I had had any such dream and said I was once again demonstrating disrespect for her intelligence. She then left in a state of dudgeon – whether that should be high, deep or great I am never sure – and I did not see her again until dinner, when she was very cool to everybody and hardly glanced at me. I cannot blame her – it was impetuous and stupid of me to try such an excuse on her at all.

After dinner, Jessie and the Baroness retired early to their rooms. I was left alone with Glen Conach in the great hall, which is to be decorated tomorrow in readiness for the harvest dance. I decided to act upon the moment. The Baron was sifting through the numerous papers and journals that were piled around his chair, as if he might have missed some vital piece of information concerning his son. When he had completed this exercise he sat back heavily and tugged at his hair, which the Baroness has been unable to get at with scissors for some while. The unconscious effect was to make his head look as if a gale had just blown over it. He stared at me and said, 'My dear Gibb, is that you? I did not see you. How long have you been here?'

'Since we both sat down after dinner,' I replied, and leapt in before he could begin a fresh hunt among the papers. 'Sir, I must beg your attention. You have been so hospitable to me in allowing me to stay here all summer. I came – you invited me to come – to see and make a translation of the *Book of Conach*, and this I have done. I had wished to present you with a fair copy of that translation, but I regret that this will have to be postponed to a later date. The fact is, I must take my leave of you, and at once – tomorrow.'

'Tomorrow?'

'Yes, and I must make a very early start, and so will not see Lady Glen Conach or Miss Milne again.'

'But you cannot leave without saying farewell. And what about the dancing?'

'It is essential that I go as quickly as possible to my mother, who I am sure is very ill.'

'You have had a letter from her?'

When he asked this I almost said yes, for it occurred to me that he would never remember whether a letter had come for me or not. His lady, however, would and, since I had spoken of a dream to Jessie, I thought it wise to stick to that story. I therefore repeated, more or less, what I had told her, emphasising the profound effect the dream had had on me and the absolute conviction I had that I must go to my mother at once. The Baron, good man that he is, swallowed it in one gulp.

'It's a powerful thing, a dream,' he said. 'We are a rational people now, of course, and have given up burning witches and seeing angels and the like, but I have heard many tales of dreams and premonitions, what the old people – the Gaelic people, I mean – used to call the second sight. Well, Charles, I must put myself in your place. Suppose that I had a dream like yours – about Sandy, for example – would I be able to resist its message? I would not. You must go, but you will miss the dancing. Could you not stay until then?'

'I should have heeded the first dream and gone two days ago,' was my reply.

'Well, I understand the need for urgency. You would enjoy the dance so much, but it cannot be helped. You will return, though, will you not?'

That, I said, would depend on the condition in which I found my mother. Even if she were well, I did not think I could desert her at once, and winter was approaching. He nodded and pondered, and while he did this I assured him that I would copy out the translation and either send it to him or deliver it in person next spring. This seemed to cheer him. 'Perhaps Sandy will be home,' he said, 'and you will meet and become friends.' He hoisted himself out of his chair and hugged me like a bear. 'My dear Charles, my dear fellow, we will miss you,' he said, and I felt as low and vile in my being as I have ever felt. He made me drink some whisky with him, and then became distracted by the newspapers again, and I crept away to my chamber to write this entry. I am almost done. I will wrap this journal and all the sheets relating to the *Book* in oilcloth, pack my satchel and try for a few hours' sleep, then leave before dawn comes and the house awakes. And so, farewell, Glen Conach! Despite my promise to the man who bears your name, I do not expect to see you again.

Book of Conach

Chapter 15

Of some miracles wrought by Conach

On another occasion, winter was so long and harsh that even Conach and his servant were forced to take shelter in the village, for they had neither food nor fuel left in their cabins, and they the most frugal of men. The people welcomed them but warned that they too were in a parlous state, with most of their stores consumed and their animals left with no fat upon them. They were surviving on a little oatmeal mixed with the blood of cattle, which they let from the beasts in small quantities every day. Yet now they feared that this practice could not be continued, for the cows, which had some while since stopped giving milk, would be calving in the spring, and would need all their strength until then.

Then Conach said to the head of the house where they were, 'Give me two pails,' and to Talorg his servant he said, 'Make your knife as sharp as you can, and give it to me also.' They did as he bade them, and he said, 'Let me be alone with your cow.' So they left him alone with the beast and retired to the other end of the house, and for a long time they saw him not but heard him singing quietly, and it was neither psalm nor milking song but a strange chant in a tongue unknown. And then he called to them, 'Come hither and take these pails, for they are too heavy for me.' And they went and found him in the darkness, and the one pail was full to the brim with blood and the other was full to the brim with milk. And the cow was as fat as if she had been grazing all day in a spring meadow.

The people marvelled at these things, and one of them said, 'With what did you feed her?' He said, 'With dreams of summer.' And another said, 'To release all this blood, how deep you must have cut her! She will surely die.' Conach gave the knife back to Talorg and said, 'Where have I cut her?' And they searched and found no wound upon her. Even the scars where they themselves had drawn blood could not be discerned.

Then a third said, 'We have not enough oatmeal for all this blood.' Conach said, 'Go to the girnel and fetch more.' They knew it to be empty and none would go but one small child, and when she went she cried out, 'The sides of the girnel are broken,' because the meal therein was too much to be contained.

Conach performed many other miracles, which were attested to by honest witnesses, yet because their names, except that of his servant, are not recorded, some have questioned the truth of the events which I will next record. More questionable, though, is how such doubters will enter the Kingdom of God. For heaven's gate opens only after death, but is forever closed to those who lack faith while they tread the dust of this earth, even if they be monks or priests. Therefore it is as fruitless to dispute the occurrence of miracles as it is to argue against the love of God and the life everlasting.

One day, some men were fishing the river with a net. They saw Conach walking on the bank and called to him, but he did not hear them. When he came closer he seemed to notice them for the first time, and said, 'Friends, will you give me and my servant a fish?' They said, 'Father, we have been toiling all day and caught nothing.' He said, 'Cast your net further upstream, at the place between two rocks, and when my servant comes, give him what fish you can spare us.' And he went on his way up the glen. So they took their net from the water and cast it at the place between two rocks, and in a while the net was so heavy with salmon that it took six men to haul it from the river. Then they looked about them, and saw Conach's servant Talorg coming towards them. 'Take these, the two biggest fish in our net, to your master,' they said, 'and give him our thanks, for without him we would have had nothing.' Talorg said, 'What has my master to do with it?' They said, 'He told us where to fish.' Talorg said, 'You are mistaken, for these last two days he has been deep in meditation in his cabin.' They said, 'He was here not an hour since, and you must have passed each other on the path.' Talorg said, 'I passed no one. I swear to you, it is two days since he came forth.' And they were alike confused. But Talorg took the fish they offered, and went back up the glen.

When he returned to Conach he found him tending a fire, and told him what had happened. Conach said, 'I was asleep, and dreamt I saw you carrying the fish, and I awoke and made this fire to cook them on.'

On several occasions Conach mended the wings of birds and the legs of animals by laying his hands upon them. He cured a man of the palsy by washing him in the river with his own hands, and he cured a woman of lameness by touching her with a stone plucked from the bed of the river. He healed children through prayer when their fever could not be touched by natural remedies. The people who saw these things knew him to be a holy man, and were eager to worship the God he worshipped. And Conach taught them and baptised them with oil, and when he had no more oil he baptised with water.

Thus it can surely be said that if Conach wrought one miracle he wrought many, not least the bringing of so many souls into the arms of Christ. The power of the Spirit was in him, and though he was not sanctified by the Church he was blessed by God, and especially because he was not free of sin, but stumbled in the dust and rose again.

Yet sometimes Conach grew weary, and was impatient with the people because they expected him always to be strong, and their belief wavered when he was not. 'You must have faith even in adversity,' he told them. 'Indeed, I tell you, in hard times you need faith more than ever. When the tree sheds its leaves, only faith will restore them. When the land freezes, only faith will melt the ice. When disease carries off your mothers and fathers, only faith will convince you that you will not also die. When your enemies kill your sons and enslave your daughters, only faith will bring you more children.' And if they still complained, he said, 'How did you live before I came here? Did you not rise from the sickbed and labour again? Did you not make repairs after the flood or the fire? And will you live in less hope now that you know Christ and are assured of eternal life?' And he left them, and was not seen among them for many a day.

Chapter 16

Of solitude and silence

These are the words of Conach as they were told to me by an old man, who learned them from his father, and he from his father, and seven generations before that.

'When a prisoner breaks his bonds, the shackles are still about his limbs. When a dog snaps the chain that has tethered him, he drags a portion of it with him wheresoever he runs.

'Thus when I left the monastic life and sought solitude, I took with me some of what I left behind, and not least I took myself.

'When I arrived in this place I gave loud thanks to God, and sang psalms to Him, and praise-songs of my own making.

'I went into the wilderness in search of solitude, and found that I was not alone. Birds and animals are always around me. The lowly toad and the mighty eagle are alike my companions.

'So too I went in search of silence, but far though I am from the tumult of crowds there is quiet neither at night nor in the day; for a wolf and a stag, an owl and a madman call in the moonlight; birds sing from dawn until dusk; all manner of creatures make noise as they move through the forest; the forest itself rustles and cracks; and wind and water make constant music, sometimes gentle, sometimes fierce.

'Yet I perceive that this is solitude, though I share it with others. And truly this, though there be sounds within it, is silence. It is the silence of the bell that rings without its clapper; the silence of the slow, dark river's flow; the silence of a deer grazing on the far hill. It is the silence that crowns all, the silence of God before He created the heaven and the earth. I have learned in these my old years that to pray aloud to Him is not to pray at all; that to sing praise-songs is not to praise Him. I have learned that the highest form of prayer is to listen in silence to God; that speech is as shallow as time, silence as deep as eternity. I have learned that I must be a deer grazing on the far hill, a slow, dark river flowing, a bell without its clapper. These I must become to enter the eternal kingdom.'

Conach and the Wild Man

(School of Scottish Studies Sound Archive: Geordie Kemp, Glen Conach, Angus, recorded by Dr Ken Clavers, 1985; transcribed by Dr Matthew Tybault, 2020)

Noo I mind hearin a story that Conach wisna the first hermit in the glen. In Conach's day it wis a gey different place fae whit it is noo. Nooadays there's roads an fenced-in fields an ferms an the like, but back then it wis whit they cry the Dark Ages and that wis on accoont o there bein a lot mair ignorance an a lot mair trees aboot. The trees werna lined up in raws like they are noo, they were mair spread oot an grew whauriver they wanted tae growe, an they merched higher up the glen an aa. The forest then wis aa kind o trees – pines an oaks an rowans an birks an siclike – an there wis aa kind o beasts bidin in it. It wis an awfie wild place that maist folk steyed awa fae, an that wis fine for Conach, he wid gang there tae offer sangs an prayers tae God, an the wilder it wis the mair he likit it. An whiles he wid sing the words fae his hert, an whiles he wid tak oot his psalter, the book fu o sacred verses and bonnie decorations that he himsel had made, an he wid sing fae thon. An there's somethin else ye should ken: whitever tongue it wis that Conach had, it wisna the wey we speak nooadays. Mibbe he had the Gaelic, I dinna ken, but mibbe it wis an even aulder speak nor that, that's lost tae us noo. Onywey, there's a wee bit Gaelic in this story, but I'm no certain that it really belangs.

This ae day, Conach wis busy singin awa when suddenly he saw a craitur runnin oot the trees, an it wis a man, a wild, hairy, mad-lookin chiel aa covered in glaur an cuts an bruises, wi nae a steek on him but a croon o thorns on his heid. He cam richt up tae Conach gey fierce like, an Conach hauds up his hand an says tae him, 'In the name o the Faither, the Son an the Holy Ghost I say tae ye, stop, an tell me yir name. How is it that ye bide here in this dowie place wi jist the beasts an the birds for yir companions?'

'Aweel,' the craitur says, 'my true name is lost tae me, but the birds ca me Fear nan Coilltean.' (That's the bit o Gaelic I mentioned, an it means Man o the Widds.) 'Langsyne I wis like you,' the craitur says tae him, 'a Christian an a man o noble bluid, but since the madness cam on me I couldna bide amang ordinary men sae for mony a year I hae bedd here whaur naebody can find me. An I beg ye noo tae gang awa an lea me in peace.'

'An how did this madness come on ye?' Conach spiers.

'There wis a great war on,' says Fear nan Coilltean, 'an there wis a great battle atween twa muckle armies, though I canna mind noo wha wis on the ae side an wha wis on the tither. But I wis in the mids o this battle, an aw o a sudden the clouds pairtit an a voice like thunder spoke tae me fae heaven. "Man, man," it says tae me, "the guilt o the bluid o the slain is upon ye an on nane ither, an you alane maun pey the price. Fae this oor tae ye dee, ye are banished tae the wilds tae live oot yir days amang the beasts o the forest." An I wis gruppit wi a terrible fear an I couldna dae ocht but flee awa as fest's my legs wid cairry me, tae at last I cam tae this dour place whaur I maun bide until daith. Sae it has been ever sinsyne, an I implore ye no tae bring the wrath o God doon upon my heid again, but gae yir wa's and lea me tae my fate.'

Weel, Conach wis hert-sair tae hear sic a tale, but he wisna for gaen awa and he tellt this tae Fear nan Coilltean, an promised tae pray tae God on his behalf. Then Fear nan Coilltean gied a great greetin skirl an fled awa intae a secret pairt o the forest whaur Conach couldna follow. But the next day, when Conach begun tae pray an sing tae God again, did the wild man no appear wi his hands ower his lugs an the bluid poorin doon whaur his flesh wis riven wi the croon o thorns, beggin Conach tae lea him alane? An the guid saint wis hert-seik for the man an prayed tae God for mercy upon him, but there wis nae mercy gien an Fear nan Coilltean fled awa intae the forest again. An on the third day, when Conach begun tae sing his psalms, it happened that the wild man wis nestin in a tree abune his heid, an he drapped doon an seized the precious psalter an ran awa wi it, an he wis that angry at Conach that he ran the lenth o the glen an when he cam tae the widest pairt o the river he flung the book intil it an it sunk oot o sicht. Syne he cam back tae whaur Conach wis waitin an said, 'Noo, will ye gae yir wa's an lea me in peace?' An Conach said that he widna. 'Aa this time I hae been prayin tae God tae hae mercy on ye,' he said, 'an you repay me wi this evil deed. Ye're a thrawn chiel, but I tell ye I am mair thrawn than you are, an I winna gang oot o this glen.' Then Fear nan Coilltean said, 'Ye mak my penance ten times waur nor it wis, but I canna defeat ye. Sae I will awa tae the benmaist pairt o the forest, and ye will see me never nae mair until my daith is upon me.' And awa he gaed, yowlin an howlin, an for mony a day Conach saw him nae mair, an wis left tae his ain sel amang the trees. But whiles he wid hear a doolsome skirl fae the benmaist pairt o the forest, an he kent it wis the madman in his torment.

But a strange thing happened atween whiles, an it wis this. An otter that wis huntin in the river brocht the psalter up fae the mirk an cairried it tae Conach, an the lines an letters o it werna spoilt in the least.

Weel, time gaed by an on a certain day when Conach wis in the forest the madman appeared on a craig abune him, an he wis fell sair an seik-lookin. He set up sic a yellochin an skirlin an sae deaved Conach that he couldna pray or sing or dae onythin. An Fear nan Coilltean wis threapin that he bude tae dee, an that as he had aince been a Christian he wanted tae receive the bluid an body o Christ afore he left this world. Conach didna ken if this madman should receive the sacramental breid an wine, an forby he didna believe whit the man wis sayin, sae he retired tae his ain wee cabin tae pray. But efter a while he wis vexed, an he sent his servant tae spier o the madman whit mainner o daith he wid thole an if this wis the day. 'Tell yir maister that this is the day,' Fear nan Coilltean says, 'an it is by stane that I will dee.'

Sae the servant reported tae Conach the madman's words. An Conach said, 'I doot he disna ken whit he is sayin. Awa an spier o him again the mainner o his daith an if this is the day.' An this time Fear nan Coilltean says, 'Tell yir maister that this is the day, an it is by widd that I will dee.' When the servant gaed back tae Conach wi this, Conach said, 'Aye, I wis richt. He is as gyte as ever he wis. But spier o him again an see whit he says.' Sae the servant gaed tae the madman a third time, an Fear nan Coilltean says, 'Tell yir maister that this is the day, an it is by water that I will dee.' Weel, Conach wis certain sure then that he wis either mad or tellin lees, for how could ony man dee a threefold daith like yon, an he widna gie him the sacraments. An aa day the yowlin an skirlin rang through the forest, tae Conach thocht that he himsel micht be driven mad wi it.

As the eenin cam on, Fear nan Coilltean grew quiet, an drew closer tae the cabin whaur Conach wis at his devotions. He stretched himsel oot on the grund an in a maist pitiful voice he says, 'Maister, hae mercy on me. Soon my penance will be by wi, an I will be taen up tae heaven. I beg ye tae let me confess my sins, an syne gie me the sacraments that I may gae my wa's an never fash ye mair.' An the tears ran doon his wretched face an body even tae his fingers an taes, an Conach wis sair moved an saw that he wis no lang for this world an gied him absolution an the breid and wine that in the auld faith wis the bluid an body o Christ. An nae sooner had he done this than Fear nan Coilltean louped up an ran awa doon the glen. An when he wis close by the river some laddies seen him an chased him, an ane o them threw a stane at him an it hut him on the heid, an he slippit an fell doon the bank intae a fish-trap, an wis pierced wi a widden stake that wis stickin up in the water, an his body bent ower an he drooned. An sae whit he had prophesied aboot himsel wis true, an he dee'd three daiths on the same day, by stane, by widd an by water. An that's aa the story I ken aboot Conach an the wild man, Fear nan Coilltean.

Journal of Charles Kirkliston Gibb

Saturday, 30th September 1809

Today I take up my pen and it has in it the weight of a stone. I can scarcely bear to wield it, nor to open this book again, but I must, if only to break the bleak spell that has descended on us. There is a line in the poem *Gertrude of Wyoming*, when the tragedy has occurred, and the Indian chief stands silent witness to the young hero's grief – 'but words had none to soothe the grief that knew not consolation's name'. The poet might almost have been here in this glen when he wrote that.

Yes, I have returned. It proved more difficult to leave than I could have imagined.

Yesterday morning – only yesterday! – I awoke when it was still dark, dressed quickly and quietly, took my belongings down the stair, stepped over the dogs now so indifferent to me that they did not stir, descended to the kitchen for some oatcakes and a lump of cheese, then let myself out and began to walk. The dew was heavy on the grass and the air was cool, yet so fresh that I thought myself cleansed just by striding through it. Soon the light was filling the sky before me – another happy augur, as I thought – and I even began to sing a few notes, caring less about where my destination lay than that it lay somewhere. Meanwhile, I was a man at liberty, free once again of all responsibility. I felt sound in my body, and my conscience, which had given me a few buffets of late, grew lighter with every pace. After half an hour I paused, ate my breakfast, took some handfuls of water from a burn, and continued on my journey. I remember thinking, as the sun began to heat the day, how great was the contrast between this weather and that through which I had struggled when I came into the glen. Charles Kirkliston Gibb, I told myself, you are a rascal and a vagabond and always will be, and you have done the right thing by leaving those honest, settled people to their honest, settled lives.

It was about eight o'clock and I was still a mile distant from the mill at the Brig o' Conach when, coming over a little rise, I saw a horseman approaching. As we drew near each other I discerned, first by his red tunic and then by his grey breeches, that he was a soldier. When we were but a few yards apart I spied, hanging at his side, a sword in a scabbard, and hanging from his saddle, a military hat with the black feathers, chequered band and red hackle that marked him as an officer of the Black Watch. This is Sandy Milne come home already, I thought – what speed he has made! And at the same time I dearly wished that I had stepped off the track and hidden behind a boulder rather than have to introduce myself to Miss Jessie Milne's brother. In another moment, however, the soldier steadied his horse and disabused me of my mistake.

'Friend, am I right for Glen Conach House?' he called. He had black hair, a black moustache and a Highland voice. He seemed weary.

'You are,' I said. 'Six or seven miles straight up this road. Do you come with news, Sir?'

'I do,' he said. 'Are you from the house yourself?'

'I have been a guest there,' I said, 'and am now on my way south. If you bring word from the war, I know you will be welcome.'

He stared at me as if I were impertinent. 'And who is it I am addressing?'

I gave him my name. 'Mr Gibb?' he cried. 'Then I have a letter for you. Last night in Forfar, when they heard where I was bound, they fetched it to me. Wait now.'

He swung down from the horse and rubbed at his thighs and stretched himself. He was a man of impressive stature, and probably of great strength. 'God, but I think I will never get straight again,' he said. 'I have been three days in a coach and three on horseback, and am damned if I know which is worse. And I wish you were right, Sir, but I think I will not be welcome at all. I think they will wish me away to hell when they hear the news I have.'

'Is it of Captain Milne?' I said. 'I thought, when I saw you coming, that you were he.'

'Then you don't know him?' he replied. 'Ah, but you know his family. Well, Mr Gibb, if you can tell me something about them, perhaps I may find a way to soften the blow, although it will be hard enough even at that.'

His words disturbed me greatly. I asked, at once fearful of hearing his reply, 'He is wounded?'

He shook his head. 'I wish to God that was it.' He wiped the sleeve of his tunic across his brow and held out his hand, which I shook. 'I am Captain Donald MacKay,' he said. 'Captain Milne was my comrade, my fellow officer and my friend. I bring the worst possible news of him. I have come as fast as I can, so that they hear it from me and no one else – but, Mr Gibb, now that I am so near I find my courage ebbs at the prospect.'

The last words burst from him and were accompanied by a gruff bark or sob, which in so powerfully built a man sounded most pitiable. I said, 'Captain MacKay, you have made a long journey on your own. Will you not sit down for a minute, and tell me? That may make it less hard for you when you reach the house.'

'Thank you, Sir,' he answered, 'but if I sit I may never get up again. And I did not come all the way alone – I left a sergeant and a corporal at Forfar on regimental business. Do not take offence when I say that you are a stranger to me and, from what you have said, to Captain Milne too. My first and only duty is to tell his mother and father, nor do I wish that duty to be less hard than it must be. I am used to duty, and the harder it is the more I stick to it. I swore to him as he lay dying that I would do this, and I will.'

A thin, trickling burn ran beside the road just where we stood, and he crouched beside it to splash his face and drink, then let the horse take its refreshment. Only after this did he resume his tale.

'As soon as we landed at Deal I requested leave of absence to convey the news. My commanding officer said that it was not possible, my duty lay with my own Company. I said that I had put the care of my men in the hands of my junior officers and that not only were they content for me to go, they urged that I should. My commander said that he did not heed the urgings of lieutenants, ensigns and the like, to which I replied that either I would resign my commission or if he preferred he could have me shot as a deserter on my return, but I would go in any event. He relented – by God, they cannot afford to lose any more of us – but I must be back with the regiment in ten days. Oh, but I forgot your letter!'

He went to his horse and extracted an envelope, somewhat crumpled, from one of the saddlebags. I tore it open. It was from Oxenfoord – a brief note to say that Sir John could not extend an invitation to me to visit as he was most unwell and did not know when he would be better. I folded the letter – I might as well have dropped it on the ground – and put it in my pocket. I was deeply shocked by what Captain MacKay had told me.

'Sir,' I said, 'if you will permit me to walk beside your horse, I will escort you to Glen Conach House and introduce you to the Baron.'

'But you said you were leaving,' he said.

'I find, with the news you have brought, that I cannot go,' I replied.

He took my hand again. 'I am obliged to you, Mr Gibb,' he said. 'We will walk together.'

And without delay, he leading the horse, we set out on the road back to whence I had come.

True to his intention, he did not speak about the campaign or what had befallen Sandy Milne. For long periods we strode in silence, each consumed by his thoughts, and with the horse blowing its breath between us. Captain MacKay had a brisk, rough manner, no doubt the result of years of soldiering, but I thought there was a heart somewhere beneath that stony exterior. From time to time he remarked on a feature of the country which, he said, was not unlike the part he was from, north of Inverness. I made a few observations about the glen and its people, and the Baron and his family, but I noticed that each of us volunteered our information only in passing, and not in response to any direct question from the other. For two hours we made these halting exchanges while in contrast our onward march was steady, until the house came into view.

'I would be obliged if you would walk on, Mr Gibb,' he said, halting. 'I will ride in from here.' And he began to adjust his uniform and fix his hat upon his head.

I did as he asked. He waited until I was nearly at the door, which was wide to the day, before he urged his horse forward. The Baron's dogs came to bark at the stranger and this brought out the Baron himself, who must have been in the hall. He stopped and gave me a look of astonishment, and was about to speak when he saw Captain MacKay ride up and dismount. Sight of me, I think now, made him aware that something untoward was afoot, and the sombre expressions of myself and the Captain must also have disquieted him. The Captain dropped the reins, and the horse stood patiently while the dogs sniffed about it. The soldier approached the laird and, standing before him, removed his feathered hat and bowed his head.

'Sir,' he said, 'my name is Captain Donald MacKay of the 42nd Regiment of Foot, the Black Watch. Have I the honour of speaking to the father of Captain Alexander Milne?'

'You do, Sir,' the Baron said. Already his eyes were filling with dread, and I saw that he grasped at the word 'honour' as if it might shield him from evil. 'Do you bring a message from my son?'

'I regret to report, Sir –' the Captain continued '– I regret to be the bearer of such tidings, but I have come to tell you this myself – it is my most unhappy duty to inform you that your son, my comrade-in-arms, has died in the service of his king and country.'

At this the Baron let out a long, low moan and, suddenly transformed into a man ancient beyond his years, staggered a few paces. MacKay and I rushed to support him and between us we carried him inside, still uttering that awful moan.

The scenes which ensued will be vivid in my mind for as long as I live. The commotion brought everybody then in the house to the hall, and from there the word spread rapidly to the clachan and even to the men and women out on the land. I have never heard, and hope never to hear again, such sobs and cries as issued from the lips of father, mother and sister, and indeed from the servants and others as one by one they learned the bare bones of the news. Captain MacKay was urged to give the circumstances and manner of Sandy's death, which I will set out below, and his answers occasioned renewed anguish and weeping. Glen Conach, his head in his hands, lay so low on his chair that he was half on the floor, and rose only to reach out weakly and ineffectually to his wife and daughter. Jessie paced like a caged beast, weeping and wringing her hands and going towards first one parent then the other only to stop as if an invisible barrier lay between them. The Baroness, so self-controlling by habit, could not be consoled by husband or daughter, but waved off their vague caresses as one might wave away wasps, and sat like a pale statue with tears coursing down her face. Elspeth was caught in the middle, neither wholly family nor wholly servant, but she was as racked by lamentation as any. Captain MacKay stood like a craggy mountain amid it all. I was quite helpless. There was nothing either of us could do or say to relieve them of their agony.

Relief did come, though, and from an unexpected airt. Mr Dunning arrived after a quarter of an hour and, by a force of character which even his recent manners had not led me to suspect he possessed, began to establish a measure of calm. He moved from one person to another, hardly speaking and never above a murmur, and when he had been round the room once he went round it again. He did not raise his voice, nor seek to unite everybody in prayer, nor deliver anything remotely in the form of either eulogy or sermon. He came even to me, saying not a word but clasping my hand and looking with a kind of stern kindness into my eyes. Everything was forever changed, yet somehow Mr Dunning began a process of – what may I call it? – restoration.

The family were destitute of spirit, but around them their people gathered themselves to action. Kate Nicol and Norah repaired to the kitchen to make food. Davie Nicol took away the Captain's horse and fed and groomed it. Men who had begun to set chairs and stools in the hall for the dancing quietly removed them. I took Elspeth aside and said that Captain MacKay would require a chamber. She said that only Sandy's was fit for a man like the Captain, but she feared to put him in it lest it upset her mistress. She began to cry again, and was so distraught that I put an arm around her, which I did not do from any motivation but sympathy. The Baroness glanced up and saw this, and rose from her seat and took Elspeth from me and held her in her arms, saying, 'Ah, lass, lass, what a sair thing this is for us all,' which I thought a great kindness. And when it came out about the room she said at once, 'Mak the bed wi fresh sheets for the Captain, Elspeth, and show him where he is to sleep. We'll no hae that room empty the nicht.'

By and by, some order returned to the day. Daniel Haddow came in and was most solicitous of everyone, and spoke long and gravely with Captain MacKay. Elspeth, a little recovered, lit the fire, for although the day stayed dry the warmth had gone out of it. Mary came from the manse and she, Kate and Norah laid out food, both hot and cold, on the dining table, and we came and went and helped ourselves as we pleased, for there was no thought of all sitting down together. The Baron roused himself to fetch wine from the cellar, and ale was brought in, and for a while the hall was a thorough democracy, and none who came was turned away or denied food or drink.

But as the afternoon advanced only a few were left. The Baron, the Baroness, Jessie and Captain MacKay were in a group around the fireplace, while the rest of us – Mr Dunning, Mr Haddow, myself, Elspeth and the Nicols (Mary having returned to the manse, and Norah gone to her bed) – sat quietly a little way off. And it was necessary then to have the Captain tell again exactly what had happened, and he did as he was bidden and, manfully and honestly in his own gruff manner, supplied all the information he could and spared no detail, which is supposed to be a comfort to those who receive sudden bad news of this sort.

I have been writing all afternoon and must now go to dinner, but will continue this evening and recall, as nearly as I can in his own words, the story that he told us, and the effect it had on his listeners.

Sunday, 1st October 1809

I had hoped to write more last night but events overtook me. I have scribbled some notes concerning these, but am determined to keep a true chronological order to this journal and so, anxious though I am to set down what has occurred lest I forget some details, I return first to Captain MacKay:

Captain MacKay's Narrative

My father was a soldier and so too his brother, my uncle, in this same regiment to which I belong. My uncle having a little land in the county of Ross-shire, and no sons of his own, he provided the funds to enable me to buy a commission, and I have been an officer in the King's army now for seventeen years. I was in Saint Lucia and Saint Vincent and then in Egypt where I fought against the French at Alexandria, and latterly in Gibraltar under Sir John Moore before we were posted last year to Portugal. It was in Gibraltar and the Peninsula that I became closely acquainted with Captain Milne – your son,

Alexander, or Sandy as he was known to me. He rose from Ensign to Lieutenant in my Company and then transferred to another Company when he too was made a Captain. His conduct during the Peninsular campaign and especially on the retreat to Corunna was of the highest standard. He displayed great bravery and determination, and set a fine example to his men, for whom he was ever a firm but considerate officer, and earned their loyalty and devotion accordingly. I can say no more about him than this: when he departed this life it was for the men in his Company as if they had lost a father, although many were older than him by some years.

The expedition to the Low Countries, from which many of us have returned and others return daily, was a very great enterprise, with forty thousand troops, two hundred and forty vessels of many sizes, six thousand horses, a vast quantity of artillery, munitions, wagons, and so forth. Our regiment was part of the 2nd Division under command of the Marquess of Huntly. We set sail on 28th July, and the next day were off the coast of Holland, but we could not disembark as planned on the island of Kadzand since it was discovered that there were not enough boats to carry us all ashore. While others made landings on the island of Walcheren, we were obliged to remain on board for another whole week. You may imagine that this was good neither for the men's spirits nor for their health, owing to the cramped conditions on the transports and the rolling movement of the sea. But at last there was a change of plan and we got on to the island of South Beveland and marched across it without resistance until we reached the river opposite the port of Flushing, the capture of which was the expedition's first objective.

As we were setting up our quarters in barns and other buildings we became aware of an evil smell, and a strange, milky mist drifting towards us from Walcheren. We learned that the French had opened the sluices on that island and flooded the ditches to hamper the movements of our troops there, and the water was foul with decayed matter and animal waste. The situation was not improved by a tremendous thunderstorm one night, which threatened to wash us all away and made the foul water rise. However, the bombardment commenced a few days later, and by, I think, the 17th or 18th of August the garrison of Flushing was obliged to surrender.

It was the brigades on Walcheren who entered the town on the next day. We on South Beveland had very little to do as a foot regiment but try to keep ourselves dry and ward off the mosquitoes, a kind of gnat very numerous there, whose whine is most aggravating to the ear although its bite is as nothing to a cleg's. I learned in Egypt that smoking is effective in dispersing these creatures, so puffed away incessantly, and even those who were not smokers took up a pipe. And the tobacco fumes were always pleasanter to breathe than that milky mist, which had a most offensive taste.

('My son was not, at that point, involved in any of the fighting?' Glen Conach asked, although by then he knew well the answer. 'He was not, Sir,' Captain MacKay replied. 'We none of us were.' Glen Conach had eaten a little food and drunk one bottle of claret, and kept another at his side further to dull the pain of his sorrow.)

The day after the fall of Flushing, I became aware that something was not right among us. Several men in my Company who had been sentries during the night were taken ill with a fever, which came on with a rapidity I had never seen before. They burned with heat one minute, and the next the very sweat on their bodies turned to ice, and they shook with such violence that it was all they could do to hold on to their muskets, or even to stand upright. I had these men separated from the rest and saw that the surgeon gave them every attention, for they could do nothing for themselves. They could neither eat bread nor drink grog or water, and complained of stomach pains and severe headaches. There were half a dozen of them, all as sick as each other, and it was evident that they were in a very bad way.

I sought out Captain Milne, whose Company was quartered only half a mile away, to see if any of his soldiers had become ill. The first man I met was a sergeant who was known to me, a man from my own country. 'Well, Sergeant,' I said, 'how do the men fare, and where is your Captain?' 'Oh, Sir,' he said, 'as for the men they are fatigued with having had no combat. And as for the Captain, you had better see for yourself.' He led me to the house where your son was billeted. I went inside. He was lying on a couch and as soon as I set eyes on him I knew that he had the same fever as the others. He looked at me and said, 'MacKay, is that you? My head is so sore I can hardly see you. But I will be better after a day's rest.'

(Captain MacKay halted and made growling noises. When his host asked what was the matter, he said that he did not wish to distress the family with too close a description of Sandy's condition, but Glen Conach insisted that they would, and must, hear all. MacKay later told Daniel, however, who in turn told me, that he did spare them the worst of it, such as the sick men being so reduced to helplessness that they could not stir even to void themselves and had to lie in their own filth, while at the same time they swelled like barrels or dead beasts left in the sun. And he said that Sandy Milne was not exempted from these humiliations, and that he, MacKay, did what he could more than once to clean him and try to ease the excruciating pains in his legs and stomach.)

A surgeon had already attended him, had bled him a little and given him an infusion of bark. The Sergeant promised to let me know of any change, and I returned to my own Company. I had been gone no more than an hour. In that time another ten of my men had collapsed with the same symptoms as their comrades. I immediately went to report what was happening to our headquarters. When I got there I found several others on the same errand, and one or two even of these had the same pallid skin and shivers that indicated that they would soon be in a like condition.

I never saw an army so laid to waste in so short a time. Two days after the first casualties, in my Company of eighty men not half were able to stand. For the poor lads that were stricken it was an agony to move their muscles, and many of them suffered from a kind of dropsy too. We had very few doctors to tend to the sick, and the doctors also began to succumb, so that it was all we could do to lay the men out on the floors of barns or even outside. We obeyed the instructions of those physicians who were not themselves sick. Mostly this amounted to forcing a little port wine into the patients, bleeding them, covering them with their greatcoats to sweat the fever from them, and giving them bark and mercury. But supplies of the latter were insufficient, and even if a man made a recovery and returned to duty, he remained so weak that the slightest exertion would cause him to fall sick again.

A week after the capture of Flushing, we learned that the French had greatly reinforced Antwerp as well as two forts that lay between our positions and that city, so that it would be almost impossible to overcome them before the onset of winter, even were we not under attack by this other, secret and more deadly enemy. The orders were soon given to evacuate from South Beveland to Walcheren Island, and from there the vast bulk of the army would return to England, with the sick being taken off first. This, after all the preparations for the campaign, seemed too swift a retreat, an abandonment of all that we had meant to do. I see now that it was the only sensible action, for though we had lost few men to the French, the fever was by then carrying us off by the score. We buried our dead by night, and without pomp, to avoid demoralising those already sick or those who dreaded that they soon would be. Soldiers will always rise above their fears and fatigue when called to battle, but they do not know how to fight an enemy like that disease.

('But Sandy was in his prime,' Glen Conach said, swallowing another glass. 'From what you say, he was among the first to become ill. I would not have believed that, if you had not told us.' 'That is why I came here in person,' Captain MacKay said. 'Your son was struck early, and resisted longer than most. He fought until he could fight no more. He never gave up.' Mr Dunning said, in an attempt to offer solace, 'He was not alone, Glen Conach. There were dozens who died alongside him.' And the Captain said, 'Not dozens, Sir. Hundreds. I believe that before this is over we

will number the dead in their thousands.' This prediction was greeted with incredulous gasps, but Captain MacKay was insistent. 'The 42nd alone set out nearly eight hundred strong,' he said. 'Barely two hundred were fit for duty when I left it.' And when pressed as to how many had died of the fever, he said, 'When I left, four officers and some thirty-five in the ranks. I do not doubt it will be more by now.')

I am astonished that I myself did not come down with the fever, nor even exhibit the mildest symptoms. I am no medical man, but that I was not affected suggests to me that it was not a disease carried from one man to another, but that it emanated in some way from the ground, or the air, or the water, or the insects. It is common enough in a hot, damp climate for the air to become unwholesome, what the Italians call *malaria*, and for this to cause sickness. And yet this fever spread so quickly that perhaps it did pass among the troops by breath, or touch, or blood, or other matter. I do not know. I think though that in some part of my own history – perhaps in the Indies or Egypt – I gained a strength that protected me from whatever that poison was.

I went when I could to see Captain Milne. This was not often for I was too much taken up with looking after my own men. On my second visit, I found that the sergeant who had met me before had himself been struck, and like many others was stretched out on the floor, as white as a ghost, and also delirious. He did not recognise me and when I came again the following day I learned that the poor fellow had raised himself in the middle of the night, cursed and cried in a most demented way and dropped down dead. Captain Milne, I was glad to see, was somewhat improved. He knew me and said he was not in such pain, but he too was very white and his tongue had a white coat upon it which made me think of that horrible mist. 'We must get you home,' I said. He would not countenance it, and was determined to go forward to Antwerp in a day or two. I came back next evening and he was on his feet, dressed and attempting to buckle on his sword, yet so shaky that he could not manage it.

'Come, Sandy,' I said, 'you must rest again.' He admitted that he was tired, and sat down and soon fell into a drowse. I thought – I hoped – that the crisis had passed, and I went away, but in the morning he was worse again, and scarcely knew me. This was the day we marched to the ferry and crossed to Walcheren, with wagons conveying the sick, your son among them. Another march brought us to the coast, where we waited two days to be re-embarked and brought home. It was in those days that he entered his final decline, and was so weak that I had to lift his head to let him sip a little port wine. He was sometimes in a dream, and sometimes very lucid, and in both states of mind he spoke of this glen and wished me to convey to you that he loved you dearly and that he had never disgraced you. He hoped he would recover enough to get home, and then to serve his country again, and it was in that hope that he breathed his last, which was on the seventh day of this month of September. We had sixteen men of his own Company, which were all that were well enough and could be spared, to form the guard of honour at his graveside, and the chaplain said prayers for him, and there he lies in that Dutch island. The next day we set sail for England, and once I had got my men into barracks or into hospital and could do no more for them, I set out to bring you this news, since I could not bring you your son.

'Ah!' the Baron exclaimed, when Captain MacKay had finished. 'To think that had he only managed one more day, he might have come back to England and lived.'

'Do not dwell on that possibility, Sir,' MacKay said sharply – it was almost a command. 'I believe he would not have survived the crossing. There were several who expired on board, and were committed to the deep, which to my mind is a more desolate resting place.'

'Oh, I could not thole the thought of him in the cold sea with the fish swimming about him,' Jessie cried, the first words she had spoken for an hour. I could not help but imagine, when she uttered them, the fish not swimming but nibbling at her brother's flesh. Captain MacKay bowed his head to her and stroked his black moustache. I thought she held his gaze for a few moments and I was, even in that gloomy hour, struck by a pang of jealousy, and wondered why I had been so determined to walk away from her. She chose not to look in my direction, to which neglect I could hardly object.

The Baroness had sat still and silent all through MacKay's narration of these events. She stood up now, and thrust some wood on the fire with a sudden vigour. 'This great expedition,' she said, 'this vast naval and military operation that must have cost so much money, and has cost so many lives and is likely to cost many more, and that great and clever men have expended so much of their greatness and cleverness to plan, and that has achieved so little; I cannot think but that it has all been a colossal waste – of everything.'

She did not address the Captain directly, perhaps because she did not mean him to be the target of her bitter words. Her husband, however, could not tolerate the implication that their son had died for no good purpose. 'No, no, you must not say that,' he said. He took off another glass and refilled and muttered again, 'You must not, *we* must not say that.'

'I do say it,' she replied. 'And you must not drink any more wine. You will do yourself harm.'

At this the Baron was incensed. 'I must not drink? I must not *drink*?' He drank again in defiance. 'And what else must I not do, to keep myself from harm? Am I not to breathe? Am I not to bleed? Am I not to be bitten by a cleg? Am I not to mourn my son? Oh, to think of him taken off by this – this fever! Slain not by sword or shot but by a sickness. He could have stayed at home and died of a sickness. Oh, if he had only died in battle!'

Then it was the Baroness's turn to vent her despair.

'In battle! If he had only died in battle?' She strode to the foot of the stair and turned again. 'He *did* die. Our son is dead, Sir. Deid.

And with him *we* die. All of us here are deid. Does it matter how he died? It matters only that we will never see him again.'

And with these words, which seemed to be torn from her by some external force, she hurried up the stair and Jessie, weeping, followed after her.

We were all shocked, at first into silence and then into action. The Nicols slipped away to the basement and from there no doubt to their room over the stables. Mr Haddow stood and said he would be on his way, and Mr Dunning said he would go too, and Captain MacKay said he would step out with them and get some fresh air.

The Baron said, 'Gentlemen, I beg you to forgive me any embarrassment I have caused. I spoke with too much passion. It has been a vexing day, a terrible day. I will go and apologise to my wife – she aches as much as I do, but guides herself better. Whatever I am, she is a mother and has lost her only son.'

He stared into the fire and drank again, then suddenly started to his feet.

'Good God!' he cried. 'I have clean forgot my own mother!'

Elspeth, who seemed minded to go with the others, came over to him and put a hand on his arm. 'Dinna fash,' she said. 'Granny Ally will ken. A'body in the clachan kens.'

'But I must go to her,' the Baron said. 'Elspeth, lass, come with me, and you must stay the night with her after we have seen her. Quickly now, we will go with the gentlemen. Good God! It is late enough already.'

It was by now approaching seven o'clock, and growing dark. One minute there was a small gathering in the hall, the next I found myself alone. I almost ran after everybody as they set out for the clachan, but I had begun very early that morning and, with all that had happened, was overcome with exhaustion. I therefore sat down in the Baron's chair in front of the Baron's fire, drank off the rest of the Baron's bottle of claret, and mused on the circumstances which had brought me back to the Baron's house and would shortly see me climb the stair to my familiar bed in its blue room. Not least, I mused on what had for some reason never occurred to me until that moment: that the old woman in the clachan, the laird's mother – Alison Murray as she once was, Alison Carnegie as she is now – had not one granddaughter but two, Elspeth and Jessie, and a grandson, Sandy, who she had learned that very day was dead.

Tuesday, 3rd October 1809

Let it never be said that life is predictable. The wheel has spun so rapidly these last three days that I have had no time to write here, and now I have so much to write that I do not know where to begin. Begin I must, though, for all is changed beyond reason or repair.

Five days ago I walked almost clear out of this glen. Another hour and I would have been free. My determination then was never to return. Now it appears that I may never leave.

On Saturday, which should have been the day of the dance, I came downstairs about eight o'clock to find all signs of the previous night's activities *redd up*. I was the last to breakfast – Lady Glen Conach had been up at six, I learned, and the Captain too, but Jessie and her father did not make an appearance until dinner. The sky promised rain, and I felt too tired to try my departure again. I made a new plan that I would go on Monday – that is, yesterday! I thought it best to keep to myself in the meantime, and made my way to the library, intending to take one or two books and retreat to my room. I also meant to write in this journal, which I accomplished, as shown by the entry above the last.

Captain MacKay was in the library, perusing the shelves as if he were inspecting his men. He paused every so often to straighten a spine or buff a morocco binding, but he did not seem interested in the contents of the volumes. I had entered quietly and he did not notice me at first. I wished him a good morning and he spun round, clicked his heels and wished me the same. I asked if he had slept well and he said only fitfully, being a man who was not used to a soft bed. He looked me up and down, judging me, I thought, to be a man who was, but he made no comment.

ME: 'I do not mean to disturb you. I am here for a book, and then I will be on my way.'

MACKAY: 'You do not disturb me at all, Mr Gibb. I have seen too much to be easily disturbed. I understand from Mr Haddow that you are a very learned gentleman. I suppose you have read a great many of these?'

ME: 'I have, though not as many as Mr Haddow.'

HIM: 'I am not a reader of books. In my opinion the old blades and guns next door, even in their poor condition, have greater utility. Books are an encumbrance to a soldier, and don't do well in hot countries. Furthermore, I have never been good at sitting still, which is essential to the reading habit. If there were any books on military affairs, I might have a look at them.'

ME: 'There is nothing much of that kind. There are some good maps, which perhaps would interest a soldier.'

HIM: 'I find maps of interest if I am trying to find my way about a particular country, but not otherwise. It is the same with books. If I open one, it must be for a practical purpose. I feel that a book steals my time and my energy. As soon as I open one, I want to close it and do something else.'

ME: 'You should speak to Mr Haddow about that. He is of two minds about books and learning. He worries that we are not the men our warrior forebears were.'

HIM: 'Some of us are, some of us are not. Mr Haddow and I discussed it last night. We convoyed the minister to the manse, and on my return he invited me to share a dram with him at the schoolhouse.'

ME: 'He keeps a very fine whisky.'

HIM: 'Tolerably fine. He is a healthy, youthful man but, as he confided in me, not half so young as he looks.'

ME: 'Yes, I believe he is in his forties.'
HIM: 'He is nearer fifty than forty. I told him that he could pass for half that. He said he could not account for it but he had always kept well. You too are a healthy-looking man, Mr Gibb. Do you keep well yourself?'
ME: 'My sojourn here has done me no ill.'
HIM: 'Have you ever thought of a soldier's life?'
ME: 'Enough to know it would not suit me.'
HIM: 'I always ask. I am going to stroll over to the clachan this morning, and ask there too.'
ME: 'There are plenty of lads that have gone for soldiers from the glen. I think that Glen Conach would not be happy if you ensnared any more, especially after what has happened.'
HIM: 'I am not a press-gang, Mr Gibb. I don't force it on any man. I don't like anybody to miss the chance, that's all.'
ME: 'To be blown to bits by grapeshot, or die of a fever far from home? I'll happily miss such chances, Captain MacKay.'
HIM: 'Well, Mr Gibb, I see *you* are not to be persuaded, but there was no harm in my asking.'

He had a twinkle in his eye while we spoke, and we parted cordially enough, but I liked him less than I had the day before. I remembered also that he had mentioned leaving two men at Forfar, and understood now that they must be recruiting. I thought that this, and not his offer to be shot for desertion, might have been what persuaded his commander to let him come north. I went to my room and did not see him again until dinner time, nor anybody else either, the house being quiet and solemn and anybody who moved about doing so like a mouse. I once opened my door because I thought I heard somebody outside it, but there was no one. All afternoon I wrote a long screed in this journal. Before going down for dinner I put it back in its hiding place.

I wrote in that entry that on first receipt of the news of his son's death the Baron seemed to age in the instant. Later, he became animated and angry, and when he left the house to go to the clachan he was full of eager anxiety. But when I saw him at table on Saturday he was a changed man again. All his genial eccentricity was now turned to dotage, and his wild gestures and looseness of limbs were reduced to the tottering movements of senility. He gazed upon us as if upon strangers; toyed with his food and sipped at his wine as if he had never tasted such stuff before. The Baroness watched over him with concern, and had clearly forgiven him for his offence, if indeed she thought he had offended. Jessie too paid him much kind attention, but was otherwise absorbed in her own thoughts.

Captain MacKay made short and efficient work of the courses, and made short, efficient contributions to what little conversation there was among us. He said that he would attend church in the morning and then, unless his travelling on a Sunday was disapproved of by his host or Mr Dunning, he would take his leave and ride to Forfar, the first stage of his return journey. I was tempted to ask if his sergeant and corporal were strict Sabbatarians or if they would be going about the town recruiting after *they* had attended church. But I did not wish to set off that firework unless I was sure that the Captain meant to take any young men with him from the glen. If he did not, I concluded, I had better not interfere in his regimental affairs. I was surprised by how protective I felt of this place.

Elspeth was not present, and the dishes were brought to table by Norah and Mrs Nicol. After we had finished eating, the Baroness and Jessie assisted Glen Conach to his chamber, and MacKay went to see that his horse was fit to be ridden the next day. As I had not been out all day and it was still light, I decided to walk over to the clachan. I had not gone half the distance when I met Daniel Haddow carrying a tall pile of books. He requested me to take some from him before he dropped them, and to accompany him to the library. He was anxious to return the books to their right places, he said, after which, if I would walk back with him to the schoolhouse, he would offer me a dram and an explanation.

All this we did, and settled in front of his cold hearth as before, myself in the chair and Daniel hauled up like a boy on the cutty-stool. He brought forth the pig and glasses, and poured the drams. 'There are just a few drops left, Charles,' he said, 'and you do me an honour in sharing them with me. It is as well to leave everything neat and tidy if it is within one's power to do so. But I must ask for your discretion. In fact, I must ask you to say nothing of this until I am gone.'

I said, laughing, 'Nothing of what, Daniel? You are too mysterious. Are you dying? Do you wish me to witness your will?' To which he laughed back and raised his glass. 'No, no, I have never felt more alive in my body than tonight. My mind is a little dizzy but I assure you it too is well. And it is quite made up – about my going, I mean.'

'You had better tell me what you do mean,' I said. 'This loss of the laird's son must be borne by all here, not just by the laird. That was what Lady Glen Conach meant when she spoke those words last night. Without an heir, what will happen to the house, to this glen? And yet, life continues. You will have your students back soon, now that the harvest is in, so what is this about you going somewhere?'

'My students will not have me,' he replied. 'I am leaving the glen. It is Sandy's death that has decided me. I cannot stay any longer. Lady Glen Conach was right. We are all dead here.'

'But leaving to go where, and to do what?'

'To enlist in the army,' he said. 'I go tomorrow with Captain MacKay.'

I stared at him in amazement, choked on my whisky, and even laughed in his face. I tried to argue him out of his stated intention. No matter what I said, however, he would not be diverted from it. He had wrestled not for months but for years, he declared, with the problem of how a man might best acquit himself in his life on this planet – a life which, as he told me before, he believed would be succeeded by no other. He had tried to find a balance between philosophy and deeds, between thought and action, between prevarication and decisiveness. He had wanted to believe in Glen Conach as a place where that balance could be maintained, but he no longer had that belief. He wanted to follow in Sandy Milne's footsteps, not to avenge him but to emulate him. To be a soldier was to be heroic, he said. That was what he desired – to be heroic.

'MacKay has put you up to this,' I said. 'Had he not come – had we had the news of Sandy's death by letter – you would never have thought of this.'

'You may be right,' he said. 'Captain MacKay is an impressive man. He and I talked very long last night. He says my age does not matter. What matters is the health of my mind and of my body. He says I will do very well.'

'You can be Hector or Achilles or any hero you choose,' I said, 'but a cannonball will blow you apart just the same. This is madness, Daniel. If you are lucky you will last five years and if you are unlucky you will last ten. Then what will you do? There's nothing heroic about living off a soldier's pension.'

'You are right again, my friend. I do not expect a pension.'

'Daniel,' I said, 'has anything passed between you and MacKay? Has he gained knowledge of you and threatened you with it?'

He shook his head, smiling at me. 'Nothing of that, Charles – on his part or mine. Even if I felt something of that nature, I assure you I would not put myself in his power. I told you before, I am neither heroic nor pure. Now I have a chance to be both.'

'And you will leave tomorrow, trotting after MacKay on his horse, without a word to your friend and benefactor, without saying farewell to your bairns, or the men and women you have taught, or to the sister of the young man you say you wish to emulate? I would not have thought you capable of such treachery.'

He looked at me, still with his friendly smile. 'Oh, Charles, that is a very fierce word, especially coming from your lips. What will I be doing that is so treacherous? Only what you tried to do. You think you are unnoticed, but you are not. I rise early every morning, and regardless of the weather I take myself for a long walk. I saw you slip away yesterday. My thought was, who – forby myself who am of no importance – has not been bid farewell by my friend Mr Gibb? Has he thanked Glen Conach for his hospitality? Has he kissed the hand of Glen Conach's wife, or that of his daughter? Then, later, I saw you return with the Captain. Well, I will not criticise you, but that is not how I will go. They have been good to me here. I ask your discretion only until I have spoken with Glen Conach, and then with everybody else, which I will do tomorrow after kirk. I cannot delay but, as I said, I wish to leave everything as neat and tidy as I can. Once I am gone, what remains will be in the hands of those who also remain.'

Thus he put me in my place and, although we talked a little longer, I saw that to argue with him was futile. It was then that he told me the details that MacKay had withheld from the family. He also said he had some letters and instructions to write concerning the school, and so after half an hour I shook his hand and made my way back to the house. The evening was by then drawing close around me, and with the darkness came a chill in the air, presaging the coming season. Despite my conversation with Daniel, I resolved to be away myself on the Monday morning.

Nobody remained downstairs. I went directly to the blue room and lit some candles, intending to write before going to bed. I was hardly settled when I heard a scratching at the door. I opened it and little Norah the kitchen maid almost fell in, fluttering and twittering like a bird: 'Oh, Sir, oh, Sir, dinna be angry at me, but I didna ken wha to come to. I couldna gang to the maister and I daurna gang to the mistress, and Miss Jessie thinks I'm stupid but I'm no, and syne I thocht o' yirsel and that ye micht hear me oot, and I hae been hoverin and hotchin at yir door the leelang day and ilka time I got up the courage to chap it anither pairt o' me wheeched me awa again, but I thocht I wid ettle aince mair afore Elspeth wins hame frae the clachan, for she fills my lugs wi it a' and I ken she'll be angry gin I clype on her but I'm feart it'll be a sin gin I dinna. Oh, dinna be angry at me, Sir.'

I calmed her and hushed her as well as I could, and assured her I was not angry, and had her sit in the chair while I sat on a side of the bed, and implored her to keep her voice down and tell me what was troubling her. It took some time to disentangle her tale from the panic and worry that beset her, but in the end I had it, and it amounted to this: Elspeth, having her particular sorrows after the death of Sandy, could not share these with any of the family, and so Norah had become her unwilling confidante. Norah seemed not fully to comprehend the familial ties between Elspeth and the Milnes, and thought that Elspeth was *far abune hersel* when she voiced her special grief and her fondness for the young master. That was partly the fault of the Baron (Norah said) because he was too soft with Elspeth and treated her like a pet, and let her away with things that she, Norah, would have been scolded for, although she was not complaining since he was kind to her too, she could never wish for better master or mistress than she had, and she hoped she would never rise so *far abune hersel* as to forget it. But still she was shocked when Elspeth hinted at intimacies between herself and Sandy and spoke of Miss Jessie as jealous and a hindrance to their companionship. And Elspeth told her she had always had it in mind to woo or be wooed by Sandy, and when he ceased to be a soldier she intended to be his wife and in time the next Baroness – though that (Norah said) could surely never be, for whatever else he was, alive or dead, he was still a gentleman and Elspeth a common bit lassie. But now that he *was* dead, Elspeth's dreams lay in ruins, and she went from weeping in one breath to raging in the next, and said there was nothing for her to live for any more, not if she stayed in the glen. She had waited for a soldier, she told Norah, and the one she had waited for would never come, so she was minded to go away with another and seek her fortune in the wide world, and if Norah uttered a word of this to anybody she would get a pillow over her face and it would be the last word that left her lips.

That, in short, was Norah's story. Once she had finished I asked if she felt better for sharing it with me, and she answered that she did except that now she feared to go to the attic in case Elspeth guessed where she had been and murdered her in her sleep. I said she need have no such fear, because I would wait for Elspeth to come home and tell her that if she laid even a finger on Norah I would know it, and if she murdered her she would be hanged. I admit that this last remark, which I tried as a jest, was ill-judged and nearly brought on a fit in poor Norah, but she did at last stop wringing her hands and cheeping, and I told her to go to bed. Then I took a candle and went down to the hall, blew out the flame and waited for Elspeth until I was cold to the bone, but she did not come. So I gave it up and retired to my own bed.

I must have slept soundly enough, but twice I awoke, and each time to noises further along the passage. The first time, I believe I heard Glen Conach call out, an uncanny cry more like an animal's than a man's, and a door opened, and I heard his lady's voice as she went into him, as a mother goes to a child afflicted by the nightmare. And some hours later I heard another door, and low, whispered voices, and I hastened from my bed and cracked open my own door, and there was the Captain in his shirt, and a lithe, bonnie figure was slipping away towards the back stair, and I thought then that there was little I could do to save Elspeth Carnegie from herself, any more than I could save Daniel Haddow from himself. And so I crept back under the covers, and if I had dreams of anything I do not remember what they were.

Tuesday, 3rd October 1809 (continued)

Everybody was at kirk on Sunday morning. The people were there in a great, dark crowd, sombre and respectful. As the family passed through the bodies, men stepped forward and shook Glen Conach's hand and bowed to the Baroness and Miss Milne, not in a deferential way but to show sympathy for their loss. Captain MacKay and I took our seats alongside the Baron, who seemed quite detached from the whole occasion and spoke not a word to anyone. The Captain avoided my eye, as did Mr Haddow across the aisle – not that I made any effort to catch theirs. Elspeth and Norah and the other folk from the house were behind us. I did smile at Norah to acknowledge that she had not been murdered but she gave me a blank look in return, and Elspeth would not look at me at all. I felt quite invisible.

Mr Dunning – I find I admire Mr Dunning more and more – performed most excellently. He did not whine or howl, nor did he preach, nor did he drag out the proceedings, but gave the concluding blessing less than forty minutes after he entered the pulpit. He led the congregation in psalm-singing and his voice was strong. The first psalm sung was the forty-sixth, which includes the verse

Unto the ends of all the earth
wars into peace he turns:
The bow he breaks, the spear he cuts,
in fire the chariot burns.

I thought the swell of voices then might have lifted the roof off the old kirk. Mr Dunning read, from Isaiah, the passage that speaks of people beating their swords into plowshares and their spears into pruninghooks, and nations not learning war any more. I thought it a noble vision even if a futile and possibly a treasonous one. He offered prayers not only for Captain Milne but for all from the glen who were absent, those who had gone to be soldiers and those who had gone to make new lives in far-flung parts of the world. We had had news of the dead, he said, whom we lamented, but we had not had news of the living, whose lives for months or years at a time were a mystery to us. Yet in our ignorance lay faith and hope. It was fitting therefore that we should pray for their health and happiness and that they were cared for by a just and loving God. For the dead were safe now in the bosom of Christ, but the living had yet to enter that place of eternal rest we call paradise.

Altogether his words were very moderate and kindly; there was a certain poetry about them which I hoped might somehow find its way through Glen Conach's ears to his mind, and give him comfort. And although John Dunning made no mention of his own dead wife I could not but think that he was remembering her, and I felt that I had misjudged him. I thought, if I had been going to stay longer in the glen, that I would have made an effort to understand him if not to befriend him. And then I said to myself, Charles Kirkliston Gibb, you are falling under some kind of enchantment that is softening your brain, and it is high time you were on your way.

When the service was over and folk were lingering outside the kirk, I saw Daniel approach Glen Conach. They stepped aside and Daniel spoke earnestly to the old man but I was not able to hear what was said or what reply, if any, was given. Then Lady Glen Conach gathered her husband and daughter, and the minister joined them, and they began to walk through the clachan towards the house, with Daniel following a few yards behind, and all the people gave way before them. A little apart from that group was Captain MacKay, and a little apart from him was Elspeth Carnegie, who had her grandmother on her arm, and in another group were the Nicols and Norah and Mary, the Maid of the Manse. It occurred to me that everybody was separate and yet all were connected, some without quite knowing what connected them. There was something biblical about the scene – a painter could have made a great canvas of it. Then the people began to disperse. I walked back alone. Yes, even I was separate, yet not entirely unconnected.

Captain MacKay, after a private meeting with the Baron and Baroness, mounted his horse and took his leave that afternoon. He went alone, and I wondered if Daniel had had a change of heart. But it transpired that both he and Elspeth had had the same notion – that, being on foot, they had better get a distance ahead of the Captain.

She had slipped away after the service, and he had hurried off after concluding matters at the house. MacKay overtook them some miles along the road to Forfar. Daniel and Elspeth were each surprised, not to say dismayed, to discover the other's plans, and disputed as to who should go forward and who turn back, but neither would give ground, and when they saw MacKay riding up they fell into a sullen truce lest he dismiss them both.

We learned all this because there was a fourth on the road, a young lad called Hugh Pirnie. He too had decided to enlist, and followed his old schoolmaster despite Daniel urging him to give up the idea; but, when they met, first with Elspeth, and later with Captain MacKay, the enormity of the adventure he had begun overwhelmed young Hugh (who has never been out of the glen in his life) and he deserted them and ran all the way home.

That evening's meal – more an early supper than a late dinner – was a most subdued affair. There were just Glen Conach, the Baroness, Jessie and myself at table, and Norah bringing the dishes to us. Hardly a hundred words were spoken, and none of them by the Baron. He had his dogs at his feet and occasionally fed them by hand, and neither he nor they were admonished for it. The dogs, ever since the arrival of Captain MacKay, have demonstrated their sympathetic intelligence by tucking their tails between their legs and staying out of the way, only creeping to their master with canine sighs and groans when they perceive that he is settled in one place for a period. I feel sorry for those dogs. They do not understand what has come over their master, and seem to be patiently waiting for his true self to return to them.

It was widely known by then that Daniel had resigned his post and gone off with Captain MacKay. That Elspeth had also gone was no secret, but mention was made of neither of them. I am sure that the Baroness ordered this silence so as not to distress her husband. In truth, she herself did not look well. I am in some awe of the effort it must cost her not to give way to her emotions.

We retired to the upstairs parlour, where there was a fire lit, and Jessie played some gentle and mournful tunes on the spinet and I listened, as if with rapt attention, while her mother sewed and her father stared at the flames. After half an hour of this, and as I was about to excuse myself and retire, the Baroness said that she was going to her bed and suggested to the Baron that he might want to go with her. He acquiesced without a murmur, and they departed.

No sooner were Jessie and I alone than she, still seated at the spinet, requested me to go to the dining room and bring a decanter of port wine that I would find there. I did this and poured us each a glass. She ceased her playing and sat on one side of the fire, and I took my seat opposite her.

'Well,' she said, 'what is to become of us? I do not mean you and me, Charles. I mean, how are we to get on, here in the glen, now that Sandy is dead?'

I began to answer, but she held her hand up to silence me, and continued.

'Sandy lies in a Dutch island, and will never return. Captain MacKay came with his news and now he is gone, and we will see him no more. As for the runaways, what is there to be said of them? They are not children, they may do what they wish. I don't know if the Captain and Mr Haddow are to fight over Elspeth, or if she and Mr Haddow are to fight over the Captain, but I do not foresee a happy resolution. Do you? Elspeth's bloom will soon fade once she has been discarded, as she surely will be when she complains, as she surely must, that life is not fair. At least Mr Haddow will not be discarded, no matter how poor a soldier he makes. They will keep him until he is killed, I suppose. And all because my brother caught a fever.'

I ventured again to give an opinion, but she would not be interrupted. I was there only to listen, it seemed – and to refill our glasses, which I did twice. Jessie sat and stood and walked about, like an actress rehearsing her lines – the lines of a drama as yet unwritten, and one with a disjointed and at times contradictory plot. Her father was destroyed, she said. He could not do without her mother, and her mother in turn could not do without Jessie. There was nothing for it but that mother and daughter would have to manage the affairs of the estate. Jessie must take lessons in housekeeping and accounting from the Baroness. She said that her father's visit to Edinburgh last year was to raise money in exchange for the deeds of some property he had there, but the money was all but spent and the property would now probably never be recoverable. She and her mother must together study the economy of farming, and better than her father ever had. Since there was now no male heir, in time the estate would come to her. Now she was truly the Maid of Glen Conach, she said, with a look that dared me to bring evidence disproving that title.

In the afternoon she had been to see Granny Ally, whom she had observed being supported by Elspeth after kirk. Old Alison, shaken to the core by the death of her grandson, Sandy, was further dismayed by the news, which Jessie brought her, of Elspeth's flight. But, the old woman said, Glen Conach was a good father to his people and would look after his own. Glen Conach was not well, Jessie told her; it might be beyond his power to look after his own. Then, Granny Ally said, as Sandy and Elspeth were both gone, it behoved Jessie to marry and have bairns of her own. How else could the glen be saved? Jessie came home with this question burning in her head and it smoulders there still. How else can the glen be saved? She knows not how to answer but, she insists, she will not marry against her will. Once, when her mother was fretting about not finding a husband for her, her father said, 'Lass, if ye dinna want to marry I'll no mak ye and I'll no blame ye.' Yet, if she were to die without issue, the estate would have to be sold and the glen would fall into other hands. Lord Finbeg, the distant neighbour, has long coveted the land. Her father detests Lord Finbeg. Lord Finbeg has a son. Jessie detests the son, who is brutish and coarse and thinks Jessie beneath him, but Lord

Finbeg would happily force him upon her in order to add the glen to his own property. Then they would turn all the people out and she will never allow that. Why should she marry if she does not love a man and he does not love her? Why should she provide that man with an heir? She will live to a grand old age and by then she will have found a solution, perhaps even somebody who *deserves* to inherit. 'Do not look at me in that way, Charles,' she said. 'We will get on very well, I do not doubt, but we have already established the terms of our relations. You may marry if you wish, but you will not marry me.'

'How will we get on at all?' I asked. 'I am leaving tomorrow.'

'I forgot, you dreamt that your mother was dying. Well, here we have had a real death, and I only wish I could wake and find I had dreamt of it. You cannot go tomorrow, Charles.'

'Why not?'

'My father desires you to stay. He thinks of you, almost, as a son. Of course, he is not himself. My mother too is greatly changed. All their hope rested on Sandy. Now they must place their faith, if not their hope, in me. But you could also be of service to them. You could repay their kindness to you. Perhaps you could persuade my father out of doors and encourage him to regain something of himself. You could help him finish the dyke in the high park.'

I gave an involuntary snort of laughter. 'I detest that dyke,' I said.

'But you do not detest my father,' she said. She stood with her hands on her hips, and in the flickering light she presented a striking figure. 'Are you really to leave us, Charles? I know that that was your intention, but do you have anywhere to go? I do not think you have. Will you not stay a while?'

'A day or a week, what difference will it make?' I asked.

'I thought,' she said, 'you might wait somewhat longer than that – at least until the spring – before you made up your mind.'

'Until the spring?'

'We are in need of a schoolmaster. Mr Haddow has left several pages of advice for his successor.'

I did not know what to think or say. Her suggestion appalled me. The dyke was bad enough, but to be the dominie in such a place – the prospect of a living hell! And yet, she was not wrong. I had nowhere to go, and to stay through the winter would not prevent me leaving at the end of it. Even now as I write these words my senses are confounded, although I have since given my answer. Everything I have written heretofore seems petty and inconsequential, mere dalliance, a game of cards the night before a duel or an execution. At that moment as she stood in the candlelight, I was quite unable to speak.

'Say nothing now,' she said. 'Refill our glasses, consider it, and you can tell me your decision when we wake in the morning.'

*A Note on Charles Kirkliston Gibb's Journal**

The journal of Charles Kirkliston Gibb ends abruptly, halfway down the last page of the volume in which it is written. If he continued his narrative elsewhere it has not been discovered. However, we know from another source what decision he made.

It is difficult to determine how much of Mr Gibb's journal is truth and how much invention. Taken in isolation, it is a document that might not bear much scrutiny. Some aspects accord with known historical facts relating to Glen Conach at that period; but others, such as his depiction of the behaviours and opinions of Daniel Haddow, of the Reverend John Dunning and even of his host, Mr Thomas Milne, seem much less credible. His claims regarding his relationship with Jessamine Milne may also simply be the fantasies of one who was, by his own admission, quite untrustworthy.

Evidence does exist, however, which might corroborate at least some of what he wrote down, but equally which might undermine it. For example, one Daniel Haddon [*sic*], Private, 42nd Regiment of Foot, was killed in action at Quatre Bras on 16th June 1815, two days before the Battle of Waterloo. This soldier is described in the muster rolls as a 'Clerk, Forfarshire', but nothing else is known about him. The name Captain Donald MacKay does not appear in the medal roll for the Waterloo campaign, but a Lieutenant Donald Mackay [*sic*] of the 42nd Foot is listed. Of Elspeth Carnegie, the other 'runaway'

* Extracted from Dr Matthew Tybault, 'Symposium Review: The Strange Case of a Celtic Non-Saint' in *Studies in Scottish Medieval History,* Volume 32, 2020.

(the term used by Jessamine Milne according to Gibb), the historical record is silent.

More relevant, and more persuasive, are three extracts from *Annals of an Angus Glen in the 19th Century* by William Williamson (Montrose, 1900). These are self-explanatory, and so are reproduced without further comment:

There had been a school in the glen from at least the early 18th century and probably, in some primitive form, long before that. As far as can be ascertained, it was always located in or near the clachan. *The present school is very recent, having been erected only twenty years ago. The previous building was deemed to be inadequate after the passing, in 1872, of the Education Act, which required all children between the ages of five and thirteen to attend school. Prior to this date the school, and its schoolmaster, had been sustained partly through the support of the Kirk and partly through the patronage of the Glen Conach estate. There are at present nineteen pupils enrolled, and for the first time the school is presided over by a schoolmistress, Miss Brown, who commands both respect and affection from her charges.*

Within the last few years there were still living in the glen two or three persons who were pupils at the school when the dominie was a Mr Gibb, and indeed one redoubtable lady, Mrs Strachan, now in her eighties, can even today recall learning her letters from this gentleman when she was just ten years old. This was during the 1820s. It appears that Mr Gibb was a strange, erudite, often cold yet sometimes kindly man. He was a great friend of the old minister, Mr Dunning, then in his sixties. According to Mrs Strachan, the two of them used to go for long walks, or stravaigs, *across the hills, no doubt supplementing their physical exercise with vigorous discussions of a philosophical or political nature. Yet despite their intimacy, it was common knowledge among the glen folk that Mr Gibb, whilst ever the dedicated pedagogue, and a man of otherwise impeccable moral character, had little patience with the formalities of religion and was seldom seen at kirk, unless to pay his respects on the occasion of some person's decease. When Mr Dunning died, in 1829, and another minister came from Kirriemuir to conduct the funeral service, Mr Gibb was a pall-bearer. After he had helped carry his old companion to his final resting place he declared that he would never again cross the threshold of the kirk.*

Mr Gibb lived a simple life, but was not without his eccentricities. He had only two suits of clothing, one with a grey coat and the other with a black, and his charges believed that they could tell his mood – 'gloomy' or 'gloomier' – according to which of these he was wearing when he entered the schoolroom. Yet despite his reputation for a lack of humour he was very patient and seldom lost his temper even with the dullest of children, and the most physical punishment to which he ever resorted was to throw a piece of chalk at the head of an inattentive pupil, which caused great hilarity among the rest of the class, especially if his aim were true.

It was told that he had once been a frequenter of learned clubs and societies in Edinburgh, and had been acquainted with Adam Ferguson, Henry Mackenzie, Francis Jeffrey, Walter Scott and other literary luminaries of the day; but, his brain having been overheated by so much intellectual stimulation, he had come to Glen Conach House on the invitation of the then laird, Mr Thomas Milne, to recuperate; and, finding the glen conducive to his health, he had chosen to remain when the position of dominie, then vacant, had been offered to him. His salary was small but he requested three supplementary benefits: first, that he would always be allowed to borrow books from the extensive library in Glen Conach House; second, that a woman from the clachan would once a week clean his accommodation and wash his linen; and third, that half of his first year's salary be paid in advance, as he wished to send that sum to his aged mother in Linlithgowshire.

These requests were granted and honoured, and he was the dominie for more than twenty years. After the death of Mr Milne, Baron of Glen Conach, in 1815, and then of his wife in 1819, Mr Gibb became a favoured friend of their daughter, Jessamine Milne, referred to in an earlier chapter, who did so much to maintain the estate despite economic difficulties and the departure of many of the glen's inhabitants to new lives in other parts of the Empire. Miss Milne, even though she inherited the title of Baroness, always styled herself 'Maid of Glen Conach'. Mr Gibb was a trusted adviser to this redoubtable lady, and frequently dined at the 'big house'. It was even rumoured that there might have been a romantic outcome to their friendship but alas (as we have already recorded) Miss Milne died in 1832, at the age of forty-seven, in the terrible fire which devastated much of the house and about which we have written elsewhere. In that same year, Mr Gibb, heartbroken some said, resigned his post and left the glen. He seems to have settled in or near Edinburgh.

We have elsewhere made mention of the Book of Conach, *a medieval manuscript which for many years was kept in the library of Glen Conach House. This unusual document, a life of the hermit sometimes, although erroneously, known as 'Saint Conach', was presumably preserved in the vicinity of the glen for several centuries after its creation, perhaps in a priory or other house of religion, until the Reformation, at which time it may have been passed to the then Baron of Glen Conach for safekeeping.*

It was only in the early 19th century that a translation of the Latin original was made by Charles Kirkliston Gibb, of whose connections with the glen we have already written. According to a note attached to the manuscript of this translation, in the hand of Mr Douglas Bartholomew (see below), it was first intended that it would be published, alongside the Latin text which was its source, with funds raised by subscription. However, not enough subscribers could be found. In 1824 the work was offered to the newly formed Bannatyne Club but rejected by its management committee for reasons unknown.

The medieval manuscript was one of many precious items consumed in the fire of 1832. About ten years after this tragic event, Mr Gibb made an arrangement with the Antiquarian Field Club of Forfarshire (fl. 1837–1914) to publish his translation together with the original Latin, of which he had made a transcription, but owing to a disagreement between the parties over who would bear the costs of printing, this plan too came to nought. It seems that at some time during this dispute the Latin transcription became separated from the English translation, and the *former was destroyed when it was accidentally used as kindling by a servant of the Field Club's President. The Field Club's records state that the President wrote a letter of fulsome apology, offering to compensate Mr Gibb with a modest financial sum for the loss, but at the same time withdrawing the Club's offer to publish what it now regarded as an incomplete work, the provenance of which could not be substantiated. Mr Gibb was far from satisfied and threatened legal action, but to no avail, the Antiquarian Field Club of Forfarshire being immoveable and, moreover, probably unimpressed by the threats of a man whom they knew to be impecunious. After Mr Gibb's death in 1851, through the offices of his executor, Mr Douglas Bartholomew, an advocate of Edinburgh, the translation MS was deposited, along with sundry other papers, in the Library of the Faculty of Advocates, where it remains to this day, a curiosity rather than a document of any historical significance.**

* It was transferred to the National Library of Scotland when that institution was constituted by Act of Parliament in 1925.

Maja

I hope she made it, that's all. I hope Elspeth made it.

Whenever I think of her I see her, even though I never saw her in my life. How can this be? I never saw her in my life or in hers, but I see her now. She is walking out of the only world she knows, heading into another, stepping out bravely even though she must feel fear inside. How could she not feel it? But hope, too. Fear and hope go together, and the combination makes her tremble with excitement. She is going down the road that wasn't even a road then, just a track. I see her bonnie face, her black hair, her hard wee feet. She has no shoes on, but she must have taken some. Just one pair of shoes. Did she have them in a bag? She had some kind of bag, surely? She was taking her whole life away with her, and she wasn't coming back. Elspeth wasn't a tail-between-her-legs kind of lass. She couldn't get what she wanted by staying at home, not with Sandy dead, so she took off. There was no hope left in the glen for her, if there ever had been, and not much fear either; only the fear of growing old and not having seen that other world, not having been in it. The glen was not a sanctuary for Elspeth, it was a prison. She had to go. And once she was away, she was away.

She ran off with a soldier; they probably said that about her whether it was true or not. I am sure there was plenty said about them: the soldier and the maid; the wicked Captain and the silly lass; the bold MacKay and the strumpet. But maybe she was not so wanton or stupid or innocent; maybe she only went with him because she knew she would need a man to begin with, she would need him for protection on those first steps into that other world. Was that it? Did she just lean on him for a while? Maybe he forced himself on her, maybe she resisted. Maybe she let him have his way, maybe she wanted him, welcomed him, maybe he let her have *her* way. Maybe he made her happy! Maybe he was a decent man and didn't take advantage. It need not all have been bad, even if it ended badly. But maybe it ended well. Maybe whenever she got to wherever she was going he was still with her, maybe he wasn't. Maybe they parted on good terms, maybe she ran away from him. Maybe she found what she was looking for, maybe she found something else that was better. Wherever she went, wherever she stopped – Dundee, Edinburgh, Newcastle, London, Lisbon, Paris, Boston, Sydney? – maybe there was something worth stopping for. I don't know.

But one thing I do not see: Captain MacKay and Elspeth Carnegie, together, years later. I don't see that.

Did word ever come back about Elspeth? Did somebody recognise her face, still bonnie but with new lines on it, her black hair streaked with grey? Did she have bairns at her feet, another at her breast? Did somebody say, 'Is it you, lass? What are you doing here?' And, some time later, was the news of her carried homeward to the glen?

Maybe. But I don't see that either. I think she was away for good, or not for good, and she was not seen again. She became an *other*. She was not herself any more.

I like that idea, that her escape was permanent. I hope she kept herself safe, if safety was what she wanted. Maybe it wasn't. Maybe she knew fine that she wasn't heading for safety, and danger was what she wanted. Not like Hugh Pirnie, the young lad who took fright and turned for home and whose descendants were still here a hundred and fifty years later. No turning back for Elspeth. If she did want to live dangerously, I hope she didn't come to regret it. It's not a choice, that's the trouble. Risk is a choice. Danger is what happens when you don't have a choice.

And then there was the schoolmaster, Daniel, who went looking for the lions' den. After Sandy died, the glen changed for him just as it did for Elspeth. What did he find when he went out of it? Another man's love? A bayonet in the belly? Comrades shoulder to shoulder, or blown apart by grapeshot? Who knows?

Maybe he and she stayed together for a while, safe with each other. Maybe they became friends, strong because they were not lovers, because they did not have to be lovers. Elspeth and Daniel.

I hope things worked out for them both, whatever happened.

Maybe, maybe, maybe. So many maybes. And what does that mean, *things worked out*? Things were, things are. There is no plan or system, divine or scientific or any other kind. No way of knowing if things 'work out'. A plan that nobody thought of makes even less sense than God, I think. God didn't have to have a plan. God could just have created everything and set it going and then sat back to see what happened. God doesn't have to know any better than the rest of us how things will be.

I don't believe in anything except this one thing: *where you are*. Everybody has a place: that's all I believe in. Whether you call it home or not, whether it is where you end up or where you started or somewhere in between, everybody has a place. Like where animals go to hide, to sleep, to die.

One day you wake up and it's the last day of your life, though you don't know it. Not in that moment, maybe not later, maybe not even in the moment that is the end. More maybes. Do you get a presentiment? Not even that, a hint? I wonder if Geordie Kemp got a hint when he sat down with his dram at the end of that last day of hard labour.

One day you wake up and you are an old woman and you *do* know it. *I* know it. An old woman. If Elspeth lived long enough that realisation would have come upon her: *I am old*. That's not such a bad thing to know, that you survived. I hope she found her place to hide, to sleep, and I hope she had some days or maybe even years to appreciate it, to be able to close her eyes and say, thank you for having me. Before it was time to go.

But still there is the dumb lass. I will come to her. Or she will come to me.

It was after a war that the dumb lass came to the glen. Imagine what it is like after a war. Even after one battle. Imagine the night of Waterloo, the ground covered with bodies, dead men and wounded men from so many countries, so many towns, villages, cottages. Thousands upon thousands of men lying dead or dying, thousands of horses too. Moonlight glinting on the steel, men moaning and weeping and screaming. And the next day other soldiers went among them and brought out any who might still be saved by the surgeons, who sawed and sewed with their arms red to the elbows, who for every one arm they amputated cut off sixteen legs, who saved some men to be beggars and killed others because they did not clean their implements between one patient and the next. But the living soldiers were not permitted to bury the dead, there were too many; the living soldiers were ordered to march away. The local peasants were paid a few coins to dig trenches and throw the bodies in, and if they refused they were told they would be shot and thrown in the trenches themselves. And by then another army had been over the field through the night and in the misty morning, an army of ghouls, sometimes the same people who would later dig the trenches. They had stripped the dead and the dying of their boots and belts, their shirts and tunics, they took their purses and rings and tobacco pouches and if there were some who protested too loudly their cries were stifled. No waste! And all the dead heroes and all the dead cowards and the ones who were neither but who were also dead, all robbed of their clothes and their dignity, all naked when they were rolled and shovelled into the pits. And although the battle was over, shots rang out through the day as they slaughtered the torn, broken horses and left them turned with their legs to the sky so the farriers could recover their shoes. No waste! And it was June, and hot, and days passed and there were too many soldiers still to bury, so they built their naked bodies into funeral pyres and set them alight, and later the peasants spread the ashes on their fields for the next year's crops. No waste!

I am wandering. I have had books about Waterloo from the library and I remember the details but I can see the battlefield as well, the way I can see Elspeth. If Captain MacKay stayed with his regiment he would have been there. If Daniel Haddow did become a soldier, if they let him enlist because he looked young enough, and if he survived for five and a half years, he would have been there too. Even Elspeth might have been there, a camp-follower, a soldier's wife, perhaps a picker of dead men's pockets. I can see it, that carcass-strewn field, like something out of the Bible, stretching away to the horizon. One battle.

Now imagine that multiplied over and over, across a whole continent. Not thousands of dead, but millions. Millions of displaced, millions of homeless people. Homes flattened in flattened cities, ruined towns one after another, ruined roads between them. Homes from which families were ejected, never to return, or if they returned they found others living in them. Homes people occupied and made their own, only for the tide of war to turn and wash them out again. Roads crowded with convoys of lorries, lines of people walking, old, young, sick, crippled, blind. Blinkered horses and lame donkeys pulling carts piled high with broken lives. Broken men and women in a broken world. Broken, filthy, starving children. Children keeping their heads down, people avoiding eye contact. People made mad by what they had seen, by what had been done to them, perhaps by what they had done. People crying, arguing, shouting, fighting. People speaking in different languages, or not speaking because their language would mark them, betray them as the oppressed, or as the oppressors. People with suitcases and bags or with nothing. Children clutching broken toys. People with their papers hidden from sight, but ready if they should need them. People with no papers, no identities, no proof of who they were. They were not themselves. How would they manage if they were not themselves? How would they repair themselves? How would they make themselves into other people?

Even before that war, in the weeks before that grave announcement came over the wireless, *I have to tell you now that no such undertaking has been received, and that consequently this country is at war with Germany*, but especially once war was declared, bairns came to Glen Conach. But these ones were still themselves, they had not lost their identities, they came checked and labelled, carrying their little cases and their gas-masks. Mostly they came from Dundee, which expected to be bombed. Thousands of Dundee bairns put on trains to Fife, to Perthshire, to Aberdeenshire and to Angus. If you took in an evacuated child you were paid a weekly sum, if you took in a second or a third you were paid a smaller sum for each one. I have read all about this and had it told to me too. So folk in Glen Conach did their duty and calculated that they would not be out of pocket but they had not reckoned on the Dundee bairns, a separate tribe altogether from their own. The Dundee bairns spoke a different language from that of the bairns of the glen, and each tribe regarded the other with wonder and suspicion. The glen bairns were clean and apple-cheeked and knew how to live here; the Dundee bairns had nits and impetigo, and were disturbed by the hills and the wild-eyed cattle. There were some taken into cottages and some into the Big House and none of them had their mothers or even their big sisters with them, for the mothers and sisters were all at work in the factories of Dundee. After a week or two of nightmares, wet beds and other incidents and accidents, things settled down, but it was not a happy time for most of the city bairns. Later, when it became clear that Dundee was not to be bombed after all because, so it was said, Hitler had a granny from Dundee and had forbidden it, they went home again, and they were hardly back when the Germans tried to destroy the Tay Bridge but their bombs landed on the West End and some buildings were hit and some people killed. But for all that none of those bairns came back to Glen Conach.

The dumb lass, though, she came after the war. Sometimes I find myself wondering, which war? Sometimes she seems unreal to me, more myth than flesh and bone. It is as if she has been walking into the glen all through history, with her ragged grey dress and her dirty hair and her bare legs. She's like somebody not from modern times at all. And when I see her like that she is barefoot, like Elspeth on her way out, but the dumb lass came from so far away it seems impossible that she could have walked the whole distance without shoes. Just thinking of the journey she made, hundreds of miles across Europe – the roads she was on, the bridges she crossed, the deranged countryside, the sullen towns, the kind people and the cruel – just thinking of all that is exhausting. And not to know where she was going but to keep going anyway, always into the setting sun. And not to ask for help or guidance once she was on her own because by then she could not speak to ask for anything. As if she sleepwalked her way across a continent. Just to imagine it is heartbreaking, but actually to have done it! I think of all the wars she could have come from, all the violence and suffering she could have witnessed and experienced and escaped, and it doesn't seem to matter much which war or which century or which continent. An innocent child walking through the valley of the shadow of death, and then into the glen of Conach, the place that would be hers, the place to hide and sleep and maybe in the end to die. Like a pilgrim, or a person seeking refuge. Maybe Shirley Darroch is right when she talks about a retreat. Maybe it's not the spirit of Conach she feels, but the spirit of the dumb lass.

But then I have to shake myself because that is not how it happened. She did not walk in shoeless, she came on a bus. Such an ordinary method of travel when so much else about her was extraordinary – even the fact that she came at all, that one day she was not here and the next she was. Found on a bus! That is what she was, a foundling. How can such a word exist? Children are born, not found.

And yet the fact that it does exist shows that she was not quite so extraordinary. There have always been foundlings, and there always will be. We humans have our waifs and strays like any other species of animal. We probably have far more.

Now I am tired again. These thoughts make me tired. She will have to wait a little longer. There is still time. Not as much as there was, but it is still out there in the trees, sniffing about.

Book of Conach

Chapter 17

Of a blind girl whose sight was restored

At another time some men brought a young woman who was blind to Conach's cabin. They wanted him to cure her blindness. Conach was not there. Talorg said that his master had gone into the forest to pray, and he did not know when he would return. Those who brought the girl were fierce and warlike men, unknown to Talorg, and they spoke in a coarse tongue that he could hardly understand. They reminded him of those men that Conach and he had encountered long before in the mountains, but they were not the same men. They said that they were on a journey to the north, and had heard of Conach's power of healing. They were impatient to be on their way and, because the girl would slow them down too much when they crossed the mountains, they proposed to leave her there until they came back. Talorg told them that they could not do this, so reluctantly they took her with them, but when they had gone on a little distance they abandoned her, and later Talorg found her weeping piteously because she could not find her way through the trees. His heart was filled with anger at those men, and with grief for the girl. He consoled her but he could not understand her speech at all. So he took her to his cabin and fed her and let her sleep on his bed while he kept watch outside. And it was summer, and the nights were short and the days full of sunshine.

The next morning, Conach returned. When Talorg related what

had happened, his master said, 'You did well, but she cannot stay with us.' Talorg answered, 'She cannot leave us unless I take her, and where shall I take her? She is not of the glen and she speaks in a strange tongue. Can you not use your power to heal her blindness, and then she can go her own way? For I do not believe the men she was with will come back for her.'

Then Conach said, 'Talorg, how often must I tell you that I have no power but that which comes from God?' Talorg said, 'Then do whatever God allows.' Conach said, 'Bring her to me.'

Talorg brought her, and she knelt before the blessed man. He tilted her head in order to look at her eyes, and he asked her to say her name.

She spoke. Talorg said, 'Do you understand her?'

Conach answered, 'Yes. Her name is Meta, which is the pearl from the oyster. She speaks the same language as we do but it is not her first tongue. She learned it in a place beside the sea where the salt wind has shaped her mouth in a manner that makes her speech strange to your ears. Turn your right side to the sun and you will be facing the sea. Then you will hear her more clearly.' So Talorg turned his right side to the sun and in a little while he began to understand her.

The girl told them that she could formerly see as well as anybody, but some time ago her eyelids began to flutter like birds' wings and shadows fell across her vision. Now her eyelids were as heavy as iron bars, and she could not open them.

Conach said, 'Why did your people desert you? Had you no father or brother to protect you?'

She said, 'They are not my people. I am their slave and their possession. I come from another land, and if I have a father or a brother I do not remember them.'

Then Conach put his hands to her temples, and touching her eyelids with his thumbs he prayed aloud, 'If it be your will, O good and merciful God, let this woman be a witness to your power and to my weakness.'

And straightway her eyelids were freed and she could see again. And she wept with tears of joy and said to Conach, 'How can I repay you?'

He said, 'You owe me nothing, yet you will repay me in full, for on account of you my imperfection will be revealed, and thus you will make my penance complete before God, before whom I must suffer naked and alone.'

She said, 'Who is this god? And why should I be the cause of your suffering?'

He said, 'It is why your sight has been restored to you, which was done by God and not by me. And though you are ignorant of Him now, you will come to know Him before you die.'

She said, 'When they return and find me healed, they will enslave me again.'

He said, 'Do not be afraid, for they themselves have been captured in the north and taken into slavery. This I have seen.'

Then, after she had rested out of the sunlight for some hours, he told Talorg to take her from his presence and deliver her to the people of the glen, who were to treat her as one of their own.

Chapter 18

Of Talorg and Meta

Now, as they were going down by the river, Talorg looked upon Meta, and she was beautiful in his sight. Her skin was darker than any he had ever seen and her eyes were pools of light in the darkness. And he was afraid of what stirred in him. But she, laughing, said, 'There is nothing to fear. What is life if there be not love in it?'

Talorg said, 'Do not tempt me. This is why my master sends you away from us.'

She said, 'But did he not send you with me?'

It being midsummer, the sun and the moon shared the sky, and the night was neither night nor day. And Talorg and Meta lay together and were happy.

In the morning, when Talorg brought her to the village, she said, 'Would you be with me or with your master?' He said, 'How can I choose between you?' She said, 'Do not torment yourself now. What is to come will come, and what is to be will be.'

So he left her with the people of the glen, and went back to Conach with a heavy heart. But often after this Talorg and Meta met secretly in a safe place, and joyful were their meetings.

Chapter 19

Of the madman's death

That wild man who inhabited the glen had not been seen for a long time, nor even heard howling at night. One day, however, filthier and more like an animal than ever, he waited for Conach at his cabin door.

'Art thou still a wicked man?' Conach asked.

'No wickeder than thou,' he answered.

'What dost thou want with me?' Conach said.

'I have come to tell you two things,' the mad creature replied. 'First, that your servant has betrayed you, not once but many times. Second, I come to tell you of my death, which is at hand. And for these truths I ask in return only that you absolve me of my sins before I die.'

'God alone can absolve you,' Conach said, 'and He is not to be bargained with.'

'I bargain only with you,' the madman said. 'Are you not curious to learn of your servant's treachery?'

'No,' Conach answered, 'for I believe him and not you.'

Nevertheless, the venerable hermit's heart was troubled, and when the demented one ran off, returning and rushing forward again like a dog, he followed him. And they came to a path that led to a cave in the hillside, and they spied Talorg, his servant, and Meta, the girl that had been blind, issuing forth from the cave. And Conach put his hand upon the madman's mouth and kept him still, and they were not discovered.

After Talorg and the woman had gone, the madman said, 'I have told you one thing that was not a lie. Now, if you promise to give me absolution I will tell you of another: my death, the time and the nature of it.'

Conach said, 'Though I give you what you ask, the gate of heaven will not open to you if you are a deceiver.' For he thought that the Devil possessed the madman, and sought to trick his way into paradise.

The demented one said, 'My death shall be by stone, by wood and by water, and I shall not see another dawn.' Then he knelt before Conach, who put his hand upon his head and blessed him. And a peace came upon the man such as he had not known for many years. And he and Conach wept together before they parted.

Then, as I have been told, the man went to the river to wash himself. And while he was in the river, some boys from the village saw him and cast stones at him, and wounded him sorely, and he fell into a faint. And the river carried him away until he came to a fallen tree which ensnared him in its branches, and he was drowned. And thus his prediction came to pass.

When Conach heard of this, he grieved for him. The people of the glen were ashamed of what had happened, and brought before Conach the boys who had thrown the stones. But, remembering his own error, he would not permit them to be punished. For, he said, they were but the unwitting instruments of God's will, and indeed they had assisted the man on his journey to everlasting life.

Maja

Over Christmas and New Year, Lachie came to see me several times. A lot of the Darrochs' friends called on them during the holidays. Some just came for an afternoon, others stayed a night or two. There were a few children, but the guests seemed to be mostly grown-ups. They were loud and sometimes a fair amount of drink was taken. Even from here, I heard occasional cheers and shouts. Bagpipes were played at midnight when the year turned. When the noise and jollity got too much for Lachie during the daytime, he would slip away and come to me.

It was quiet in the clachan. Julia was away to her parents, Sean was offshore and Kristina was putting in extra shifts at Tesco in Forfar. Lachie wanted calm, but his brain needed to work too. So I taught him how to play rummy. It became a routine: I'd make the tea while he shuffled the cards, and then we'd begin, hardly saying a word as we played game after game, and at the end of an hour or so he'd go home.

It wasn't for me to mention his ghost. I knew he wouldn't have forgotten her, and if he didn't want to talk about her that was his choice. But I did wonder.

School restarted a few days after New Year, and Lachie didn't come again for almost a fortnight. When he appeared on a Sunday afternoon, quietly taking his place at the table, finding the cards and beginning to shuffle them, I realised that I had missed his presence. Those short midwinter days are not good for drawing or painting or reading. The light is poor and my eyes struggle. I listened to the radio but without much interest, found ordinary tasks quite exhausting, and kept wanting to sleep. I stood at the door every morning, as always, but I did not linger long, even though it wasn't particularly cold. I knew I wasn't ill, but something was changing, and I felt – not lonely, but a little too much alone. So when Lachie came, full of young, intense life, I was glad to see him.

We played rummy. Neither of us showed the other any mercy. The look of pleasure on his face when he won, which he did more often than he lost, was itself a delight. Eventually, when he had beaten me three times in succession, I put my hand over the deck.

'Well, Lachie,' I said, 'you don't have to tell me, but have you seen her again?'

'Not since before Christmas,' he said at once.

'When you saw her in the high park?'

He frowned. 'That was the time before. I saw her after that. Did I not tell you?'

'No.'

'It was the last day of school,' he said. 'We were coming home on the bus.'

'She was on the bus?' I felt my heart beat a little harder.

'No,' he said, '*I* was on the bus with the others, and just as we were about to get off I saw her standing on the pavement. Like she was waiting for me. I thought she was looking in the window but by the time I got off she'd gone.'

'Nobody else saw her?'

He shook his head. 'I don't think they can.'

'And what was she like this time?'

'Just the same. The same dress, and no shoes. It was the closest I'd been to her but there were probably too many of us and she got scared. I think ghosts do get scared. Anyway, I've not seen her since.'

'That's a few weeks.'

'Yes, but just because I don't see her doesn't mean she isn't here.'

I said, 'That's interesting. Do you think ghosts can exist even if nobody sees them?'

'Of course they can. Just because I don't see you for a few days doesn't mean you're not here, does it? Ghosts are the same.'

'Why do you think you can see her but nobody else can?'

He shook his head again. 'Don't know. I'm not special or anything.'

'Well, you are,' I said, 'but maybe not in that way. You don't have special powers, is that what you mean?'

'Well, I'm not Harry Potter,' he said, in as deep and sarcastic a tone as he could muster. I could not contain my laughter, which gave him great satisfaction.

'You know what you said before, about an echo?' he said. 'I think maybe ghosts are dead people who don't want to be forgotten. So they hang around trying to get live people to notice them. They just want to say, look at me. *Please* look at me.'

'They just want to say, I was here?'

He smiled. 'Yes, that's it.'

'You've still not said anything to your mum about this, have you?'

'No, and I'm not going to. And you've not to either. Promise?'

'I promise.'

'Because it wouldn't be fair on her.'

I would have hugged him if he would have let me. I thought, I hope you live to be an old man, Lachie. I hope when you're eighty you remember this. I thought, if you do, you'll have lived a whole life between now and then, and may it be a good one.

I kept thinking about those people from the glen of long ago. Charles Gibb and Jessie and Elspeth and Norah, and Mary from the manse, all of them. I wondered what had happened to them after Charles Gibb's journal came to an end. I thought that Lachie, when he was older, should read that journal and make of it what he could. That made me think of Dr Tybault, and the recordings of Geordie Kemp that were held in some archive in Edinburgh. There was so much for Lachie to find out, if he knew where to look.

January went by, and February, and the first three weeks of March. The light was better every day. Lachie came over once a week, sometimes twice, and we played rummy and drank tea and ate biscuits, and I taught him a few ways to make his drawing better. I left it to him to bring up the ghost girl, or girl ghost, and he chose not to. Every time he was with me I knew myself to be blessed.

But one day in late March his visits came to an end. The coronavirus was the cause of it. For weeks the virus had been in the news. It was gathering pace, it was on the move. When I put on the radio I could hear it in the background as it made its way out of China and round the world, on planes and boats and trains. It moved in silence yet I heard a kind of hiss, like a leak of water or gas. It arrived in Europe, country after country succumbing to its seeping advance. The news, first from Italy, then from Spain and France, from so many places, was terrible. The virus seemed a long way from our glen, but it was coming.

One Wednesday the government announced they were closing the schools at the end of the week. Lachie came over on the Sunday and we played cards, and he talked about the virus, quite cheerfully. He wasn't frightened, he said. It probably wouldn't get anywhere near us. He was sorry about being off school and having to spend more time around his sister but at least the house was big, and here nobody was going to stop him going outside. Everything would be okay. 'I'm sure it will be,' I said. Then he looked at me and said, 'You're not to worry,' and I realised that all his bright talk was to make me feel better. He'd worked out that if the virus did come this far I'd be its number-one target. 'I'm not worried, Lachie,' I said. 'Honestly, I'm not.' And that was how we left it.

The next day the lockdown began. And the day after that Shirley came over. Was there anything I needed? She or Peter would be going into Forfar every week as long as the situation lasted, and they would get me whatever I asked for in the way of food or anything else, if it was available. I thanked her. I said that Julia had already made the same offer that morning. I was well stocked-up and I didn't eat much. I'd let Julia or her know if I was running short of anything.

'You're pretty tough, Maja. You'll get through this.'

'We all will,' I said.

Then she said, 'You know Lachie won't be able to come and see you until it's over. All this stuff about keeping our distance – we're all going to have to do it.'

I wasn't surprised, but something in me made me kick against her words.

'Even here?'

'Even here. Different households have to keep apart.'

'But I never leave the glen,' I said. 'The last time I was out of it was when you took me for my birthday meal, and that was at least a year ago. I can't possibly have it. The virus, I mean. Lachie would be completely safe.'

'You can't say that,' she said. 'Anyway, what about you? What if he gets it? It doesn't seem to affect children badly, but he might give it to you.'

'But he won't be leaving the glen either.'

'He might already have it and not be showing any symptoms. Or one of us might get it, pass it to him but not know we had for a week or more, by which time . . . I admit it's unlikely but that's the whole point, isn't it? We just don't know. And you're a vulnerable person, Maja. You'll probably get an official letter telling you so.'

'Me, a vulnerable person? Shirley, you are mistaking me for somebody else. You just told me how tough I am.'

'Well, I'm also telling you, we're all going to have to keep our distance, not just Lachie. We'll try to get you whatever you need. We'll bring it to your door, and of course if you're ill or need help of any kind we're going to be here, and Julia and Kristina too.'

'I think you're overreacting,' I said, at which she snapped back at me, 'We have to stick to the rules or there's no point in having rules. I'm sorry.'

I don't know why I was arguing. She was right. And I wasn't even arguing, I was just being stubborn. She stood there with her hands outstretched in a kind of pleading way, but she didn't come towards me for a hug.

'Well, at least it'll be spring soon,' I said. 'Maybe we'll all shout to each other. Can Lachie come and shout at me if he stays outside?'

'Yes, we'll organise a weekly shout,' Shirley said. By which I knew that he wasn't going to be allowed to come on his own.

She was being perfectly reasonable. She was his mother, and he was only eight. I keep forgetting that.

Shirley came to my door one day, a year ago – or was it two? – and asked, as if it had just occurred to her, 'Maja, do you think you are eighty yet?'

I had been giving it some thought myself. I said, 'Yes, I think I probably am by now.'

'Peter and I would like to take you out for dinner. A celebration. Would you like that?'

I wasn't sure if I would. She added, 'We'll ask Julia too. Just the four of us. Not a crowd.'

'That would be fine, then,' I said.

Peter drove us to a fancy restaurant in Dundee. I hardly knew such places existed in Dundee. I tried not to look at the prices since I was not allowed to contribute. It was midweek and quite quiet. Not long after the waiter took our orders a man and a woman came to the table next to ours. The waiter brought them menus and they ordered their meals and drinks. The man had a bottle of beer and the woman had a glass of white wine. He took out his phone and she took out another gadget with a screen and they sat there fingering and thumbing and sweeping, heads down. For fifteen minutes they did not exchange a single word. Even when their food arrived they kept at it, with their gadgets laid beside their plates where the serviettes had been. I found it hard to concentrate on my own food or on the conversation at our table. I silently condemned those people for being stupid, for being inhuman, for not liking each other, for not caring about each other – but then I told myself not to be so self-righteous. They were only doing what the dumb lass did for years. They had retreated into themselves and become mute. Why? Because they were damaged. Damage had been done to them. You could say that they had a choice and the dumb lass didn't, that she was a child and they were adults, but still it was not really their fault. It was what had been done to them. Their behaviour was not inhuman. It was completely natural.

That evening, after Shirley had been to say Lachie couldn't visit me any more, Julia came in with her bottle of malt whisky. It is a little ritual of ours. Every once in a while I take my bottle to her or she brings hers to me. We have two drams each, one from each bottle, and that is that. One of my few luxuries, when my bottle gets low, is that I hand Julia some cash and she buys me an interesting replacement. It's the only alcohol I keep in the house.

'After this,' she said, 'we'll have to be good for as long as it takes. Not long, I hope. I don't like drinking on my own.'

'I don't think I ever have,' I said, remembering that final dram I'd had in Geordie's front room. 'I'll not start now.'

'We could always toast one another across the wall when the weather gets better,' she said.

'Dangerous,' I said. 'I'll wait till it's over.' And I thought of her cat, Tam, who would continue to walk along the wall as if nothing in the world had changed. And in his world, nothing would have.

Julia is the office manager of a housing association in Dundee. She said she would be going in the next day to organise work-from-home schedules for the staff, and after that she too would be working from home. She was worried about some of her clients and how they would cope with lockdown. She would miss some of her colleagues, but not all of them. She wasn't sure how disciplined she would be when her desk was only a few steps away from her bed.

She sounded like an older version of Lachie.

Julia's parents are in Ayrshire. Her father hasn't kept well for some time. She was concerned about not being able to go and see them, about how her mother would manage without friends and family coming in.

I said, 'People are resilient. They will get used to almost anything after a while.'

'Not everybody,' she said. 'If it's just Mum and Dad on their own they'll drive each other crazy, but they've been doing that for years, so you're right, up to a point. But getting used to something isn't a virtue. If you're stuck in a bad situation, you only get used to it because you don't have any choice. Otherwise you'd get out.'

Julia has been a very good neighbour since she came to live next door ten years ago. She has become a friend in that time, but that too is through circumstance rather than choice. We've exchanged a lot of information about ourselves, but also withheld some. I don't know much about her past life or any relationships she may have had, and I am not that interested. She knows some of my story, but not all of it. But, then, neither do I.

At some point that evening, while Julia was speculating about how long the lockdown might last, I remembered Dr Tybault, sitting just where she was sitting, taking out his mobile phone to record what I was going to say. I thought, if I had a recording device maybe I could try to tell the story of the dumb lass, so that Lachie could hear it, hear my voice telling it. But I knew I would get stuck. I would start in the wrong place, or leave some important detail out. Or I would say more than I meant to, or more than I actually knew.

Just having those thoughts made me realise that I didn't want to go out of the world without leaving the story of the dumb lass in it.

For Lachie, or perhaps for somebody else I couldn't imagine, a hundred or two hundred years into the future. But now, because of this virus, I couldn't tell it to him. I would have to write it down, the way Charles Gibb had written things down in his journal. And it might survive or it might not. Anyway, if not now, when? I was about to have a good deal more time on my hands than usual – even Frank would not be coming in his library van with books for me. I had an unused sketchbook with decent-sized pages of good-quality paper without lines. It would almost be like drawing.

'What do you think?' Julia said.

'I'm sorry. Think about what?'

'You're tired,' she said. 'I'll be off in a minute. I was saying that maybe this coronavirus thing is nature redressing the balance. The world saying, enough is enough. Is that too far-fetched?'

'Not at all,' I said. 'And maybe not just the virus. Maybe it's everything – floods, fires, chopping down the rainforest, clogging up the oceans with plastic. Enough is enough. Why not?'

'There are too many of us,' Julia said. 'If most of us were wiped out, the planet would be okay.'

We nursed our whiskies in silence, in a glen with only forty people in it, and it was hard to believe that there were too many of us or that we should be wiped out. The logs in the stove glowed and crumbled. In 1809, all the fires burning in the world made no difference to the world, but everything was changed now.

Book of Conach

Chapter 20

How Conach was led into temptation

Now I come to the hardest part of my history, when I must give a true account of the holy man's temptation by the Devil, who preyed upon his weakness and caused him to stumble. And herein lies the reason for the Church's disregard of Conach, for it prefers the lives of our saints to be as pure as new snow. Although all men are sinners, the Church makes the goodness of the saints shine so brightly that their sins can no longer be discerned. But Conach's life, as I here record it, retains its blemishes as well as its beauties, and this I believe will endear his memory more to those who know his name than if he were robed all in white.

After the death of the wild man of the glen, Conach was much troubled by what he had learned of Talorg and the girl, Meta. He loved Talorg as a son, and wished neither to lose him nor to hold him against his will. He could not forget the promise Talorg had made, to forsake all and go with him as his servant. Yet neither could he forget that Talorg was a young man who had not dedicated himself to God as he himself had.

One day he said to Talorg that he was going into the forest to be alone for a prolonged period of reflection and prayer, and would not return for a week or more. Then he took his leave and departed, but he did not go far. This was a great lie that Conach told, and I cannot deny it.

He became like the wild man, creeping and hiding as he watched over his servant. Talorg did what work he had to do, and then he went down to the village. Conach waited, and in a while what he both dreaded and desired took place: Talorg returned, and with him was the girl. Painful it was for Conach to hear the laughter of this pair, and especially to see Talorg's face, for he had never seen his servant smile so happily. And he crouched in the bushes like a fox, and groaned with the hurt that was in him.

For three days he hid, and could not avert his eyes from the young man and young woman, who grew so confident of being alone that they went naked everywhere. And the Devil was beside Conach in the form of a snake, and praised the beauty of the woman and the virility of the man. So Conach crawled closer, and saw and heard the pleasure that Talorg and Meta took of one another, and was both envious and lustful. And he caressed the Devil and spilled his seed upon the ground.

On the third day, when Talorg went a little way from the clearing where the cabins stood, he heard snoring in the bushes and discovered his master asleep. Talorg was greatly shocked and cried out. His master awoke, and they saw into each other's eyes and were equally mortified. And Conach fled into the forest.

Talorg returned to Meta and said, 'Get dressed, because my master is nearby and he will be angry with us for what we have done.' She replied, 'What have we done that he should be angry?' He said, 'We have sinned, and he will know it in our faces.' So they put on their clothes.

Then, hearing cries of great anguish and hastening towards the sound, they found Conach naked in a thicket of briars, tearing open his flesh upon them. Even as the blood gushed from him he threw himself ever deeper among the thorns. They begged him to cease, but he paid no heed, asking only that he be left alone to chastise himself before God.

So they departed, and the woman said, 'Why does he so hurt and abuse his body? Surely this is a great offence to his god who made him?' But Talorg said only that his master was closer to God than either of them, and knew what would please or displease Him. And the woman pondered these words in her heart.

Then Talorg sent her back to the village, telling her to wait until such time as he should come to her again.

When she had gone, the young man beat his fists upon his chest and wept. But in a little while he calmed himself, and waited until the cries of his master ceased. Then he took his knife and went to him, and found him hanging upon the briars in a state of utter torpidity. He cut him free from his fetters and carried him to his cabin and tended him there for many days. But even when Conach regained some of his strength, they did not speak of the things that had passed.

Chapter 21

Of Conach's act of sacrifice

From this time forth, once he had recovered, Conach spent but little time with his servant. Nor did Talorg have any communication with Meta, the woman whom he loved and whose blindness Conach had miraculously healed. But one day she came in great distress to the place where their cabins were. As it happened, both the hermit and his servant were present. She told them that the band of desperate men who had enslaved her had appeared in the village, demanding that she be surrendered to them. They had stolen the beasts and chattels of the people and abused some of the women, and when two of the village men resisted, they had killed them. The people of the village believed that Meta was the cause of this calamity, and feared that if they did not give her up worse things would happen to them, but before they could seize her she escaped and came to Conach and Talorg for sanctuary.

Conach sighed and said, 'Now I am repaid for my wickedness. I saw in a vision that those men were made slaves in the north. But God blinded me so that I did not see that they would return here, and I am sorry for it.'

The woman said, 'Wherefore did this god, who gave me my sight, make you blind?'

He said, 'Because I was consumed with lust and envy, and this is the consequence of my sin. Where are those men now?'

She said, 'They will be here soon. Am I to be taken by them again because of your sin?'

'No,' Conach said, and without hesitation he instructed Talorg to take the woman to the cave in the hillside, to stay with her and guard her. 'For,' he said, 'you are made to be her shield as you have already been a blanket over her.' Talorg said, 'Will you not come with us, Master? If you stay, they will surely kill you.' Conach said, 'I will stand before these men, and God will decide if I am to be killed.'

Then Talorg said, 'Master, I shall remain with you, as I chose long ago.' Conach said, 'My son, you have made another choice. You have chosen this woman. Take her, and may God be with you and with her. Only, leave me your knife, and see that it is sharp.'

So Talorg sharpened his knife and left it with him, and he and the woman went and hid in the cave.

In a little while, the men who had enslaved Meta came to Conach's cabin and found him at prayer. They handled him roughly and said, 'Where is the girl we left with your servant? For they have told us you cured her blindness, and we have come to get our property back.'

Conach said, 'You lie. You did not leave her with my servant. You abandoned her in the forest. You have no claim on her.'

But they said again, 'Where is she? She is ours.'

He said, 'You yourselves were slaves in the north, yet now you are free. Do those who enslaved you have a claim on you?'

They laughed at him, saying, 'Old man, we are free because we killed our captors. They have no claim on us, but we demand what is ours. Tell us where she is.'

He said, 'She is not here.'

They said, 'Old man, we heard that you were wise and had miraculous powers, which was why we brought the girl to you. But now we see that you are both foolish and powerless, or you would not defy us. Tell us where she is.'

But he said only, 'She is not here.'

Then they released him and said, 'Go to her now and when you draw nigh to the place only nod your head and pass on, and we will spare you.'

He said, 'She is not here.'

They said, 'Must we torture you until your tongue speaks in spite of your obduracy?' And they made to lay hold of him again.

He said, 'No, for my tongue is not yours to command.' Then he drew the knife from his robe, and with his free hand he grasped the end of his tongue and with the blade he severed it and offered it to them in his hand. And they were appalled by what he had done and shrank from his offering. The blood gushed from his mouth like a fountain, and he cast both knife and tongue to the ground and stood before them.

When these bold men saw that he neither would nor could tell them what they demanded to know, they fell out among themselves. Some wished to kill him and some to hunt for the woman, while others wished only to leave as quickly as they could. And while they disputed among themselves what to do the people of the glen, who had come in pursuit to avenge their sons and daughters, fell upon them in a great fury and slew them, every one.

As this was happening all around him, Conach did not move but stood with his arms outstretched and his face turned to heaven. Only when the slaughter was over did his mouth cease to issue blood. Blood-red was he, from head to toe. And his tongue lay on the blood-soaked earth, and no man would approach it.

Then Talorg and Meta descended from the hillside and saw what had occurred. Meta lifted the tongue in her hands and held it before Conach, saying, 'Twice you have saved my life. You restored my sight but I have not the power to restore your speech. Only your God, in whom from henceforth I put my faith, has that power. Put your tongue back in your mouth and if your God hears my prayer He will mend it.'

She knelt before Conach as if to pray but he touched her brow with his bloodied fingers and shook his head, by which she understood that she was not to beseech such a remedy from God. And in that very moment she was filled with the love of Christ and was converted in her heart, although Conach could say nothing to her.

Now it happened that the leader of the band of wicked men was lying a few feet from her, and was not yet devoid of all life. He reached for Talorg's knife where it lay and with the last of his strength he stabbed Meta in the back, saying, 'No other shall have you.' And before they could strike him down he expired.

Then Talorg gave a great howl and gathered the woman into his arms, and took the knife from her back, but the life ran out of her and she died without further speech. Great was the consternation of the people who witnessed these things, and who saw the pain of Talorg who was a friend to them all. And Conach came and put his hands upon the shoulders of his servant, and for hours they were as if turned to stone, without movement but for the tears which coursed down their faces like rain.

At last Talorg stood and, turning to Conach, he said, 'Today you are not my master, but from tomorrow I will serve you again until death separates us.' He fetched water from the river and washed Meta, and the women of the village brought a winding-sheet and he wrapped her body in it. Likewise he washed the tongue of his master and wrapped it in a cloth. He dug a grave for Meta and placed her body in it and the tongue beside her. And Conach made no intervention until Talorg handed him the spade, and he took it and filled in the grave while the other sat and watched.

Chapter 22

Of Conach's last years and of his death

After these events Conach lived for a dozen years or more, ever more reclusive in his habits. Refusing to desert his master, his servant Talorg built a new cabin for himself some distance from that of Conach, and from that time was not only the hermit's servant but also his guardian, protecting him from the world as well as providing him with whatever he required, which in truth was little enough. Sometimes the two men would sit together in silent companionship. More often, however, Conach wandered the glen by himself, barefoot and clad only in his customary robe of coarse cloth.

No longer able to speak or sing, Conach from the time of his sacrifice did not permit himself even to make sounds, but maintained a complete silence for the rest of his days. He communicated with Talorg by signs and by touch, and acted likewise with any who came seeking him. At first there were many such pilgrims, but when it became evident that God had removed Conach's healing powers, they ceased to come. Even the people of the glen left him in peace, which was not neglectful but their way of showing respect for him. And in this peace and solitude, as I have been told, Conach became, if not the happiest of men, then wholly placid and free of all passion, impatience and ill temper. He was beloved of God and of the birds and animals that lived in the forest.

There came a time, and it was approaching winter, when Conach's old and deformed feet no longer supported his frail body, and he was unable to walk. Then he made Talorg to understand that he did not wish to lie helplessly on his bed waiting for death, but would rather begin his final journey at once; also, that he did not wish his body to be interred. Talorg was to carry him up the mountain, and leave him there to die, and afterwards to let his flesh be exposed to the cold, the wind and the rain, to be food for the wolves and other creatures. So

Talorg obeyed his master, who was by then as light as a child to him. He took him upon his back and carried him high into the hills, and laid him in a place where he could watch the sun rise in the morning and the stars shine at night, and there, after they had shed many tears, they parted for the last time. And Conach died looking out over the glen which now bears his name, and was received by Christ at the gate of paradise, and blessed is he in our memory even though the Church remembers him not.

Talorg abandoned his own cabin and was given shelter in the village. During that winter, he told over and over all that he knew of Conach's life, all that they had faced together and all that his master had taught him. He did this, so I believe, in the hope that Conach's name would not be forgotten by ordinary people even if the Church had no interest in preserving his memory. And so it has proved to be, for how else can these tales have come into my care?

In the spring, when the snows melted, Talorg went back to the mountain and found those bones of his master that had not been carried away by animals, and gathered them together and brought them to Conach's cabin and buried them nearby. Over them he put a stone which he carved with a cross, which may still be seen to this day, though the cabin and all other physical evidence of Conach's presence have long since gone. Then Talorg himself said farewell to his friends and left the glen, and of where he went and what became of him I am entirely ignorant. No doubt, in time, the stone marked with the cross, which I myself have prayed beside, will also disappear, and only this book will be testament to Conach's story. And this is the purpose of my toil in writing down these words, to show the life of a good man who was not however without faults, who lived and died in Christ, and all to the greater glory of God the Father, the Son and the Holy Spirit, in whom we trust in this world and in the next.

Yet should a day come when Conach's name is forgotten, or a day when God's name is unknown or despised in this world, or a day when war, pestilence, flood and fire rage unchecked across the earth, even in such a day shall hope abide in human hearts, that to each and every one, and to creatures of all kinds, a place of refuge and tranquillity is assigned; and if that place be found in this life then blessed beyond all blessings is the finder, and if it be not found then hope itself is the name of it, and the only door that closes upon hope is called death. Amen.

Story of the Dumb Lass

Dear Lachie

I am missing our weekly games of cards. It was good to see you, your mum, dad and Rosie the other day, when we stood in that big circle and shouted and laughed, but it wasn't the same as when just the two of us meet. Anyway, as we don't know how long the lockdown is going to last, I have decided to write a story for you. I suppose I could add 'just in case', as I am very old and who knows what might happen in the next few weeks? You told me not to worry about the virus and I am taking your advice: I would rather it didn't come here and I certainly don't want to catch it since it seems to be very hard on old people, but at the same time I am not worrying about it. There isn't much point. In return, I don't want you to worry about me. It won't do either of us any good.

The thing is, this story of mine is a true one. I will try to tell it as well and as truthfully as I can, although there are parts missing and parts that are probably not quite right. But there is no one else left who knows as much of it as I do, so where there are gaps you will have to use your imagination to fill them in. That is what I have done when my memory has failed me.

And probably, as I write, I will sometimes forget that the story is supposed to be for you. My mind will go for a wander and I will just write things down as I see them. So don't worry if you don't understand every word – that will be my fault, not yours. If I haven't finished writing it before we meet again I won't give it to you until I have. And if I have *finished it, I might decide to keep it until you're a bit older, even perhaps until I am not around to get in the way of you reading it.*

Because if you had any questions I probably wouldn't be able to answer them, and that would be frustrating for both of us.

Well, we will see.

With love
Maja.

The story starts on a Tuesday in September 1945, the year the Second World War ended. There was a bus then too, that took the children of Glen Conach to school. They had to go to Brig o' Conach, just as they do today, because the school in the glen had closed twenty years earlier. The bus driver was a man called Sam Dawson. Every weekday morning, he drove the bus up the glen to collect the bairns and after he had taken them to the school he drove the roads to Forfar and Brechin and Montrose, picking folk up and setting them down at farm road-ends and villages all along the route. In Montrose he had his dinner break, and then he drove back, stopping at Brig o' Conach for the bairns to come out of school, and brought them home again.

Mr Dawson was always dour, and often angry. He had a red face and red whiskers and a blue uniform with a peaked cap. He barked and growled a lot, like a collie dog, and the bairns would not have dared to eat anything or put their feet on the seats while they were on his bus. Mr Dawson had once put a boy off, and the boy had had to walk two miles home in the dark, and when he got home his father asked why he was so late and the boy told him he had been put off the bus. The father asked what he had done, and the boy said he didn't know, which may have been true. And the father said that he must have done something, and took off his belt and beat the son with it so he wouldn't do it again.

On this Tuesday afternoon in September, about four o'clock, Mr Dawson drove his bus into the clachan. There were six glen bairns on board, sitting halfway down the bus in a group, chatting and laughing but not too loudly. When Sam Dawson pulled up outside the post office four of them got off, and two brothers stayed on because they lived further up the glen. There was still a post office then. Apart from the Big House it was the only building that had a telephone line. Nobody had phones in their houses, and mobile phones hadn't been invented. You could buy stamps and postal orders at the post office, and collect pensions and other payments, and you could send a telegram if you had to, or receive one if there was bad news, although a telegram was a rare event indeed – it was an expensive way of getting an urgent message to somebody. So the four bairns got off the bus, and the two brothers who were staying on were changing seats to be together when all at once they began to shriek, and ran to the front of the bus just as Mr Dawson was about to drive off. He yanked the handbrake on and shouted at them to sit down but they wouldn't. 'Mr Dawson, Mr Dawson, there's something back there under the seat!' 'What do you mean?' 'It's a cat or a monkey or something,' the older brother said. Mr Dawson told him not to talk nonsense, but he went to have a look.

Well, there was something. It was stuck in below the seat at the very rear of the bus. Mr Dawson put his hand in and grabbed and pulled. Out it came, and it wasn't a cat or a monkey, it was another bairn. It didn't seem to be moving. Mr Dawson yelled at his two passengers to stay at the front, and picked the bairn up and set it on its feet and yelled at it. 'Whit the blazes were ye daein' doon there?' (He spoke in the local dialect of Scots, as others in this story did, and I will write it down as well as I can.) The bairn fell over and he set it up again, and found that his hands were covered in coal dust. 'Whit's your name?' he yelled. 'Whar are ye fae? Whar did ye get on the bus?' He'd been driving the bus for years and he knew every bairn along his route but he'd never seen this one before. But the bairn didn't answer, it seemed to shrink away from him. Mr Dawson seized it by the arms and half carried, half dragged it out on to the road where by now all six glen bairns that had been on the bus were waiting in a state of excitement, and he started yelling at the new bairn again, so red in the face they thought he was going to burst.

The new bairn didn't do anything. It didn't cry or swear or spit or try to run away, it just slumped to the ground. It wasn't like a bairn, it was like a small animal trying to look like something else, and Mr Dawson was like a dog barking at it.

I think now that's exactly what he was – a dog that barks at something not because it's angry but because it's puzzled and a little afraid. And the more the bairn did nothing, just lay there in the road, the more puzzled and afraid he became and the louder he barked. After a minute or two Mrs Pirnie, the postmistress, opened her door and said, 'What's all this?' When she saw the bairn she said to Mr Dawson, 'That's enough now, can you not see the poor thing is absolutely terrified?'

Later Mrs Pirnie would wonder why she had said that, because the bairn didn't look to her as if it had any emotion in it at all.

'You take these children home, Sam,' Mrs Pirnie said, 'and come back here, and by then perhaps we'll know what this is all about.'

Mr Dawson wiped his hands on a cloot and got the two brothers that lived up the glen back on board, although they didn't want to go, and the bus drove off, and Mrs Pirnie sent the other bairns away. All this time the new bairn was lying curled in the road. It seemed to be watching and yet at the same time not watching. Mrs Pirnie lowered herself till she was almost lying on the road too, and held out her hand. 'Now,' she said, 'there is no need to be frightened. Nobody will hurt you. If you will come inside with me you can have some cake and a glass of milk.'

The bairn's eyes stared at Mrs Pirnie's hand. Those eyes were great white saucers with small black centres. Its hair was short, thick and matted, as if somebody had chopped it weeks before in a great hurry and it had never been attended to since. The bairn had no socks or stockings and the shoes were so far gone that its toes were sticking out of the left one. It had on a smock or dress and a woollen jersey on top of that, both of a greyish colour but smeared black with coal. Everything about it – its clothing, its arms and legs, face and fingernails – was utterly filthy. If it hadn't been for the dress Mrs Pirnie would not have known if it was a girl or a boy, and even then she wasn't certain.

Mrs Pirnie ran the post office in an orderly and strict manner – she had done so right through the war after her husband, the postmaster (whose family had been in the glen for eight generations), had caught pneumonia and died – but she had a soft heart when it came to bairns. She had had three boys of her own, they had all grown up and gone to the war and one of them had been killed in the North African desert and the others were still overseas. So now she squatted there with her hand outstretched until the bairn reached and took it and then, gently and slowly, without pulling, she led her into her house, which was the other half of the building where the post office was. She put a cushion on one of her wooden chairs and a tea towel over it to protect it from the coal dirt and she lifted the bairn up on to the chair. Mrs Pirnie was shocked by the lightness of her and the feel of her bones beneath the dress, and also by the smell of her. She began to regret the cushion, which was decorated with a fat hen and three chicks that she had embroidered herself. She poured some milk into a cup and cut a slice of cake for the bairn, and watched as she drank and ate greedily. Her mouth had several teeth missing. Mrs Pirnie said, 'And what do you say?', not really expecting an answer, let alone a thank-you, and she did not get one.

Mrs Pirnie went into the post office to use the telephone. She kept the door open so that she could glance through every so often to check on the bairn. She called the Big House (where you live now, Lachie) and asked to speak to Sir Gregory Grant. Sir Gregory was not at home, but his wife was. When Lady Grant came to the telephone Mrs Pirnie apologised for disturbing her. Something unusual had happened, she explained. A strange child had appeared out of nowhere, on the bus, and she wasn't sure what to do about it. As Lady Grant had taken evacuee children during the war and as Sir Gregory was a Justice of the Peace, she felt that they would know the right course of action to take.

Lady Grant said that this was not a convenient time. 'But what am I to do with her?' Mrs Pirnie asked. 'It's a girl, is it?' Lady Grant replied. 'Can you not keep her until tomorrow? I will call in in the morning.' Lady Grant had a clipped, commanding accent which made her sound impatient with everything and everybody.

Mrs Pirnie made another call to the post office at Brig o' Conach, where the postmaster was Arthur Dunn, whose sister, Effie, was the district nurse. Mrs Pirnie told him the situation and Mr Dunn, who lived with his sister, said he would get Effie to cycle up in the morning, but he couldn't say what time. Mrs Pirnie said, 'Could you let Wull Macfarlane know as well?' Wull Macfarlane was the local policeman. He also stayed at the Brig.

By the time Sam Dawson returned, the bairn had drunk a pint of milk and eaten another slice of cake. Mrs Pirnie did not want to give her more for fear that she would not stop. When Sam came in, the bairn suddenly became still – like an animal sensing danger and playing dead, Mrs Pirnie thought. She asked Sam to stay on the other side of the room and to take his cap off and not to raise his voice. 'She's afraid of you,' she said. 'It's because you shouted at her before.'

'The wee gype shouldna hide on buses if she disna want shouted at,' Sam said. 'It's no my fault.'

Mrs Pirnie said, 'Nevertheless, Sam, we must try to find out where she has come from, so we can get her home. Can you think where she might have got on? It must have been when you were away from the bus doing something else.'

Sam had left the engine running at a few farm gates while he dropped off parcels or picked up eggs, but he didn't think it could have been at any of those places. The bairn couldn't have just climbed out of a hedge. And most of the time there was a passenger or two on the bus, so they would have spotted her even if he hadn't. He thought it must have happened in Montrose, when he was on his dinner break and the bus was lying empty at the station. 'There was tinkers hingin' aboot,' he said. 'That's a tinkie quine if ever I saw ane. Scrape the dirt aff her and she'll be just as dark below. She'll be hoatchin', Mistress Pirnie, and if ye dinna pit her oot quick your hale hoose will be infested.'

'Never mind about that,' Mrs Pirnie said. 'But why would she have got on your bus?'

'Either she sneaked on to see if there was onythin' she could steal, or they pit her on to get shot o' her,' Sam Dawson said. 'I doot there's something no right wi her. She'll be a imbecile or something. They're heartless, the tinkers, when it comes to that kind o' things.'

Now, the war had only been over a few months, and Mrs Pirnie had read the newspaper reports of what had been done to Jews and gypsies and the like in the German concentration camps and once, at the cinema in Forfar, she had seen a shocking newsreel of the liberation of one of those camps. She said, 'Sam, she's just a bairn,' and she remembered the feel of the skin and bone beneath the lassie's dress.

Sam looked a little ashamed, but he said he couldn't take her all the way back to Montrose now. It was too late, and anyway if it was tinkies who had put her on the bus they would be long gone. The police would have to be told, and the bairn would have to go into a children's home until they found the parents, *if* they could find them and *if* they didn't deny she was theirs.

And all the time they were talking the bairn did not move a muscle or make a sound.

'Why is she covered in coal dust?' asked Mrs Pirnie.

'Maybe she's been hidin',' Sam said. 'Maybe she's been hidin' in somebody's coal cellar.'

'Sam,' Mrs Pirnie said, 'you'd better be on your way. But before you go would you step across to Molly Skene and ask her to come over? If I'm to keep this child tonight she'll need to be bathed and that might be more than I can manage on my own.'

Once Sam was gone, Mrs Pirnie thought that the lassie relaxed slightly. 'You've not uttered a word,' she said. 'I wonder what's going on inside your head.'

The bairn jerked forward suddenly and vomited milk and cake across the table, and as soon as she had done this she slid off the chair and crawled into the corner furthest away from Mrs Pirnie and crouched in it with her arms over her head, as if she expected to have the daylight beaten out of her. And Mrs Pirnie was never going to hit her, she only wanted to comfort her but some instinct stopped her from going too close and frightening her more. She stood beside the table saying, over and over again in as soft a voice as she could manage, 'It's all right, I'm not going to hurt you, I'm not going to hurt you.' And she was looking at the mess she was going to have to clean up, and then she saw the cushion with the hen and her chicks, dark and sodden where the bairn had been sitting.

You should understand that none of this was remembered by the dumb lass. She had it told to her later by Mrs Pirnie and Molly Skene and others who had different parts of it. She had no memory of how or where she had got on the bus, or whether she crawled under the seat at the back or somebody put her there. She had no memory of Sam Dawson pulling her out and shouting at her, although she was always a little afraid of Sam. No memory of the milk and the cake or being sick or wetting the cushion. No memory of Molly Skene coming in with her daughter, Janet. No memory of Mrs Pirnie telling them to wheesht and Janet saying in a trembling voice, 'Is she deid?' No memory of Mrs Pirnie trying to loosen the arms and legs that she had clamped tight around her own body, while Molly tried to get the jersey and dress off her. No memory of trying to beat them back with tiny, fierce fists, or of how she suddenly went floppy, or of how they had to use scissors to cut her out of the clothes, or of how the clothes went straight into a sack and Janet was told to take the sack to her father and get him to burn it with all its contents. No memory of the tin bath filled with water, not too hot, and the two women lifting her in still curled like a shell upon herself, and Molly holding her while Mrs Pirnie began the slow, soft business of soaping and rinsing, changing the water, soaping and rinsing again, and the way they shook their heads when they saw the bruises she had on her. No memory of Molly gently massaging the tightness out of her arms and legs and saying, 'Oh, lass, there's naethin' o' ye,' and Mrs Pirnie saying in an awed voice, 'Terrible things have happened to this child.' No memory of the nappy Molly made for her out of an old towel, and the blankets Mrs Pirnie sorted into a shakedown bed in front of the fire, and the pillow – an old one that she could afford to throw away if she had to – they put under her head. No memory of Wull Macfarlane, who cycled up that evening and wrote ponderously in his notebook and said he would pass his report on to the station at Forfar and they would look into it. No memory of any of this.

Nor of how Mrs Pirnie sat up through the night, fearing that if she went to her own bed the bairn would wake and fall in the fire, or take herself off and be hit by a motor car or Sam's bus coming up the road in the dark of early morning. Nor of how she slept without moving for eight hours, and Mrs Pirnie kept having to check that she was not dead. Nor of how Molly came with some old clothes of Janet's for her, and how when she woke she clenched up again and made it so difficult for them to get her dressed before Lady Grant came. The dumb lass remembered none of it.

She had to learn it from people who told her it was all true, but how did she know it was true? It might have happened to some other wee lassie and they just said it was her. But why would they lie about it? They weren't people who told lies. And if it wasn't true, why else was she here in the glen? That was all she knew when she began to look around herself: that she had arrived, that she was somewhere. For a long time she knew nothing else, and maybe not even that.

*

Lady Grant said, 'She is not very lively. Is she abnormal?'

Molly Skene said, 'She was lively enough yestreen, Ma'am, but we gied her a guid wash and we think they're awa noo.'

Molly was talking about the lice that were in the dumb lass's hair and on her body. If Lady Grant understood what she meant she did not acknowledge it. She found it hard enough anyway to understand Molly, who had an accent that was very different from hers.

Mrs Pirnie said, 'I don't think she is abnormal, Ma'am. Quite the opposite. I think she has suffered terribly and is in a state of shock, and that's normal.'

Lady Grant did not really believe in shock as a state. She thought *a* shock was something that took you by surprise and then you got over it. On this, and not only this, her views differed from those of her husband, who had fought in the First World War.

'Is that what you think?' Lady Grant said. 'Well, what is it you wish from me?'

'I just thought you should know that she is here, Ma'am. And Sir Gregory too, in case there's anything official to be done.'

'Yes, yes, I see.' Lady Grant shifted in the armchair in which she had been invited to sit. She did not find it comfortable. They all looked at the lass, who was sitting on the floor and seemed not at all interested in the new clothes she had on, nor that there were three women in the room with her. She stared at an empty space a foot away, or perhaps she didn't.

'Has she not spoken at all?' Lady Grant asked.

'Not a word,' Mrs Pirnie said. 'Not even a sound. It's uncanny.'

'Child,' Lady Grant said, 'do you know your name?'

After a few seconds she said, 'Can you not say something?'

And after a few more she said, 'Can you hear me?'

'I did wonder,' Mrs Pirnie said, 'if she was deaf as well. I mean, as well as dumb.'

'Mibbe she disna ken English,' Molly Skene said.

'Well, we can hardly try her in every language until we find one that suits her,' Lady Grant said. 'You have been very kind to her, Mrs Pirnie, and I am sure she is much better now than she was when she was discovered. But she doesn't belong here, does she, although she must belong to somebody. Have the police been informed?'

'Yes, Ma'am. Constable Macfarlane came last night. And the nurse is coming to look at her this morning.'

'Well, you have done everything you could have done. We are very grateful – more grateful, I fear, than the girl's family will be. She is a gypsy, I take it?'

'I don't know,' Mrs Pirnie said.

'But it's surely very obvious what we are dealing with,' Lady Grant said. 'If the child has been neglected or mistreated, then her father and mother must be found – if they can be – and held to account. Wouldn't you say, Mrs Skene?'

'Na, I widna,' Molly said boldly. 'The gaun-aboot folk are awfie fond o' their bairns. I dinna think they would treat ane o' their ain like that.'

'I hope nobody would,' Mrs Pirnie said. 'Not theirs or anybody else's. But some do.'

Lady Grant rose majestically from the chair. 'Well, no doubt the police will look into it,' she said. 'And if the parents cannot be found, then I suppose the child will have to be taken to a home. Now, I must be getting on. Do let me know if there are any developments.'

When Mrs Pirnie came back after showing her ladyship out, Molly could not hold her tongue any longer. 'Stuck-up cow,' she said. 'Ye should hae brocht her a basin so she could wash her hands, even though she never touched the bairn.'

Mrs Pirnie was not the sort of woman to criticise her social superiors, not out loud at least, but she smiled to show that she saw Molly's point of view. Molly passed the smile to the bairn. The bairn didn't smile back. She had watched Lady Grant go but now she was staring at the space again.

The bell over the post office door rang. The bairn turned her head. Mrs Pirnie and Molly both saw it.

'Weel, she's no deef,' Molly said. 'Away ye go. I'll stay wi her.'

When Effie Dunn, the district nurse, arrived she found Molly Skene sitting on Mrs Pirnie's parlour floor with her back against the settee, playing Pelmanism with an old pack of cards. The cards were spread face down. Molly turned them up two at a time, and if she got a matching pair she put them aside and if she didn't she put them back with their faces to the floor. The dumb lass was cooried in at Molly's left side, very still. Her head hung forward like a broken doll's. Her eyes were open but Molly couldn't tell if she was watching the game. Molly kept turning the cards, she had them in a half-circle around her so she didn't have to stretch far and so dislodge the bairn. When a matching pair came up she said quietly what they were. 'Twa fours.' 'Twa nines.' 'Twa quines.' She put the pairs in front of the bairn, leaving the court cards face up so she could see the pictures, if she wanted to. Molly had been at this for an hour. She didn't know if she was doing any good but the bairn was calm at least. She'd eaten some porridge too and had not been sick with it.

Mrs Pirnie came through from the post office, which was quiet, as it usually was. Effie Dunn was good at her job but she had an abrupt manner and a *raucle* Aberdeenshire tongue. Mrs Pirnie was anxious that she didn't frighten the bairn.

Effie said, 'Pit her on the table so I can hae a gweed look at her.' Molly stood up, lifted the bairn and carried her to the kitchen, and Effie, quite gently for her, began to check her over.

Everything was going well until they tried to undress her. First she went rigid, then she started kicking and punching so that they had to hold her down, then – just as suddenly – she went completely limp. Effie moved a finger across her vision; the black pupils followed it. They took the clothes off her and Effie felt the little body over.

'Dear God, dear God,' she said. 'See these bruises? These are recent. There's naethin' sinister aboot them, it's jist wi the ruch wey she's been livin'. But look at this airm. It was broken in the past. It's healed but it wasna set properly. Mibbe it wasna even set. I doot her ribs has been cracked and a'.'

'I want to kill somebody,' Molly said.

'I ken, but let's get her back into her claes,' Effie said. 'That'll be mair use to her the noo. We'll awa ben to the parlour, she seemed to like it fine there.'

They went through. Molly sat on the floor again and brought the bairn into her side.

'What do you think set her off fighting us like that?' Mrs Pirnie asked. 'And then, when she stopped – I thought she'd fainted.'

'Aye, but she hadna,' Effie said. 'Did ye nae see her watchin' my finger? I think fit she was daein' was tryin' nae tae be hurt. Her instinct tells her to fecht, but then something else beats her instinct. She's learned that resistin's nae use and it hurts less if she disna fecht.'

'But we weren't meaning to hurt her,' Mrs Pirnie said.

'*She* didna ken that. She micht, though, next time. See foo she is wi Molly. Fit's learned can be unlearned, and something else learned in its place. It jist taks time.'

Mrs Pirnie asked, in a quiet voice, 'Has she been . . . violated?'

'There's nae sign o' that, thank God,' Effie said. 'But she's been in the wars, and somebody's been fell cruel to her at sometime. It's nae wunner she's nae spikkin'.'

The others were themselves silent. There was nothing they could say.

Molly started to gather up the cards. 'I'll need to get hame,' she said. 'I've things to dae. Will I tak her wi me?'

'How old do you think she is, Effie?' Mrs Pirnie asked.

'Hard to tell, she's that wee. I would say aboot eicht.'

'D'ye think she wid come wi me?' Molly asked. A card slipped from her hand to the floor. The bairn reached out and grabbed it. She clutched it into her bony chest.

'Ye like that ane, dae ye?' Molly said. 'Are ye keepin' that ane?'

The bairn's watchful black eyes looked around the room, then slyly at Molly. Her hand was tiny but wrinkled like the hand of an old person. Suddenly it pushed the card on to Molly's lap and let it go.

'For me?' Molly said. 'Well, thank ye. The Quine o' Herts tae. That's braw.'

'Aye, she'll gang wi ye,' Effie Dunn said.

Wull Macfarlane came back the next day. He didn't cycle this time. An officer from Forfar drove as far as the Brig and gave Wull a lift. They were both big men, between them they took up half of Mrs Pirnie's parlour. Molly brought over the bairn, who shrank back at the size of them.

'I think she's afraid of uniforms,' Mrs Pirnie said. 'She didn't like Sam Dawson in his.'

'Maybe she's jist clever, and didna like Sam,' Wull said. 'How did ye get on yestreen, Molly?'

'No bad,' Molly said. 'We listened to the wireless, and she watched while I got Bob's tea ready. And when Bob cam in he was richt cannie wi her and she seemed fine wi him, and Janet played at the cairds and the bairn even picked oot some o' the pairs, so that was a' guid. And she'd scrambled eggs and plenty o' breid for her tea.'

The Forfar policeman's name was Inspector Brand. 'I've made some inquiries,' he said. 'Nobody's reported a missing child anywhere in the county in the last three days. Of course if she's a gypsy they might not anyway. Well, it seems some folk did see a child wandering about at the harbour in Montrose on Monday. I don't know if it was this child. There are quite a lot of children who loiter down there, mostly boys I would have to say. We could take her there and ask our witnesses if it was her they saw but that won't get us very far even if it was.'

'She looks different since we cleaned her up,' Mrs Pirnie said.

'Constable Macfarlane says you don't know anything about this child and that she isn't able to speak. Is that right?'

'She *doesn't* speak,' Mrs Pirnie said. 'I don't know if she is able or not.'

'You wonder,' Brand said, 'how a child that can't speak manages to get itself all the way from Montrose to here. What age would you say she is?'

'Eicht or thereaboots,' Molly said. 'That's whit Effie thocht.'

'Aye, that looks about right. Constable Macfarlane says there's a possibility she might be foreign and off a boat,' the Inspector said. 'What do you think of that, lassie?' he said, suddenly turning on her. 'You're a stowaway are you, eh?'

The bairn stared at him, unblinking.

'She'll no answer,' Molly said. 'Shouting at her disna change that.'

'I wasn't shouting,' Brand said.

'You raised your voice.'

'I was wanting to see if she was really deaf.'

'Ye mean, ye were tryin' to catch her oot?' Molly made a noise in her throat like porridge when it's cooking. 'And wha said she was deef?'

'Molly,' Mrs Pirnie said warningly. Molly kept an arm around the bairn and the bairn seemed to appreciate it.

'She was very dirty when she was found on the bus,' Mrs Pirnie said. 'She was covered in coal dust.'

'Aye, Constable Macfarlane wrote that in his report. It could be significant. There was a coaster up from Leith docked on Monday morning. What was it carrying? Coal. So maybe you were a stowaway on that boat, eh, lassie? If she got on at Leith she could be from anywhere, especially if she's foreign. But that coaster took a week because it stopped all the way along the Fife coast, so maybe she got on at Dysart. And coal's not exactly a rare commodity, so who's to say she was on that coaster at all? We're not any further forward, are we?'

'I think she is foreign,' Mrs Pirnie said. 'I think she has come from the continent.'

'Any particular reason?' Brand said, a slight aggression in his voice, as if he didn't think Mrs Pirnie had any right to this opinion.

'Her ears have been pierced. The holes are nearly closed up, which means she hasn't had any earrings in them for a while. The piercing must have been done when she was very young. I don't know any local girls of any age who have pierced ears. Do you, Inspector?'

'Gypsies,' Brand said. 'We're back to gypsies again. Well, if you're right that's going to make identifying her almost impossible. Do you know how many folk there are wandering about Europe? Thousands of them. Tens of thousands. The Russians don't want the Ukrainians, the Ukrainians don't want the Poles, the Poles don't want the Jews and nobody wants the Germans. Then there's Romanians and Slovaks *and* gypsies and God knows what else. And if this one's somehow got across the North Sea and wound up halfway to Braemar I don't think anybody's coming after her to take her back. So what's going to happen to her?'

'She can stay wi me,' Molly said. 'For noo.'

Inspector Brand rubbed his chin. 'I suppose she'd be classified as an alien,' he said. 'Maybe as a refugee. I'll check. She'll need to be classified as something.'

'She's no a spy,' Molly said. 'Can ye no jist classify her as a bairn?'

'It's not that simple,' Brand said. 'She'll have to be registered.'

'Suppose ye jist gaed back doon the road and didna register she was here at a'? That'd be simple.'

Inspector Brand gave Molly a look.

'I'll make a report,' he said. 'There's no point in me taking her away until we know what's to happen to her. You can keep her for now. I wouldn't get too fond of her, though. Mrs Pirnie, will you make sure this is all done in a proper way?'

Mrs Pirnie said she would.

'Good. Right, Macfarlane, I need to be getting on. I'll let you out at the Brig.'

The Inspector stood to go, shook Mrs Pirnie's hand, nodded at Molly Skene, wagged his finger at the dumb lass. 'You be good, lassie,' he said. 'These folk are being very kind, so don't you forget it. You've landed lucky, do you know that? No, I don't think you do. You don't know how lucky you are, and we don't even know your name. What a world, eh? What a world.'

After the policemen had gone, Mrs Pirnie asked Molly how the bairn had been during the night. 'She slept better than I did,' Molly said. 'I was up every oor to check on her and mak sure she didna pee the bed. There was jist aince, aboot five when Bob was stirrin', that we had some trouble wi her. She must've got into a bad dream and this soond cam oot o' her, a kind o' squeal like a rabbit caught in a trap, oh it was horrible. It was neither speech nor cry and Bob said it made him think o' the banshee. I'd rather hae her scream the hoose doon than that, it wasna human. I jist bosied her ticht until it wis oot, and that was a whilie, and syne we were baith done in, sae I took her into my bed and we slept till Janet cam in and tellt me it was efter eicht o'clock. Whit was that yon polis said aboot no gettin' ower fond o' her? The damnt cheek.'

'One thing he was right about, though,' Mrs Pirnie said. 'We don't have a name for her. I think it would be good if, when we talk to her, we could call her something. What do you think?'

Molly said, 'Aye, I was thinkin' that mysel. I was thinkin' Flora, at least until we ken ony different.'

Mrs Pirnie said, 'I think that would be very good, but only if you're sure.'

'I'm sure,' Molly said. 'I'd better check wi Bob, though.'

*

As I wrote before, I am making a lot of this up. I don't know the story of the dumb lass in *that* much detail. I am telling it as bits and pieces of it were told to me by others and over the years my mind has filled in the gaps. It comes to this in the end – a mixture of memories and imaginings and I am not sure which is which. I don't know which spaces were always blank and which were ones where things were rubbed out, and whether the rubbing-out was conscious or not. I have pictures without sound and voices without pictures. I can still hear Molly's voice. She's been dead a long time now, but once she started to speak it was hard to stop her and she told me the parts she knew often enough so maybe I am not making up as much of it as I think. And Mrs Pirnie, I can hear her voice too although I have almost forgotten what she looked like. Her first name was Joy but she was always 'Mrs Pirnie'. I remember Effie Dunn's voice too, but nothing of her face or shape. I remember Sam Dawson but not Wull Macfarlane or Inspector Brand. Strange, how I remember some but not others. But then, maybe it's not so strange. I mind Bob Skene of course, and Geordie Kemp and Sir Gregory Grant and Lady Grant. In later years Geordie would sometimes mention somebody else from that time, and when I looked blank he would say, 'D'ye no mind him? Ye must, surely?', but there was nothing there except the space where a memory might have been.

They are gone now, every one of them. I have outlived them all. When that Dr Tybault came to see me, he said I was one of the oldest inhabitants of the glen but he was not quite correct. I am *the* oldest. This was why your mother sent him to see me – because once I am gone the last link will be broken.

Well, back to the story. Dr Logan came to the glen a day or two later. He came to see Lady Grant, who had something the matter with her, and while he was at the Big House she happened to mention the recent arrival and wondered if he should have a look at her in case she was carrying any diseases. She would telephone Mrs Pirnie at the post office and ask her to have the child ready for inspection. Dr Logan could hardly refuse such a request but also knew that he was not expected to add his time examining the child to her ladyship's bill. (This was before the National Health Service was created.) He was therefore somewhat short-tempered by the time he parked his motor car outside the post office.

When the dumb lass was lifted on to Mrs Pirnie's table she reacted in the same way that she had to Effie Dunn, only this time she didn't even struggle, she went straight into a state of limpness. Molly Skene, who had brought her over, thought this was perhaps because Dr Logan was a man. He listened to her chest and looked at her tongue and down her throat and said he was satisfied that she was free of tuberculosis. As to any other diseases or infections she might have, he could not say. She needed feeding up but seemed healthier than many children he saw. Her bruises would go away in time. If her arm had been broken it was mended now. He looked in her ears and said he could see nothing untoward in them. He did not know why she did not or would not or could not speak, as he could find no physical reason for her dumbness. Dr Logan seemed to be less interested in the dumb lass than in getting home for his dinner.

'As to what mental and emotional damage she has sustained, I do not know enough about that,' he said. 'We all know more than we used to, because of the wars, but I am not a specialist. Even leaving aside her dumbness she is unnaturally quiescent. She is probably retarded and will not do well in the ordinary run of things, for example in a normal school. I expect she will have to go somewhere she can be looked after properly.'

'Whit d'ye mean?' Molly asked. She glanced at the bairn, who had revived and was on the parlour floor playing with the cards. 'You mean a home?'

'A children's home, yes, where they have specialists who can help children like her.'

'And whar wid that be?'

'Wherever there is space,' Dr Logan said. 'Quite likely it would be in Dundee, or possibly Aberdeen. I have no idea.'

Molly said, 'Oh no. Ye're no takkin' her.'

The bairn grouped the cards in different ways. She put the red cards together, then the face cards, then just the queens, then the black cards that weren't face cards.

Dr Logan said with irritation, 'I'm not taking her anywhere. It won't be up to me. If I am asked, I will recommend what I think is best for the child, but it will not be my decision.'

'Please dinna tak her,' Molly said.

'It is really no business of yours,' the doctor said. Something in Molly's face stopped him. 'Having said that,' he continued, 'she seems quite at ease with you. It is clear you are taking good care of her. In any case, I doubt whether there would be a place for her just now. They are very stretched. But so long as she remains dumb, I don't see how you could cope. In the long term she must be placed where she can receive the best care possible for her needs.'

'I ken thae places,' Molly said. 'She'll no get care. She'll get pit in a corner and forgotten aboot.'

She watched to see if the bairn was listening as she sorted the cards. But even if she was she wouldn't know what was being said. How could she?

'That is simply not true,' Dr Logan said, gathering his things. 'There are some good homes where the children are made as happy as they are capable of being. It is not like it was in the old days.'

I imagine that, when he said that, Molly made the sound of porridge again. It was one of her endearing habits. You always had warning when she was about to boil over.

Very few people knew then, but Dr Logan may have been one who did, that Molly had been in a children's home herself. She only told me years later, and even then she wouldn't speak about it. She didn't speak much about Flora either, her first daughter, who died of meningitis aged three. It was odd that she wanted the dumb lass to have Flora's name, and that Bob agreed to it. Or maybe it wasn't.

Many people have reasons for not speaking some of the time. Fewer people have reasons for not speaking at all.

These days a doctor would not use the word 'dumb'. It is not acceptable. He would use another word, such as 'mute'. Language has its fashions like everything else. One day 'mute' will fall out of favour and be replaced with another word. But back then everybody spoke about 'the dumb lass'. It wasn't considered unkind or incorrect. If somebody had suggested it was, people would have been astonished. 'What are you talking about?' they'd have said. 'She's dumb. That's just a fact.'

The day after the doctor's visit the dumb lass took herself off. Made herself scarce. She was skilled at doing this. Making herself scarce was how she survived. It was how she had ended up in Glen Conach.

That first time she disappeared into the glen was maybe the first time she knew, really knew, that she was there. She remembers it. Nobody else does, nobody told it to her, so is it a true memory? It starts with a bad dream in the night, always the same dream. A dream about running and being caught. In the still-dark hours, only half awake, she finds herself struggling between the fold of Molly's embrace and a fear she cannot speak, can only let out in a squeal like that of a terrified rabbit. Molly gets her back to sleep at last. In the morning she seems calm. Molly leaves her to rest. Before Molly comes back she wakes and knows at once she has to go. She pulls her dress over her head and slips barefoot outside and away.

There are stone walls, trees and bushes to cover her. She doesn't have to think about staying hidden, she just knows to do it. It is dry but she could cope with wet. It is mild but she could cope with cold. She moves like a shadow of herself away from the cluster of low cottages. The trees are shedding but still not naked. Deep drifts of dead leaves from other years fill hollows and dips in the land. They remind her of something. She goes on. Some small animal scurries from her. That reminds her of something too. Things from somewhere else creep in around the edges of her thought as she moves away from any sight or sound of human life, looking for a place to be unknown.

She finds a hollowed-out spot where the roots of a tree have spread themselves around a rock. It has a musty smell, a powdery feel. Leaves have blown in there over time. The roots and the mossy turf make a low roof over her. Animals come here too but for now she is alone. She curls up and listens. The only sounds are not ones that threaten. She feels herself going over into sleep. She hears a voice and wakes again, but there is nobody. This time when the voice comes she knows she is dreaming or remembering, one or the other, and the voice is safe. It is Tomas's voice.

Tomas. He was bigger than her, stronger. He took care of her. When Tomas said, 'We must walk,' she walked. When he hushed her, she was silent. When he said, 'In here,' she went in. When he said, 'Eat,' she ate. When he said, 'Sleep,' she slept.

Somewhere further and deeper beyond Tomas were Mama and Tata and a horse. There was a kind of street, she could almost see it but not quite, it was too far. Little low houses scattered about. Something was about to happen, they were loading all their things into a cart, the horse was between the shafts and Tomas was holding the reins. There were other people also packing up, they all looked afraid. Men were coming, Mama and Tata heard the engines, they told Tomas to take her and run. Nobody else ran, they were too old or too afraid or didn't have enough belief that the bad things they feared would really happen.

Tomas led her into the forest. There were leaves in thick banks.

That is what she is reminded of. You burrowed in and when you were lying quiet the leaves would still let you breathe and you wouldn't be found. Tomas and her together in the deep leaves. They were not found.

Hours later they came out and brushed themselves down, sneezing and giggling. Tomas put his finger to his lips. They went back to where the house was. Evening was coming on. Only that morning they had been living there but nobody lived there now. It looked as if nobody had lived there for a while. One day, and everything was changed. The door was smashed in, the horse and cart, Mama and Tata and everybody else – gone.

Tomas said, 'They have taken them away.'

'Where?' she asked. In those days she spoke, mostly to Tomas. He pointed.

'Can we go after them?'

'No. It's not safe.'

'Are they not safe?'

'No.'

'Can we not save them?'

'No.'

'Will God save them?'

'I don't know.'

'Will God save us?'

'I don't think so. We must go the other way,' Tomas said.

They started to walk in the opposite direction.

Tomas had a good sense of where they were and a good sense of what was happening. He was older than her by five years. No longer a little boy, not yet a man but he acted like one. He told her the Americans were coming but nobody knew when they would arrive. It would be better if they came before the Russians did. Tomas said that what would be even better and safer would be not to wait for them but to go and find them. He pointed towards the setting sun. 'This way.'

'How far is it?'

'I don't know. A long way. If we keep going we will meet them coming.'

'The Americans?'

'Yes.'

'Will they save us?'

'Yes.'

Sometimes they walked in the daylight, sometimes only in the evening or at night. When they stopped and slept, they curled up together, Tomas tucking himself in at her back. But sometimes Tomas went off alone and came back with food. He said, 'No matter how long I am away, no matter how frightened you are, you stay here.' And she did, and after a few times she wasn't so frightened because he always came back.

They each had a little, thin book with writing in it. They kept these books out of sight, next to their skin. Tomas said, 'Don't lose it. It is who you are. One day you will show it to somebody and you'll be safe.'

'To the Americans?'

'Yes, to them.'

'Where are they?'

'They are getting closer every day.'

'But where have they come from?'

'Across a big sea. If we kept walking we would come to the sea, and if we got in a boat it would take us to America. That's where they have come from. But we won't have to go that far. We'll meet them long before then.'

Tomas said, 'Don't speak to anybody else unless I do,' but there was nobody to speak to anyway because they kept away from people as much as they could. She learned to listen instead. She could pick up tiny changes in the air, shifts of sound that alerted her to this or warned her of that. Tomas was a good listener, but she was better.

And she learned to look. She saw motion where there appeared to be none. When a human or an animal moved she saw the shape that was left where they had been. Echoes. She saw shadow and light and how they played against each other. She looked at the world and was both in it and not in it, but her eyes recorded everything that passed before them.

She wakes up in her root-roofed hole to the sound of voices. They are calling her, even though they don't know her name. They call, 'Flora! Flo-o-o-ra!' She recognises Molly's voice but she does not show herself. She hardly breathes, even though they can neither see nor hear her. It is not that she doesn't want to come out. She wants that very much, but Tomas said it was better to stay hidden, and he was right so often before.

She hears an animal noise. She is so still that even the animal does not know she is there. A mouse maybe, or a hedgehog. What she remembers then is a hole under a house. The house was like all the other houses nearby, a heap of rubble with a few walls standing. You could hardly tell where one house ended and the next began. They crept into the hole and there was a space with old things in it, a pram and broken chairs and empty wooden crates. Everything was coated in thick grey dust. It was daytime but very little light got into the hole. Tomas said, 'You stay here,' and went to look for something to eat. While he was away she heard an animal close by. Her eyes had adjusted to the gloom. The animal was a very big rat. It was grey but not from the dust like her, grey was its colour. She did not like rats. The first thing she wanted to do was get away from it and the second thing she wanted to do was kill it. There were loose bricks and stones lying around. She lifted a brick and waited. The rat snuffled closer. Her arm and hand ached with the weight of the brick. If the rat had any sense of the danger it was in it did not show it. When it was only two feet away and she was about to hit it with the brick the rat stopped and stood up, nose twitching. In the half-dark its eyes glinted and she thought that her eyes probably glinted back. In that moment she realised the rat meant her no harm. She put the brick down. The rat went on its way.

After a while, when all is quiet, she finds herself thinking about going back to Molly's house. She wonders if they will stop being kind now. There is only one way to find out and it is getting cold and she wants to be in bed again.

She waits till the sun is almost below the trees and then starts back, the way she came.

Molly did not stop being kind. The bairn she called Flora – the bairn that had made her distraught when she found her gone, that she had searched and shouted for along with Bob and their neighbour Jenny Kemp – ran away for a reason, and Molly knew about reasons for running away. She was home when she heard the back door open, but she had the presence of mind not to rush, she stayed very still and waited. It was half-dark, she had just lit the fire. Bob was still out, he'd been late to his work after searching for the bairn. 'She's awa, love,' he'd said, after they'd given up. 'I'm sorry but she's a sprite or a changeling, I doot. She'll no be back.' But Molly thought she would be. She lowered herself to the floor and watched the flames licking round the coals and the coals beginning to glow. She was conscious of the bairn's creep, pause, creep, as if she was playing a game, but it was no game. Every half-step was a judgement on whether to take the next one. At any moment the desire to stay might be beaten by the need to flee. Molly hardly allowed herself to breathe. She sat with her face to the fire, trembling, until she could feel the bairn inches away from her. Molly slowly stretched out her hand. After a long moment the bairn came into her. To feel that hard, matty head against her breast was almost more than Molly could bear. She said nothing, but somewhere in the fire's whisper she could hear the name she had given her. *Flora. Flora.*

Next morning, at the table in the kitchen, Molly said, 'I'll never hurt ye, Flora, and I'll no let onybody else hurt ye either.'

The dumb lass stared at her. There was almost a smile, something like trust. But Molly knew they had a long way to go.

She said, 'If ye run awa again, I'll no be angry at ye. Just come back safe to us, that's all. This is your hame noo. D'ye ken whit I mean by that? Hame.'

She put her palms together and laid her cheek against her hand in imitation of sleep. 'Hame,' she said.

She fetched some paper and a pencil, and drew a simple picture of a house, with a door and windows and smoke spiralling from the lum. She drew a stick woman and a stick child holding hands beside the house. 'Hame,' she said again, laying the pencil down.

The dumb lass took the pencil. She gave Molly that same stare, then redirected it at nothing. Molly thought, she doesn't want me to watch. She went to make a pot of tea.

When she came back there was another house on the paper next to the one Molly had drawn. It was crudely done but the dumb lass had shaded in some parts and left others blank, so it seemed real compared with Molly's cartoon. Where the roof should have been wooden beams were sticking up in the air, and part of the front of the house was missing. There were no people, there was no door and only one window, which Molly thought was like a half-closed eye looking at her.

She turned the paper over and tried again, this time drawing a fir tree with sloping branches. 'Tree,' she said, and this time she wrote the word in capital letters. While the dumb lass drew with the pencil Molly rummaged around until she found a box of eight coloured crayons that Janet had not used for years.

At first she was disappointed when she saw the trees the dumb lass had drawn. They were more like telegraph poles than trees, a row of them getting smaller up the page. Then the lass put in some more lines, and Molly realised that the trees *were* telegraph poles, alongside a road going into the distance.

It seemed that Molly's picture of a fir tree was not very good.

The lass did not write any letters under her drawing.

Molly placed the box of crayons on the table. 'Ye'd better hae these,' she said. 'You're better at it than me.'

Mrs Pirnie had a telephone call from Sir Gregory Grant. A gentleman from the County Council, who had received a report from Inspector Brand about the child, was coming to Glen Conach House the next morning. Sir Gregory understood that the child was now staying with Bob and Molly Skene. If Mrs Pirnie would bring her to the house at eleven o'clock he would be grateful. He was sure it would be all right to close the post office counter for an hour or so. If it would be helpful for Mrs Skene to attend, in case the child was frightened or Mrs Pirnie needed to get back, that would be quite in order.

Sir Gregory was better-liked than Lady Grant. He did not talk down to people as she did. He was handsome and polite and genial and had a habit, when he paid a visit to one of his tenants' cottages, of bringing a half-bottle of whisky with him and leaving most of it behind when he left. He had been on the Western Front in the 1914–18 war, and it was said that the experience had had a great effect on him.

He was still the laird, though, and therefore of a different species. It was intimidating to be shown by the maid into his study, an enormous room, lined with bookshelves, spread with rugs, and hung with large paintings of stags, lochs and snow-capped mountains. There was a fire roaring in the marble fireplace. Sir Gregory, in green tweed, came out from behind a desk and invited them all to sit down on a hard, brown-leather sofa. Molly took the lass on to her knee.

Sir Gregory crouched down in front of the dumb lass. 'Hello, you,' he said, and smiled. He had a very warm smile, like an actor's. He could have been a film star. The lass at least did not turn her face away, although she flinched when he put his hand out as if to pinch her cheek. Sir Gregory checked himself, stood up and returned to his chair.

'Mr Travers from the County Council is due in a few minutes,' he said. 'Before he arrives I would like to ask how you are all getting on. Lady Grant has told me something about the situation. This child has been here now for, what, a fortnight?'

'A bit longer, Sir,' Mrs Pirnie said.

'And she still has not spoken?'

'Not a word in my presence.'

'Mrs Skene?'

'Naethin', Sir.'

'It is not uncommon if something very distressing has happened,' Sir Gregory said. 'In the last war, for example, we had soldiers who suffered from shell shock. We had men for whom the bombardments and machine-gun fire and so on were just too much. They closed in on themselves. They were accused of malingering, but they simply could not help it. They had to be taken out of the trenches and sent home. With time and rest and sympathetic care, some of them got better.' He smiled again at the bairn. 'Do you have a name for her?'

'We cry her Flora, Sir,' Molly said.

'Why do you call her that?'

'It was my mither's name. And I had a bairn that dee'd. She was Flora tae.'

'I'm sorry. It's a lovely name. Perhaps if she hears it often enough she will come to think it is hers. How is she in other respects? She is very small. Is she eating well?'

'Aye, Sir. She's pit on a bit o' wecht.'

'Do you think she is happy?'

'I'm no sure I would say happy, but she's better than she was. She's no sae feart.'

'Oh, she was frightened, was she?'

'She had awfie bad dreams, Sir. She still does, but they're no like whit they were when she first cam.'

'Not so extreme, you mean?'

'Aye, Sir. She's mair settled. I'm tryin' to get her into a routine. She's a guid bairn, but she disna aye ken whit's richt and whit's wrang.'

'I see. Well, we can hardly hold her responsible for that. Lady Grant said she thought she might not be quite . . . normal.'

'Weel, she's no. But she's no daft, if that's whit your wife meant.'

Mrs Pirnie looked a little nervous, but Sir Gregory only said, 'Do we know if Flora can read or write?'

'She kens whit a book is, Sir, but I dinna think she can read, even if English isna her ain language. And she's never written doon ony letters either, but she can haud a pencil and she's braw at makkin pictures.'

'Well, that's encouraging. What about you? You don't mind having her?'

'I like it, Sir. I dinna want her taen awa.'

'And your husband, Mr Skene – he's the roadman, isn't he?'

'Aye, Sir, and he works on the estate as weel, hedgin' and ditchin' and the like.'

'Yes, of course. A very good man. How does he feel about your having taken the child in? There'll be an extra expense.'

'No that we notice, Sir. Nae offence, but we've little enough onywey, and she's a wee thing as ye said yirsel. Bob's fine wi it.'

'You have a daughter – Janet, is that right? What does Janet think?'

'She's fine wi it tae. It's guid to hae a bairn aboot the hoose. We a' like it.'

'I can tell you're already very fond of her, Mrs Skene. It's important for me to have a full picture, you see.'

There was a knock at the door, and the maid entered. Molly and Mrs Pirnie knew her, but it was not for them to speak to her there.

'Mr Travers, Sir.'

'Thank you, Meg,' Sir Gregory said, standing up again. 'Come in,

Mr Travers. Mrs Pirnie, Mrs Skene, this is Mr Travers from the Forfarshire County Council. Mr Travers, this is the child, Flora. Mrs Skene has taken her in for now. Please sit down. Now, you've come about Flora obviously. What can you tell us?'

Mr Travers sat, and gave the two women nods. He did not smile at the dumb lass as Sir Gregory had. In fact, he seemed hardly to notice her. He had a briefcase, from which he extracted a single sheet of paper. After glancing at this, he began to speak, in a slow, doom-laden voice.

'There is no name mentioned in the report submitted by Inspector Brand,' he said. 'On what grounds are you calling her "Flora"?'

'Jist here and in the clachan,' Molly said. 'We've no been onywhar else.'

Mr Travers raised his eyebrows as if he thought she might be making a joke. He saw that she was not and sighed. '*Why* have you chosen to call her that?'

'It was my mither's name,' Molly said.

'I see,' Mr Travers said. He did not seem impressed. 'The Inspector's report says that she cannot speak.'

Mrs Pirnie stepped in. 'That's not correct,' she said. 'She *doesn't* speak.'

Mr Travers made a mark on his paper. 'The police have her listed as lost, but have been unable to identify where she comes from,' he said.

'If she was simply lost,' Sir Gregory said, 'somebody would surely have reported her missing by now.'

'One would think so. Inspector Brand says that she may be an alien, who has entered the country illegally.'

'Do you think that?' Sir Gregory asked. 'I mean, look at her. How could she?'

'She may have been smuggled in by persons unknown.'

'But for what purpose?' Sir Gregory asked. 'It's surely more likely that she has been abandoned.'

'Well,' Mr Travers said in his funereal voice, 'whatever the truth of the matter, she is a minor and must receive appropriate care and protection. That is the responsibility of the County Council, specifically in relation to the administration of poor relief, education, lunacy and mental deficiency, and public health. As the County's representative, that is why I have come to see you.'

'Yes, well, as one of the County's Justices of the Peace I am very glad you have,' Sir Gregory said. 'What do you intend to do about young Flora?'

'The first thing will be to arrange for a medical examination. Then we will have to seek suitable accommodation for her, in a children's home perhaps. Unfortunately, that will not be easy.'

The dumb lass was very still. Although she could not know what the man was saying, Molly felt that she was anxious; as if she somehow understood his power, and feared it.

'Just a moment,' Sir Gregory said. 'She has already been examined by a doctor.'

'I was not aware of that,' Mr Travers said. 'Can you tell me which doctor?'

'It was our own GP, Dr Logan,' Sir Gregory said. 'Do you know him?'

'I don't think I do,' Mr Travers said.

'He has been my family's doctor for twenty-five years. He examined the child at the request of Lady Grant. My wife,' he added, giving Molly a faint, sly smile.

'I see. We have not received a report from him.'

'Did you ask him for one?'

'How could I, since I didn't –'

Sir Gregory turned to the postmistress. 'Mrs Pirnie, I believe you were present when Dr Logan carried out his examination. Did he tell you what his conclusions were?'

'He did, Sir,' Mrs Pirnie said. 'He said that she did not have tuberculosis. He said he could find no physical reason for her dumbness.

He said she seemed healthier than many children he saw, she just needed feeding up a bit.'

Sir Gregory turned to Molly. 'You were saying to me, Mrs Skene, before Mr Travers arrived, that Flora was eating well.'

'Oh aye, Sir. She's pittin' on wecht.'

'Mrs Pirnie, did Dr Logan say he was going to make a report about Flora?'

'Oh no,' Mrs Pirnie said, wide-eyed with surprise. She could have been in a film alongside Sir Gregory. 'I imagine he didn't think it necessary since she was in good health and also in such good hands. Mrs Skene's, I mean.'

'Oh, he said that, did he?'

'Yes, Sir. He said it was clear that Mrs Skene was looking after her well and that the bairn liked her.'

'Well, Travers,' Sir Gregory said, 'you can see why Dr Logan didn't go to the trouble of sending you a report. He had nothing *to* report. I don't think you need concern yourself with another medical examination – unless of course you want to check with Dr Logan, who as I said I have known for twenty-five years?'

Mr Travers looked more downcast than ever. 'I am sure that won't be necessary,' he said.

'Now, as to the matter of accommodation,' Sir Gregory continued, 'had you anywhere in mind?'

'No, Sir.'

'I think you said it would not be easy, owing I assume to a severe shortage of places in orphanages and the like?'

'That's correct.'

'Well, we have a ready-made solution. Mrs Skene is willing – is happy, in fact – to keep Flora here. Flora is being well cared for by Mrs Skene, her husband and her daughter. All in all, it seems to be an ideal family situation in which to place a child without her own family. I can of course vouch for Mrs Skene, a lady of excellent character. Her husband is a tenant of mine, and also works as a roadman for the

Forfarshire County Council. I think the County Council would be very glad to have this matter taken off its hands, don't you? Speaking as its representative?'

'It's a wee bit irregular, Sir,' Mr Travers said. 'If it transpires that the child is not British, for example, something would have to be done.'

'What, for heaven's sake? Wherever she has come from, she is here now. You could write a new report, I suppose. Look, Travers, let's not make this complicated. You have nowhere to place her at the moment, so leave her where she is settled. If things get too difficult for Mrs Skene she will tell me and I will tell you. But it sounds to me as though you don't need another homeless child to deal with. Of course, if somebody is searching for her and can prove that she is their child, Mrs Skene will have to give her up. But in the meantime, she is surely in the best possible place?'

Mr Travers scratched his head. He had some other papers in his briefcase. He took them out and looked at them, and put them away again. In the end, the logic of Sir Gregory's argument, and the fact that it was he – Sir Gregory Grant, JP, of Glen Conach House – who was making it, proved decisive. Mr Travers agreed to leave things as they were. If circumstances should change, he would rely on Sir Gregory to inform him.

Meg, the maid, showed Mr Travers out. Sir Gregory put another log on the fire and rubbed his hands with satisfaction.

'I almost thought I had overdone it when I made that comment about writing a new report,' he said. 'Would you care for a sherry, ladies?' They declined. 'Well, I very much doubt that Mr Travers will trouble us again. The only thing would be if Flora's family were to turn up. That would be awkward. Mrs Skene, I want you to promise that if that happens, or if you have any other problems, you will come straight to me. You must not hold back because you think I would not be interested. I *am* interested. I have a son of my own, as you know, and I cannot bear the thought of him being in such an unhappy situation as this little lass must have been. Do you promise?'

Molly nodded, because she could hardly speak.

'Now,' Sir Gregory said, 'I cannot lower your rent because that would be unfair to the other tenants, but I will make a small payment to your husband every month so that this great generous act of yours does not make you poorer. Mrs Pirnie, I thank you for all you have done.' He hunkered down again in front of the bairn. 'I hope one day you may be able to tell us your story,' he said, and from one of his pockets he produced a half-crown and held it out to her. A half-crown was a very large, weighty coin. Even a child that had never seen one before would know it was worth something. The dumb lass looked at Molly, who nodded, and the lass took the coin and closed her fist around it.

'I'm sorry she canna thank ye,' Molly said, finding her own voice.

'Well, perhaps she's saving up her thank-yous for when she can,' Sir Gregory said.

Molly Skene had always had a low regard for the gentry, although her husband's livelihood depended on them. She never did care much for Lady Grant, but from that day onward she would have died for Sir Gregory. She told me this herself. It was a sorrow to her, years later, to see the son that he spoke of so fondly drink himself to death and bring the estate to such a condition that it had to be sold to pay off his debts. She was glad that Sir Gregory was not alive to see that. And she always remembered the last thing Sir Gregory had said that day as he ushered them from his study. She believed that it explained why he had been on their side when it came to the dumb lass.

'The trouble with the soldiers who had shell shock,' he said, 'was that they were taken away from the war to get well again, and once they were well they were sent back. I remember one chap who, two days after he returned, was in the same state he had been in before. He wouldn't go over the top. He *couldn't*. But they didn't send him home a second time. They court-martialled him and shot him for being a coward.'

They were walking through a war. There were others like them, moving in different directions, trying to stay clear of danger. Tomas was determined they must keep going towards the setting sun, even though that seemed to lead them towards some of the worst fighting. Marching soldiers and columns of vehicles overtook them or passed them coming the other way. Sometimes they were shouted at or shoved aside. For the most part, they were not noticed at all.

She had two ways of speaking – the way she spoke to Tomas, Mama and Tata and all the people who had been taken away, and the way she spoke to other people. But now she spoke to no one except Tomas. As they went further on their journey even he found it difficult to understand what people were saying. Sometimes she would linger to hear the strangeness of their voices but she was too small for them to pay her much attention. That was a good thing, Tomas said. Sometimes they slept under trees, sometimes in holes under broken houses, sometimes in barns. If there was a cow they knew how to get milk from her if she would let them. They knew about cows and other animals, farm ones and wild ones.

People's eyes were either very shiny or very dull. She tried not to be caught looking. All the trees were bare now. It grew colder. Snow fell. They huddled together at night, teeth chittering, their whole bodies shaking. Tomas said they had to find somewhere warm. 'If we go to sleep here we won't wake up again,' he said. She thought that would be nice.

They were in a town full of lorries and soldiers. Everybody was shouting. Aeroplanes droned like huge bees through the night. Often the sky was lit up with flashes. There were bangs so loud they made her fall over. She put her hands over her ears until Tomas tugged at her to make her stand up. They walked on.

In one part of the town men were gathered round a big drum full of fire. They could feel the heat of it and smell hot food. Tomas said, 'Wait.' She stood at the edge of the heat while he walked up to the men. She saw him making signs at them, and them laughing at him. Somebody handed him something which he put in his mouth. He turned round and waved to her. She went towards the fire. The heat hurt but it was the best thing for days. One of the men held out something in his fingers to her. She took it, it was black and greasy, she did not hesitate, she ate it whatever it was.

The fire turned all of them into flickering shadows. Tomas tried for more food. The men didn't laugh now, they shooed him off. He tried again. One of them pushed him and he slipped on the snow. Another man kicked him. Tomas scrambled to his feet and came for her. He took her hand and quickly led her away.

Later. Maybe it was the same night, maybe not. Maybe it was another town. There was still snow. For the first time Tomas did not seem strong to her. He kept coughing. He shuffled rather than walked. Her own feet were so cold she could not feel them. She remembered the old people who hadn't run away. They were moving, both of them, the way those old people used to.

They were indoors, in a loud, noisy room. Tomas must have decided they had no choice. It was dark outside but the room was bright as daylight. Women were there as well as men. A woman noticed them crouched by the door. She made them sit at a table and brought them bowls of soup. The soup was too hot, it burned through her whole body when she swallowed and made her dizzy. The woman sat next to her and asked questions she did not understand. She could see a man talking to Tomas, maybe asking the same questions. She had a bad, sick feeling and wanted to go outside, but when she stood up the woman stopped her. She wanted to fall asleep and maybe she did.

Then they were somewhere else, another room. The woman was not with them but the man was. Other men too, like soldiers but with different uniforms. One of them sat next to her on a wooden bench. He put his arm round her shoulders and talked to her, he didn't seem to mind that she didn't answer. It felt nice, she wanted to go to sleep again but something wasn't right. She looked for Tomas and saw him very small and getting smaller, as if he was far away. The man from the first room was shouting at him. There were metal tables and chairs, and pipes running round the walls. The candles hanging from thin ropes in the ceiling dazzled her, she could not look at them. Tomas put his hand inside his shirt and brought out his little book. The man who was holding her saw this, he said something and signed for her to give him her own little book. She dug around under her clothes and pulled it out. He took it and laughed. She thought she was dreaming because it didn't make sense that her man was laughing and Tomas's man was shouting. She said, 'Are you the Americans? We are looking for the Americans.'

Maybe they didn't understand what she said. Maybe she shouldn't have said it but she was so tired. Now the other man was standing over Tomas and suddenly Tomas jumped up and fell down, and only afterwards did she realise that the man had hit him so hard he had lifted him off his feet. Tomas lay on the floor. She tried to go to him but the man holding her squeezed her tight until she stopped struggling. She went limp. The other man picked Tomas off the floor and hit him across the mouth. Then he put him on a chair and talked into his face and punched him and shook him. The man jabbed a finger in her direction. Tomas was crying, shaking his head. She couldn't remember ever seeing him cry before. Blood poured from his nose and mouth. The man who had hit him signalled to the other one to bring her over. She tried not to go but she was not strong enough. Tomas's man seized her wrist and held her hanging in the air in front of Tomas and pointed at her. He jerked her up and down until she thought her arm would come off. Tomas was sobbing and pleading with the man to let her go. The man was very angry. He did something that spun and twisted her, and then he threw her in the air and she landed upside down on the floor and a jolt of pain went through her. She had never felt pain like it. Her face was against the floorboards and she heard a cat screaming. The man's boots were near her eyes. She noticed how polished they were just before she was sick on them. This made him even angrier. He started kicking her. She tried to curl up but her arm was too sore. He kicked her anyway, over and over, as if she was a ball that had burst, that had no further use. After a while she didn't hear the cat any more.

For a long time every part of her hurt. It hurt to breathe, to eat, to lie down, to stand up, to walk. It hurt to speak. Silence was a blessing.

Do you know what chronology is? Chronology is one thing happening after another. For the dumb lass time wasn't like that, it was all mixed up. Between whatever happened in that room – what she remembers happening – and finding herself under the spreading roots of the tree in the glen, was like a heap of jigsaw-puzzle pieces. No picture, no box, just pieces. Maybe she and Tomas escaped or, more likely, those men let them go. It was as if they just hurt them for fun, because they had nothing else to do. They needed the flimsiest of excuses and she gave them one when she said 'Americans'. It could have been worse; the men could have killed them.

Odd how, later, she almost felt sorry for those men. They must have known the end was coming. They must have believed they were going to lose everything. Why else would you take your fists and your boots to children?

She never again saw the little book that according to Tomas was who she was. Maybe the men kept it. Maybe she and Tomas threw the little books away because they had not been made safe by them after all. In some way she did not understand, they had been betrayed by them.

Jigsaw pieces. Snow, mud, rubble. Broken lorries, cars, tanks. Lying in the dark for days and nights, nights and days. Soft bread, hard bread. Dirty snow in her mouth. Tomas whispering to her but she couldn't hear him. She heard explosions, gunfire, aeroplanes, engines, dogs barking, but not Tomas whispering. Lying still, pain in and out when she breathed. Rain. Grey people wandering about like ghosts. A dead house with soldiers in it but the soldiers weren't there, only their empty shells. Tomas crawled over them and put his hand in their pockets for coins. He had a black eye and his nose was not straight. He coughed all the time now, his chest rattled. She saw Mama and Tata one night. They were waving from the back of a lorry.

I don't have much more than this, Lachie. The thing is, there is a distance between the dumb lass and me, a vast, open, empty space. The war was over by the time she and Tomas had got to wherever they were. As far as I know, they never met the Americans. They must have passed them, going in the opposite direction. But if the war was over it left its trail everywhere, it had neither beginning nor end, the wreckage of it seemed to go on for ever.

One morning she woke up and Tomas was beside her but he would not wake up no matter how much she hugged and kissed and shook him, even when she pinched and poked him he would not stir. He was as cold and gone away as those soldiers. She was angry with him for leaving her alone. Later she realised it wasn't his fault or his choice. She put her hand in his pocket and found a few coins. Then she said goodbye. The sun was shining on one side of her face. She knew which way to go.

I think she probably ended up in Antwerp or Zeebrugge or Rotterdam – one of those ports, or another like them on the western seaboard of Europe. Surely somebody must have noticed her. Surely somebody must have helped her. She had nothing, not even speech. I have a vague picture of huge boats, cranes, clanking machines, the busyness of a port. The world was beginning to repair itself, return to something like normal – not that she knew that, or what normal was. Not that normal existed. Nothing could be as it had been. I have another vague picture of the sun setting over the sea which, eventually, she crossed. But from that coast, if it was that coast, where did she cross to? Harwich? Hull? Newcastle? Did she come by sea to Leith, to Montrose? Or maybe she made only one sea journey, and the rest was on land. Did she think she had reached America? How did she find out about getting on buses? Was it hard or simple? Did she work out that the worst that could happen was she would be put off again, and that if that was the worst it was nothing? Did she think that she would survive from one bus to the next for ever?

I don't know. But one day in Montrose she got on to Sam Dawson's bus, and it took her to a place where there was no next bus. And there – here – her long journey ended. Out of one world and into another. She arrived, and she stayed.

You might ask, 'Was she never curious? Did she never want to go back, find out where she came from, what happened to her family?' Of course, she often thought about Tomas, and wondered who had found him, and what they had found when they did. She thought about Mama and Tata. Where were they taken, and who took them? The Germans? The Russians? She was sure they must have been killed, but did she need proof? No. Was she curious? No. Did she want to go back? No, never. There were too many empty holes, too many blanks. She did not want to go looking for those missing pieces. She did not want to disturb the place she was in. She wanted what she had, the one thing she could believe in: where she was.

It is not surprising to me that we are making such a mess of our planet. There are too many of us who insist on living beyond the world's means. No wonder the planet is kicking back – drowning us, ripping our defences to shreds, confounding us with its heat and raging winds, its fires and floods. And now this pestilence. Three generations ago, when the dumb lass was born, most of humanity lived without electricity or piped gas or plumbing. And 'most of humanity' then was a small fraction of all of us now.

Electricity didn't come to the glen until 1957. It was the first time the dumb lass lived with it. Those candles on their ropes that blinded her in that terrible room had been new to her. In fact, the dumb lass *never* lived with electricity because by 1957 she had regained her ability to speak, or gained a new way of speaking. She was long enough without either, though – electricity or speech. Nineteen, maybe twenty years without the one, four or five years without the other. Long enough. But when her old self looks back at her young self, when her speaking self remembers her mute self, she knows she could survive without either again, if she had to. She doesn't have to, and for that she is grateful, but she doesn't waste energy or words. Never leaves a light bulb burning if it's not needed, never puts the kettle on to boil and forgets it. Often sits in the dark if she has no reason to switch on a lamp. Does not speak unless she has something to say. Does not speak, sometimes, even when she has.

She has lived on almost nothing for so long that she needs almost nothing to live. All those years she got by on seasonal farm work, odd jobs, helping out at the Big House, a few sales of her paintings, the occasional charity of Sir Gregory Grant, and the constant, patient giving of Molly and Bob Skene.

Some instinct in Molly understood that she would speak one day, but that she could not and should not be rushed. Bob and Janet took their cues from Molly. They were amazing people. They had never been anywhere but they knew about the world and they knew more about the dumb lass than she knew herself.

Maybe it was because of the daughter she lost, but it was as if Molly recognised her. She should never have been here. She should have been dead. She came back from the dead, unlike Tomas and

Mama and Tata and so many others. Unlike Flora, Molly's first-born. The dumb lass became Flora, her third-born. She was Flora Skene, whenever her existence needed to be recorded. But that was only a name, a convenience. She knew this, and Molly did too. They both knew that one day she would tell who she was and it would be nothing to do with records or reports or papers. I think it was because Molly understood this that she never considered formal adoption. She sensed that it was neither necessary nor appropriate, and she was right.

Sir Gregory was right too about Mr Travers and Inspector Brand. They never bothered about the dumb lass again. They had more important matters on their hands. The glen adjusted to her having arrived. Time has an irregular current, now rapid, now barely moving at all. In retrospect, she hardly made a ripple.

She went to the school at Brig o' Conach after Molly and Mrs Pirnie had schooled her themselves for some months. They had worked out that she could hear. They also believed she had a hungry mind, so they fed it. They read to her, sang to her, spoke to her, and she listened. Mrs Pirnie taught her how to connect the squiggles on the pages of books with the sounds she heard the two women making. The sounds Molly made did not relate to the words in most of the books they put in front of her, but Mrs Pirnie's sounds did. By the time the dumb lass went to the school she could read pretty well, and was beginning to write too.

It was not easy at the school. Some of the children bullied her for not speaking, although the bairns from the glen protected her when they could. In the first days she was the cause of several fights. Sometimes she herself hit out. Other times she made herself as limp as a rag doll.

The teacher tolerated her rather than encouraged her to learn. I think that teacher believed, in spite of everything Molly and Mrs Pirnie told her, in spite of everything she should have known as a teacher, that the lass was stupid. 'Retarded', to use Dr Logan's term. When she was sitting at the back of the class, not joining in with the others, it was as if she were somewhere else. The teacher let her be, left her to read and to draw. She recognised, at least, that when the dumb lass was reading or drawing she was at her calmest.

Sometimes she *was* somewhere else. There were nights when fear of the dream kept her from sleep, when she knew she could not go to school the next day. The following mornings Molly would find her bed empty, or she would disappear at the last moment when it was time to get on Sam Dawson's bus. Then she would not be seen all day – unless, as occasionally happened, Bob or somebody else working up the glen glimpsed a figure emerging from or vanishing into the cover of the trees. But even then they could never be sure it was her. Bob turned a blind eye. He entered into a conspiracy with Molly, and she in turn conspired, without acknowledgement or admission by any of them, with Sam Dawson and with the schoolteacher. Nothing was said and nothing was done. The dumb lass was special, she was not like other bairns. Molly and Bob believed she would come to no harm in the glen. She had had her share of harm already.

What did she do on these days, alone for hours at a time? Nobody knew, but when she returned, usually dirty, sometimes wet, always hungry, she was no longer distressed.

A year went by. Janet, her 'big sister', was not unkind to her, but became indifferent. She was probably jealous of the attention Molly gave the dumb lass, and why should she not have been? Janet became more her father's daughter than her mother's. But Bob was also the dumb lass's friend. She had landed among good people. She knew she had. She never forgot it.

And then Jenny Kemp's son, Geordie, came home. He had been conscripted at eighteen but the war was over by the time he finished his training. He was moved around various army barracks and camps in different parts of the country but they never sent him overseas. After two years he was demobbed, and back to the glen he came, and got a job on the estate farm. Geordie had been friendly with Janet Skene but about the time he came home she left, first going to work in Manchester and then on to London. So when Geordie came to Molly and Bob's after that it was them he came to see, them and the dumb lass.

He was twice her age and he shouldn't have wanted anything to do with her but something struck up between them at once, an empathy of some kind. They enjoyed being together. He was impressed by the dedication and concentration she gave to her drawing and painting. She liked his sense of fun, his laugh, how he could turn his hand to most things. They were easy in each other's company.

On Sundays, or if he had a day off, they would go on long tramps across the hills. Geordie never minded her silence, and she never minded his incessant chatter; he talked away at her as if he were on the wireless. There was no end to his stories. He told her of witches and whisky smugglers, Jacobites and cattle reivers, he told her the legends of Conach and took her to Conach's Linn and the cave and the place where he had lived in his cabin. They would stand in the mouth of the cave, looking down the glen. 'Is that no braw?' he would say, and she would smile and nod but she could not say she agreed, she could not speak it. Even when he made her laugh it was a silent laugh, more like a smile that made her shoulders shake, and usually she brought her hand up to her mouth to cover it. And he reminded her of somebody and it was on one of those hikes that she remembered who it was. He reminded her of Tomas before they started walking towards the sunset. And some pieces of that old jigsaw puzzle clicked together, and some of what she saw when she shuffled them around began to make sense.

She lost a bit of her heart to Geordie. How could she not have? But his was set on Betty McLeish from the Brig o' Conach, and she could not blame him, because even she fell in love with Betty. Still, the dumb lass grieved a little when they got engaged a year later. Six months after that, the wedding took place. She made them a painting of the glen for a gift, and when it was done Bob measured it and made a frame for it. And he was checking to see that it fitted right and saying how much Geordie and Betty would love it, when Molly said suddenly, 'But ye hinna signed it, Flora. Ye canna gie it to them unsigned, it widna be richt.'

What was she then, eleven or twelve? Molly used to say she hardly recognised her from the bag of bones she had been when she came. She was still small, she would only ever be small, but her hair was long and her skin was brown and something like light showed in the dark centres of her big eyes. She gave them a smile and Bob took the painting out of the frame and handed it to her.

It was the next day before she brought it back so that Bob could fit it in the frame and seal the back of it. She had signed in red paint in the bottom right corner. She had copied what she signed from something on one of the jigsaw pieces in her head. She wouldn't have known how to spell it otherwise, her name, although she could hear it in Tomas's voice. But there it was on the jigsaw piece, a scrap of the little book she had once carried next to her skin. Tomas used to point out the letters to her. 'That's you,' he said. 'That's how your name looks written down.' And with a supreme effort of memory, she pictured the four letters and took her thinnest brush and dipped it in the blood-red paint and signed the painting.

Maja.

Molly said, her finger poised over the word, 'Is that you? A' these years we've been cryin' ye Flora and this was your name? Is that you?'

She nodded. The shy smile.

Molly put her hand to her mouth. After all this time.

She said, 'But I dinna ken how to say it. I dinna want to get it wrang.'

The dumb lass seemed to be staring at the painting but maybe she was looking at something else.

Molly said, 'Majja?'

She said, 'May-ja?'

She said again, 'Majja?'

She said, 'Please, my love, I need ye to help me. Just nod your heid when I'm richt.'

The dumb lass did not nod her head. She shook it. And then – so quiet and quick it was almost gone before Molly heard it – 'My-a,' she said.

And again, with more certainty, '*Maja*.'

Janet married and settled on the south coast of England, and seldom came home. In time she had three children. Molly and Bob made long trips to see them, and once Janet brought the grandchildren to the glen. Then Molly and Bob died, within a year of each other. Now Janet is dead, and I don't know where her children are. I am the only one left from those times.

So now you know as much as I do, Lachie, or as much as I am able to tell you. I have had my voice again for seventy years, give or take a year. Many people's lives do not last nearly as long as the years I have had since I got over that difficulty. I call it a difficulty, not a disability. A disability may be accommodated, it may be eased, its effects may be reduced through therapy, assistance, equipment. But I do not think a disability can be cured. It would need a miracle to 'cure' most disabilities. I do not believe in miracles. There is a verse in Mark's Gospel, if you should ever read the Bible, when Jesus miraculously heals a man who cannot speak: 'And straightway the string of his tongue was loosed.' Well, it took a little longer for me than 'straightway', but the string of my tongue was loosed and my muteness ended. So it was a difficulty, a barrier, and one day I broke through it.

I have been thinking a lot about the girl you saw, the one you think might be a ghost. I wonder if you have seen her again. When you first told me about her I thought she might be the dumb lass, but I couldn't see how that could be, since I was still here. But the dumb lass and I were so far apart that it was maybe possible. Then

I read about another girl who was here in the glen much longer ago, somebody I hadn't even known existed, and I changed my mind: it might be *her*. And then you said something else. You said you thought ghosts are people who don't want to be forgotten. And that feels right. They see other people in the places where they used to be and they want to say, 'Yes, I've been here too, I know what it's like.' But they can't say it, so instead they show themselves. So whoever the girl you saw was, maybe that's what she was doing, and once she was sure you had noticed her she could go, she could disappear.

No doubt that's all an old woman's nonsense, but I find it helpful. We're all ghosts really, whether we know it or not. We come and go, and after a while we go for ever, and only a few memories and stories are left behind with other people. And even those go eventually.

Yesterday evening I walked over to the old kirkyard. Do you ever spend much time there? You should. Any graveyard is full of stories. In our one, nearly all the stones are fallen and the words on most of them are hard to read or gone altogether. There is one stone for a man called David Gillespie, who was the minister here two hundred and fifty years ago. It is still just about readable. There is a stone for the minister who came after him, who was called John Dunning. And there is another, quite large stone that bears the names and dates of Thomas and Margaret Milne, who used to live in the Big House that you live in; and it also has on it the name of Alison Murray, who was Thomas Milne's mother; and that of Thomas and Margaret's daughter, Jessamine, who died in the great fire of 1832. Under her name and dates it says only 'The Maid of Glen Conach', which was how she was known. Then there are other stones that mark the graves of people who lived and died in the glen after that. The last of those are from about a hundred years ago. The church closed between the two world wars and the graveyard was full so, for a hundred years now, glen people have been buried out of the glen, or these days, mostly, their bodies go to Friockheim or Dundee to be cremated. My friend Geordie Kemp, who is in that photograph I showed you, he was cremated, so there is no marker here to show that he was ever in the glen, even though this was where he was born and where he lived all his life and where he died. And all those more recent stones with names on them – well, the names are beginning to fade and one day nobody will be able to read them. I know this is probably all a bit depressing to read but what I am trying to say is that even a physical object like a stone, with words on it that say, 'I have been here' – even that won't stop you being forgotten when enough time has passed. That's just what happens.

Well, I was standing beside the old ruined church, looking at the gravestones, thinking about all this. It's a lovely, peaceful place to be, a place to let your thoughts roam. And what did I see? I saw a deer. A beautiful roe deer, with her dark flanks and her white backside, picking her way through the stones. It was nearly nine o'clock, the light was going fast. I stood very still. She was grazing, keeping alert for danger, but she must have known she was safe enough. She came within about twenty feet of me. I was like a statue. Maybe she thought I was a gravestone. If she sensed I was there, she wasn't frightened. She stopped next to one of the old stones and rubbed herself against it, first one side then the other. She must have needed a really good scratch because she was at it for quite a while. I watched, thinking she was playing her part in making the stone unreadable. After a while she trotted off down to the river and I lost sight of her. It was almost as if I hadn't seen her, as if she hadn't been there at all. But she was there. I'm telling you now and I'm writing it down now. I saw the deer.

Then I began to make my way home. I took my time because I couldn't see the ground very clearly and if I fell and couldn't get up I would be in trouble. I kept thinking of that deer. It occurred to me that, although she was there and I had seen her, she could have been a ghost. And then I thought, *I* could have been a ghost to her. I felt the cold air, and when I touched one of the stones I felt its dampness, and when I reached my garden gate and had my hand upon it I felt that too, so I didn't really believe it could be true. But maybe ghosts feel such things too. And, anyway, would I know?

Until this virus happened there were people on the move all over Europe, all over the world. Have we learned nothing since the dumb lass and Tomas walked through that war? It seems obvious that there are too many of us but that was also said all those years ago, or at least some people believed that there were too many of the wrong kinds of us, and they acted on that belief and did terrible deeds. Now the planet is telling us to change our ways. Can we change? When this time is over, when the virus has gone or we have learned how to live with it, people will set off again on their long journeys looking for safety, shelter, food, water, work – whatever it is they do not have. They will be trying to leave behind whatever it is they do not want, which may be just a lack of things. It is not these people's fault that they are on the move: they want only to make other lives for themselves and for their children; to make life less terrible, more bearable. The world is a great plain criss-crossed with pilgrimages, hejiras, exoduses, flights; it is an ocean of refugees and pirates, and a few brave vessels that sail on into the setting sun. There are bones scattered across the plain, there is wreckage floating on the sea. Where life once was, only the ruins of life remain.

I am wandering again, Lachie. I have not moved for hours yet I too am on a long journey. My hand aches, but I have almost finished writing. Everybody has a place – a real place or a memory of a place, or a dream of a place. And some never find the real one from one end of their lives to the other, they have to go into themselves because they have nowhere else to go. I was lucky. All those years ago I was lucky.

One day you will wake up and it will be the last day of your life.

You may know this or you may not. You may want to know it or you may not. Either way it will not be in your control. But if you are in your place when death comes calling, so you don't even have to get up and open the door, then you are blessed indeed, whatever else has befallen you in the days and years that went before.

365

JAMES ROBERTSON

In 2013, James Robertson wrote a story every day. Each was 365 words long. A year later, on a daily basis, the stories were published on the *Five Dials* website. Now the 365 stories are gathered in one volume. Some draw on elements of ancient myth and legend, others are outtakes from Scottish history and folklore; there are squibs and satires, songs and ballads in disguise, fairy tales, stories inspired by dreams or in the form of interviews, and personal memories and observations.

Underpinning them all are vital questions: Who are we? What are we doing here? What happens next?

'A masterclass in the ventriloquism of fiction. Overall, there's a powerful sense of a fertile mind and a great generosity of ideas'

Guardian

'An anthology of possibility about what the short form can do'

Stuart Kelly, *Scotsman*

'What can you say in a few words? Everything, it seems. 365 worlds pressed between two covers'

Ali Bowden, *Scotsman*

WWW.PENGUIN.CO.UK

TO BE CONTINUED

JAMES ROBERTSON

Douglas Findhorn Elder is in a sorry state. He's turning fifty, split up with his girlfriend and been pushed out of his job at the local news rag. But on the night of his birthday, he makes an unexpected new friend: a talking toad.

Setting aside the obvious problem, Mungo the toad is the most sensible person Douglas has met for years. And when the man gets embroiled in a wild-goose chase that leads him out of Edinburgh and across the country, naturally the toad goes with him. Awaiting the duo at crumbling Glentaragar Manor are a hundred-year-old firebrand grandmother, a split-personality alcoholic/teetotaller, an elaborate whisky-smuggling conspiracy, and maybe even a shot at redemption . . .

This gloriously surreal romp proves once and for all that the important things in life – friendship, romance, a funeral hearse stuffed with crates of bootlegged whisky – come when you least expect them.

> **'Robertson manages to skilfully join the quirky with the serious; the surreal with the real. His take on contemporary Scotland is insightful, eccentric and highly readable'**
>
> *Scotsman*

> **'A wildly eccentric tale laced with dry, deprecating wit'**
>
> *The Times*

> **'*To Be Continued*, with its harum-scarum scenarios and surreal twists, was written to entertain'**
>
> *Sunday Herald*

WWW.PENGUIN.CO.UK

Acknowledgements

My sincere thanks go to the following for their support and help during the writing of this book: my agent, Natasha Fairweather, at Rogers, Coleridge & White; my editors Simon Prosser, Hermione Thompson and Hannah Chukwu at Hamish Hamilton; and my copy-editor, Sarah Coward.

I am grateful too to Stephen Fitzpatrick and Alexandra Radbil, who suggested that I read *The Hermit in the Garden* by Gordon Campbell (2013). Other books I consulted include *An Angus Parish in the Eighteenth Century* by William Mason Inglis (1904); *Warlords and Holy Men: Scotland AD 80–1000* by Alfred P. Smyth (1984); *Glenesk: The History and Culture of an Angus Community* by Margaret Fairweather Michie (2000); *Scotland's Merlin: A Medieval Legend and Its Dark Age Origins* by Tim Clarkson (2016); *Conceiving a Nation: Scotland to AD 900* by Gilbert Markus (2017); and *The Scottish Clearances: A History of the Dispossessed* by T. M. Devine (2018). I also learned much about various campaigns during the Napoleonic Wars from online sources, for example Ian Yonge's 'The Walcheren Expedition of 1809' at www.waterlooassociation.org.uk.

Thanks, finally, to Joan Bowden for checking my Latin and to Donald Meek for checking my Gaelic (any remaining errors are not their responsibility, but mine); and, as ever, to Marianne Mitchelson for providing sound criticism of early drafts, and for her continuing patience and love.

James Robertson, Newtyle, February 2021

THE PROFESSOR OF TRUTH

JAMES ROBERTSON

Twenty-one years after his wife and daughter were murdered in the bombing of a plane over Scotland, Alan Tealing still doubts the official version of events surrounding that terrible night. He is sure that the man convicted of the atrocity was not responsible, and that he himself has thus been deprived not only of justice but also of any chance of escape from his enduring grief.

When an American intelligence officer arrives on his doorstep with information about a key witness in the trial, Alan decides to act. He travels to Australia to confront the witness, whose evidence he has always disbelieved. Will this encounter end only in more distress and disappointment? Or might it lead to the truth for which Alan has waited so long?

'A beautiful rendering of grief and intangible truth'

Laura Marney, *Herald*,
Book of the Year

'Sensitive but provocative . . . confirms Robertson as one of Scotland's great contemporary storytellers'

List

'Robertson is a very great novelist'

Alexander McCall Smith,
Guardian

'Robertson offers up some powerful philosophical asides on truth versus justice, cynicism versus hope, and the nature of romantic love'

Hannah McGill, *Scotsman*

WWW.PENGUIN.CO.UK

AND THE LAND LAY STILL

JAMES ROBERTSON

Michael Pendreich is curating an exhibition of photographs by his late, celebrated father, Angus, for the National Gallery of Photography in Edinburgh. The show will cover fifty years of Scottish life but, as he arranges the images and writes his catalogue essay, what story is Michael really trying to tell? His father's, his own or that of Scotland itself?

Tracing the intertwined lives of an unforgettable cast of characters, James Robertson's new novel is a searching journey into the heart of a country of high hopes and unfulfilled dreams, private compromises and hidden agendas. Brilliantly blending the personal and the political, *And the Land Lay Still* sweeps away the dust and grime of the postwar years to reveal a rich mosaic of twentieth-century Scottish life.

'A brilliant and multi-faceted saga of Scottish life and politics in the second half of the twentieth century . . . a powerful and moving novel'

Sunday Times

'*And the Land Lay Still* weaves engrossing individual storylines against the broader stripes of cultural shifts such as the birth of Scottish nationalism'

Daily Telegraph

'Bold, discursive and deep, Robertson's sweeping history of life and politics in twentieth-century Scotland should not be ignored'

Ian Rankin, *Observer*,
Books of the Year

WWW.PENGUIN.CO.UK

THE TESTAMENT OF GIDEON MACK

JAMES ROBERTSON

For Gideon Mack, faithless minister, unfaithful husband and troubled soul, the existence of God, let alone the Devil, is no more credible than that of ghosts or fairies. Until the day he falls into a gorge and is rescued by someone who might just be Satan himself.

Mack's testament – a compelling blend of memoir, legend, history and, quite probably, madness – recounts one man's emotional crisis, disappearance, resurrection and death. It also transports you into an utterly mesmerizing exploration of the very nature of belief.

'Overwhelmingly compassionate and thought-provoking'

Irvine Welsh, *Guardian*

'A powerful and compelling read'

Anne Donovan, *Sunday Herald*

'A sly, baffling and deeply subversive stunner'

Scotland on Sunday

'A hugely gripping tale and a fascinating examination of the difference between faith and belief'

Financial Times

'A masterly piece of storytelling (and Scottish soul-searching)'

James Naughtie, *Herald*

WWW.PENGUIN.CO.UK